Stephen A. Benjamin

2014, TWB Press
www.twbpress.com

Acknowledgments

I want to thank all who have read the various drafts of this novel, including my colleagues in the Northern Colorado Writers' FantaSci critique group, for their encouragement and invaluable suggestions. The book would not be what it is without their input.

Most of all, I am grateful to my wife, Barbara, for her unfailing support and patience, particularly the latter, when writing consumed more of my life than it should have.

CHAPTER 1

I JUST DID IT AGAIN, shot off my mouth while surrounded by the tavern's myriad of flapping ears. Too much ale was no excuse.

The behemoth in front of me dominated my vision. I underestimated him because of his worn laborer's clothing, and he demolished my self-composure when he said, "And you believe your experience supersedes that of the Torah?"

"You're twisting my words," I said in loud debate, hoping the volume of my voice would support my big mouth. "The Old Testament is not meant to be taken literally. More than four thousand years of experience has changed the context of what was written."

"God gave Moses the Torah." Goliath's laugh boomed across the room. "I was not aware that the word of God had need for a context."

A chorus of patrons echoed his mocking laugh. Even so, I sensed many of them supported my views but would not voice that support—for good reason. They had seen the three rebbes watching our conversation. I had not.

The rebbes rose from their table and headed straight for me. My heart jumped as they glared at me from beneath the brims of their traditional black flat-brimmed fedoras.

A hush came over the crowd, and the commentator of a free-fall soccer match on the giant plasma screen thundered against the silence. The overhead bioluminescent lights felt like heat lamps. A trickle of sweat ran down the back of my neck. People rose and scuttled for the exit as if afraid the black-coated enforcers of religious purity might target them next.

I swallowed hard. "Good evening, rebbes."

The rebbe closest to me had a scar that ran from the corner of his left eye to the middle of his bearded cheek. The eye twitched as his fiery anger seared my empathic perception. My stomach wrenched as it always did when struck with strong emotions, and I had slammed my mental empathic barriers into place too late. As I quashed the incipient nausea—I did not need to lose my dinner in front of everyone to add to my chagrin—the inevitable headache stomped into my brain. Closing my eyes accomplished nothing against what seemed like an explosion of fireworks in front of my optic nerves. I opened them again and squinted at the rebbe. "Is there a problem?"

"You should heed the words of a man who knows the path of true faith." The scarred rebbe glanced at the giant who had stepped away from us, and then back at me. "I shall see more of you, I think." He turned and stalked out of the tavern with the other two rebbes in tow.

Oh, shit. I'd really screwed up this time. What started as a disagreement over a government entitlement program had ended in my denouncement of the dogma of the Rebbinical Council and the tyrannical theocracy that ruled Dovid's World. My big mouth could send me straight to the Inquisition.

Subdued conversation resumed with the exit of the rebbes.

A touch on my shoulder accelerated my heartbeat

again.

My recent opponent stood over me, his voice now soft and serious, not mocking as it had been. "You okay? You don't look good. Come on, I'll buy you a drink." He put a huge hand on my shoulder and steered me to a table in a corner.

I was in no condition to argue further.

He frowned as we sat. "You're a fool. Your words could put you in prison. You need to use your brain before your mouth."

Yeah, I knew that, but it never seemed to help much. Already in a lousy mood and feeling awful, I did not need someone else pointing out my flaws. Although angry at myself for my stupidity, it was easier to direct my anger at the most convenient outlet, so I glowered at the man in front of me. Goliath's bright brown eyes studied me, in turn.

As the headache faded, I cautiously lowered and peeked over my shields, all I could do without incapacitating myself. I sensed an aura of curiosity, but not the hostility I expected considering his attack on my heretical statements.

He turned and addressed the barmaid who came to our table. "An ale for me. A cider for my friend." He raised an eyebrow, dared me to contradict him.

I didn't argue. Still queasy from the rebbe's emotional assault, I knew that too much alcohol had taken its toll, though I did not appreciate the reminder.

The man thrust his bear-like forepaw across the table and smiled. Full lips peeked out from within a sandy beard and moustache, topped by a broad, crooked nose. "I'm Furoletto Cohen. People call me Fur."

I stared at his hand and rolled the name around my brain; I did not recognize it. Fur fit his impressive facial shrubbery. I was envious. The law said that men of age must wear beards. I barely managed an anemic lawn of chestnut fuzz.

"I'm Cy Berger."

His hand engulfed mine. "Well, Cy Berger, perhaps turning your inappropriate tirade into a clownish performance might save you worse trouble. Didn't you see the rebbes sitting in the back? We can hope that a laugh at your expense will make them less likely to take serious action." He tugged at his beard.

"Why should you care?" After all, he had just humiliated me in front of the entire tavern—some of my fellow students included.

"Why? A good question. Wait. Here are our drinks." He took his and downed half the mug in one swallow.

I sipped my cider and wondered what the guy's angle was.

Cohen wiped his mouth. "I wouldn't see *anyone* subjected to the Inquisition. You should learn to keep your political opinions to yourself...at least in public." He smiled, perhaps to blunt the edge of his criticism. "Tell me about yourself. I might as well know whom I tried to save."

Mortification compounded by annoyance made me curt. "I'm a student at the Academy College of Veterinary Medicine."

"Congratulations. Not an easy profession to get into. What about before that?"

Though the compliment sounded sincere, I was still leery of the guy. Why this change in attitude toward me? What did he want? "I grew up on my family's dairy farm, throwing bales of hay and shoveling kilotons of shit. What's it to you?"

He smiled despite my hostility. "What do you do for recreation? Besides drink."

"All right. What is this? *Your* version of the Inquisition? Why don't you just *kish mein tuches*?"

Even as the words poured out, I regretted them.

His brows pulled together, his eyes narrowed, and he slammed his mug onto the table. My cider glass jumped and teetered before I caught it. My hands shook and slopped cider on the tabletop.

He took a deep breath before he spoke. "Look, Berger, I tried to help you tonight. Maybe that was a stupid thing to do, considering you don't seem to give a shit. I thought perhaps you could learn from a bit of advice, but that looks to be a lost cause. Fine. I'm finished. Maybe I'll see you again when the Rebbinical Council gets done with you—if there's anything left to see."

God, I could probably piss off that ancient icon of forbearance Mahatma Gandhi, if I had the chance. Cohen's words hit too close to home. My breath caught as I recalled horror stories about the Inquisition. As he started to rise, I grabbed his arm. "Wait. Don't go." At least his presence made me feel like less of an isolated target. "I know you tried to help me. It's just...how you did it."

He sat down, though his frown did not clear until I began to talk.

To be truthful, it never took much to get me started. Shutting me up was a bigger problem. I watched my fingers make wet circles of cider on the tabletop as I spoke about myself. "...so, aside from my studies, I read a lot, and I have a thing for watching ancient vids from Old Earth."

"Like what?"

"I read and watch anything available on microchip from the ancient Greeks to the present. History, philosophy, fiction. Recent books I've read have been on political systems, particularly religious tyrannies." I glanced around to see if the rebbes hovered behind me. Many of the tables had emptied. "Don't get me wrong. I don't reject Judaism. I treasure our traditions. But I *do* have a problem with dictatorships and oppression."

"I would never have guessed." Fur's mouth curled up at the corners. "Veterinary medicine makes sense with your background, I suppose. I don't think politics would suit you."

He looked around "It's late. I have to go."

Despite our disagreement, I liked the big man, but I still was unsure about his motives. "Hey. I've given you my life story. What about yours?"

"Perhaps another time." He scowled at me. "Until then, you might keep your mouth hidden behind your textbooks."

We shook hands, or rather, I let my hand disappear within his and move up and down without my assistance. He threw a bill on the table and trudged off.

As I stared at the iconic picture of a rebbe adorning the bill, a frisson ran up my back. I finished my cider and I left the tavern. As I stepped out the door, I came face-to-face with two members of the Palmach, the government's elite police force. Their stealth-powered armor disappeared into the darkness, and it seemed as if their faces and hands floated disembodied before me. One flipped his visor down and then back up, as if to ensure himself of my identity before he spoke. "Mr. Berger, you are to come with us."

My first thought was to bolt, but for once my brain recognized the stupidity and futility of such an action. I felt like I had a mouth full of chalk dust, and it took a couple of tries to get any words out. "Wha -what for?"

"You will be informed." He motioned with a laser rifle for me to move.

The other guardsman took hold of my arm in a painful grasp, and they marched me off as our smaller moon joined the larger moon above the rooftops. I wondered if I'd ever see such a sight again.

CHAPTER 2

W HEN THE GUARDS MARCHED me up to the infamous headquarters of the Inquisition, I almost lost control of my sphincters. Fortunately, I did not add utter embarrassment to my heart-pounding fear.

They locked me in a tiny cell and disappeared without another word. I alternately sweated and shivered as I listened to a variety of moans and sobs, punctuated by an occasional scream, from voices I assumed were other prisoners. I recalled the vids I had watched that featured all sorts of torture and wished I had stuck to the Walt Disney shows.

Hours later, a taciturn Neanderthalic guard packing a very large blaster unlocked my cell. I assumed it was morning, but they had confiscated my comm unit, and the room had neither a window nor a chronometer. He marched me up a flight of stairs and down a corridor then shoved me into a small room furnished with a plasteel desk and three chairs. My glance slid behind and above the empty desk. A veritable museum of torture instruments decorated the institution-gray wall. I had visualized many of them during the night: thumb screws, branding irons, spiked whips and scourges, electric prods, and more. As my mind wrapped itself around their meaning, I heard the door close and turned.

The rebbe who addressed me the previous evening

in the tavern stood by the door. His face had haunted me in my cold cell all night. The reality was worse, and my gut clenched.

He smiled through his chest-length black beard, a smile that belied his underlying hostility. I kept my shields firmly in place; I did not need a repeat of last night's nausea and headache. His beard contrasted with the shiny bald head he unveiled when he doffed his fedora to me.

I did not return his smile.

He replaced his hat. "I am Reb Levi Schvartz, a member of the Rebbinical Council. You may address me as Reb Levi." His voice grated like rough ball bearings against rusted steel.

I assumed he knew my name and did not respond.

Built like a fireplug, the man looked to be in his early forties. His midnight black attire—suit, shirt, tie, socks, shoes, and hat—seemed to suck the light from the room. His matching black eyes sat above a large, hooked nose that, as prominent as it was, could not rival the size of *my* mammoth schnoz. His pale scar gleamed against his ruddy face and disappeared into his beard.

He moved behind the desk and sat in the only padded seat, then motioned me to a straight-backed metal chair across from him. I surreptitiously looked for electrical connections before I sat.

A knock preceded the entry of a third person. To my amazement, the Dean of the College of Veterinary Medicine appeared. I had met him twice, both times when I had challenged the intelligence or the personal habits of one of his faculty members. He was a gray man—like the walls. He would not meet my eyes as he moved to sit in the hard chair next to me.

Reb Levi rubbed his fingers over his scar. "Mr. Berger, your seditious diatribes have caused considerable consternation among the members of

Rebbinical Council."

The Dean coughed as if the rebbe's words had choked him.

My gut writhed like an eel in a net.

"Last night was just the latest of your transgressions."

I felt the blood drain from my face. The Dean's sallow face turned even paler, and I wondered if mine looked the same.

"The Dean tells me that you are at the top of your class, academically. Commendable. He also tells me that you are a *kochlefff*"—he used the Yiddish word for troublemaker— "even at the Academy. You realize that you could be subjected to the Inquisition, do you not?" He raised his right eyebrow and his scarred left cheek twitched in response.

My heart skipped a beat. I glanced over his shoulder at the wall of torture implements and prayed it was only a museum display, although the past night's sounds suggested my prayer would not be answered.

He waited for a response, although I was not sure what I could say. Recant my "seditious" pronouncements? I would not back down on my beliefs—well, at least not yet. Be tortured? That fear played more games with my sphincters. I'm no hero; I'm a chicken when it comes to pain. Disappear like others before me? Scuttlebutt said two radical students who dropped out of school last year had not been seen since. But if they were going to get rid of me, why was the Dean here? My hands twisted around themselves as if they had a life of their own.

The silence lengthened until the Dean cleared his throat and spoke. "Mr. Berger—"

"No," Reb Levi said. "Let *him* speak."

For once in my life, I could not. I froze. I could not clear my mind of the old vid images of torture victims. I don't know how long the silence lasted before I broke free of my paralysis. "Wha-what do you want from me? Are you going torture me, for God's sake?"

The Dean gasped.

The Rebbe's eyebrows bunched up like some huge black caterpillars. "Despite your blasphemy, we have no wish to torture you, Mr. Berger. Not if you accede to our wishes. On the contrary, we might have a job for you." His smile reminded me of Dracula inviting a victim to rest in his coffin. His antipathy seeped around my mental barriers.

A *job*? What in hell did that mean?

Reb Levi tented his fingers. "Mr. Berger, you are a challenge, for your professors and the Rebbinical Council. Because of your sedition, the Council would see you leave Dovid's World...permanently." He stroked his scar.

My heart bounced off my diaphragm. Exile? My family—

Before my thoughts went further, Reb Levi added, "Or, perhaps, if you were to remain you could be taught to see the error of your ways." He smiled and followed my glare over his shoulder to *The Wall*. It had taken on a life of its own in my mind.

My body trembled. The man exuded malignant pleasure as he watched me, and my stomach twisted again, despite my shields.

"I see either option as a waste," he said. "You are among the brightest young persons at the Academy. Therefore, we have proposed a compromise." He turned to the Dean and nodded. "You may explain, Dean Altschul."

Altschul cleared his throat. "Mr. Berger, the Council has suggested several things. First, they would like to see you gone from Dovid's World within a month."

I felt like I had been gut-punched. When I caught my breath, my next words were comical considering my situation. "But I have final exams...and graduation."

"Yes, yes." The Dean waved off my outburst. "There is no problem. You could fail all your finals and still graduate with honors. The Rebbinical Council has ordered the Academy to waive your examinations and confer your degree early." He stood and held out his hand. "Congratulations, *Doctor* Berger."

My mouth hung open. Was he serious? Things were happening too fast. Had I just gone from the Inquisition's prisoner to a full-fledged Doctor of Veterinary Medicine in the span of minutes? I finally stood and shook the Dean's hand, confused but not so befuddled that I didn't know to wait for the other shoe to drop.

Dean Altschul sat again and I followed suit.

"As Reb Levi said, we have a job for you. One that will not entail your *permanent* separation from our world."

I let out the breath I had held, but took particular note of the "we" and waited for more.

"As you may know, our College of Veterinary Medicine once had many students from other worlds, but for various reasons we now have no students from offworld. We need someone to go to other planets, to seek out and recruit students, to entice them to enroll here. It is important to the, um, finances of our Academy. Income from other planets has been lacking since our government—" Altschul snapped his mouth shut and glanced at Reb Levi. His fear that he had said too much permeated the room.

Reb Levi's eyes did not change, but a wave of disapproval radiated from the man's brow.

After an uncomfortable silence, Altschul coughed and began again. "Dr. Berger, you are a persuasive speaker as you have shown both inside and outside the Academy. We feel this would be a good opportunity for you."

Anger began to replace my fear of Reb Levi. Blood pulsed in my temple. Good opportunity? Leave my home, for God's sake? And why me if I was such a pain in the ass? The obvious answer hit me like a bucket of ice water. No matter how they cut it, they were getting rid of me.

"We will empower you to offer scholarships to accomplish our goals."

Your goals, not mine.

"What do you say?"

Was I supposed to agree to give up my plans and aspirations for my own veterinary practice? The farmers and ranchers in my home county needed a veterinarian, and I had planned to go home to fill that role. Was I to Leave Dovid's World and my family? Like hell, I would. I conveniently submerged any thought of my precarious situation.

"No thanks. I'm not leaving my home."

Reb Levi's voice cut through me like the parting of the Red Sea. "The Council would *very much* like you to take this assignment, Dr. Berger. Though you have spoken harsh words about our government, there is no evidence that you are an active revolutionary. This appointment will give you a chance to prove yourself."

"I don't need to prove anything—"

"And to see that your family remains in good health."

My heart clutched in my chest. I turned to him. His face was smooth. A slight smile curved his lips. His blunt fingers stroked his scar as his left eye twitched. I did not need my empathic ability to read him. I was now responsible for my mom and dad, whether or not they would become targets of the government, victims of the Inquisition. This was torture in itself. My fists clenched. I had to restrain myself from attacking him bodily. I had trained in martial arts as a teenager, and I wondered if I could take him. He looked strong as a bull.

The Dean must have taken my silence as acquiescence. "Ah, good. Good. I knew you would be willing, Dr. Berger. We can work out all the details later. See my Associate Dean for recruiting. She will train you."

I glared at Reb Levi, fists balled. What I saw made further protestations moot. His eyes were narrow, and he nodded once, sharply, as if to shake something unpleasant out of his nonexistent hair. His demeanor was clear: Take it or suffer—you *and* your family. There were no alternatives.

"One last thing," the Dean said. "You will have a companion on your travels."

I arched my eyebrows.

"Reb Levi."

I glanced at the smiling rebbe and shuddered. I'd rather share a spaceship with a giant Antarean scorpion. I wondered if only one of us would return from this journey.

CHAPTER 3

THE FRONT DOOR OPENED and Lucky, our chocolate Labrador retriever, rocketed through and bowled me over. He straddled me, tail wagging like a jet-propelled windshield wiper. He expressed his joy in a thorough tongue washing of my face. He also laughed.

Yeah, dogs laugh, but because of my empathic ability, I'm the only one who can hear them. Lucky thought knocking me down in greeting was hilarious.

Our ginger tabby, Einstein, looked out the door at me, meowed once, and disappeared. Cats laugh, too. But dogs laugh with you; cats laugh *at* you.

I hugged Lucky then pushed him away. I missed him as much as he missed me. We had the twelve-year-old dog for almost half my life. Our time together had been limited since I'd gone away to school.

I rose and faced my smiling parents in the doorway. My mother opened her arms, and I hugged her before we moved inside.

"Sit," my mother commanded. "We want to hear all the details of what has happened. This whole business is quite extraordinary."

I picked at a hangnail as I spoke. "This is an honor. Because I'm at the top of my class, I've been appointed Assistant Registrar for Recruiting for the Academy

College of Veterinary Medicine. The university wants offworld students. There haven't been any in recent years, and they need the revenue." I had to convince my folks that the whole thing was kosher; Reb Levi ordered me to say nothing about the Inquisition or the threat against my parents. "They chose me because I'm a good speaker."

Mom and Dad looked at one another. Their skepticism was tangible. They well knew my political leanings.

"Assistant Registrar," Dad repeated. "Sounds fancy enough. But will you have the opportunity to practice medicine? That's something I know is important to you. You'll be giving up your own plans."

"I'll run an interstellar veterinary service in a ship outfitted as a mobile clinic. I haven't seen it yet, but I'm told it has great equipment."

"*Mazel tov*, darling. I'm sure that will be exciting. How long will you be gone? Will you be able to return home regularly?" Mom looked at me expectantly, but concern leaked through her happy façade.

My dad's steel gray eyes probed me as I answered, as if he sought something beneath my words.

"I'm not sure what the schedule will be. I haven't been given an itinerary. But I'll send you hyperwave transmissions whenever I can. Promise."

"I'm sure you will," Dad said. He stood. "Come with me. Let's have a drink while your mother gets dinner on the table."

I followed him into his study. In an age where most databases were digital, an impressive library of cloth and leather-bound books covered the shelves. This was where I got my love of literature. He motioned me to one of two leather-covered armchairs and doled out a couple of glasses of schnapps.

"Okay, let's have the truth. Who put the

thumbscrews to you?"

I choked on my schnapps. "Wha-what do you mean?" A vision of *The Wall* skewered my brain. How could he know—?

"I don't need your empathic talent to know what you told your mother and me is *drek*. You did not get chosen because you're an expert speaker or because you're a good student. This is *mishegas*. It makes no sense."

Mom and Dad were among the few people who knew about my empathic ability. I sensed the emotions of animals and my empathic connection allowed me to soothe stressed beasts. I also perceived human emotions—I sensed what I call auras, for lack of a better term. Rarely, powerful human emotions came through as a fleeting vision, but I was *not* a telepath. I did not read minds. I certainly couldn't influence people in the way I could animals.

Animals' emotions caused both physical and psychological reactions, but people were worse. If I let them through, strong emotions caused nausea, vertigo, and headaches. A psychiatrist, a family friend, helped me learn to deal with my ability, but I had to develop my own mental shields by trial and error, and they were not perfect. In the inevitable fistfights of youth, I was doubly handicapped. Along with any physical beating, I got an emotional one from the anger of my opponent. While I avoided reading human emotions, leakage was all too common. One of my veterinary college professors knew of my empathy for animals, but kept the secret. I did not want other faculty and students to see me as a freak. After reading Asimov's *Foundation* books, I worried I would be looked at like his Mule character, and that people would fear and shun me. So I kept my secret close.

However, I never could hide anything from my

parents, and I often wondered if they had some of the same talent and could read me as well as I read them.

"But that's it..." I came to a halt under my father's hooded stare. "Dad, please. I can't say anything more."

"You're in trouble again, aren't you?" He sighed. "What did you do this time?"

I hunched my shoulders, but looked him in the eyes as I answered in a small voice. "I blew it. I shot my mouth off in front of some rebbes." I held up my hands, palms forward. "I didn't know they were there." I knew that was a miserable excuse and dropped my eyes. "Now, the Council wants me out of their hair—way out."

My father's lips thinned. "I've told you a hundred times, Cy: All the intelligence in the world is useless without common sense. You know the Test-Lits don't tolerate dissent."

Yeah, I knew. For the past eighty years, the fundamentalist Testamentary-Literalist party ruled our planet with an iron hand and had become an oxymoron, an evangelistic Judaic tyranny—with an Inquisition, yet. Our people left Old Earth more than a thousand years ago, refugees from an oppressive Islamic world government. The age-old enmity between Hebrews and Muslims became intolerable and forced what Jews hoped would be the final stage in the Jewish diaspora.

My voice shook. "Reb Schvartz is a member of the Rebbinical Council. He...he threatened me with the Inquisition—you and Mom, too—if I don't do as he says."

Dad's face creased with pain. "Reb Schvartz. From what I've heard, he's the most sadistic of the Inquisitors." He shook his head. "You really know how to pick them."

"How can they justify what they do?" I cried. "The Inquisition was a church tribunal to torture heretics, particularly Jews. To have Jews use it to torture their own people..?"

Dad frowned. "The Test-Lits' use of the term Inquisition is deliberate. Even two thousand years later, the original Inquisition echoes in the fears of Jews throughout the galaxy." He opened his arms.

I stood and stepped within his embrace. Tears filled my eyes. I felt his strength. I had attained his above average height, but not his muscular physique. I stepped back and looked at him. I saw myself in his reddish brown hair, his gray eyes, his chiseled face, and the hook of his prominent nose—the latter, unfortunately, even more exaggerated on my face.

"One more thing," I said. "Reb Schvartz is going with me."

Dad's rush of fear washed over me, roiling the small amount of schnapps I had managed to swallow.

"That is a dangerous man, Cy. You need to keep your wits about you. You need to control your quick temper."

"I can take care of myself."

Dad shook his head. "I know you are a fighter. We had to pull you out of enough scrapes as a kid. But I'm not talking about your martial arts training. You can't let it come to something like that. You cannot antagonize Schvartz. Promise me, son. Don't start a fight you can't win."

I swallowed hard and nodded.

"Say nothing of this to your mother. Come. It's time for dinner."

It was Friday night and we lit the candles and recited the *shabbos* prayers. I no longer attended synagogue—the Test-Lits brand of religion had put me off that—but the traditions I had been raised with meant more to me now than they had at any time in my life. Mom had prepared my favorites: matzoh ball soup, brisket with potato kugel, and rugullah pastries for dessert. Dinner sat in my stomach like lead.

On Saturday morning, I promised my folks that I would visit before I shipped out. I merged my land drone onto the autoroad, let the autopilot connect with the road's traffic system, and sat back. I watched the pastoral scenery flow by. Golden grain fields and hay meadows stacked with bales were interspersed with verdant pastures dotted with cattle, goats, and sheep. Those animals and chickens came from earth during the diaspora in the giant, multi-generation seedships. They allowed Dovid's World to develop as a self-sustaining agricultural ecology. Even now, other than the roads, vehicles, and farm machinery, much of our world would have been familiar to Terrans of a thousand years ago.

Since the takeover by the Test-Lits, the latest technology was difficult to come by for the average citizen. The government and military restricted the use of winged aircraft, whirlydrones, and hovercraft to *approved* personnel. Antigravity propulsion technology was even more restricted, and space travel was out for all but the military. Most people made do with wheeled land drones. The Test-Lits monitored movement between local districts to keep tabs on revolutionaries, who were always thorns in the side of the government despite official pronouncements that they were of no concern.

Even as I thought this, my vehicle slowed for the first of a half dozen military checkpoints I would negotiate before I reached Jerusalem City. A camouflage-clad Zionist Guard member motioned me to roll down my windscreen. I wondered at the ubiquitous camouflage uniforms of the military. Did they hope someone might miss them standing in the middle of the road so they could unlimber their blasters to fry some rebel?

He stuck out his hand. "Papers."

I guess military mothers never taught their kids to say please. I handed over my documents. The guard looked at the folder, looked at my face, glanced back at the papers, and then returned them. Without another word, he waved me through.

The fields blended to an aureate blur and I closed my eyes. I wished I could be more like my dad, stoic and wise, never one to speak without careful forethought rather than the impulsive idiot I tended to be.

At school, I had never missed the opportunity to show off my smarts, which antagonized most other kids. My ability to read human emotions went beyond facial expressions and body language. I sensed what lay deep within, feelings no one was willing to show. This was more a curse than a blessing, since I perceived the hostile vibes I engendered. I learned that even supposed friends harbored negative feelings.

I isolated myself because I did not know how to deal with the perceived antipathy, and the resulting constant queasiness and headaches were intolerable. As an only child, I became a loner and a compulsive reader and watcher of Old Earth books and vids when I didn't have chores.

Almost everything ever written and filmed was preserved in digital format. Fortunately for me, that included even bad vids: some of those were a kick to watch, particularly the old science fiction flicks predicting the future I now inhabited. I laughed at the Fourth-of-July sparkler spaceships of Flash Gordon, the ubiquitous and clunky robots, the inevitably big-headed aliens. I marveled at the predictions of the writings of Verne, Wells, Clarke, and Gibson. I shed tears at Simmons's portrait of a father watching his daughter aging backwards in *Hyperion*.

I remained a loner and, in some ways, looked forward to the isolation of space travel, though the thought of Reb Levi as my companion made my heart pound all the way to Jerusalem City.

***

Levi lectured me on my assignment in his office at his headquarters. I had never been in Government House. The Palmach storm troopers in every hallway sent shivers through me, but at least it was not the Inquisition prison. Levi's office was less intimidating than the interrogation room. It even included a generic landscape painting and a potted plant—no torture instruments, thankfully. He sat in a chair in front of a window, a black silhouette against the light.

"You will pursue your clinical duties and recruit students for the Academy on each world that we visit. I will tell you where to go. Our ship is well-equipped, so I expect you to impress the worlds we visit with veterinary medicine on Dovid's World. I will set the fees for these services, after all, we must pay for our travels.

"I will be your veterinary assistant, but remember *I* am in charge. You will obey my orders without question. You are responsible for what happens to your parents. Is that clear, Berger?"

I could only nod. The man had no clue as to what a veterinary assistant's job entailed. I looked forward to his education: how to collect urine and fecal samples and how to express infected anal sacs, among other grisly tasks.

My hospital ship—a converted space yacht from a time when private citizens could have space yachts— looked a bit like a giant, inverted "T," with the engines at the bottom of the cross-bar. It had been fitted with the latest antigravity drive for use within planetary atmospheres, an anti-matter drive for interplanetary travel, and an interstellar hyperspace jumpdrive. This voyage was obviously important to the Test-Lits. No way would we ever pay off the cost of this thing with veterinary services and new students. I puzzled over that quite a bit, especially since I assumed most human-settled worlds would already have veterinarians.

A wheeled land drone chassis with a rear compartment fitted as a combined examination room, surgery suite, and laboratory would give me mobility on planets. On the side of the spaceship and on the side of the land drone cabin was the symbol of veterinary medicine: the letter V super-imposed on the staff of Aesculapius. It overlaid a picture of a spiral galaxy and blood red letters surrounded this: *Galactic Circle Veterinary Service.*

The name seemed a bit presumptuous, but I liked it nonetheless. I thought of the ship as the *GCVS.* If not for the specter of Levi and the Inquisition, I would have been ecstatic. As it was, I felt like an ancient cartoon character I had seen: a man with a permanent thundercloud over his head who was the earth's greatest jinx.

***

As I nursed a drink in my favorite tavern, Furoletto Cohen asked to join me. I had not seen him since my arrest.

After some small talk, he said, "I worried about you after the night we met."

I told him about my opportunity. I did not mention the Inquisition, of course.

"That's remarkable. It says something about your

abilities that they will speed up graduation and send you off on a mission of such importance. Congratulations." He looked at me with a furrowed brow. "But I'm confused. That night in the tavern, a member of the Rebbinical Council tore into you for your heresy. Why the change in heart?"

I took note that he recognized Reb Levi, but I brushed that aside and gave him part of the story, otherwise it would look as phony as a three-dollar bill, as the ancients used to say. "The Council decided I was better off someplace where I couldn't spread my seditious ideas. This was a way to get me out of their hair without making a martyr out of me. But it is a great chance for me to get experience."

Fur smiled. "I'm glad you didn't get targeted by the Inquisition."

"Um, yeah. Lucky, I guess."

Fur pursed his lips and tugged at his beard. "I almost envy you."

I snorted. "Yeah. Envy the fact that I am exiled—" I snapped my mouth shut. It had overridden my brain once again.

Fur leaned back in his seat. When I looked away and fiddled with my beer mug, he spoke. "Okay, you've got my attention."

"An experiment. That's what I meant. It's an experiment sending a new graduate on such a mission." My phony grin felt more like a grimace.

Fur stared at me.

I blinked first. Something about the big man's general demeanor and aura inspired my confidence, and I made a snap decision. I hoped I would not regret it as I did with my decisions all too often. In a low voice I said, "I'm being exiled. My parents and I have been threatened with the Inquisition if I don't do as they say."

Fur sat forward. "But why are they outfitting you for this space voyage?"

My hands trembled as I rolled my mug between them. "I've thought a lot about that. I'm guessing that it's a ploy to get a rebbe to other worlds as a spy. Reb Levi Schvartz is going with me as my assistant."

Fur's lips twisted in a grimace. "You might be right. Political representatives from Dovid's World have been *persona non grata* on other planets since the Test-Lits' attempt to subjugate Sammara." He referred to the only other inhabited planet in our solar system.

Too late, my caution kicked in and I started to panic. I grabbed his arm. "Please, don't say anything. I'm not supposed to tell anybody. I don't know what they'll do to me or my folks if Levi finds out."

Fur's paw covered my hand. "Don't worry. I won't get you in trouble." He let me have my hand back and shook his head. "Schvartz, huh? Not the most companionable of traveling partners."

I looked over my shoulder. Paranoia closed in on me. "You obviously recognized him. How well do you know Schvartz?"

"By reputation only."

"What have you heard?"

"That he's the top man in the Inquisition. He's a nasty piece of work. I knew a guy who was pulled in and interrogated. They thought he was a member of the resistance."

"Was he?"

"No, but he was crippled by the time they released him."

That did not ring true. Fur was not telling me something. I wondered if the guy in his story *was* connected to the resistance. Either way, the story gave me the creeps. Reb Levi was pure evil. I shuddered.

We spoke a bit more about the trip before I needed

to leave for an appointment. As I rose, Fur asked if we might meet again. I sensed a strange excitement behind his words. I agreed.

The next couple of weeks, the Associate Dean for recruiting kept me busy. I had to learn all about the finances of the Academy, how students were selected, and how I was to act as the Academy's agent on the worlds that we would visit. I found that it was far more complicated than I had realized. The Associate Dean gave me speeches for different audiences. My spiel to students would be different from those I gave to school officials or local veterinary societies. I was not nearly as thrilled about that aspect of my job as I was about the real medical challenges I would face. After all, veterinary medicine is what I had studied for the past four years, not how to sign up new students. The Associate Dean finally cut me loose saying I was as prepared as I could be. That remained to be seen.

***

When I met Fur again, he seemed nervous. He finished his beer and lowered his voice, not an easy thing for him. "Cy, I-I have a request of you."

"Yeah?"

He looked around the room, then back at me. "Ten years ago I enrolled in the vet college, but I dropped out after two years. I decided that there were more important things than becoming a veterinarian. Family matters, you know? I settled for being an assistant."

I nodded, though I detected evasion in his thoughts.

"I've been working at a private clinic as a veterinary technician. I'm a damned good one, too. I want to go with you."

"It's not up to me—"

"I'll never get this opportunity again."

"I don't know."

"I can watch your back."

Astonished and not sure what to say, I sat silently for a few moments, but some of his excitement rubbed off on me. "Let me ask about it."

We finished our drinks over small talk and exchanged commlink data. I promised to get back to him.

I gave his offer lots of thought. I wondered what motivated the big guy. There was a deeper story than he was telling. If he knew that Levi was a sadistic son-of-a-bitch, why would he subject himself to a space voyage with the rebbe? On the other hand, it was easy to make the case for a real veterinary assistant besides Reb Levi. I would train and utilize the rebbe for routine tasks, but I doubted he would meet all the needs of my practice. I still needed someone like Fur to hold animals, to assist in surgery, to run the lab, and more, like watch my back.

I checked into Fur's background and confirmed his story about vet school and his job as a veterinary technician. His references were outstanding. He was the perfect choice; he had the background and there were few animals the big guy couldn't handle—or so I thought.

Levi remembered him from our tavern debate and was thrilled to have someone else along who saw eye-to-eye with him, at least with respect to religious matters. Fur passed the Rebbinical Council's screening, so I gained a real assistant and a badly needed ally. Maybe someone to keep Levi's venom from poisoning the whole trip.

***

Our spaceship had a brand-new Artificial

Intelligence, although the ship itself was a reconstruction job. I guessed that was okay. They wouldn't put an expensive new AI and fancy drives in a questionable hull, I hoped.

As the first with access to the AI, I programmed and customized the interface. I added something that I did not tell anyone about: an override that would make the AI accept only my commands in case it came to a battle between me and Reb Levi, something I feared. I also named the AI *Ruthie* and gave her a seductive female voice to annoy the stiff-necked Levi.

"That is not acceptable," he fumed at me. "This is a computer. Computers do not have *names*."

Before I could respond, Ruthie chimed in. "But Cy gave me a name and I like it," she said in an excellent approximation of a whine.

Shit. That did not help. I switched off the AI's voice circuit. "A name will make it easier to give the ship commands," I argued. "Saying 'computer' all the time is awkward."

Levi scowled at me, but I did not back down, and the name stuck. I hoped I would not pay for that victory somewhere down the line, but I could not resist pulling his chain to achieve even a minuscule quantum of control.

The three of us, Levi, Fur, and I, took a crash course in operation of all the ship's systems. Although the AI handled everything, there was the outside chance that we humans would have to intervene. What if the AI failed? That fear lost me one night's sleep to a dream where the ship flew into the sun while Ruthie seduced me. "We will go out in a blaze of orgasmic glory," she said in her sexy contralto.

My first erotic nightmare, and I hoped the last.

Fur was more mechanical-minded than me. He said he had grown up fixing all the machinery on his farm, and been good enough that neighbors frequently enlisted him for help. He had also operated and repaired the medical equipment at his clinic. Levi came in a distant third in that regard. We sat around a small table in a room at the spaceport.

Levi pointed to a parts schematic of the air-processing unit. "What is this, here?"

His voice grated on my nerves. The trip hadn't even started yet and already his sour disposition and unpleasant aura bugged me. "That's the grabmitz valve."

I sensed Fur suppress a laugh at the name I'd pulled out of thin air.

"What does it do?" Levi asked.

"It's critical for the freebwhanil to scrub carbon dioxide out of the recycled air. If the freebwhanil fails, we suffocate to death."

"Suffocate?" Levi's voice rose as his eye twitched. He looked at Fur. "Can that happen?" He looked back at me, black eyes probing. "Is this one of your jokes, Berger?"

Fur remained mute as if to let the tension ratchet up a bit then jumped to my rescue. "It's no joke, Reb Levi. If the air scrubbers fail, carbon dioxide levels would rise and the air would become toxic."

He omitted reference to the grabmitz valve and freebwhanil because they did not exist. "The main thing we need to know is the oxygen-carbon dioxide ratio. That shows on the screen over here." He pointed to the drawing. "If that's good, we don't have to worry about the workings of the equipment. I'll handle repairs in case of a problem."

Levi nodded. "That is good. I will be busy with spiritual matters. They are just as important as the mechanical ones."

Right. I would grab the extra oxygen tank while he

prayed for deliverance.

***

Reb Levi had to make some major changes to accommodate his new role. It began with a clothing change, no more Darth Vader black-on-black like the old vids. He wore a white shirt, dark gray suit, and an over-the-top splash of color—a dark blue tie. His new look included a shave, but he looked uncomfortable shorn, and his scar stood out even more. However, his head was never without his fedora or a *yarmulke*, both black of course.

Levi's lessons as a veterinary assistant took place in the laboratory of the *GCVS*.

I motioned for Levi to move closer.

He flinched when I raised a scalpel to his face. "What are you doing?"

"Relax. I'm just going to take a skin scraping, for God's sake."

He scowled and adjusted his *yarmulke*. "Your continued use of our Lord's name in vain does you no good, Berger."

"Sorry. Just hold still."

I scraped the greasy, blackhead-dotted skin beside his nose. Nauseating, but worth the effort, I hoped. I had him place the scrapings on a slide and instructed him in further preparation of the sample. He examined it under the dual-headed microscope. I wondered that he could even focus through the eyepieces, his left eye twitched so violently.

"What is *that*?" He recoiled from the microscope.

"Those are mange mites. The *Demodex* mite is a common inhabitant of the skin of people and animals. Ugly little things, aren't they?"

"They were in my skin?" His mouth turned down at

the corners.

"They creep around in there and feed off your dead cells."

His ruddy face paled.

"Now let's take a look at the cultures you prepared from your skin a couple of days ago."

I brought out the Petri dishes from the incubator. Numerous bacterial colonies in sickly whites, yellows, browns, and blues dotted the gelatin surfaces of the plates.

As he stared at them, his face paled even more. "Yech," he mumbled.

His almost palpable queasiness delighted me even though I felt it as he did. I showed him how to make smears and stain them. At the microscope again, I said, "Those little round guys in chains are streptococci," as he peered into the lenses. "They can cause sore throats and meningitis."

His cheeks puffed out, fighting back his nausea.

"The round ones in bunches are staphylococci. They cause abscesses with thick nasty yellow pus."

I could *hear* faint gurgling in his stomach.

"Those rod-shaped ones are *E. coli*. You know, fecal bacteria?"

That did it. He stood, slammed his hand to his mouth, and rushed out of the lab.

Fur, who had observed us, said, "Our rebbe is not the only one with a sadistic streak, you know that? Be careful you don't take it too far."

"I don't know how else to fight back." I swallowed hard to remove the acid taste in my own mouth; my actions to gross out Levi was not without its side effects on me.

I sensed a rush of indecision from Fur, as if he were on the cusp of a major decision to reveal something, but it receded as quickly as it came.

Whatever that meant, he was right. Inconsequential triumphs like these did nothing but feed my need for revenge against Levi, and that could spell trouble for everyone.

***

My final visit to my parents was short, but difficult. Mom could not stop her tears no matter how I tried to assure her things would be fine. I wondered how much Dad had told her about my predicament.

My stomach squirmed and my head ached as I envisioned my failure to protect my folks. The thought of them subjected to torture made me fight to keep my own tears under control.

Mom forced a smile. "Just take care of yourself, darling. We're going to miss you at graduation."

Dad put his arm around her. "Cy is not going to be gone forever. He'll be back before we know it."

She looked up at him, then at me, bleary-eyed, as if uncertainty and fear clouded her mind.

Dad hugged Mom with one arm. "The college will present your diploma to us in your stead, but it's unfair not to have you there. They could have delayed your trip for another month." A touch of anger colored his thoughts. His eyes told me to say nothing more.

As I left, Mom cried in my dad's arms.

Would I ever see them again? My breath caught at the real possibility that I might never return home. I desperately wanted to turn back, to stay with them, protect them, but I was powerless. The lump in my throat did not leave for a long while. I prayed there would be no further reasons for Mom's tears.

CHAPTER 4

THE SHIP'S ANTIGRAVITY DRIVE quashed my childhood vision of blasting off the planet on a tail of flame. Although antigravity thrust could ramp up to four-g during liftoff, the drive also supplied artificial gravity and kept the occupants in a one-g environment. We took off as comfortably as any atmospheric craft. For the long space voyage, artificial gravity was a major physiological blessing. For someone like me who got sick on a merry-go-round, no zero-g was a godsend.

Once we reached orbit around Dovid's World, the vista made up for any disappointment. Emerald forests, sapphire seas, and umber deserts winked from beneath pearlescent clouds, all hung on a sable canvas. I imagined that the refugees had the same reaction when they first looked upon Dovid's World more than a thousand years ago and named their new home for a heroic spaceman who had saved one of the colony ships at the cost of his own life.

"Beautiful, isn't it?" Fur said.

Even Levi was moved, his tone reverent. "God's handiwork is always magnificent."

I turned to the two men who would share my extended journey. I looked forward to whatever adventures awaited me, but was fearful of what might happen—to me and my parents—if I did not fulfill the desires of Levi and the Rebbinical Council.

Despite that, hope remained in the back of my mind. My philosophical beliefs had not changed because the Test-Lits held my folks hostage. I dreamed that someday I would return to help free my world from oppression, although I was clueless as to how I might accomplish that. I glared at Levi's back as he gazed out the viewport. I wondered what his ultimate plan was for this voyage. He never openly stated his intent to spy on the worlds we would visit, but he had dropped enough hints to be obvious. I sure as hell did not want to be involved in anything like that. What kind of information did he expect to gather?

The command chairs on the bridge molded themselves to our bodies as we settled into them. Levi gave orders to Ruthie.

"Computer. Take us to orbit around Sammara." He refused to use her name.

Sammara was the other inhabited world in NewSol's solar system. The Dovid's Worlders were not very inventive when they named our sun. The antimatter drive kicked in for the interplanetary jaunt. Once out of a planet's gravity well, the antigravity drive's efficiency wanes quickly. So I got to ride a tail of antimatter flame, but the acceleration and ride were anticlimactic.

When Sammara hung below us, just as impressive from space as Dovid's World, it had the added thrill of an unfamiliar world. Levi and I were alone on the bridge.

He said, "Computer, contact the authorities so we can land."

"Wait." I turned to him. "Reb Levi, I have to be the one to make the official contact."

His ruddy face became darker as he faced me. "What?"

I ignored his red-faced glower. "I have to be Captain of the *Galactic Circle Veterinary Service*. I'm the Doctor of Veterinary Medicine and this is a veterinary clinic ship. How could my assistant be Captain? That makes no sense."

"I am in charge of this expedition." Levi's tone was low and dangerous. His left eye twitched as he rubbed his scar with his left hand.

"Well, yeah," I conceded. "But don't you want to keep your ability to collect information intact? You can do that better if you aren't in charge. You'll be undercover, so to speak."

"You do not know what I am going to do," he snapped. "Remember your place and what is at stake."

I did not respond and I felt the gears grind in his polished dome as he scratched beneath his *yarmulke*. "But I suppose it does make some sense that I am free to explore the worlds we stop on. The Council will want reports about them. But you follow my directions. Is that understood?" He pointed a stocky finger at me like a firearm. He then looked at the comm board as if it was the core of the AI. "Is that clear, Computer? I give the orders."

"Certainly, Reb Levi," Ruthie responded in a prim and businesslike voice rather than the sultry intonation she used with me. It made me wonder just how intelligent this AI was to pick up on the differences in our personalities.

I said, "Fur will be co-captain and you the mate." I continued before his temper could explode. "That makes sense, too, since Fur is the real veterinary technician. He needs to be at my side for all medical activities, whereas you can go off to do other things. After all, who would worry about a mate?"

Levi's glare intensified. "I am not a 'mate,' I am a member of the Rebbinical Council, and don't you forget that. You can be the Captain in name, but that means nothing. We know who is *really* in charge, no matter what the titles."

I smiled at him. "Of course."

***

About thirty minutes after contact with the Sammaran spaceport, a small, sleek and obviously military spaceship pulled up alongside and extruded a boarding tube to link with our ship. Another disappointment. As a fan of the ancient vid series, *Star Trek*, I longed to have someone materialize on my deck, accompanied by the famous "Beam me up!" command. Alas, transporter physics had proven to be fictional.

A well-starched young officer greeted us and asked a million questions about who we were, why we were here, what we intended to do on Sammara, and how long we would stay. I assumed he had some sort of recording device, though I could see none. He finished without one change in his expression.

"You will be contacted," he said and left.

I looked at Fur with raised eyebrows. He shrugged. Levi scowled. We dared not say anything suspect, since we had no idea of Sammaran surveillance technology. The officer could have left the *GCVS* bugged, for all we knew. So we waited. And waited some more. A day passed before anything happened, and not what I expected.

The comm lit up, and Ruthie's sultry voice announced, "Galactic Circle Veterinary Service. Thank you for calling. We are here to serve you. Please pay attention since our menu has recently changed. For Captain Cy Berger, press or say *one*. For Co-Captain Furoletto Cohen, please press or say *two*. For Mate Levi—"

A gravelly voice broke in. "What the hell is this?" The voice rose. "I am Colonel Glazer. Sammaran security. Who the hell are you?"

Ruthie responded, "Sorry, I did not understand your response. Please press or say *one* for Capt—"

"I'll be pressing something you don't like in one minute. Get me the Captain." A string of oaths followed.

When I programmed Ruthie's interface, her name was not the only place where I was creative. I made her sound like a receptionist I'd heard on an ancient vid when everyone had something called telephones. But this comm greeting was not one I had programmed. Where in hell did the AI get it from? Before the colonel's lack of patience could get any worse, I jumped in. "Um, sorry, Colonel. This is Captain Berger."

I resisted the urge to announce, "Captain James T. Kirk, here,"—no one would have understood, anyway.

"Captain Berger," the colonel barked. "Get your ass down here."

"So we're cleared to bring the ship in?"

"A ship will pick you up. Just you. It will rendezvous in five minutes. Out."

Levi had sputtered in the background during this exchange. He now shouted, "I forbid it. You cannot go to the surface alone. I *must* accompany you. The Rebbinical Council demands it."

I faced him. "Do *you* want to call him back?" I jerked my thumb toward the comm board.

He took my meaning and shut up. How could he, as a mate, override his captain and maintain the secrecy his spying demanded?

Levi took a deep breath and walked to the bridge hatch. There he stopped and addressed me. "I want an exact transcription when you return. Use those." He pointed to a bulkhead compartment and left us.

Levi had stocked a number of tiny recording devices for his own use. I retrieved one and stuck it in a small pocket in the lining of my tunic.

Fur raised one shaggy eyebrow and pulled on his beard. He said nothing, but I sensed his internal laughter.

"Shut up. I know what I'm doing."

***

The same officer who had questioned us on the *GCVS* led me through the spaceport. The terminal was far busier than any transportation station I had seen on Dovid's World. People of every size, shape, and skin color were clothed in tunics and bodysuits of bright pastels and fluorescents never seen on my world, where black was the approved garb. Crowds scurried in and out doors and up and down moving walkways. Some of the old sci-fi vids did not miss by much that this would be a typical spaceport in the future. We left the public area through an exit flanked by two armed guards. The sign read: *Official Business Only*. We walked until we reached a door marked with a plaque: *Colonel Glazer*.

I took a deep breath and let it out slowly

My guide opened the door, motioned me inside, and then closed it while staying outside.

A gray-haired woman behind a desk directed me to another office door. When I opened it, a haze that resembled the effluvium from a pile of manure on fire enveloped me. A smoke-shrouded figure spoke. "Well, don't just stand there like a donkey. Get your ass in here." He laughed at his own pun.

I stepped forward and held my breath for fear of asphyxiation.

"Shut the goddamned door."

I did as asked, then took a breath to speak—a mistake. When I stopped coughing, I croaked, "Sir. I'm Cy Berger of the Galactic Circle Veterinary Service." My heart pounded like racehorse hooves in the stretch run.

"C'mere. Siddown."

The man sat in an old-fashioned rocking chair, for God's sake. The smoke emanated from a large brown cylinder that protruded from his mouth. How someone could put something as vile as that in his mouth, much less smoke it, I couldn't fathom. My stomach clenched, both from the fumes and from my dread.

"Humph. You don't look like one of them orthodoxies. I said *siddown*."

I found a chair and sat.

"What in hell do you think you're doing here? We have no love for you Dovidians." Though his words were angry, I detected underlying amusement. His protracted silence made me realize it was my turn.

I recited the spiel given me by Levi and the Deans about recruiting for the veterinary college and staying away from anything that sounded remotely like it was connected to religion, although my voice quavered and broke like a teenager asking for a first date. The colonel sat poker-faced. When I finished, he pointed to my lapel and pantomimed me to remove something. It took me a moment to realize he not only knew about my recording device, but he wanted me to give it to him. They must have run some sort of body scan. I gave it to him and he put it in a small box on top of his desk.

"That's all bullshit," he said.

I swallowed, a sound I imagined the secretary could hear through the closed door. What in hell was going on here? My knees knocked and my hands shook. I clasped my hands between my knees to quiet both.

"Okay. Enough fun and games. Now tell me the

truth. This thing won't pick up anything more," he gestured at the box, "and we can record some fake crap later. Your government is a bunch of fucking idiots. We're aware that you have a Test-Lit spy on board, this Reb Schvartz character, and that Cohen is a member of the Sons-of-David resistance. So what the fuck is *your* role in this goddamned circus?"

I could only imagine my expression as my mind corkscrewed in confusion.

Glazer reached into his desk, pulled out a bottle, and poured dark liquid into a glass. He handed it to me. "If you're going to sit there with your mouth hanging open, you might as well put something in it. You look like you need this. Drink it." It wasn't a request.

I followed orders but coughed up the first swallow. The stuff was vile. Fortunately, I turned to the side and didn't spray the colonel. Whatever it was, it burned its way down to my already squeamish stomach.

"Don't you dare puke on my desk. Shit. You guys can't even take your liquor." He looked over my head. "Esther. Get in here with a couple of towels. And bring a glass of water."

Esther came in, gave me the water and a towel, made a few cursory swipes over the rug with the other towel, then left. She must have watched my performance on a monitor.

I took a drink of water and wiped my chin. I could not believe it. They knew about Levi. What had I gotten into now? Sammaran jail? And Furoletto Cohen a member of the Sons-of-David, the most active underground resistance group to the Test-Lits on Dovid's World? What was *my* role? My mind was unable to come up with a response.

Glazer stared at me as his vile beverage tried to claw its way back *out* of my gut.

"Are you really as clueless as you look? Is that

possible?"

I choked out, "I-I'm being blackmailed!"

The colonel sighed. "Let's have it. The whole story."

As I spoke, his eyes and mouth tightened. I felt his anger grow, fortunately, not directed at me. I struggled to keep my empathic shields intact.

His voice was less harsh when he addressed me. "Let me tell you what you are going to do next."

***

Sammara, colonized later than Dovid's World, was farther from NewSol and had a colder climate. It had a much smaller population, most living in the equatorial region. When the Test-Lits invaded, the Sammarans called for help, and several other worlds from different star systems responded. This led to an ignominious back-down by the Dovidians. There was no love between the two worlds, as Glazer had said.

Most émigrés from my home first ended up on Sammara. The Test-Lits had driven out not only those of other religions, but many liberal Jews as well, before they clamped down on travel. Sammara had a large Jewish population. Judaic sects were varied, including Reform, Conservative, and Orthodox, but the more traditional and reasonable forms of the latter than the Test-Lits' evangelical fundamentalism. A much broader range of humanity and religions had settled the world, as well. Since the invasion, Sammara had expanded its military, not enough to take on the Test-Lits alone, but enough to hold them off until their allies could respond.

Colonel Glazer was reluctant to have Reb Levi step foot on Sammara, but he did want Fur to have an opportunity to contact the Sons-of-David command on the planet. Since Levi was unlikely to allow us to go anywhere without him, Glazer suggested an option and said he would make it happen. I returned to the *GCVS*.

That night, I cornered Fur in his cabin. "Furoletto Cohen. You lied to me. You're a Son-of-David and a son-of-a-bitch to boot. You're putting my family and me in danger. What the hell do you think you're doing?"

His face grew red. His voice was a low rumble—soft for him. "I'm sorry. I didn't like to deceive you, but it was necessary. The SOD kept an eye on you after we first met. Some in our party thought to recruit you for your brilliance, and you obviously believe as we do. But because you were in the Rebbinical Council's sights and because of your tendency to be...less than circumspect, it was too risky to sign you up."

"Crap. I don't give a damn about your Sons-of-David. I care about my parents. And me. If the Council thinks that I had anything to do with this—"

"Cy, when you told me you were offered this job, it was too good an opportunity to pass up. The SOD leaders wanted to keep watch on your overseer. My veterinary and mechanical background was perfect for that. I could stand up to the Council's scrutiny.

"Schvartz made it clear to me that he's in charge of this expedition. He didn't tell me he was a spy, but he insinuated that." Fur grimaced. "The man can't help but crow about how important he is. I'll stay undercover and not do anything to threaten your situation."

"You'll stay undercover? How will you do that with Reb Levi poking his nose into every nook and cranny? You're going to get us killed."

"Calm down. I promise—"

"You promise?" I shouted.

Fur winced, and I realized I could draw Levi's attention. I lowered my voice. "I don't trust your promises. You lied to me once, how do I know you're not lying to me now?" I stopped ranting, drew a deep breath, and let it out. "God help us both—if He isn't on the Test-Lits' side."

I turned and stalked from Fur's cabin. I slammed the hatch behind me. From a simple student with no greater goals than a rural veterinary practice when I graduated, I had become a subject of the Inquisition, the patsy for a Testamentary-Literalist spy, and now the cover for a counterspy. I faced an interstellar voyage sandwiched between a sadistic representative of the government I hated and a member of the underground resistance that I could not afford to support.

I sure hoped God would help me.

***

Ruthie set the *GCVS* down on a vacant pad at the edge of the spaceport outside of Sammarak, the capital city. A young man in a blue and white uniform met us when we disembarked.

"Captain Berger? I'm Lieutenant Clarrett. I've been assigned to assist you."

Reb Levi frowned, muttered something inaudible, and started to walk toward the terminal. Clarrett's jaw clenched, and the muscle bulged and twitched as he watched the rebbe move away.

I glanced at Fur. I had not spoken to him since the previous night and did not intend to now. As repugnant as Levi was, at least he had never lied to me. In the back of my mind, I realized the ridiculousness of that thought, but my anger submerged the absurdity.

Clarrett quickly caught up to the rebbe. Fur and I followed.

After a quick tour of the terminal so we could find our way around later—the busy concourses, shops, hotels, and administrative offices were well-marked—

another officer named Ranu joined us. I didn't catch his rank, but he had one less stripe on his sleeve than the lieutenant. We headed into town on a monorail.

Clarrett engaged Reb Levi in conversation and was quite civil despite Levi's petulant manner and his known history.

We passed through well-kept farmland before we entered the city proper. The buildings were relatively new, mostly plastrete structures with lots of glass. Gleaming hovercraft swooped along tree-lined roadways and occasional aircraft glided overhead. This activity, far greater than the norm for Dovid's World, suggested that Sammara's economy well exceeded our own.

"This section of town is new," Ranu said to Fur and me. "It was destroyed in the invasion thirty years ago and rebuilt." He said this in a flat tone as he stared out the window.

I looked over at Levi, but he and Clarrett were talking and had not heard the comment. Out of curiosity, I kept one ear directed toward the Clarrett-Levi dialog.

"...and you do not worry about security issues outside the spaceport? Interesting. What about your standing armed forces, don't you use those for security in the city?" Levi's spying was so obvious it was comical.

Clarrett said, "No. We keep our standing forces to a minimum. It costs far too much to maintain a large army and navy when they aren't needed."

"Yes, I see." Levi's head bobbed up and down as he unsuccessfully attempted to suppress a predatory grin as they discussed military and security issues.

Stunned, I wrenched my attention away from the two. Ranu asked me a question I didn't catch. "Sorry, what was that?"

A smile fleeted over Ranu's lips. "What in particular would you like to see today? Are you interested in entertainment? Shopping? Sightseeing? We'll get off at the city center."

"Uh, sightseeing is fine," I replied.

We got off the rail at the center of town, and Clarrett and Ranu pointed out some of the sights. Again, the buildings were new and modern.

"This is the tallest building on the planet," Clarrett said. He pointed upward. "One hundred and ten floors. Graphsteel reinforced, like all of our new buildings. The glass facing is nano reinforced, as well. It's commercial, but the top ten floors have luxury condominiums—and I mean *luxury*." He laughed. "A week in one of those would cost me half a year's salary. Let's walk around to the next block." He surreptitiously glanced at Levi. "There's something I think you might be interested in."

I caught a brief grin from Ranu.

As we moved through the crowds, people entered and exited businesses all along the street. Besides the color of garb, the thing that struck me most was the absence of head coverings on most of the men. Ancient Jewish law required a man to cover his head during prayer, although a head covering at other times for Orthodox males was custom. On Dovid's World, while not required by law, the vast majority of males wore hats or *yarmulkes*, even outside of synagogue. While neither Fur nor I wore a head covering when not in prayer, Levi would not dispense with his hat or *yarmulke*, undermining his ridiculous masquerade.

The lieutenant, the rebbe, and I forged ahead of Ranu and Fur. Still fascinated by the dynamics between the two men, I did not want to miss anything.

"And these buildings are designed to resist bombardment, you say?" Levi asked.

How could he be any more transparent? I couldn't believe him.

"Oh, yes." Clarrett looked at Levi with a bland expression. "We have learned from our experience."

That comment seemed to fly right over Levi's head.

"Here, this is our main military intelligence center," Clarrett said.

We stood in front of a plastrete and graphsteel building that had few windows. Levi's mouth hung open and his eyes glazed over.

Clarrett grimaced as he watched the rebbe. I saw the muscle in his jaw bulge and twitch again, but he swallowed and spoke, "Would you like to go in?"

Was this really their intelligence center? Levi was so eager that he was laughable. I mulled over Clarrett's performance. It had to be a sham, a ploy to feed Levi a bunch of false information.

I looked around for Fur and Ranu, but they were nowhere in sight. I turned to Clarrett. "Hey, what happened to Ranu and Fur?"

At my words, Levi spun around. "What do you mean?"

I bit my tongue, hard. The ferric tang of blood forced me to swallow and collect my wits before I responded. I knew that Fur would be spirited away for an SOD meeting, but my mouth overrode my brain again. When would I learn?

"Um...well...they were right behind us." I wanted to crawl down the nearest sewer drain.

Levi turned to Clarrett and dropped his submissive pose. "What has happened to them?" he snapped.

Clarrett shrugged. "I have no idea. We didn't have any particular schedule or route. Maybe they missed us when we turned the corner back there. Don't worry about them. The city is very safe, and Ranu knows his way around."

Stephen A. Benjamin

"That is not the point," Levi barked. "I need to know—" He stopped short, squinted his left eye in an attempt to control its twitching, and then forced a smile. "Well, I suppose that they will be fine." Neither his expression nor his emotions reflected his words. His eyes darted to each new face that appeared out of the crowd.

Clarrett said, "Would you like to go in, Mr. Schvartz?"

The rebbe's head swung back toward the lieutenant, then to me, then back again. "Why yes, that would be of interest." His voice inveigled once again.

Could he actually believe that anyone would swallow his act whole?

As Clarrett started up the steps of the building, Levi sidled up to me. "Mr. Cohen will hear from me later. *You* had better stay close."

I said nothing and followed the rebbe as he trailed in Clarrett's wake.

In an anteroom to the main entry, a vidshow on a large plasma screen about an outbreak of epidemic pustular dermatitis in cattle in the south of the continent caught my interest. EPD is a nasty disease, and I had never seen a case on Dovid's World.

I caught Levi's arm and pointed to the screen. "Levi,"—we dropped the Reb title when in company— "would it be all right to stay here and watch this show? It's about a cattle epidemic. I'd like to learn about that. You could stay with me if you don't want me out of sight."

He frowned. It had become clear that the rebbe hated anything to do with real disease. I wouldn't get *any* useful technical help out of him. He glanced at Clarrett. I could almost feel his brain fracturing between the desire to keep me close or continue his spying. "You may stay here," he hissed, "but I expect you to be here when I return." With that, he wheeled and stalked over to Clarrett, and the two of them disappeared around a corner.

I took a chair in front of the plasma screen and tried to calm my roiling stomach. I hoped Fur would not get in trouble, and me by association. A woman's voice narrated:

"EPD is a highly contagious virus that causes skin lesions similar to the pox virus diseases of old Terra. The virus also attacks the lymphoid system and reduces immunity, so the animals are prone to develop secondary bacterial infections at the sites of the blisters. If the bacterial infections are not treated, septicemia often results, leading to death."

The camera rolled over herds of thousands of cattle. The voice-over continued:

"Sammara's cattle herds are one of the mainstays of our economy. Cold stasis-preserved beef is a delicacy and a major export to other worlds. EPD, if unchecked, has the potential to destroy seventy to eighty percent of the herds. Veterinarians and other government personnel are working around the clock to enforce effective quarantines..."

***

The show was over by the time Clarrett and Levi returned. Levi asked me, "Have you seen Cohen?"

"No."

He gave me a dirty look, as if I was responsible for the disappearance of Fur and Ranu. My mouth wanted to explain Fur's absence, to cover for him, but for once, my brain intervened. I could say nothing that would not raise Levi's level of suspicion even more. I did not even have to bite my tongue again.

Since entering the building, clouds had rolled in and

a light drizzle now descended. We had no raingear, so we waited inside as Clarrett went to arrange for transportation.

We returned to the spaceport where we had accommodations in a luxury hotel. This turned out to be a suite with sitting room and three separate bedrooms. After Clarrett left, Levi muttered and paced the main room. He ignored me, and I retired to my bedroom to get away from his execrable aura. I sat down on my bed, a pillow propped behind me, and turned on the vid. I flipped through channels and fretted over the situation. The news that caught my attention was more about the EPD epidemic. I really wanted to learn more, maybe see it first-hand. When I heard Ranu's voice, I turned off the screen and went back to the common room.

"Yes, I apologize for losing track of you. We continued toward the waterfront. When it started to rain, Mr. Cohen and I took refuge in a tavern."

Fur chimed in. "Katz's has some of the best brews in town and an electroboard player and singer was performing."

"I'm afraid we lost track of the time, as well. I am sorry if you were worried about us."

Ranu gave a masterful performance, and Levi never had a chance to get a word in edgewise.

Before Ranu left, I asked if it would be possible to see the EPD outbreak. He said he would pass on the request.

Fur asked Levi, "And what did you see, Reb Levi? Was it interesting? Quite a city, yes?"

Levi evaded Fur's questions and stormed out.

I retired to my room again and collapsed onto my bed. I had not blown Fur's cover, thank God. My earlier anger at the big man had evaporated, and I was left with nothing but dread. What would happen to my parents and me if Levi learned that Fur was an SOD member? I was not sure I wanted to know.

Stephen A. Benjamin

CHAPTER 5

LIEUTENANT CLARRETT SHOWED UP early the next morning and found us at breakfast. "Sorry to interrupt, but Dr. Berger asked if he could observe the EPD outbreak down south. Do you still want to do that?"

"I sure do," I replied and I looked at Fur and Levi. Fur nodded his agreement.

Levi muttered, "If I must." He obviously did not like the thought of having one or both of us out of his sight again.

We piled into a whirlydrone that had landed on the roof of our hotel. The view of the city as we flew over was a dramatic contrast of new construction interspersed with older, dingier areas. A military-type pilot flew the aircraft, so Clarrett served as tour guide again.

"You can see the difference between the old and the new areas. Striking, isn't it?"

When no one answered, Fur asked, "How long is the flight?"

"About two hours," Clarrett replied.

I enjoyed the scenery. Levi was truculent since Clarrett declined to discuss military matters further.

We flew over well-ordered farms and pastures. Fences and brush rows cut the land into a neat checkerboard, and copses of woodland separated farms. They had not followed the unfortunate practice of my world in recent years of cutting down most of the forests to maximize tillable acreage.

As the drone approached our destination, plumes of sepulchral smoke dotted the countryside like heralds of disaster. Below us, a large chamber on the bed of a trailer belched inky fumes. "That's a mobile crematorium." I had given my companions a rundown on the nature of EPD, but hadn't discussed the management of outbreaks.

"We haven't advanced that much from procedures used a thousand years ago for diseases like foot and mouth disease and EPD, although EPD is a much newer disease than foot and mouth. Back then, the only recourse was to quarantine infected herds, slaughter them, and burn or bury the carcasses. We're more efficient with the incineration now, but that's it. You deal with animal disease based on different principles than human disease."

Even when I understood the need to euthanize and incinerate the herds, it was a painful thing to see, and I cringed inwardly. "Even with our modern antivirals and antibiotics, the cost of treatment of tens of thousands of cattle in a major outbreak isn't economically feasible."

Clarrett and Fur's faces were grim, but Levi seemed unmoved, his face frozen in its usual sour expression.

When we landed, I jumped down and ducked under the rotor blades. In a landscape of rich crop and pasture land, the only animals in sight were in a corral adjacent to the crematorium.

From that direction approached an incredible vision. I could not remove my eyes from her. Tall, only a few centimeters short of my skinny frame, her close-cropped, curly hair had auburn highlights. She wore blood-spattered gray coveralls that did not hide her ample curves. Smudges of black soot on her face, including one on the tip of her thin, straight nose, only seemed to enhance her beauty by contrast. She caused my tongue to stick to the roof of my now very dry mouth. Magnificent. A Goddess.

"Good morning," Clarrett said to her. "Do I have the pleasure of addressing Dr. Simon?" Clarrett was tall and handsome in a stuffy military way and I was jealous of the smile she gave him.

"My pleasure, Lieutenant. And these are our guests, I assume?"

Her green-eyed gaze on me had my tongue wrapped in a Gordian knot. I had never been good with the ladies. My ability to sense emotions worked against me. I was used to indifference, or outright disdain, from the opposite sex, which made it difficult to hold a reasonable conversation, much less anything intimate. This encounter was worse. I couldn't remember anyone who had affected me to this degree. Her response to me was friendly and curious. Fur and Levi introduced themselves, and everyone waited for me to speak. Dr. Simon's amused grin did not help one bit.

I finally unglued my mouthparts and stammered, "Hi. I'm, um, Cy. Dr. Berger, I mean. Call me Cy. Please. Um, glad to meet you."

"I'm Roxanne. Let's walk over to the barn," she pointed to a building adjacent to the corral, "where we can talk."

Roxanne? I couldn't believe her name. It took me a moment to wrap my mind around that and to get my feet moving. I followed the group toward the building.

Dr. Simon—Roxanne—took off her protective outer clothes and dropped them in a barrel before we went inside. We found seats, and she continued. "I understand you are from Dovid's World, Dr. Berge—Cy—and that you haven't had EPD there for more than a century. You're fortunate." She gestured toward a window with her head. "This has been anything but fun."

"Yeah," I replied. "I learned about it in school, but that's as close as I've come."

We proceeded to a technical discussion about the disease, differential diagnoses, confirmatory tests, and so forth, which put me more at ease.

Fur asked, "This has got to be hard on the farmers and ranchers. What will they do now?"

"We have improved cloning techniques, stasis cryostorage of embryos, and new forced embryonic maturation equipment, so the herds can be repopulated fairly quickly. While it is painful to see your animals subjected to euthanasia and the economic impact is severe, those technologies moderate the losses. It is cheaper to repopulate than to treat all the affected animals, especially since losses would be more than fifty percent even in the treated groups."

Intrigued by her comment about the forced maturation, I made a mental note to follow up on that. Clarrett was silent, but followed the discussion, while Levi stared out a window. He did not even try to look interested. I could almost taste his impatience.

After some further discussion, Roxanne asked, "Would you like to examine the cattle?"

"Sure would," I said.

"Okay, let's get suited up."

Roxanne, Fur, and I donned disposable protective coveralls, plasboots, gloves, masks, and head covers. Clarrett and Levi declined the opportunity. No surprise with respect to Levi. He did not trust Fur or me out of his sight, but he wanted no part of the diseased animals.

We walked to the corral where Roxanne opened the gate then closed it behind us. The cattle were black Hebrides, a beef strain developed on Sammara for their vigor and high quality meat. Fur and I moved over to a cow and examined her from a short distance.

"That one's relatively early," Roxanne said. "Only mild secondary infection as of yet."

The skin lesions ranged from early vesicles to a few full-blown ulcers. The latter showed the purulent exudate typical of bacterial infection. The lesions were present over the entire body. The animal had her head down and her breathing labored. I looked at Roxanne. "You call this mild?"

"They do get viral pneumonia, but it's not enough to kill them unless they get secondary bacterial invaders. This lady has more problems than is typical for the viral phase alone."

"Yeah, looks like it." The cow hardly reacted to me when I moved closer. I lifted the cow's lips. There were no mucosal ulcers. I bent down and checked her hooves, but could see no lesions below the hocks. I looked to Roxanne again. "No mouth or foot lesions."

She nodded. "The lack of those lesions is a major feature that differentiates EPD from other blister-forming diseases like vesicular stomatitis and foot and mouth disease."

We looked over a few more animals in various stages of the disease then Roxanne said, "They're ready for this group now."

Several coveralled men herded the cattle out of the corral into a chute that led up to the chamber on the flatbed. I could feel the discomfort of the animals. For many, it was a general malaise due to the illness, accompanied by some degree of fear—a diffuse, nonspecific dread. Herd illnesses stressed my empathic ability the most. I could deal with single animals better; then I had a chance to soothe them. Cattle packed the chute and, as the first animals were euthanized, the overall level of herd fear rose, as did my uneasiness.

Animals lowed plaintively. The euthanasia was painless, a quick laser beam through the ear and brain, but it seemed like the laser cut through me at the same time. My stomach writhed, and I turned away, staggering slightly.

My face must have shown my distress. "Are you okay?" Roxanne asked. "You don't look good."

"I-I'm fine." I gritted my teeth and fought off a wave of nausea and the inevitable headache. I hated that she might think I was a wuss.

At that moment, a gust of wind swirled and blew the acrid smoke over the crowded cattle. In seconds, the level of fear in a few animals jumped to panic, as infectious as the disease. With frenzied bellows, several animals bolted in the only direction they had available to them—straight at us. The herd followed. I stumbled as emotional vertigo hit me. I didn't think I could make it to the fence. Maybe Fur could.

"Take Roxanne and run," I yelled to the big man.

Fur picked up Roxanne as if she were a child and sprinted for safety, but I never moved.

I heard Roxanne scream, "Cy."

I put everything I had into controlling my negative reactions, then I concentrated on the lead cattle, the ones headed straight for me. Once, years before, I had prevented a stampede when a predator had gotten into our corral at home. I prayed I could do it now. I targeted my thoughts to calm the lead animal, despite my own terror, nausea, and pounding skull. Time seemed to slow as I projected even harder. The horns of the lead steer gleamed. Sweat soaked my shirt. I dropped to one knee. The steer came to a halt within a body length of me, and the rest of the herd split and bucked around him in a black wave. The back of the stampede had broken and the herd now milled while they gasped and huffed.

Stephen A. Benjamin

As the coveralled workers herded the cattle toward the crematorium once again, I staggered toward Roxanne and Fur. Fur met me, grabbed my arm, and led me to an overturned water trough, where he sat me down. "I've never seen anything like that. Amazing."

Roxanne stared at me as if I had grown horns myself. "What in blazes did you do? And how?"

I shook my head and did not answer.

Roxanne's eyes fixed me with a glare that said she expected an answer. After a moment, she went to help the men with the cattle. A few minutes later, she returned. "You okay now?"

"Yeah. Maybe I'd better explain."

"I think that might be nice."

I held hard to my shields as concern, tinged by perplexity, radiated from both Roxanne and Fur. I looked at the ground as I spoke. "I'm a bit unusual."

Fur snorted.

"I'm empathic for animals. I feel something of what they do and perceive their mental state, and I can make myself felt by them. I'm not sure how better to put that into words, but I can calm distressed animals. This was...a bit more."

Fur pulled at his beard. "A bit more? You call that a bit more? You just stopped a goddamned stampede."

"Mr. Cohen said it right to begin with. Amazing." Roxanne shook her head. "Can you diagnose specific problems in animals? Locate internal disease sites, like liver versus kidney?"

"Mostly it's just a general impression. If an animal has severe and very localized pain, I sometimes pick that up. It's useful when I palpate an animal. I feel when I elicit pain without having to interpret the animal's response. That allows me to spare them some discomfort. The most useful aspect is the ability to soothe. Makes it easier to deal with a stressed patient. I

~56~

concentrated on that lead animal and calmed him down."

"Incredible. I've never heard of anything like that." She looked at Fur. "Have you?"

"Nope. Our Dr. Berger is unique, so far as I know."

"Does this work with people?" Roxanne asked.

"No! No. Not with people. Only animals." I knew I'd overreacted when I got a narrow-eyed look from Roxanne. "When this first manifested, I was a mess for a while. A family friend, a psychiatrist at the medical school, helped me. He ran me through all sorts of tests, but he never found anything other than some strange electrical activity in the hippocampal region of my brain. It did make veterinary medicine a logical career choice, but I don't tell people. I don't want to be seen as a freak."

Reb Levi and Clarrett joined us. I shook my head at Fur and Roxanne before I turned away, hoping they would get the message to keep my secret. Levi had returned to the whirlydrone while we examined the cattle. Now I guessed he felt obliged to find out what had happened. He must have seen the stampede.

"Did you stop those cattle? How?" he demanded in his usual imperious manner. He peered at me. His eye squinted and his scarred cheek twitched.

"It wasn't really a stampede," I said. "The cattle were just nervous."

"Nervous? They were charging you." He glowered at me, and his mind radiated a lack of understanding of what had happened.

"You have to understand animals," I said. "They can sense fear, in their own kind and in humans. If you are calm, they will get that vibe. By standing firm without fear, it caused the lead cattle to come up short. You only have to stop one, then the others will calm themselves."

Levi shook his head in disbelief. "That does not seem possible."

"Well, seeing is believing, right?" I paused to look back at the condemned herd. "But, you know, the most interesting part of the whole thing was examining the cattle. I've never seen a disease like epidemic pustular dermatitis. Just like the name says, the early lesions often get infected, and then they get all pussy—the thick greenish-yellow kind of pus. If it goes on too long, they can develop gangrene. We could use samples for lab testing, and you can help me collect those."

Levi paled and turned an unattractive shade of green. His queasiness added to my already unsettled stomach, so I cut my fun short.

I glanced at Roxanne, whose brow creased in a quizzical expression. I shrugged.

We finished up with a few pleasantries, and then Lieutenant Clarrett herded us toward the whirlydrone. I was relieved that he showed no interest in Dr. Simon other than as our guide. I hung back as we boarded, long enough to say goodbye.

I hemmed and hawed, felt my face heat, but finally got out, "Um, Roxanne, do you think it would be okay if I contacted you...if I come back through here? I mean if you're not, er, taken...or anything."

God. I felt like a buffoon. I braced myself for a response that could wither a cactus, what I usually got in such circumstances. Either that or outright laughter.

I had a pleasant surprise when she gave me a delightful smile—she had very cute dimples and I didn't even notice the soot on her nose any longer—and said, "I'd like that."

I was at a loss for words. My weird performance had not put her off. Her aura was actually positive toward me. It did not even cause me a hiccup.

"I have to be in Sammarak tomorrow morning, after

we wrap up here." She touched my arm. "How about getting together for dinner?"

I could hardly believe my ears. I nodded, once, twice, three times, then stopped my head before it bobbed right off my shoulders. "Um, great," I exclaimed. "Tomorrow. Evening. Right."

She laughed, and I heard Fur snigger behind me.

"I'll call when I get done with my meetings. Where are you staying?"

I couldn't recall the name of the place, but Clarrett jumped in and rescued me. I don't remember much about the flight back, but I do recall what I had sensed from her.

She *liked* me.

* * *

Back in town, Reb Levi made a big deal about his transmission of a message back to Dovid's World. He looked at me as he spoke. "I have discussed our visit here with the Rebbinical Council, Dr. Berger. They are very pleased with what I accomplished. I did inform them of your effort with the cattle. They were impressed. They feel that gives our world a good name. They also indicated that your continued assistance in my efforts will be helpful in assuring the, ah, *favorable treatment* of your family. You want to make sure that is the case, right, Berger? You may give me a message for your parents, if you like, and I will send that."

His smirk signaled not humor but satisfaction at making me squirm. I might have throttled him right then, if not for the consequences to my family. My pulse pounded in my temple, my thoughts warring between ignoring him or getting a message to my folks. I took a deep breath to gain control. "Tell them I'm fine and I miss them. And that I hope *they* are fine, too." I turned and strode away before I stuck my foot in my mouth. I trusted this guy as much as an angry cobra.

***

"Good morning." Reb Levi beamed as he walked up to our table in the dining room. His good mood, no doubt, related to his report to the Test-Lit Rebbinical Council. They probably thought he was a super spy and collected all sorts of great intelligence data. I wished he could break his arm from patting himself on the back. I was sure the Sammarans had fed him a load of *drek*.

I did not respond. Levi's sadistic threats against my family had eaten at me all night. He *enjoyed* my reactions. The *putz*.

Fur returned the rebbe's greeting and kicked me under the table.

"Fuck off," I muttered under my breath, just loud enough for Fur to hear, but not Levi, who now stood at the buffet. He poured enough cream in his coffee to support Sammara's dairy industry single-handedly.

I could not do anything about Levi, but I sure didn't have to talk with him. I got up and left, my breakfast half-eaten on the table.

I heard Levi's grating voice as I walked away.

"What is wrong with Berger? Is he not well this morning?"

I did not hear Fur's response, if any.

***

I had one more charge to dispense with before we left Sammara. I needed to put in place the system that sought candidates for our veterinary college. I looked forward to this, as I saw no downside to recruitment of good students for my profession. Until the invasion, Sammara had relied on my home world for their veterinary education. Now, they had to send students farther afield, and that we might accept, and even support, Sammaran students was something I could use effectively, I hoped.

I had two meetings set up for that day. I met with the local veterinary association, told them what we sought, and asked them for their assistance. I was not surprised at their minimal enthusiasm for the Dovidian educational system, but I made my case and left it at that.

I then met with guidance counselors and advisors from the local secondary schools and colleges. I spoke of the opportunities at our Academy and had a similar negative response. However, when I described the scholarships available, faces of my audience began to light up. Perhaps this *would* work. I left them with the contact information for the Academy and set up a session with interested students for the following day.

***

The door opened on a vision of beauty that exceeded the recollection of my hormone fogged brain. Roxanne wore an ankle-length emerald dress that hugged her body in just the right places. A white shawl draped across her bare, shapely shoulders and covered a demure neckline. The dress matched her eyes and turned her auburn hair into a crown. I'm not sure how long I stood in the hall, mouth open, but long enough that she had to prompt me.

"Good evening, Cy. Are you going to come in, or do we order dinner to eat in the hall?"

"Um, what? Oh, sorry. Sorry."

I moved into the room as she stepped away from the door. "You...you are lovely this evening."

Her smile dimpled as she responded. "Hmm.

Meaning I wasn't yesterday?"

"No. That's not what I meant."

She laughed. "I know. I'm just teasing you. Thank you very much." She made a mock curtsey. "And you look very...dashing."

I looked down at my garb, a midnight purple tunic with lots of gold braid, and grimaced. "Sorry. This was the best I could do. It's my Captain's ceremonial dress. It's supposed to impress the residents of all the worlds we'll visit." I shrugged.

She wrinkled her nose delightfully. "Please have a seat." She motioned to a divan. "I'll just be a few moments."

I sat as she moved out of the room. I felt like a total idiot. Pull yourself together, Berger. She'll think you *are* a loser. My mouth was dry and my heart pounded a staccato beat. I took a deep breath and tried to think of what to say next. I wished I could change my clothes; coveralls would be better.

Lost in my thoughts, I started when she said, "Ready." I had not noticed her return. She had added an emerald pendant with matching earrings to her ensemble.

As I jumped up, I almost knocked over a floor lamp. Oh God, what was I going to do next? "Oh, sure. Let's go." I paused heading for the door. "Where're we going?"

She laughed again.

I didn't need to be an empath to feel her amusement. What a fool I was making of myself.

"I have reservations at the Pinnacle. It's one of our nicest restaurants. The food is excellent, but the view is even better. You'll see."

***

The restaurant stood atop one of the tallest buildings in the city, and was the kind that revolved. Our window seats afforded a three hundred-sixty degree view of the capitol and countryside. We settled in and sipped at martinis while we watched the sunset go from tangerine to lavender and finally to night's indigo. The red and green safety beacons of aircraft flitted across the darkening sky as the myriad lights of the city winked into being.

"Beautiful," I breathed.

"Told you so." Roxanne smiled and picked up a menu.

I followed suit and perused the selections. "This menu is overwhelming. Why don't you order for both of us?"

She arched an eyebrow and nodded. "I'll be happy to." To the waiter, "We'll have the smoked whitefish for the appetizer, and then the Cenurian pepper beef with baby roasted potatoes and grilled asparagus for the entree. A bottle of the '07 South Coast Cabernet Sauvignon would go well with the beef." She looked at me. "That okay?"

"Sounds great."

"Excellent selections, Madame. I will serve the wine and appetizer right away."

"No hurry," Roxanne said. "We would like a leisurely dinner."

"Certainly." The waiter moved away.

"I've never heard of Cenurian peppers," I said.

"Cenurus is a tropical world that exports a dozen different peppers and tropical fruits, all delicious."

I shook my head. "I'm afraid Dovid's World has been pretty well insulated from the galaxy for a long time. We don't see much in the way of imports."

Roxanne was quiet, brows drawn together, as the waiter delivered our smoked fish and poured the wine.

We let the wine breathe as we finished our martinis and dug into the fish. It was even better than I expected, the flesh white and flaky, the smoke flavor subtle. I smiled and nodded to Roxanne, my mouth full.

"It *is* good," she replied. "May I ask you something? I'm puzzled. Just why are you here on Sammara? I know you're on a recruiting trip for your vet college, but the cost of outfitting a medical spaceship for that purpose alone seems prohibitive."

I swallowed and hesitated before I spoke. "This is sort of a trial balloon, if you get my meaning. See if we can get enough interest in our university to make the trip worthwhile. And I hope to bring in enough credits by our veterinary services to make it pay." I sensed uncertainty.

She frowned. "And something else, if you don't mind?"

I took another bite of fish and nodded.

"Your relationship with your assistant, Levi, seemed...uncomfortable. He was rather uninterested and...squeamish for a veterinary technician, and he was peremptory and...belligerent. Can you tell me what's going on? If you can't, I understand."

Roxanne was not in the loop with respect to our arrangements with the Sammaran government. I sensed that her questions were honest and believed she was trustworthy and on our side, but that might have been my hormones talking. I desperately wanted her to like and respect me, so I made an impulsive decision, even as my brain urged caution. I hoped the consequences of revealing my story would not ruin our wonderful dinner.

I leaned toward Roxanne—not a distasteful act in of itself. "This is sort of complicated, but I'll be honest with you and trust you to keep this to yourself. You're familiar with the political system on Dovid's World, right?"

She nodded.

"It started the day I met Fur..." I told her the whole story, about Levi, the Test-Lits, the Inquisition, my folks, Fur and the SOD, everything, as we ate our appetizers.

When the main course arrived, that shut me up for a while. My first bite of the Cenurian pepper beef set my mouth ablaze. It hurt just as much sliding down my esophagus and into my stomach. Two glasses of wine later—alcohol is a better emollient for the hot oils of peppers than water—I took a deep breath.

"Oh, I am so sorry, Cy. I didn't realize the peppers would be as hot as this. They usually aren't. They must have used a different variety this time."

"S'okay," I breathed. The depth of her concern added another ingredient to the cauldron that passed for my stomach. "I shouldn't have shoveled in a mouthful without tasting first."

I ate around the peppers and we polished off what was left of the wine. After the martinis, no doubt that helped loosen my tongue, an all-too-common effect on me. A credit to the restaurant, they made us feel like there was no rush to get out, despite the fact that all the tables were full.

Roxanne shook her head and took a deep breath. "You're a surprising person."

I felt my face get warm.

"You downplay your role in all this, saying that you've been forced to act as you have, but I don't see it that way. Even the way you responded to Levi today is not the response of someone who is beaten down, cowed by the oppression of the Test-Lits. You're selling yourself short."

I hung my head. "Shit. I've done nothing but accede to their demands, do whatever they want."

"That's not true. Just by having Mr. Cohen onboard with you and not disclosing his mission is a challenge to their government. And I don't believe you won't fight back. I just don't believe it."

I looked at the magnificent woman across the table but could not meet her eyes. "I'd like to believe that. All I feel now is fear for my family. I can't afford to make any missteps. They could be killed." I tapped the tabletop in frustration.

She reached across the table and grasped my hand. A thrill coursed through my body, unfortunately accompanied by my usual negative reaction to her admittedly positive response to me. Talk about mixed emotions!

"There are few people who wouldn't feel that way. Remember that you have allies. I can't believe they won't look out for your parents." She squeezed my hand before she released it.

The waiter reappeared. "Can I interest you in some dessert and coffee?"

I was happy to break off the uncomfortable conversation. Roxanne recommended a crème brulee for me and a fruit plate for herself.

"Well, what about you?" I asked. "You've heard my life story. You deserve equal time. Why did you become a vet?"

She thought for a moment before answering. "It took me a while to make that decision. I had no obvious talents like yours. Like you, my folks were farmers. I loved animals, especially horses, as a girl, but that made me no different from half the girls on this or any other world. Science and medicine fascinated me, but again, those were not the only things that held my interest. I made my choice before my last undergraduate year. My interests in medicine and animals were the deciding factors. Since I had to go offworld to vet school, I needed a sponsor; I couldn't afford it otherwise. One of my professors hooked me up with a philanthropist, and he footed the bill. I studied on Setaa III with the proviso that I return here to Sammara to ply my trade in public service, otherwise I would have to pay everything back. It would have taken me twenty years to break even." She snorted.

"I can't say that my life has been even a tiny bit as exciting as yours." She smiled. "Not that I need that kind of stress. I started this job about a year ago and it has been much more interesting and more of a challenge than I feared." The corners of her mouth pulled down. "I suppose a major epidemic will do that. Oh, here's our dessert."

I polished off my crème brulee and sat back. "That was fabulous. Thank you for your suggestions." I wiped my lips and put down the napkin.

She smiled. "I thought the crème brulee would be a bit more soothing after the peppers."

I chuckled. "I wonder about something else, if you don't mind my being nosy."

"No. Go ahead. It's only fair for you to have a turn."

"How long has your family lived on Sammara? They predated the Test-Lit invasion, right?"

"Yes. My great-great-great-grandparents emigrated to Sammara from Cantos, one of the Aldebaran worlds. They had a small farm there, but saw the opportunity to expand their opportunities on a less densely populated world. Sammara offered land for a pittance if the family agreed to farm it for at least two generations. My brothers have every intention of continuing that heritage."

"Then the Test-Lits haven't had the kind of impact on you—"

"Not true. I had an uncle killed in the Test-Lit

invasion. So even my family has a bone to pick."

"Sorry to hear that."

The waiter returned with the check and I reached for it, but Roxanne was faster.

"This is mine. It's on the government veterinary service tab. Orders from my boss. He was quite impressed when I told him about your exploits. That was the last farm quarantined in the area. If those cattle had gotten loose and spread the epidemic even more, we would have really been in trouble. As it is, we got the region under control quickly."

I felt my face heat again. "So long as you're not paying. You didn't tell him about—"

"Your empathic ability?" She shook her head. "You said not to, and I could tell you didn't want Levi to know. Now that you've explained, I understand why."

"Thanks."

"But I'm not quite buying your story." She frowned.

"Wha—?"

"Come on. You couldn't have been more transparent when you denied that you could sense human emotions like you can for animals."

She was not happy and my stomach and head felt it. "But I can't—"

She put up a hand. "Please. This has been a delightful evening. Let's not spoil it with lies."

My head and heart pounded like triphammers. I'd just blown everything. I could not leave it like this. The thought that she might hate me for my talent took my breath away.

After too long a silence, I said, "Roxanne, this is something I never reveal. There are only three people who know I'm empathic for humans, my parents and the psychiatrist I mentioned. Four, now." I hesitated. "I perceive emotions. Rarely, I get a flash of an image accompanying a very strong emotion from someone, but I don't read minds. I can't tell what you are thinking."

Roxanne put her hand out across the table and squeezed mine. "I understand. This must be a difficult burden for you to carry. I trust you."

I sensed that she meant what she said. I had to be honest with this woman. She affected me more than anyone I had met before.

"Sometimes it's hard. I can't help but get messages on the nonverbal level. Strong human emotions affect me badly with nausea, vertigo, and headaches, so I try to block them as much as possible, but I could tell that you are sincere. Earlier, that helped me decide to level with you about my mission and Levi."

She smiled. "I won't hold that against you. You are a very special person, you know."

Roxanne took a powder room break and as she walked away, I thought that holding her against me would be just dandy. What I learned about her character only enhanced the initial physical attraction I felt. This was an extraordinary woman, and I did not want the evening to end.

When she returned, I said, "I remembered something you mentioned yesterday about new forced embryonic maturation technology. Would there be some way for me to get that? I could see it as useful in some circumstances. I have no idea what kinds of challenges we face on this voyage."

She nodded. "I don't see why not. I'll talk to my boss. We owe you more than just a dinner, in my view."

"Thanks. That would be great."

The rest of the evening went far too quickly, and soon I found myself at her door.

Roxanne stood framed in the doorway. "Thanks for a delightful evening. I enjoyed myself."

"Same here. I-I'd like to see you again. If I could?"

She smiled and her cheeks dimpled. "I'd like that, too."

"But I leave late tomorrow. I don't know when—"

She put a hand on my arm. "I understand. Whenever is fine. Let's keep in touch. Let me know where you will be, and I'll try to leave a hyperwave message."

"Yeah. I'll do the same." I didn't know how to end the evening. My hands felt like extraneous appendages.

As she stepped close to me and rose up on her toes, face upturned, I momentarily panicked. There was no way our lips could meet without my huge nose getting in the way. But they did and our emotions blended and soared. For the first time I experienced that joy can be implicit in perceiving an emotional response instead of nausea and pain. When the door closed, it seemed like I floated back to my hotel.

***

Other than the constant of Levi's sadistic threats, the stop at Sammara had been successful. I did not do anything with respect to veterinary medicine—other than stop a stampede, which they don't teach in vet school—but I learned a good deal about EPD. My meeting with aspiring veterinary students had turned up several who I thought had real potential. I gave a recruiting report to Levi to send back to the Academy.

And I met Roxanne. Despite Levi being such an overbearing *putz*, I was elated. As a teenager, I had fallen in love with an ancient actress named Ingrid Bergman in the vid, *For Whom the Bell Tolls*. I mistakenly thought Bergman was Jewish, but that was not important. She was the most enchanting woman I had ever seen. Roxanne could have been her stand-in. And her name—Roxanne! That had to be a coincidence, right? Of course. It had to be.

CHAPTER 6

AFTER SAMMARA, Reb Levi laid out his itinerary.

"We will go to Crother's World, then to Makan, then to Wolath," he intoned in his most officious voice.

All three were human-settled worlds within Newsol's sector out near the edge of our galaxy. They also happened to be worlds that responded to Sammara's call for help when the Test-Lits invaded. I wondered about that and mentioned it to Fur.

The big man smoothed his moustache before answering. "That's by design, I think. Those worlds have sizeable Jewish populations. Not as many refugees from Dovid's World as on Sammara, but enough that the tyranny of the Test-Lits is well-known."

I thought about that for a moment. "Then why does he want to go there? I can understand gathering military info on Sammara. The Sammarans and the Test-Lits are mortal enemies. What in hell does he want on Crother's World and the others?"

Fur shrugged his shoulders. "Probably the same reason as Sammara. Find out what the Test-Lits might face militarily if they decided to invade or, worse, get allies to support their brand of despotism. But that's why I'm here. I can help you on the medical end, but I've got to learn what Levi is up to."

Fur putting us at risk brought my pulse rate up, and it must have shown.

"I'm sorry, but that's the reality," he said. "We can't let the Test-Lits either get support from other worlds or take their brand of fundamentalist tyranny elsewhere. The SOD will do everything we can to stop them."

"Don't stop them at my expense. I don't want anything to happen that could endanger my parents."

He fixed me with his brown eyes. "Not doing anything might be the very thing that endangers your parents." He turned and walked off.

***

When I examined Levi's full itinerary, I noted that most of the worlds he scheduled followed around the rim of the galaxy, staying away from the more heavily populated inner sectors. Given that, I supposed that the name Galactic Circle was not as presumptuous as I first thought. Did Levi come up with the name, or was it someone else who had a modicum of imagination?

I learned that extended space travel was downright boring. Interstellar flight involved a jump into hyperspace and took only a fraction of the objective time of normal space travel. Since a spaceship could only enter hyperspace outside the influence of any significant gravity well, it took a lot more time to maneuver into and through solar systems than it did to move between stars. Fortunately, with no significant mass involved, gravity wells did not restrict hyperwave messaging.

I've tried to study hyperspatial mechanics, but I do not understand the mathematical intricacies. When they got to imaginary numbers, string harmonics, and quantum gravitational theory, my mind shut down. I'm a veterinarian, not a theoretical physicist.

Anyway, the restrictions on hyperspace jumps left us with lots of time on our hands. I passed mine as usual; I read old books and watched old vids. Fur read, as well, but we discovered a common interest in 3-D chess and enjoyed that diversion. It almost seemed as if our AI was bored, though, of course, this could not be possible. Ruthie virtually "looked over our shoulders" as our chess games progressed. Early on, we had to lock her out from participation since she would inform us of the next best move before we could begin to analyze it. Now, she restricted herself to analyzing—very critically—moves after we made them. It bothered me that an AI could sound like it was being sarcastic, but I brushed that off as my imagination.

While Fur, Ruthie and I sparred, Reb Levi was at his wit's end. He had his scriptures, a number of vids on religious philosophy, and three hard-copy *siddurs*, traditional Hebrew prayer books. He even had a vidchip of services for Fridays, Saturdays, and special holidays so that he could pray in synch with a congregation.

Another recreation that Levi participated in was weight training. He had one corner of the rec room set up as a small gym, and he worked out every day. His blocky frame lifted a hell of a lot more than I could manage, but Fur and I took advantage of the equipment, as well. I tried to ignore Levi, but he could not pass a day without some form of threat to me and my parents, his favorite form of recreation.

Fur and I were engaged in a game of chess when Levi sought us out. He watched for a few minutes as Ruthie intoned, "That wasn't a smart move, Cy. You will lose your bishop and enable checkmate in 10 moves." She paused. "If your opponent is skilled enough, of course."

"There is something peculiar about this computer,"

Levi muttered. Then he shook his head as if to clear the thought. His eyes narrowed as he fingered his scar. "We are weeks into our journey and neither of you has made any effort to join me in services. This is unacceptable. The Council would not like to hear that you have been neglecting your devotions, Berger." A sneer crept across his lips like some obscene slug. "Who knows how they might react to such a message?"

I said nothing as my heart rate accelerated. No matter how frequently he needled me, I still reacted.

As usual, Fur was quick to calm potential conflicts. "That's a very good point, Rebbe. Cy and I discussed that very thing last evening. We realized that the excitement of the journey had pushed these important issues into the background."

That was a bald-faced lie, but I swallowed the acid that rose to my throat and added, "Yeah, but don't we need a *minyon?*"

Levi turned his cold glare toward me. "The Rebbinical Council has given me a special dispensation to make up for the seven men we are missing for a *minyon,* Berger."

I wondered if that agreed with Judaic law, which regulated services, but I nodded. "When?"

Levi's eyebrows shot up. "When? Friday evening, of course. And Saturday morning."

I placed my elbow on the table, smack in the middle of the holographic image of the chessboard, cupped my chin with my hand, and tapped one cheek with a forefinger as I looked at him. "Do you know what day it is today?" I kept my voice innocent.

"What day? Of course I know what day it is. Tonight is the Sabbath. And at six we will have services." His voice held a dangerous edge, and his eye began to twitch.

"Ah, but *is* it Friday? Hyperspace jumps don't take

into account the passage of time in normal space. I know we don't experience the time passage, but it takes place. We might have lost a day or two. That could make today Saturday, or even Sunday."

I sat back and enjoyed his reaction, first disbelief, then confusion, then anger. The eye twitch was as regular as a metronome. I kept my shields firmly in place.

His beady black eyes gleamed, and the pale slash of his scar stood out on his darkened face as he moved toward me. Before he reached me, Fur leaned between us and kicked me in the ankle, hard enough to make me wince.

"Rebbe, I think that Cy is right about the uncertainty of the day of the week, but couldn't we also have a dispensation in that regard? Why don't we keep our ship's calendar based on *our* elapsed time? So, if it's Friday for us, we don't worry whether it is so for others. This differs between planets depending on planetary rotation and solar orbit anyway, as you know."

I believed that Levi knew no such thing, but I kept my mouth shut. I had already pushed too far.

Levi's face cleared. "What you say does make sense, Mr. Cohen. We will meet at six, *our* ship's time, in the recreation room."

"Delighted," Fur said. "We'll see you then."

Levi gave me a nasty look as he left.

I looked forward to services with Levi as much as an abscessed tooth.

***

We recited prayers in unison with the vidchip congregation; we used the *siddurs* Levi had brought. I had not attended synagogue for several years, but the prayers remained familiar. I hoped that this would keep Levi off my back for a while.

Surprised at how easily I fell back into old habits, aside from the constant irritant of Levi, the weekly services reminded me that it was not Judaism itself that I had come to hate and reject, but the Test-Lits' form of Judaism. Evangelism, oppression, and intolerance were diametrically opposed to everything Judaism stood for. I had to separate the Test-Lit abomination from the thousands of years of tradition that allowed Jews to persevere throughout our turbulent history. Dovid's World's Jews had to overthrow these false prophets.

But the Friday evening and Saturday morning services were not enough to satisfy Levi. I had the religious training of any young man, including a *bar mitzvah*, but I'm no scholar. I was a heretic, at least in the eyes of the Test-Lits, and Levi seemed to think it was his responsibility to bring me back to the fold.

As I turned to leave the rec room after Saturday morning services, Levi called to me. "Stay, please, Dr. Berger."

The fact that the man would not call me by my given name was just one more irritant on top of so many others.

"May we speak for a moment?" he asked.

Did I have a choice?

"I can see that you are unhappy with me, but that need not be the case." He dripped with false sincerity. "I'm your friend. You should recognize that."

Was he kidding me? I had no response.

"I have helped give you an opportunity that most of your colleagues would sacrifice much for. Seeing the universe. Practicing your profession on new worlds."

I still said nothing.

"Do you have nothing to say? I would think you would thank me for this."

What bullshit. I couldn't hold my tongue any longer. "And my family? Do I thank you for that?"

"Cy, Cy, Cy."

Now I would rather he did *not* use my first name.

"We must recognize reality. I am *protecting* your family. Without my protection, who knows what might happen. I am your friend. Please return that favor."

"Yeah. Sure. Great. We're friends."

I turned on my heel and exited the room.

I found Fur in the commissary. I slammed the hatch shut to keep Levi out and threw myself onto the chair across the table from him.

"How in hell do you maintain such a calm face in front of Levi?" I asked. "You've got to hate him as much as I do, but you never show it."

Long moments passed before Fur spoke. "Yes, I hate him as much as you do, but he can't know that. If he did, it would blow my cover. I would no longer be able to work to undermine everything he and his coterie of zealots stand for. I can't show what I feel."

"Easier said than done." I shook my head. I could never hide my feelings. "You're the consummate spy, hidden at the bosom of your enemy until it's time to plunge the knife into his heart."

Fur laughed. "Very poetic. I hope it's true."

I wished I could have that kind of control. Or did I? My anger fed my determination. That internal fire kept me from paralysis, afraid to do anything lest it harm my family. I would do what I must to protect them now, but some day...some day, I would do more.

***

At our planned stops, the drill became a set one. We orbited a world, made contact with the authorities, and proffered our veterinary services. Turned out there was little we had to offer that was not already available on those worlds. The small number of clients I got came more out of curiosity than real need. The Rebbinical Council had spared little when they equipped the spaceship, but they were parsimonious with our budget and expected the *GCVS* to support itself. The whole idea of this mission paying for itself seemed further and further from reality and underscored the real, hidden espionage agenda of Levi and the Rebbinical Council.

The one piece of equipment that actually paid for itself was the robotic surgery unit, something a couple of the visited worlds did not have. I am not a great surgeon, but when I slid into the interface cap, I was capable of complex procedures. I performed a hip and a knee transplant in a Great Dane and a Lab, and a couple of unusually difficult neurosurgical spinal procedures on paralyzed Dachshunds, things the local vets could not do and I would not have done on my own. That gave me a bit of celebrity and a few more clients. The other thing that got a few contacts, at least, if not clients, was Ruthie's telephone operator routine. Seemed that our bizarre AI was more popular than me. Apparently, she was turning into a comic. For the most part, though, I was bored to tears.

Reb Levi knew that he could not accomplish his espionage goals as a veterinary assistant—and that cover was woefully inadequate in any case—so he often broke away on his own excursions: supply missions he called them. As I had suspected, I would get little out of the man with respect to veterinary technology duties. He considered what he did and learned a big secret. For my part, I did not care; I was more than happy to get him off my back.

If we had no clients, Fur usually followed Levi surreptitiously. Keeping tabs on the rebbe's machinations for the SOD, no doubt.

On each world, I carried out my recruiting duties. I had my pitch fine-tuned now. Many people welcomed the reopening of our Academy's school, and I signed up viable recruits on each world.

At each stop, Levi sent his hyperwave message to the Rebbinical Council and the Academy regarding our progress. On Crother's World, I sent off a missive to my family and to Roxanne. These were brief and factual; Levi censored everything I sent. He did allow me to tell them where we would be next. On our third stop, on Wolath, I got my reward in two hyperwave messages. Levi insisted that he must see my parents' message. No doubt it was already censored on Dovid's World, so I endured that, but when it came to Roxanne's message, I drew the line.

"No way. This is personal. It has nothing to do with Dovid's World and your goddamned mission. I won't allow you to stick your nose any further into my life."

Levi's face turned even darker red than usual, his scar a white slash. "Your attitude is unacceptable. You have no say in this matter, Berger. And your blasphemy will earn you no rewards."

I realized I had stepped over the line, so I backed off. "Okay. I'm sorry. It's just that I don't see how my exchange of messages with Dr. Simon has anything to do with this voyage. I have to have *some* privacy or I'll go nuts. You've got my folks, and you read everything that I send and they send me. What else do you want?"

He screwed his lips to the side and tilted his head in the same direction. With his hooked nose, it made him look like a giant black-eyed bird eyeing a questionable morsel of food. "I will be magnanimous and allow you this. As you say, there can be little to do with our mission. Remember that I am being lenient. You should be thankful."

My stomach roiled as he turned away. I wondered if

his assurance would truly prevent his reading the messages. Deep down, I thought not.

I sat down to view Roxanne's message. Her face wavered as she spoke—hyperspace introduces all sorts of interference into message holos—but it was still the most beautiful thing I could imagine."

Hello Cy,

Thanks for sending me updates on your travel. I only wish that I could experience some of the things you describe. Although I have traveled from Sammara to Setaa III for vet school, the two worlds are similar enough that it was hardly different from being at home. Your words bring other worlds to life for me. You are seeing and learning much more than I can in my position here on Sammara. Not that I'm complaining, you understand. I'm thankful I have the opportunity I do. Though I can't help but be a bit jealous. I wanted to tell you how much I enjoyed meeting and spending time with you. I look forward to doing so again. Please do keep the messages coming. They help to brighten up some of my dreary, bureaucracy-filled days. Until we meet again, I will treasure our brief time together. Keep well.

Roxanne

She packed her message with everything I could have hoped for. Her dimpled smile warmed my face and my heart. I watched it over and over, until I committed every word and image to memory. Then I saved it to watch again.

In my messages to my folks, I described where I had been and what I had seen and done. I detailed the cases I had seen—as routine as most were—then stressed the coups I had experienced with the robotic surgery unit. I let them know I was fine. I fervently hoped they were, but left that out. Their missives were factual and avoided anything that might smack of politics. Always right behind me as I sent and reccived these messages lurked the sinister presence of Reb Levi.

CHAPTER 7

"Dying. Need help."

THE FACE ONSCREEN had sunken cheeks, green-tinged scaly skin, and large bulbous eyes placed on the sides of the head. It looked like it could see in all directions, like a chameleon. Small vertical slits behind the eyes probably passed for ears. Another slit—the nose?—sat above a wide mouth lined with sharp teeth. The voice was out of synch with the mouth movements because of a delay in Ruthie's translation from Pronacian to Common.

"Death everywhere."

The transmission cut off abruptly.

The planet Pronac was not on Reb Levi's itinerary, and he objected to a detour. "This is not our business, Berger. Computer, you must stay on our determined course."

My small victory on Wolath keeping Levi from censoring Roxanne's messages left me loath to buck him again, but Fur's intervention rendered my reluctance irrelevant.

"Reb Levi, standard interstellar protocol demands that whoever receives a distress call must respond. We have no choice."

Levi grumbled at Fur's words but set course for Pronac. The planet was smaller than Dovid's World, tropical, with oceans that covered seventy-five percent of the surface. Yellows and reds dominated the continents that dotted the aquamarine seas. Banks of clouds drifted above the landmasses. It was a multicolored jewel that sparkled on the black velvet of space. Based on the transmission, however, I worried that the beauty would turn ugly up close.

In orbit, we made contact again.

"This is the Galactic Circle Veterinary Service. I'm Dr. Cy Berger. We got your—"

"Help. Hurry." Another green face. I could not begin to guess if it was the same one.

"Exactly what seems to be the problem?"

"No time. Aaiiee—"

With the scream, the communication cut off. I wondered what in hell we were getting into.

Fur cleared his throat. "What was that?"

"No idea. Let's try to contact them again."

We could not raise anything on any channels.

"This is weird," I said. "What do you think?"

Levi said, "They are not human, not our Lord's creatures. We should not get involved."

My face grew hot and my pulse pounded as I listened to Levi's bigotry. *"Kish mein tuches,"* I muttered and slammed my shields into place, anticipating his response.

He might not have heard the words, but my tone was enough.

"What?" Levi barked. His face grew darker and his scar gleamed.

I imagined his brain as a bubble of magma ready to blow through his bald volcanic dome. His twitching eye made the eruption seem even more imminent. I had to watch myself. I did not want to push him that far.

Fur spoke to forestall any further outburst. "Reb Levi, we can't leave without seeing if we can help. We need to land at the port and check things out. Please understand. These beings may be different from us, but they *are* sentient and part of God's universe. How can we do less for them than we do for nonsentient animals? I'm sure our Lord would want us to show compassion. Remember the ancient hymn:

> 'All things bright and beautiful,
> All things great and small,
> All things wise and wonderful,
> The Lord God made them all.'"

Levi opened his mouth, shut it, opened it again, but before he could speak, Fur rushed on.

"You know that most of the life humans have encountered in our galaxy bears amazing resemblance to Terran life. DNA, RNA, and proteins are the basic blueprint, machinery, and building blocks for cells everywhere. True, there are differences in anatomy, physiology and biochemistry, but life throughout our galaxy, at least, must be related."

"You say that we are *related*? Us to those...those things?" Levi sputtered. "The Lord created *humans* in his image, not some giant lizards."

Fur responded, "If the Lord created life, it makes sense that he did so everywhere, and used the same template on all these worlds, doesn't it?"

I bit down hard on my tongue. Fur couldn't believe in creationism, could he? At any rate, he placated the rebbe.

Levi was confused, and his anger had not dissipated, but at least it was no longer aimed at me. My stomach appreciated that. "That may well be true, Cohen, but these aliens are like nothing from earth. And even on earth there were beasts that we consider unclean—"

I couldn't stand it anymore. "For God's sake, Levi, they don't have to be kosher, we aren't going to *eat* them." I knew that was a mistake as soon as I said it.

Levi turned his anger toward me again. A vision flashed into my mind: a belt buckle swung at my head. I flinched and almost ducked, but the vision faded as fast as it had come. I wondered what *that* meant as I clamped down on my churning stomach.

Levi's eye twitch exceeded what I thought would be the maximum possible frequency. "You seem to think that everything can be made into some sort of joke. Unnatural beings are not funny." He drew a deep breath. "And you will address me as *Reb* Levi, is that clear?" He held me with his black-eyed glare before he turned and stomped off the bridge.

Screw that *schmuck*.

I turned to Fur. "Well done. You're a never-ending source of surprises."

***

Ruthie put down the *GCVS* in an eerily quiet spaceport. The buildings were featureless multi-bubble gray domes. A jungle of riotous color encroached on the field and buildings. The stark contrast suggested a constant battle to keep the vegetation restrained.

We saw no movement other than what looked like small winged reptiles that swooped past the ship. A few immobile lumps spotted the field between parked spacecraft. I zoomed in on one with the viewscreen. It appeared to be a reptilian sprawled motionless on the ground. Several more lumps confirmed this diagnosis.

I turned to Fur and raised my eyebrows. He shook his head and tugged his beard.

Levi stomped back onto the bridge. "I don't like this. What is wrong with these creatures? Where is spaceport security?"

"Damned if I know. Ruthie, see if you can pick up any more transmissions."

"There is nothing on any channels, Cy," she crooned.

Levi said, "We must take off. Computer, do as I say."

"As you order, Reb Levi." For whatever reason, she did not screw around with him.

"Hold it, Ruthie." I looked at Levi. "We received a distress call. I thought we settled this." I tried to keep my voice level.

Fur's deep voice cut in, "I agree. The Pronacians need help. We have an obligation to assist if we can."

When Levi did not answer, I said, "Let's use the land drone. The atmosphere is breathable, but barely, so we stay in the drone and use isolation suits outside. If this is some sort of disease—and God only knows if we would be susceptible—we need to be protected."

Levi's black eyes widened until they resembled open manholes. "Disease? You think there is a plague?" He shuddered. "But what can you do about it anyway? You are a *veterinarian*." He said this with a sneer. "As you point out, these are sentient creatures despite their ungodly appearance."

I admit that the same thought had crossed my mind, but I was damned if I would let Levi dissuade me. I answered in an even tone. "I am trained to deal with all manner of nonhumans, including reptiles. Why should sentience make a difference?"

Levi frowned at the viewscreen. He turned and said, "I forbid this. We should wait until we can contact someone. This is too dangerous and not part of our mission."

"Mission or not, we've got to help," I said. While I feared Levi's power to harm my loved ones, I could not abandon a world in trouble because of his xenophobia.

"We have no choice," Fur added.

Outvoted, Levi whined. "Then I will stay here. We must keep someone in the ship. What if something happens to you two? I need to be able to call for assistance."

What he meant was "leave," with us behind, but I needed a break from the *putz*.

"Good idea," I said. "We need to have someone here in case any of the locals show up seeking help. You should be able to take care of that, right?"

He paled.

I snorted in disgust and turned to Fur. "Let's go."

***

Fur steered our mobile land drone clinic toward the bubble domes a half kilometer away. The sun was brighter than NewSol, and ships and buildings cast stark shadows on the landing field surface. We had traversed half the distance when a figure, naked except for some sort of belt, appeared from the shadow of a parked craft. It staggered into our path, dropped to one knee, and stayed there as we approached.

Pronac's intelligent species were six-limbed reptilians and this one buried its head in the upper pair of arms, and rested on one knee and the other two hands. We pulled up short of the figure, and I switched on the outside speakers.

"Hello. We're from the Galactic Circle Veterinary Service. We came in response to your call for assistance." What came out the other end was a series of clicks and hisses, Ruthie's translation into Pronacian. "How can we help?"

The Pronacian stared at the drone then rose on wobbly legs. Without further warning, it roared, leaped at the vehicle, and landed athwart the windshield. Its body blocked more than half of the view, but who admired views when he had a Pronacian mouth to look down? The mouth was twice the size of a human's and sported an impressive set of dentures, including canines the length of my pinky. Four taloned fists pounded at the window.

"What the hell—?"

I got no more out before Fur put the vehicle in reverse then slammed it into forward, then swerved from side to side as we moved toward the domes at high speed. The third swerve dislodged our unwelcome guest. I looked to the rear in the viewscreen; the figure was just another green lump on the ground.

Fur slowed the drone and brought it to a halt.

I looked at him. "Did that thing think we were trying to hurt it? That *was* one of the intelligent race, right?"

"Looked like the one that hailed us on the comm. It might be sentient, but it sure wasn't rational. It's not moving. I'd hate to have hurt him—or her. We should take a look."

I stared at the screen, not thrilled with the idea, but how could we injure the first native we met and not try to assist?

When I did not answer, Fur snorted. "Okay, I'll go."

I hoped he did not hear my sigh of relief. I nodded to him. I am not a coward, mostly, but his one hundred-thirty kilos of muscle could handle a berserker better than I could.

"Suit up. We still don't know what's happening. Take a weapon."

Fur grimaced at me for stating the obvious.

"I was just trying to help."

Fur exited and approached the immobile figure. He spoke a few words then prodded the body with his toe. Still no movement. He reached down and turned the figure face up. I could see that the eyes were wide open. Fur turned to the drone and spoke. "Dead. He might have struck his head, but there's not enough injury to see how that would have killed him. I'm coming back in. Nothing we can do here."

"Go through full decontamination in the lock. Until we know more..." I left the rest of my morbid thoughts unvoiced.

As we drove across the field, I said, "Ruthie, don't relay our comments to Levi. We'll keep them local."

"If you say so, Cy," she cooed. Sometimes I wondered about the wisdom of my programming.

I asked Fur, "You don't believe all that crap about creation that you spouted to Levi, do you?"

He glanced at me. "To have biologically similar life throughout the galaxy, it had to have been seeded there at some time. By something...or someone."

"Yeah. I know the theories: a massive storm of intergalactic objects carrying the seeds of life collided with our galaxy, a race of powerful ancients—of whom there's not a trace—deliberately seeded life here, and a dozen other theories. But a God that made everything in six days? There's incontrovertible evidence of evolution on earth and every other world that has life. Maybe God created the universe, but I can't believe the literal translation of the Torah that the Test-Lits subscribe to. God didn't just wave a wand and *poof*, out popped every form of life we know."

Fur was silent for a few moments then said, "I don't believe in literal creationism, on earth or anywhere else. But in order to explain the basic similarities between worlds, some similar primitive life form, protozoan, bacterial, or whatever, had to get to each of those worlds to begin the process. Life spread somehow. Maybe it was a deity worshipped by humans, or maybe there was some sort of cosmic intelligence out there, a mind so vast we can't possibly conceive of it. I'll keep my mind open and consider any theory to explain the reality, no matter how unlikely it might seem."

We drove on in silence as I pondered his statement. I was not sure where I stood with respect to belief in God. I grew up with the God of Israel as a given, but my later scientific training had seeded doubts. My challenges to the literal translation of the Torah were what got me labeled as a heretic. Maybe some alien cosmic intelligence *was* out there. Could it be the supernatural, omniscient being that defined our God? I shook my head. I wasn't going there. I'd leave those conundrums to the philosophers. Veterinary medicine was deep enough for me.

We rounded the bubble domes of the main terminal complex into a street lined with smaller domes and tall trees with fern-like branches. The foliage varied from shades of red-brown to yellow. To me, they looked dead or dying, but that might have been their natural color. The rest of the surfaces were the uniform gray of everything else we had seen. More figures lay scattered in view, some in the middle of the road and others about the buildings.

Fur stopped the drone. We hailed but received no response. After a few minutes, we moved on.

Fur turned to me. "Two possibilities, I suppose, when you see dead or dying victims in the streets. One is war, but there doesn't seem to be any other destruction you might expect. The other is some sort of plague. I guess the latter."

"I agree but it would be one hell of a plague to wipe out everyone. And what about the one reptilian who attacked the drone? What disease would make it do that?"

Fur smirked. "Epidemic rabies?"

"Sure, like they're running around and biting each other. And where are the rest of the live Pronacians?"

"I think I'd be locked inside."

I called Levi. "Have you received any further contact from the Pronacians?"

"No. And what was wrong with that native?"

Not in the mood to explain, I said, "I'll tell you about it later," and shut off the comm. "Let's go farther into town," I said to Fur.

The next hour we drove through deserted streets—deserted except for a plethora of bodies, many bloated by advanced decomposition. The town of gray bubble domes and pavement, ugly fern trees, and litter of putrefying corpses was grim.

"This is enough to depress Mary Poppins," I said.

Fur's brow furrowed as he looked at me.

"She was a character in an old...Oh, forget it."

As we turned a corner, we saw two more living reptilians. One stood in the middle of a street and held what looked like a club. It leaned over another figure that writhed on the ground. It lifted the implement and swung it down hard. The prone figure stopped moving.

The weapon wielder turned to us and lurched into a stagger toward the drone.

"Uh, oh. That club could crack the windshield."

Fur jammed the gears into reverse, swung around, and hightailed it out of there. He did not slow until we were more than a kilometer away.

I looked at him. "I thought this was a plague, but that did not look like death by disease." I was beginning to wonder if we could help these beings.

Fur pulled at his beard before he spoke. "I can't believe all those people were bludgeoned to death. This whole thing is bizarre."

"Thanks. I hadn't noticed."

He booted me in the ankle. "Smartass. Let's head for the city center. Maybe we can find someone who will talk to us rather than try to slaughter us."

I had Ruthie put us through to Levi again. "Have you heard anything?"

"No. What is going on? I demand to know or return to ship immediately."

"We don't know what's going on, and we'll let you know as soon as we do. Over."

A moment later, a movement caught my eye. "What's that? By the door to that building."

The comm crackled with clicks and hisses before the translation came through. *"Who you? In vehicle."*

Fur and I exchanged glances, and I responded. "We're from the Galactic Circle Veterinary Service. We've responded to your distress call. Can you tell us what the problem is?"

"Galactic Circle, can help?"

"I'm Dr. Cy Berger. My companion is Furoletto Cohen. We need more information to know if we can help."

"We die. Need help."

"Again, please tell us the nature of the problem." I would not put us at risk until I knew what we were dealing with.

"Unknown disease. Us not infected. You safe."

Right. Like I would accept that as gospel. "Come out where we can see you."

Two figures stepped out into the harsh sunlight, one a head shorter than the other. Like those we had seen already, neither wore clothing other than some sort of tool belt hung with unidentifiable implements.

The taller figure raised an upper arm, palm toward us, a universal gesture of greeting and nonviolence. *"I named Kraznit."* It pointed to the smaller figure with the other upper hand. *"Offspring, Kraznit A. Not ill. See?"*

"What do you mean?" I asked. "You could be sick and not show it."

"No. When ill, see. Stagger—become crazed." It performed a pirouette and had its kid do the same. *"See? Balance good."*

"Very pretty," Fur said.

I was not convinced. "Any more of you in there?"

He motioned, and three more Pronacians emerged. All pirouetted gracefully and seemed to be fine; at least they didn't stagger about and club each other. I could not sense anything from them on the emotional level from within the vehicle.

Fur turned to me with a sardonic grin. "Your turn. I'll stay in the drone. They don't seem to be nuts—right now."

I grimaced at him as I moved toward the airlock. I knew we could not show a willingness to help if we stayed locked in our land drone, but I did don my suit and take a stunner. When I stepped out onto the smooth gray pavement, my heartbeat did a drum-roll of apprehension. This was my first face-to-face meeting with an alien, after all.

Krasnit towered over me, as tall as Fur, but rather scrawny, like me. At their invitation, I followed them into the bubble house they had come out of, despite my nervousness. They displayed no aggression, and their emotional state seemed calm as far as I could interpret it, but I caressed the weapon at my side as I walked through the doorway.

Multiple walled compartments subdivided the structure, although the walls did not reach the ceiling. The inside of the building was as gray as the outside. Benches rimmed two walls of the first compartment. Above them were shelves covered with containers marked with alien glyphs. The Pronacians sat. The benches were too high for my comfort, so I stood. The climate-control unit of my suit kicked down a notch. The Pronacians liked it hot.

The Pronacian beside Kraznit spoke. *"I Kraznit's gryllfrt, Zlech."*

The last two words did not translate. "Damn it, Ruthie, you can do better than that."

"She is his mate, Cy. Her name is Zlech."

I could see no evidence of gender-specific anatomical differences and guessed they had internalized functional sex organs like Terran reptiles. No doubt the three smaller Pronacians, including Kraznit A, were Kraznit and Zlech's offspring. Were the others Kraznit B and C?

"Our people die. Can help?" Zlech asked.

Krasnit nodded. I supposed that was a universal sign of agreement—if you had a head.

"I need information before I know that," I replied. "Tell me what has happened."

"Plague first in jungle town," Kraznit said. *"Spread rapid. Villagers die. No cure. You first help to come."*

The first? Maybe the dumbest. This planet could mark *our* graves, as well.

Kraznit continued. *"Victims stagger, crazy, become raged. Attack anyone approach. Then sleep, death."*

The first part matched what we had seen, but it sounded like nothing I had ever heard of. Ruthie's search of the medical encyclopedia did not help.

I addressed Kraznit and Zlech. "I'm not aware of any disease that matches the description you've given us. What we need is to get samples from some patients."

I flinched as Kraznit's eyes rolled back and forth and up and down while his nose and ear slits vibrated.

"Danger. Sick homicidal maniacs."

At least that was how Ruthie translated it to me through my comm.

A wave of fear swept through Kraznit, and despite my shields, my stomach lurched in response.

Kraznit clacked his mouth a few times, perhaps for emphasis, but all those teeth just made me more apprehensive. "Perhaps our only chance is to find someone in the final, comatose stage of the disease," I said.

Kraznit said, *"Medical facility two flurgs—center city. Go."*

Ruthie added, "One flurg is approximately 2.5 kilometers, Cy."

As I parted from the family, I heard some sort of lock clack in the entry behind me. That sound made me move a bit faster to get inside the securely locked land drone.

CHAPTER 8

FUR HAD LISTENED IN on the proceedings, so after I climbed aboard, he took off as per Kraznit's directions. I called to fill in Levi. The rebbe's image onscreen resembled the color of a Pronacian by the time I reported what we had learned.

We rolled up to the medical facility. The building was white, rather than the uniform gray of everything else. A dozen red, interlocking rings formed a triangle above the dome's doors. Both Fur and I put on isolation suits, locked the land drone behind us—it had some nasty anti-theft devices—then approached the entry. We peered through transparent panels, but saw little.

Fur tried the door, but it was locked. He knocked, and after a few minutes, a figure approached. This Pronacian wore a filthy sleeveless gray smock. I was not sure this represented an improvement over the usual nakedness.

The doors muffled its voice, but Ruthie translated. *"Who?"*

"We're medical personnel. We heard your call for help. Can we come in?"

A brown-smocked figure appeared out of the gloom. After an extended conference, Dirty Gray approached the door and a lock clicked. Both Pronacians moved back from the door. They were fearful, but not aggressive.

"I'm a doctor." I did not emphasize the veterinarian part, and was annoyed at myself for letting Levi affect my confidence. "We spoke to a family earlier and they told us of the plague. Do you have patients here? Can we get samples? Our ship has sophisticated medical equipment to analyze them. We might be able to help."

The Pronacians conferred again. Both were Healers, they said, although with different specialties, denoted by the color of their garb. Neither was an infectious disease expert.

Dirty Gray repeated the information on the plague we had gotten from Kraznit, and added, *"Medical capabilities overwhelmed. Exhausted drugs first weeks. Antibiotics, antivirals not cure."*

Brown said, *"Try grow agent, but fail. Expert growers sick—all dead."* A surge of grief came through clearly.

"What about survivors?" I asked. "We met a family who survived."

Fur added, "The survivors, do they get the disease and recover? Become immune?"

The Healers conferred again. Brown spoke. *"Get disease not survive. Any who leave plague area killed so can't spread."*

God, how barbaric. Then I recalled that ancient humans had done much the same in the face of plagues and lack of understanding. I had to watch myself. I might begin to sound like Levi.

"Did you get sick?" I asked.

"No sick. One in ten not sick."

"If there are survivors of the disease, we might be able to test them for immunity and find a protective antibody. We have the facilities to produce that in our ship. But we need samples from live patients and survivors."

Dirty Gray turned his lower pair of hands downward. *"All patients confined secure—could not harm. Now long dead."*

"We need samples." I spoke to Fur on our private circuit. "Healthy, as well as sick. If we start with these two, that will give us a baseline. We can assume that they have whatever it is that protects them from the infection."

"Or don't have something that makes them susceptible," he added.

I turned to the Healers. "Would you have a problem if we took some samples from you two? That will get us started."

We took blood, skin, saliva, and oral epithelial samples from the two healers. I let Fur do the latter two. Those teeth...I shuddered.

The blood was green.

***

When we returned to the ship, Levi blasted us with a five-minute harangue on aliens and the danger we put him in. I kept my shields on maximum and let him run down without comment as we got to work. Purged, he stood in the background and watched. A scowl never left his face. His consternation colored my own thoughts, but at least he was quiet.

Fur's brow wrinkled as he examined the data. "No iron. All the active molecules are copper-based. A hydrated form of copper carbonate is what makes the blood green, but it's a stable compound and doesn't carry oxygen. A different molecule does that."

"Let's run a genetic scan," I said. "We need a full genomic pattern of healthy Pronacians. Then we can recognize foreign DNA from any agent against that background when we get samples from patients with the disease."

A transmission lit up the comm, and Ruthie's translation came through.

"Offworlders. You help? Come five hundred kilometers northeast. Disease here now—dying soon."

"Ah, two hundred *flurgs*," I said, and detected a wave of confusion from Levi. "Let's go there and see if we can get any more information."

"And samples from patients," added Fur.

***

Ruthie flew over jungle and broad brown rivers interspersed with small gray settlements. We inspected several villages through the viewscreen, but saw no evidence of life even at the highest magnification. When we arrived, the Pronacians who had contacted us guided the *GCVS* in. A contingent waited as we landed in a small field near a group of domes.

"Follow," the foremost Pronacian spoke. Then they all turned and moved toward the buildings. They had an odd, double-jointed gait that ate ground. Fur and I could not keep up in our isolation suits on the yellow, foam rubber-like turf in the lower gravity. Fur caught me once when I nearly did a strangely graceful face-plant in the moss. Levi, of course, stayed in the ship, unwilling to face unclean aliens.

Inside the first dome stood two red-robed Pronacians, the first bright color we had seen on or around these beings. I presumed they were Healers.

One spoke. *"Healers in Gpblglph say need patient samples. Can provide."*

I assumed *Gpblglph* was where we had just been. "We took samples from the healthy Healers but we need fresh samples from patients afflicted with the disease."

The second Healer said, *"Disease new here. Few dead. Many die soon. Cannot stop."* Desperation tinged his words. *"Have tissue, blood, from patients died today."*

"You've performed autopsies? That's great." I wondered if Pronacians could interpret the relief in my voice at not having to deal with homicidal patients. "May we have those samples to analyze? And may we take more from any of you here who are healthy? The samples might help us pinpoint the cause of the plague."

I explained what we could accomplish with our equipment and they agreed. We took the samples we wanted from our healthy hosts, and they gave us several additional vials and bottles that contained blood and tissue from plague victims.

***

When he completed the new analyses, Fur looked up from his work. "There are several strange things here. There's a gene complex that's absent in the disease victims, but it's present in the first two healers we met."

"Do you think that could be the reason the first two didn't have the disease?"

"I thought so at first, but it's also absent in the healthy volunteers we just sampled. I'm not sure what that means."

"Why wouldn't *all* the healthy Pronacians have the genes? We would need a full epidemiological study to understand that."

"The second thing is a protein sequence in the infected patients that's not in any of the healthy ones. That's likely to be associated with the organism. Third, there's no unusual genetic material. I'm not sure I understand that."

"We can code the protein, at least," I said. "That may lead us backwards to the nucleic acids. But we should also try to isolate the organism." I thought for few moments. "Our isolation media are unlikely to support its growth. We'll have to use local ingredients. Let's see if our friends can help with that."

The Pronacians already had facilities and reagents for isolation of copper-based organisms, but they previously had no success along that line. Neither did we. They did tell us that infected tissue injected into the local equivalent of laboratory rats caused disease similar to that in the sentient reptilians.

***

Fur twiddled the dials of the positron microscope and grunted. "This thing is bizarre. It's not a typical virus or bacterium. It's not a cell, and it does not have any coat like a virus. It looks like a copper-based enzyme, but one that can reproduce. No wonder no one could grow it."

I looked. It was not like anything I had seen before, not even like the self-replicating prion proteins that caused spongiform encephalopathies like mad cow disease. Even Levi wanted a look.

I grabbed the proteomic readout and examined it. "This fits the signature we saw only in the plague victims. This could be our bug, but it's weird. I'm not surprised that antibiotics and antivirals don't work. They wouldn't on an enzyme. We need to prove that it is the cause and figure out how it replicates, and then find a way to kill or deactivate it.

"Next, we need to determine what organ systems are affected and how it causes injury—what it does to the Pronacian physiology—if we are going to treat the symptoms. We can assume the nervous system is targeted, but there could be others."

Fur added, "It would help to know how the thing is transmitted. It's in saliva and blood, so spread could be by contact with secretions."

Levi's voice quavered. "Is this thing dangerous to humans?"

Fur and I looked at each other and shrugged.

I felt Levi's pulse of angst. He left the laboratory with alacrity.

Fur said, "We can start with studying those experimental animals that get the disease."

"We can't grow the enzyme but we can concentrate it from the blood of the plague victims."

When we had the concentrated enzyme, the Pronacian healers supplied us with reddish-green lizard-like creatures with a body about a foot long and a similar length muscular tail. One hissed at me showing a mouthful of needle-sharp teeth.

I loaded a syringe with the enzyme in saline solution and told Fur, "Grab that sucker and we'll inject it."

He scowled at me. "Can't you calm it down?"

"I'm trying, but it's not responding. Sometimes animals' reactions are just the opposite from what I want. My empathic talent isn't perfect."

Fur grimaced and reached into the cage. The lizard was a blur as it moved. Fur grabbed a towel and threw it over the scurrying form, then pinned the edges. "Can't you stick it through the cloth?" he yelled. "Quick."

"Hell, no. I can't even tell where the head and tail are."

"So be it." He let go of the towel. "Your turn."

The towel lay in one corner of the cage and the lizard in the other. I gave Fur the syringe, and donned a pair of gloves eminently suited for extra-vehicular space walks. I took a deep breath, grabbed the lizard, and pinned it to the bottom of the cage. It was surprisingly strong for such a little creature, but at least the teeth did not reach my skin as it munched on the gloves.

"Stick him," I yelled.

Fur jabbed downward just as the beast squirmed out of my grasp and I lunged for it.

I screamed and pulled my left hand back toward my body and grabbed it with my right. "Shit. You got me, not the goddamned lizard."

The look on Fur's face brought home what had happened. The pain of the jab paled to insignificance with the realization that he had injected me with the plague.

For long moments, neither of us said a word. Then Fur cleared his throat. "Cy, I...um, don't think that the disease will be transmissible to humans. After all, the organisms are copper-based. I mean, it won't—"

"Quiet," I said. "It's not your fault. If I hadn't flinched..."

"I'm so sorry. I can't begin to—"

"Grab that alcohol and disinfect the puncture." I pulled off the gloves. I had little hope that this would do any good. The organism already inhabited my subcutaneous tissues and no amount of surface cleansing would be worth a damn, but it gave us both something to do. I squeezed the puncture area on the back of my hand and generated a drop of blood. I envisioned the organism crawling through my bloodstream.

Fur started to say something, but I waved him to silence. I thought about what we knew of the disease's course. In the Pronacians, it took less than twenty-four hours from exposure to death. One day.

Fur looked like a kid who had just lost his favorite puppy. My head and gut couldn't stand the abject guilt that leaked from his huge form like radiation from a pulsar. I retreated to my cabin.

Now, I'm not a hypochondriac. Back at our university, veterinary and human medical students went through much of their first two years of the curriculum together, covering common subjects like physiology, pharmacology, microbiology, and pathology. I had friends on the human medical side of the aisle. I did not develop, as some students did, the symptoms of just about every disease that we studied. I couldn't help but be amused by the panic that took hold of students who were convinced they had everything from amoebic meningitis to Zarathustran jungle rot.

Now, as I lay on my bunk, I was *not* amused. I took note of every muscle twitch, every minor pain that coursed through my skinny frame. When one catalogs these, there is hardly a space of ten minutes when something untoward does not occur, whether it is a grumbling stomach, colonic gas movements, a twitching eyelid, a minor muscle cramp. With each of these, my cardiac rhythm lurched. Surely the onset of...something?

Sweat trickled down my neck and pooled on my pillow.

Fever.

I jumped up. I couldn't stand it. I flung the cabin door open. Fur was outside the door, and he jumped a half meter in the air in surprise. His concern washed over me. He was desperate to help, but what could he do if I got the plague? Maybe tie me down before I could kill anyone?

Damn it, I raged, forget all that crap. "Fur," I barked.

He jumped again, like a kid guilty of some

unimaginable transgression.

"Let's get some help and inject those damn lizards."

Before I lost it completely.

We recruited the two Pronacian Healers. This turned out to be a mixed blessing. Eight extra arms made all the difference in our work. They handled our little scaled beasties with ease, but this also exposed the Pronacians to Levi's distinct brand of xenophobia.

As we worked, Levi hovered in the background, which surprised me. His motivation to be obnoxious seemed to overcome his fear of the Pronacians.

"We are wasting our time here," he said. "We need to move on to human worlds where God intended us to perform our work."

I tried to ignore him.

"Why do we care if these creatures die? This planet is no good to Dovid's World and our people."

This got a long look from both of the Pronacian Healers, accompanied by an aura of distinct hostility.

"Unclean monsters," Levi muttered.

Both healers stopped their work and faced Levi.

Too late, I realized that Levi was unaware that the clicks and hisses from Ruthie were a translation of his words. "Ruthie. For God's sake, don't translate any more of Levi's diatribes." I faced Levi. "Are you out of your mind? Are you *trying* to get us killed?"

Levi huffed. "These disgusting creatures don't belong here. We don't need to help—"

Fur grabbed Levi's arm and bodily removed the protesting rebbe from the laboratory.

I looked at the Pronacians. "Please forgive us. That is *not* how Fur and I feel. Or how most humans would feel. We do not agree with Reb Levi's beliefs or hold to his narrow-mindedness. I can't apologize enough for his behavior."

One Pronacian cocked its head and stared at me.

The other shook its head. Then I realized that Ruthie was no longer translating, so I had her resume and repeated my apology. I could sense that the Healers were now mollified.

Fur returned and said, "I explained that his words were translated for the Pronacians and he understood the possible consequences. I don't think he will be back."

We continued our work, and within four hours of the injections, the creatures were sick.

"The stages are the same," I observed. "They go through incoordination, then aggression, then coma and death, all within six hours. Much faster than the big reptilians. That's incredible. There's nothing like it in the literature."

And I hadn't shown any symptoms yet.

We took samples and confirmed that the enzyme bug was present in the sick animals, but not the healthy controls, which were injected with sterile saline. That proved the enzyme was the etiological agent of the plague. We necropsied the animals.

"Look at this," I said. "The brain is swollen, no surprise. The liver is also enlarged...and yellow. The brain makes sense considering the neurological symptoms, but what does the liver mean?"

Fur viewed the biochemical data. He pounded his ham-sized fist on the workbench. I felt the seismic tremor through my shoes. He pointed to the side-by-side readouts from a healthy and a sick lizard.

"Look at the liver data. The sick ones have increased lipid levels. We saw that in the yellowness of the tissue. And look at the alcohol and ketone levels in the blood and tissues. They are higher than I have ever seen in any species."

The epiphany hit me like a freight drone. "Oh, my God. That's it."

Fur pulled his head back and looked at me beneath a lowered brow. "What's it?"

"The organism—the enzyme. It must subvert the metabolism of the host and catalyze the production of alcohol from carbohydrates and fats. When it breaks down fats, it also produces ketones. The alcohol is toxic to the liver, and both the alcohol and the ketones are toxic to the brain."

Fur continued my train of thought. "I see. The first step in the metabolism of alcohol is oxidation to acetaldehyde, and that inhibits mitochondrial function—knocks out the cell's power plant. And acetaldehyde in the brain inhibits enzymes that are critical for nerve transmission."

"Yeah," I added. "The incoordination and the coma are due to the nervous system toxicity of the acetaldehyde and ketones. Aggression can be seen with high alcohol levels in people, but may be a uniquely uniform response of Pronacians."

My excitement left me a bit dizzy, and I panicked. Oh, no. Not now. But the wave of vertigo passed, and my heart rate dropped along with it. It was late and we were exhausted. As we cleaned up, I sensed Fur's eyes bore through my back whenever he thought I couldn't see him. I knew he watched me for any signs of alcoholic incoordination.

I could not stand it anymore. "Shit. Don't stare at me like I'm one of the goddamned sick lizards. I'm going to bed. We'll work on the cure tomorrow."

Fur frowned.

"You can lock the goddamned door from the outside if you're afraid I'll go berserk." I knew this was insensitive—the poor guy already thought he had stuck me with a death sentence—but I had reached the end of my string.

Fur flinched at my words. His voice was so very

much smaller than his size. "There's no need for that."

Whether he meant locking me in or my anger, I did not want to try to sort it out. "Sorry, Fur. I just need some sleep. We both do. See you in the morning."

The "I hope" hung unvoiced in the air.

In my cabin, I collapsed onto my bunk without undressing, other than kicking off my shoes. I stared at the ceiling. Every logical neuron in my brain said that a copper-based alien enzyme could not reproduce in my body, nor cause the same biochemical changes it did in the reptilians. Every nonlogical neuron—and they seemed to be in the majority—screamed *Doom*.

***

I awoke with a start. I was sure I had dozed for just a few minutes, but the time on my comm screen said I had slept for nine hours. Nine hours. I was alive. I did not know whether to laugh or cry, but the former took precedence. I got up with no vertigo—I was sober. I slapped my hand on the door lock sensor and there was Fur...again, hovering outside my door.

He looked at me with narrowed eyes, and I laughed. His eyes narrowed even further.

I did a pirouette. "See? Balance good. No sick," I mimicked Kraznit.

Fur's hairy face broke into a smile so broad it threatened to crack the sides of his cheeks. He grabbed me under the armpits and lifted me so we were face to face. "Yup. Just as ugly as ever." He plunked me down hard enough to rattle my teeth.

We both took deep breaths.

"I tried your door a half dozen times through the night," he said. "I was about ready to break it down." His eyes were moist. Damn, he was about to cry.

"Hell. It will take more than some Pronancian

critter to consign me to vacuum. Come on, we've got more work to do. We still don't know how to cure this thing in the reptilians. Let me get my shoes on."

All night, something had tickled my subconscious, but it had stayed hidden there. Now, the subconscious tickle had become an itch.

In the lab, I said, "Let me see the Pronacian genome readouts again."

I compared the data from the first two Healers we had met with the other healthy and sick reptilians. Something about that gene complex...

"Ruthie, can you patch into the genome database and link it with the metabolic program?"

There was a fraction of a second delay before she answered—probably equivalent to several hours of cogitation for a human. "I can do that, Cy."

"See if it can decode the genome enough to run a simulation on what that strange complex from the first Healers does."

The delay was almost a full second this time.

"I have linked the programs. The data readout is printing."

The printer whirred out two sheets. I grabbed them—and held my breath.

"What are you thinking?" Fur asked.

I held up my hand for silence as I took in the data. My breath whooshed out. "Got it." I let out a laugh and turned to Fur. "Here. What do you think?"

He took the pages and studied them as he scratched his beard. A grin beamed out from beneath the whiskers. "That's amazing."

"The first two Healers never got the disease because they were not susceptible. They have a gene complex that codes for another enzyme that deactivates the plague organism by attacking the copper-protein molecule.

"What threw me off was the fact that the healthy Pronacians at the second facility didn't have the gene complex, so I thought it wasn't important. But it was simply that they were not exposed to the disease yet. They would have gotten sick if they had been exposed. And that ten percent that don't get sick? Like the Kraznit family? Likely they all have this gene complex and the protective enzyme it produces."

Fur added, "If we give the Pronacians the capability to produce that enzyme in bulk, it's their antibiotic."

We both laughed and slapped each other on the back.

Levi, who had just entered the room with his usual scowl asked, "What are you two so happy about?"

"We've tagged our culprit," I said. "The plague organism converts body fat and carbohydrate to alcohol. The alcohol levels in the blood and tissues of reptilian plague victims are way beyond lethal levels for humans. In fact, blood levels are almost as much as in some of our alcoholic beverages."

"What are you saying?"

"These guys are—literally—dead drunk!"

***

We had saved millions of lives, and the Pronacians were suitably grateful. Levi demanded payment for veterinary services rendered. For a guy who refused to help and denigrated the Pronacians in the first place, he was sure quick to take their credits. Those went into our account at the Galactic Bank, which meant that they went to the Rebbinical Council at home. The Pronacians said they could never repay their debt, but I began to wonder about that. I told their leaders, privately, that they might hear from me again.

CHAPTER 9

I MET MY FIRST racing *phrook*. The creature was long-limbed and slim-bodied with sleek gray-brown coat almost like an otter's fur. Its head was narrow with an elongated muzzle full of needle-sharp teeth. The prominent black eyes were at my shoulder height and radiated hostility. This phrook's pain cut through me as if it were my own.

The source of the animal's pain was clear; he held his left rear leg off the straw on the stable floor. Fur restrained the fractious beast while I bent and palpated the leg.

Master Fredo, the phrook's owner stood over me as I worked. "Lightspeed is the best racer on the planet."

Fredo was flanked by Lightspeed's jockey and a few of Fredo's lackeys.

The jockey said, "He's a sure winner in the Beta Cygnus Stakes tomorrow."

"Biggest purse of the year." In a harsh whisper, Fredo added, "You fix him up and I'll give you a cut of the winnings."

I looked away from the leg and up at Fredo. The man's voluminous robes did not hide his obesity. Deceit tinged everything he said. His title, *Master* Fredo, was not lost on me. The guy cowed everyone around him.

Racing phrooks did not have legs designed for the kind of pounding they took. Their fine bones could not carry a human, even one as small as most jockeys, so drivers rode behind them in a sulky. Phrooks were omnivores with a nasty disposition, and pain made this one's mood worse. He swung his head and snapped at me several times before Fur got him under control. Everything they did was fast. I was glad I worked on the hind leg. I had no desire to add my flesh to the animal's sustenance.

"Well, whaddaya think?" Fredo asked in a loud and hearty voice.

"Best I can tell he has severe sesamoiditis. That's inflammation of the bones at the back of the fetlock. That's why he's lame."

"What causes that, anyway?" Fredo's furrowed brow told me he was annoyed that I did not give him good news.

"Usually, it's excessive stress on the legs. Often from overtraining."

Fredo's doughy face turned dark with a touch of hostility. "I'll kill that trainer if Lightspeed misses this race."

The jockey gave Fredo a worried look, as if he believed his boss would do it.

"Can you fix it, Doc?"

I was betting that the Phrook's overtraining was not the fault of the trainer. "No, I can't. This is a serious condition. The leg will need to be immobilized. He needs an enforced rest period, as much as a few months."

Fredo's eyes narrowed and almost disappeared into the folds of his flesh. "Ain't gonna happen. This guy runs tomorrow. I got too many credits riding on him. Give 'im a shot, Doc. Make 'im good for the race." His voice cajoled, but his thoughts threatened.

"I can't do that. He would risk worse injury by running on this leg."

Fredo now lost any hint of good will. "I don't give a shit about that, so long as he wins that race. If he's crippled after, I can still get big stud fees. Give him painkillers and anti-inflammatories, whatever he needs. I know you got that stuff. This guy runs tomorrow."

I stood and moved away from the phrook. "Can't and won't. Anti-inflammatories and analgesics would only mask the problem, and that would be animal cruelty."

Fredo poked a pudgy finger into my chest. "You will. I run this place. People do what I tell 'em to."

I turned to Fur. "We're done here. Grab my bag, will you?"

Fredo said to one of his lackeys, "You take that bag." One look at the giant who now held my medical supplies deterred the lackey. As we left, Fredo upbraided the man for cowardice. I hadn't noticed Fredo make any move toward Fur.

Fur and I left the stable and walked back into the nearby town. As we approached an alley, five bravos stepped out and blocked our way. I guess they figured five men were enough to intimidate a veterinarian and his assistant, but as they examined Fur, I sensed their hesitation.

"Hand over that bag," the biggest of them said. He was broad-shouldered but had to look up at Fur. Nervousness trickled out of him like water from a cracked pitcher.

"Big mistake," I replied.

Fur bared his teeth in a nasty grin. "Go back to your boss. Tell him you couldn't find us. Save yourselves a lot of pain."

The thug's eyebrows just about met between his narrow-set eyes, but he shrugged and yelled, "Get 'em."

With the odds five to two, I did not hesitate and took out the leader with a perfect karate *Mae Geri* front kick to the groin. I didn't take time to watch him go down, as a second man had lunged at me. I sidestepped and dropped him with a *Tegatana* chop to the back of the neck. A third man already writhed on the ground and moaned. Fur held another thug over his head.

"Let me go," the man pleaded, but Fur tossed him a goodly distance anyway. He lay motionless where he landed.

The moaner was up on his knees now. "You broke my arm," he cried at Fur.

"You're lucky that's all I busted."

He got up and stumbled off, cradling his limb. I saw the fifth tough sprint around the nearest corner.

I staggered, tasted bile, and closed my eyes against the incipient headache. The anger of fights really got to me.

Fur grabbed my arm. "You okay?"

"Let's get out of here."

As we walked, Fur looked at me, eyebrows cocked. "Well, Captain, you have some martial arts skill I didn't know about."

I felt my face grow warm. "I trained in karate and judo when I was younger."

The look on his face demanded more.

"Hell, when you have a nose as big as mine—"

"And combine that with an ego of like size," Fur murmured.

"It meant lots of fights when other kids made fun of me. Nobody insults my nose and gets away with it." I fixed him with my best glare. "Any comments?"

Fur put up his hands, palms forward. "Far be it for me..."

I hoped that would be the end of the violence for this trip. My stomach and head would take a while to get back to normal.

***

Back in town, I had a welcome surprise: messages from my folks and Roxanne. I had sent out messages to both earlier in the day, so the missives must have crossed in hyperspace. I amused myself by imagining they waved as they went by.

I listened to my mom and dad first. As always, they were obviously aware of being monitored, and their greetings were heartfelt but cautious. Dad brought me up to date on the farm and the crops, a safe topic, and Mom talked about our neighbors and their obstreperous teenagers. Some of those exploits were humorous. Cow tipping is an age-old urban legend that some kids got hold of. Supposedly, you could sneak up on an unsuspecting sleeping cow and push it over for entertainment. But cows didn't sleep standing up like horses did, and they weren't that slow-moving or dumb. Before it was over, an irate cow trampled a couple of kids. Fortunately, the pasture was muddy and the soft substrate minimized their injuries. I chuckled and wondered what Levi would make of that one.

My heart tiptoed through the proverbial tulips as I switched on Roxanne's message. The holovision of her was enough to mesmerize me as I drank in her words:

Hello Cy,

I hope this catches you soon. It does help having your itinerary, but I'm never sure if it will get there before you leave. We had too little time together, but hyperwave will have to suffice for now.

Things ramped up a bit after you left Sammara. We had a new EPD outbreak and were hard-pressed to contain it. We still have not figured out how it got out again, but likely on someone's clothing or shoes, I'd guess. There were no cattle movements, that's for sure. I must admit it has taken me time to get past the depression I felt about being so helpless. As a vet, I want to be able to cure every animal that's sick or in pain. I know that's not realistic, but I can't help it. I have to learn not to feel their suffering—even though I don't feel it the same way you do. I don't know how you manage it. Thankfully, that is behind us now.

I was glad she was not more specific about my empathic talent. I still did not want Levi to have that information, and I had no misconceptions that Levi did not read all Roxanne's missives, even if he said he didn't.

Now, all I have to deal with is the paperwork. The number of cattle lost is staggering, but somehow on paper they are just numbers. The need to be there to euthanize even a small number was far worse, as you well know. I have been working with the techs on the cloning and forced embryonic maturation of the replacement cattle. That, at least, feels like I'm doing something positive. I'm learning a lot. When you get to using the technology, you will be surprised at its value.

I know you've said that most of the work you have had on the new worlds is prosaic, but at least it is in an exciting setting. Hey, sorry. That sounded demeaning. I wish I could spend a few days in a clinic dealing with some routine cases. I have not used most of what I learned in school yet. Anyway, keep the messages coming. Take care of yourself. Give my best to Fur and Levi.

As always,
Roxanne

I was glad she added regards to Levi. I did not want him to think I had biased her against him, much less spilled the beans about his spy mission.

The messages had chased away the aftereffects of

the fight, so Fur and I went to the hotel for lunch before we had to follow up on more appointments. We had ordered beers when the local constabulary showed up.

"You two," a beefy officer said, "are under arrest."

I assumed an innocent expression. "Us? Whatever for, officer?"

"Felonious assault and disturbing the peace. We've got complaints from one citizen who says you broke his arm, another who is in neck traction, and a third whose back is twisted out of joint."

I smiled. "Is that all?"

"Well, there is another guy in the hospital with damage to his, um, privates."

Fur could not suppress a snigger.

"Hmm. And there are just two of you to arrest us?" I said.

The officer's face turned red. Anger and apprehension fought for supremacy in his mind.

Fur broke into our little *tête-a-tête*. "Officer, it was self-defense. Those thugs assaulted us. They tried to steal Dr. Berger's medical bag."

"Tell it to the judge," the officer said.

God, couldn't he come up with a better line than that? Maybe he watched old vids, too. "Can I go to my room to get something and use the facilities?" I asked.

The two constables looked at one another and then the leader nodded. "But don't think you can skip out on us."

"Wouldn't dream of it."

This was obviously Fredo's work, the creep. I should have gotten the clue to the political set-up here from his moniker, *Master*.

In our room, I used the john and made a quick switch of my bags. I left one behind for Fredo's cronies. The police kept us at the station for a couple of hours, long enough for Fredo to pull off his heist, then released us. They actually had outstanding warrants on two of our assailants. That let us off the hook.

Of course, the bottles labeled anti-inflammatories and painkillers had disappeared from our room. Even though I knew it would happen, I was pissed. I wanted to teach the *gonifs* a lesson. It was bad enough to screw around with people, but when they did it to animals, that was crossing the line.

***

The next morning, before the race, Fur and I watched from behind some scrub on a low hill above the paddock. I figured Fredo's people would dose his phrook about an hour before the start—at least those were the instructions on the bottles I had mislabeled. Of course, both bottles contained a sedative. It wouldn't hurt the beast, but it would make it impossible for him to run. Just what he needed in the way of care.

A few minutes after administration of the medications, the phrook staggered and hung his head. Then he sank to the ground and wouldn't budge. The jockey and trainer went nuts and yelled at each other. When Fredo showed up a few minutes later, the real fun began. The guy was no dummy. He put two and two together and screamed for some guards.

"That vet has poisoned Lightspeed. He bet on another phrook and is fixing the race. Arrest him."

It was a good story on the spur of the moment. The guards ran off, to alert the authorities, I assumed. We already knew Fredo had the local law in his well-padded pocket.

The racer would be fine now, but I had one more thing I wanted to accomplish. I raised my gas-powered rifle, took careful aim, and shot Fredo in his fat ass with a trank dart. *Then* we hightailed it for the ship.

***

I dropped into the command chair and scanned the board.

"Ruthie, get us out of here. Now."

"I must wait for Control Center clearance, Cy," she replied.

Shit. We might not have the time. It depended on how long it took Fredo to get spaceport control alerted. I had put a small trank dose in the dart; it would have done no more than make him loopy for maybe half an hour. I did not want a murder charge against me, after all. I thumbed the comm to Control. "*GCVS*, ready for takeoff. Clearance, please."

When approval came back, I let out a deep breath. The engines powered up; we were ready to lift off. Just then, the red light on the comm flashed a baleful strobe.

"Control to *Galactic Circle Veterinary Service*. Please respond."

"Ruthie, don't answer. That's an order."

"But Cy, that will create difficulties with the authorities."

"Not as much as what will happen if we stay. Ruthie, just get us out of here."

Levi entered the bridge as I said this. He looked at me, then at Fur in the second's chair. "What are you doing?"

Neither of us answered him.

The comm lit up again. "*Galactic Circle*, you are no longer authorized for takeoff. Shut down your engines immediately."

"Why are we—?" Levi began again.

"Quiet," I snapped.

I knew this would kill any return to this system, but there were plenty of others out there. I hoped there weren't any patrol ships close by. *GCVS* could outrun them once we hit vacuum, but not in the atmosphere. And we had no way to fight—not that I wanted to.

The red light blinked again and I heard Fredo's voice. "Berger, you son of a bitch, I'll kill you—"

I cut the transmission off.

"What are you doing?" Levi screamed.

I continued to ignore him as we cleared the field on the antigravs.

Ruthie announced, "Cy, a patrol craft is on an interception bearing. ETA five minutes. What shall I do?"

"Damn it. Give us every bit of lift you have. Use the antimatter drive."

"That is prohibited in the atmosphere by Galactic Convention. You know that, Cy."

I also knew that I'd see the inside of a cell on Beta Cygnus IV for the next five years if we didn't get out of there. "Just do it as soon as you can."

"If you insist..." crooned Ruthie.

I felt Levi's hands on my shoulder, digging hard enough to make me wince. "Stop this," he grated. "Computer, return this ship to the ground."

The pressure on my shoulder stopped. I looked back to see Levi in Fur's grasp. "Not now, Reb Levi. We need to leave. We'll explain later." Fur ushered him into a chair.

Even though the antigravity drive kept us at one-g, the *sense* of increased g-force stayed with me as we accelerated. I trusted that would keep Levi in his seat. My face and underarms were soaked with sweat. The bridge's climcontrol system could not keep up with my body. I watched the sensors for signs of pursuit.

Just as Ruthie kicked in the antimatter drive, the patrol ship appeared on the sensors. I hoped they would be more conservative engaging *their* antimatter drive. There wasn't all *that* much danger if the ship was above the troposphere as we were now, but a few nasty explosions had led to strict regulations. I trusted the modern safeguards to protect us. We cleared orbit and left the pursuit behind.

"What have you done, Berger?" Levi's voice was shrill. "We are not done here. You have ruined my efforts to gather information on Beta Cygnus. My contacts in the Jewish commun–" He snapped his mouth shut.

I wondered what in hell that last bit meant. Why was he reticent about contacting members of the Jewish community?

"Get us out to our jump point, Ruthie," I said. "I want out of this system. Now."

"Why is the patrol chasing us?" Levi snapped. "We had a contract. You had a responsibility to fulfill that. If you have caused us to forfeit our due payment, it will come out of *your* pocketbook, Berger."

Something besides money was at issue. I got a sickening vision of weapons and bombs, whatever that meant. I made a mental note to ask Fur if he knew. He spent enough time spying on the rebbe.

I had no patience to deal with Levi. Ruthie could handle the ship from there, so I left the bridge. Let Fur give him the story.

***

Later, I questioned Fur about the impressions I had gotten from Levi. I leveled with the big man about my empathic ability to read emotions in people and other sentient races.

His aura became deeply disturbed as I spoke. He poked his big finger into my chest. "So you've been reading me all this time without my knowing it? That sucks, Cy. I feel like I've been violated."

"Now you know how I felt about your lying to me about the SOD."

He pursed his lips. Embarrassment colored his thoughts. "Okay. Fair enough. But when I owned up, you should have, too."

"It's not something I talk about. And I don't 'read' you all the time. I get sick as hell when I open myself up to peoples' emotions." I explained my reactions. "I feel like enough of a freak when people know about the animal empathy, much less the human part. But how about we call it even and go from there?"

Fur smiled. "I may be a member of the SOD, but can you tell that I think you're a real SO*B*?"

I smiled back and punched his arm.

"Anyway, when Levi *kvetched* about not bailing out of Beta Cygnus, I got some strange vibes about weapons. Do you know what's up with that?"

Fur tugged at his beard. "Our rebbe has been contacting the Jewish communities on each place we make planetfall."

"That's no surprise, is it? I imagine he wants to worship in a synagogue whenever he can."

"Be nice if that was the whole of it. He has clandestine meetings with the underworld elements on each planet."

"The Jewish Mafia?"

Fur drew his eyebrows together in puzzlement.

"Never mind. An ancient term. Go on."

"I can't tell you exactly what goes on in those meetings, but it isn't good. I found one sleazy character willing to talk after I greased his voice with credits and booze. Levi is offering money for the gangsters to stockpile weapons and to give support to the Test-Lits should they invade that world. He promises to elevate those criminals to positions of power when their world is subdued."

I could not believe what I was hearing. "The Test-Lits are going to invade other worlds beyond NewSol? They couldn't even pull it off on Sammara."

"They're obviously testing the water before they jump in with both feet. You know a basic tenet of the Test-Lits is to spread their brand of fundamentalism. I guess the next time they'll try to undermine the society before they attack."

"God. What *chutzpah*. But what can we do?"

"I've already been doing it. I make sure that someone in each government knows about Levi and his intrigues. They are not very happy. I doubt the Test-Lits will get very far."

After our talk, I felt guilty that I had been buckling under to Levi's demands and ignoring his activities. Not for the first time, I wondered how I could do anything to oppose the Test-Lits to free my parents. Was the threat that Levi and his ilk represented enough to make the people on the worlds we visited willing to help me? Or even the aliens like the Pronacians? Maybe, but how to make that happen was another story.

CHAPTER 10

"You sit here, Captain-Doctor Cy Berger."

OUR HOST, He-Who-Eats-with-Gusto, motioned with a talon as long as my hand. I always obeyed a being that resembled a tyrannosaur with wings.

Ruthie's translation in my earbud converted the dragon's mélange of grunts, hisses, and subsonic tones to Galactic Common.

"Your food." Our host pointed again. His teeth and his sapphire scales glinted in the sunlight from the high windows of the hall.

Platters held small carcasses of something covered with a brown pelt. I gave Fur a dubious look.

"At least it's been cooked," he muttered.

Levi's eyes were wide, his mouth turned down at the corners. "This must be *trefe*."

Like he expected the dragons to keep kosher?

The dragons prided themselves on having become *civilized* by their exposure to spacefaring races. Cooking was one of the civilized proclivities they had acquired. Unfortunately, this did not extend to gutting or skinning their guests' food items. Moreover, the dragons still ate their food while it was still live.

The furred creatures penned at one end of the banquet hall bore an unfortunate resemblance to teddy bears. Dragons, all males, left their seats and lined up to

Stephen A. Benjamin

select their dinners. The line-up was by size, the largest dragon—who happened to be our host—first. He-Who-Eats-With-Gusto was not so much bigger-framed than the others, but he out-massed the next largest by a significant margin. He lived up to his name. A few altercations broke out between like-size dragons as they pushed and shoved for position in line. These were put to rest by a roar from our host, but not until some blood was spilled. This did not seem to bother the dragons at all.

Consultation on a medical problem had brought the *Galactic Circle Veterinary Service* to Dragonworld—our name for their planet since we couldn't pronounce theirs. This was our welcome banquet.

While the dragons wore no clothing, they adorned themselves with variety of necklaces, finger and toe rings, bracelets and anklets, earrings, and jewels embedded in their skin, some in quite surprising parts of their anatomy. Diamonds, rubies, sapphires, emeralds, opals, amethysts, turquoise, jade, were all in evidence. But these were no fairytale dragons that sat on an ill-assorted hoard of gold, silver, and gem-bestudded treasures. The bigger the dragon, the more elaborate the adornment, but each had exquisite taste; no clash of colors or mismatched gems, here.

Gold chains complemented by topaz stones as large as my head hung from the emerald scales of one large specimen. A great ruby dragon wore rings, bracelets, and necklaces of silver and platinum that contrasted with one large black stone embedded in the center of his forehead. A golden Goliath scintillated with a belt and earrings of diamonds that radiated every color of the rainbow. I gaped as I watched this panoply of splendor march by my place at the table.

Once the dragons sat again, I looked from their dinners to the thing on my plate and swallowed hard.

The fear that emanated from the mass of furry creatures stretched my empathic defenses to the breaking point. Our host's hunger enveloped me as he grabbed one of his morsels and popped it past his jagged array of teeth. A squeal, then a loud crunch. My stomach and brain rebelled, and I fought to retain control as I bent over in my chair.

Not so, Levi. He jumped to his feet and screamed, "Stop this, you Godless creature. You are disgusting. You and your barbaric world should be isolated from decent humans."

I presumed that Ruthie's translation projected from the small speakers pinned to our tunics was all too literal. The rumble I felt through my shoes came from the dragons that surrounded us; it was not a happy feeling.

He-Who-Eats-With-Gusto leaned across the table toward Levi. He used a talon to extract a morsel of teddy bear from between his teeth before pointing it at the chunky rebbe. *"This one looks like juicy appetizer."*

A vision of slavering jaws accompanied a surge of anger from the big dragon.

I fought my nausea and splitting headache and grabbed Levi's arm as he screamed, "Your savage, heathen world should be exterminated."

"Fur, apologize," I yelled, as I dragged Levi from his seat and toward the door. I hoped we would see Fur again. Unharmed.

Outside, I turned to Levi. No time for dominance games now. "What in hell are you doing? You can't insult anyone who doesn't meet your standards of behavior." My voice shook.

He turned to me and his eye twitched as he snarled, "Berger, watch your tongue. Remember who you are and what is at stake."

"You could get us killed. That's what's at stake. Fur

is still in danger because of you."

He looked away and rubbed his scar. "I did *not* put us in danger from those...things." He looked back at me. "Cohen will be fine." He hesitated. "But there is no Godly reason for beasts like that. We should not even be here."

I threw up my hands and turned away. "Let's get out of here before our host decides we should join the feast as the second course."

Levi shot me a look as nasty as his thought, but followed me to the road that led back to the ship. Dragonworld was a dry planet, and the hot wind blasted us like a furnace. I did not see how Levi could stand to wear his suit coat and fedora. Sweat ran in rivulets down his red face. It would serve him right to collapse from heat stroke. The thought gave me a modicum of vindictive pleasure.

The city was a contrast in splendor and barbarity. Its buildings were golden towers that seemed like a reflection of the mountain spires that surrounded us. Dragons preferred heights for their abodes, being fliers that evolved by nesting on high peaks. While the dragons wore nothing but their own colorful skins and jewelry, bright flags and banners adorned their buildings, shops, and open-air stalls. Shops and stalls held a variety of wares, including rugs, furry hides, ornate wooden chests, and an assortment of metal implements: knives, axes, saws, hammers, and the like. Many shops displayed woven wall hangings dominated by scenes of gory dragon fights or by depictions of dragons dispatching large beasts that I assumed were prey. The majority of shops displayed fantastic jewelry.

Every second shop or stall contained corrals, pens, or cages that contained an astounding variety of furred, feathered, or scaled creatures. A cacophony of honks and howls, squeaks and squeals, barks and bellows rent the air. This reinforced my distress from the banquet we had so precipitously exited. These creatures were not pets. Their apprehension level was nowhere near that of the teddy bears featured at the banquet, but the sheer number assailed my equilibrium.

As Levi and I wove our way through the crowded, unpaved streets, small, dull-hued, female dragons peered out from shops. As throngs of male dragons followed us, their polished scales glittered in the sunlight as they moved. Relatively new to interstellar society, visitors from other planets fascinated them.

The youngsters—at least I assumed they were young from their size and curiosity—circled us as we walked. Some seemed to delight in rolling in the dusty street, then scratching vigorously, like some giant bird taking a dust bath. I sensed that some of the adults viewed this activity with envy. One scratched himself when he thought no one watched. I wondered if dust baths were a traditional method for dragons to deal with skin parasites—before they became civilized, of course.

As we walked, young dragons plucked at our unfamiliar clothing. Levi screeched when a talon snagged the cloth of his suit and nicked the underlying skin.

"He *stabbed* me," Levi bleated. Blood spread on the torn fabric. "Keep away from me, you...you revolting brute, you disgusting lizard."

I grabbed his arm as I sensed a surge of anger from the crowd. "Shut up and move before you get us killed."

"Just an accident," I called to the crowd. "No problem." Under my breath, I said, "Ruthie, stop translating." Seemed I was always a few beats too late in shutting down Levi's xenophobic tantrums.

"No problem? You call these ungodly creatures, '*no problem*'?" Levi's voice rose several octaves.

I pulled harder on his arm. The dragons were a threat if only because of their size and natural armament, but they also seemed to have a very low boiling point. Aggression was a natural state of being.

Levi shook off my grasp. "Keep your hands to yourself, Berger."

"If you insult the dragons any more, you might be dealing with more than *my* hands." I strode off, and he scurried in my wake.

As carnivores, I wondered if blood had the same effect on dragons as it did on Terran sharks. I kept my mental screens in place: I did not want the answer to that question.

We made the ship with no further incidents.

***

Fur returned to the *GCVS* liberally spattered with blood.

Levi gasped.

Fur glared at the rebbe. "I'm fine. The blood doesn't belong to me."

"What happened after we left?" I asked.

He grimaced. "About what you would expect. I apologized for Reb Levi, though it took a bit of abasing myself."

Levi was smart enough to keep his mouth shut.

"What do you mean?"

"The dragons were pissed. I ended up offering myself as a sacrifice to appease them."

"You *what?*"

Even Levi stood with his mouth open.

"It was a calculated move. I figured that our host could not afford to lose one of his exalted offworld visitors. He might get chomped by his superiors. That show of bravado did the trick. The dragons have a society based on personal dominance. The bigger and tougher you are, the higher up you are in the nobility. They settled down and continued with dinner."

"But the blood..." Levi stared at Fur's tunic, his face a mask of revulsion.

Fur chuckled. "Someone has to teach them to chew with their mouths closed."

***

Fur and Levi were off on an excursion to restock the *GCVS* with water and some foodstuffs. Levi insisted on going despite his fear and hate of the dragons to make sure what Fur bought was kosher, no doubt. Levi did not make any espionage expeditions on this nonhuman world. It seemed that aliens were not worth his effort unless it was to insult them. I relied on Fur to keep our rebbe on a short leash.

As the Captain and the dominant member of our delegation, I had an invitation to a *sporting* event. My leadership puzzled the dragons because of Fur's superior size, but they accepted our strange, alien ways. The dragons made it clear they would not tolerate another breach of etiquette. I needed to regain our party's standing in the dragons' eyes. God knew what might happen if I didn't.

Dragons of all sizes and colors packed the bleachers of an open-air arena. Two large and well-matched specimens faced off on the sand arena floor. One was greenish-gold, the other brown with bronze highlights. Oiled scaly skin glinted in the sunlight. They were almost devoid of jewelry as befit a prizefight, although the green combatant wore a large diamond that glittered in the center of his chest.

I seated myself next to my afternoon's host, Valiant-Killer-of-Trybwyths—whatever   trybwyths might be.

"This fight for championship," Valiant rumbled.

I could hardly hear him through the din of hisses, grunts, and bellows of the dragons surrounding us, but Ruthie's translation came through on my earbuds. The dragons hopped up and down in excitement, and I cringed for fear of impalement on a wayward talon or of being crushed by creatures that were ten to twenty times my size. My host growled at the surrounding dragons, and they moved to give me a bit of room. One small red dragon hissed at me as he moved. He did not like making space for an insignificant twerp like me, probably because he was already at the bottom of their pecking order.

The match started as the two dragons jockeyed for position. They feigned attack and backed off, then unfurled and flapped their wings. The real action got underway when Green darted in beneath Brown's guard. A quick swipe with dagger-sized talons opened a gash in Brown's belly. Blood stained the sand. Green tried to repeat the maneuver, but that was a mistake. Brown was ready and used his wings to leap above Green and slash down with his tail. Arm-long spikes on the tail-tip tore into Green's back. This caused a roar from the crowd and a scream from Green. A tail as thick around as my torso slammed down within a hand's-span of me.

"Hey. Watch out," I cried. I looked to my host for support, but he was oblivious to anything but the fight.

Both dragons inflicted damage on the other with talons, teeth, and tails, but neither seemed to have an advantage. I kept a tight rein on my empathic talent, otherwise, the pain could have incapacitated me as it almost had at the welcome dinner. I hoped I could it maintain control with just the two fighters. I dared not leave a function again.

After what seemed like an hour of bloody sparring, the tone changed. Green stood on his hind legs and roared. At this, the crowd rose to its feet and roared in return. The cumulative bloodlust ripped through me. I retched silently but gritted my teeth and hung on, swallowing back bile.

The adversaries rose above the sand and flew at one another and met with a resounding thwack. They dropped to the sand and stayed in close combat. Talons raked, teeth slashed, and tails whistled as their spikes found flesh with sickening thuds. The damage to both was incredible. Any Terran beast would already have been dead. The vitality of the dragons astounded me.

Green pressed Brown toward the side of the arena. Brown redoubled his efforts, but to no avail. His back to the wall, Green lifted above him and struck down with his tail. Brown hunched over with his wings covering his head. The intensity of the spectators' cheers swelled as the match drew toward its conclusion. I drew myself inward as much as I could, mentally and physically, terrified of the excited dragons as they pressed in on me. I could hardly see as I narrowed my eyes against the pain in my head.

The match ended with Brown a bloody, immobile heap against the wall. All the dragons in the arena stood, flapped their wings, and roared in unison.

Valiant turned to me with a toothy grin. At least I thought it was a grin. *"That was glorious death. Loser makes suitable celebratory dinner for winner."*

I tried not to cringe. "Yes. Assuredly. Very glorious. Very suitable." I couldn't get out of there fast enough.

***

The dragons needed help with a chronic problem

that affected many of them, particularly the nobility. To be sure, some dragons who were not nobles were affected, but not to the same degree or frequency.

As we made the rounds and examined afflicted nobles, we also treated lesser dragons for a variety of injuries, including torn wings, broken limbs, and variety of other fight wounds—they did like their fights—and minor illnesses. Their own healers were capable of such efforts, but the dragons seemed to relish the attention from the strange little aliens.

A large, blue dragon, Raptor-Of-The-Skies, was afflicted with the chronic disorder. As I approached, the dragon produced a low-pitched sound that I could feel in my bones.

"Your Greatness, can you tell me what the problem is?" Dragons were big on honorific titles.

"My toes," he rumbled. *"Hurt."* As if to demonstrate, he flexed his lower digits. A leg spasm almost skewered me like a shish kabob.

I could both sense and see the problem. Both big toes, armed with talons half the length of my forearm, were swollen and red.

"How long have your toes been like this?" I asked.

"Three days," one of Blue's retainers, a small brown, whispered in a growl that I could have heard a block away. Only the top dragons had names.

I looked at Raptor-Of-The-Skies. "Have you had this before?"

Raptor nodded, eyes closed.

"How often does this occur?"

"Often," was the answer from Brownie.

"And what takes place before these occurrences?"

Brownie glanced at Raptor before he answered. *"Is usually large feast."*

"How large a feast?"

Brownie said, *"Much food. Last for days."*

Thought so. I turned to Fur. "This looks like gout. Or the dragon equivalent."

Fur frowned. "I thought that was unique to humans."

"No. Animals, particularly birds and reptiles, can get similar derangements of metabolism, though they don't have the unique localization to the toes, like humans do and these dragons seem to."

"Then what do we do?"

"I'm not sure yet." I turned to back to Raptor and his retainer who stared at me. Those reflective yellow reptilian eyes sent a shiver through me. "The pattern is the same as a disease we see in humans and animals. It may or may not be identical, so we need to do tests to determine the biochemical nature of the problem."

The dragons said nothing. I wondered if they had a clue as to what I had said.

"Can we collect a sample of your blood to find out what's wrong?" I asked Raptor.

"You can fix?" Raptor snarled. I attributed the snarl to pain. I hoped that was the case.

"I won't know until we get the test results."

"Do it."

Despite my fears, we found a nice surface vein on the underside of the tail, and Raptor-of-the-Skies never flinched, although a surge of voraciousness made me envision a tooth-studded mouth enveloping my head. I hoped I would make him as nauseous as he made me.

***

I turned to Fur and Levi with a readout in my hand. "Just as I thought. In gout, uric acid builds up in the blood if the kidneys can't excrete it, and then it crystallizes in the joints. The crystals cause the severe inflammation and pain."

"But these are not humans. They are savage beasts. So how can it be the same?" Levi's truculence had not improved.

"There are plenty of diseases that are identical in humans and animals, Reb Levi. We are very similar biochemically to most life in our galaxy. We've told you that."

He shook his head as if rejecting my statement. I gave up and spoke to Fur. "Uric acid is an end product of purine metabolism. If a person has a genetic defect in metabolism, they develop gout when they eat too much purine-containing food."

"And what is purine-containing food?" Levi's voice dripped with sarcasm. "Anything alive?"

"It's protein, alive *or* dead." I would not rise to Levi's bait.

Fur broke in. "But these guys are carnivores. How can they avoid—?"

"They can't. But what they *can* do is not overload their systems, so the kidneys can keep up with uric acid excretion. Another problem comes if they don't drink enough water. Then the kidneys don't produce as much urine and, again, they can't keep up with excretion. For the dragons, they need to avoid the kind of overeating they described to us. Another thing is to get the dragons to drink lots of water."

"What about drugs?" Fur asked.

"Non-steroidal anti-inflammatory drugs are the best treatment available. We have some powerful ones, but not enough to use on creatures that big. Ibuprofen is an old drug that's effective, and we can synthesize that in bulk. That will help for a few of the dragons, but they'll run out quickly. It's not a cure."

"I still think we should just leave them to their disgusting habits and be gone," Levi said.

"And I think we need to talk to their healers," I

replied.

***

"And that's what the problem is for your people, er, citizens with this condition." I addressed a half dozen dragons, the senior healers for the city.

"Interesting, Doctor Cyberger." The largest dragon, a golden-yellow named He-Who-Brings-Succor-To-Champions, made my name sound uncomfortably like a menu item. *"Pills..."* he held out a huge paw with tablets the size of hens' eggs in his palm, *"will reduce pain. But when gone, what we do?"*

"You can do two things. First, I've been told that these attacks are associated with severe cases of overeating." Gluttony fit better, but I decided to be more circumspect. "The huge amounts of food cause the level of the toxic chemical in the blood to go too high. Eating in moderation will prevent many attacks."

The dragons looked at one another, mouths open and tongues vibrating: perplexity, I sensed.

A purple dragon said, *"Eating much food important to nobles. Demonstrates rank."*

"Well, strike *that* solution," Fur said. "It does explain why the nobles are more prone to the disorder."

I turned back to the dragons. "The other thing that can be done is to drink large quantities of water. That will help clear the toxins out of the blood."

Another round of tongue vibration.

"Drink water?" Brings-Succor asked, his big head cocked to the side.

I asked, "Is this a problem?"

The yellow responded. *"We not drink water. Drink only blood."*

Oops. Clearly, dragons were not water-dependent; they got all their moisture needs from the animals they ate. That made sense for beings that evolved on a desert planet.

"Well then," I continued, "this is an even better drug than the pills and you won't run out of it. You guys do urinate, don't you?"

A trill of laughter encompassed the six dragons before Brings-Succor responded. *"Yes, we urinate. How better mark our territories?"*

Not exactly what I meant, but it would work. "The prescription for treatment of your gout problem is simple. The affected dragon needs to drink at least five times as much water as he usually urinates. The more, the better. That won't cure the problem, but it will help to alleviate attacks."

I could feel that Brings-Succor was not convinced. *"Water distasteful. We will pass your wisdom, Doctor Cyberger. Pills go to highest nobles."*

As we left, Fur said, "Think they'll do it? Eat less and drink water?"

I looked at him. "That's up to them. Maybe they will, if they hurt enough."

"Well, you've done as much as you can."

***

As we prepared to leave Dragonworld, I checked their one functional hyperwave transmitter on the outside hope that a message might have come through from Roxanne. I was ecstatic to find her communiqué waiting:

Hello again, Cy,

I just had to respond when I received your last message. Wow. I can hardly believe what you experienced on Pronac: a planet-wide epidemic that threatened their entire society. It sounds like a novel, not reality. Not that I doubt you, you understand. It is just so amazing. You and Fur should be knighted, or whatever the Pronacian equivalent is. You said that it was your technology that enabled you to diagnose and cure the plague. I don't doubt that it helped, but you downplay your own insight. How many people would have made the connections between a self-replicating enzyme and the biochemical changes that led to the maniacal behavior and death. You and Fur should be recognized for your work, and I am going to start a news site that documents your travels and your accomplishments. I think lots of people, medical and non-medical, will be interested in your unique accomplishments. You are too far away to argue about it. Hah!

On my front, I've been busy with herd disease testing and vaccinations. We are trying to be proactive now, the way we have never been before. We can ill afford to lose any more of our cattle. I will do a bit of crowing myself. I designed a program and helped to push it through the bureaucracy. The government will pick up the cost where individual farmers and ranchers can't. That might be the only good outcome of EPD. More good news is that I am getting a vacation. I get two weeks at the end of the month, and I'm going down to one of our equatorial seaside resorts. I'll meet my sister there. She has been offworld on Seta III at the university, and this is her first trip home in over a year. I am so excited. She is studying exobiology and should be thrilled to learn of your exploits on Pronac. Surf, sunshine—and probably sunburn if I'm not careful. My indoor work and pale complexion make me a target, but I need that sunshine.

Please take care of yourself and give my best to Fur...and Levi. Enjoy your adventures.

Roxanne

I watched it several times more and chuckled to

myself. Wait until she heard about Dragonworld. I decided to get a message off before we left and thought through what to say before I recorded it.

***

A request from the planet's emperor derailed our planned departure. We arrived at the palace, a tower that soared so high my neck hurt to look up at it. The emperor, Inflicts-Death-Upon-His-Enemies-With-Great-Violence-and-Feasts-Upon-Their-Carcasses, was by far the largest dragon we had met; he also had the longest name. His scales were a unique shade of deep rose. Though he might have preferred a description like scarlet, or crimson, or even just red, he really was pink.

I wondered what he would do if I called him that. I was less than one mouthful...without chewing. He reclined on a pile of furs that looked too much like the little teddy bears that had been the menu at our banquet. I shuddered.

Pink's mouth hung open and he writhed as he keened, a low, plaintive sound that rattled my teeth.

"Your Highness, what is the problem?" We were told to address Pink as royalty.

He grunted and lifted his massive head off the furs. *"Stomach. Hurts."*

I eyed the vast expanse of fuchsia scales. "Any particular place in your stomach?"

He raised a foreleg and pointed a talon as long as my arm to his lower abdomen.

His tenderness was in the lower bowel. I normally could not localize internal pain this well, but he was so big, and the pain so intense, that I sensed different zones of his body. I stayed well back as we spoke. While my stomach wrenched in time to his waves of pain, I did not want to lose it to accidental disembowelment by his writhing limbs.

"Sire, have you had this before?"

Floomph. He passed a huge bolus of intestinal gas. This was not sweet, herbivorous gas. Fur and I gasped for breath.

Pink replied. *"Yes. After eating staflymp."*

The name did not translate, but I took his meaning. I glanced at Fur. "I don't think we can do anything here. We need to get him to *GCVS*."

I turned back to Pink. "Sire, do you think you would be able to get to our ship? We can run tests there to determine how we might treat you."

He looked at his retainers and said, *"Do."*

***

A litter borne by six sturdy dragons brought Pink and deposited him next to the ship. We had deployed our largest X-ray unit, but still had to take thirty X-rays and stitch them together digitally to examine the images of the colon.

"My God," Fur said, as he pulled at his beard. "Look at the size of those bones. They are as big as a full-grown ox. And not even chewed up a bit. No wonder this guy has a bellyache."

I laughed. "I'd like to see whatever it was that he ate whole. That must be an amazing sight. He said it isn't the first time this has happened, just the worst."

"Yeah. Gluttony is taken to an extreme here, isn't it?" Fur shook his head.

I walked over to where Pink reclined. His moans were worse, if anything. "How long since your last bowel movement, Your Highness?"

It turned out to be more than four days. No question, then. He had a colonic blockage.

I looked at Fur. "We have nothing pharmacologic

that we can use to loosen him up and we need to do something fast. He's getting toxic, and colonic rupture is a threat."

"Surgery?" asked Fur.

I shook my head. "On this guy? Uh, uh. What this guy needs is an enema."

Fur barely suppressed his guffaw. "So much for modern medicine."

I grimaced at him. "Classic therapy has its place."

I explained this to Pink's retainers. They were aghast.

"You sure?" one asked. *"Hurt His Majesty, he eat you."*

Fur looked at me and mouthed, "Are you kidding me?"

I turned back to Pink. "We can do this, or we can just leave you and see what happens."

He suspended a talon a hand's-breadth above my head. *"Will remove pain?"*

"I sure hope so." I did not need to read his emotions to get the message that I would follow the *staflymp* if this went wrong.

Fur and I ran a four-inch hose from the *GCVS* water tank and inserted it into the nether region of Pink's anatomy. A variety of interesting sounds emanated from Pink's mouth, accompanied by the release of considerable gas from the orifice we happened to face. We staggered back and I told a couple of dragons to hold the hose. Let *them* be in the path of any reflexive disemboweling. They approached this duty rather gingerly.

I had Ruthie open the valve and waited. Water flowed for several minutes, while the cries from Pink increased in volume. I swallowed back acid as my head felt like it would split. When he started to thrash, I staggered away from him. Then an incredible explosion rent the air. An ordurous slurry liberally peppered with flying bones sprayed the countryside. The dragons assembled to watch the festivities scattered in every direction: left, right, and up, out of the path of the potentially lethal osseous missiles. Thank God the blast blew *away* from the ship and us.

The moans from Pink receded to a few bleats, and then nothing. He sat up on his litter and shook his wings. He now looked every bit the emperor as he displayed his impressive dentures.

"Captain Berger, I have relief."

I know I was relieved.

"Your magic powerful," he continued. *"Dragons in your debt."*

"I will remember that, Sire." Having dragons in my debt had to be good, if I could only figure out how. I thrust aside the image of the emperor swallowing a screaming Levi. Maybe line the whole Rebbinical Council up on his plate? I shook my head and came back to reality.

Inflicts-Death-Upon-His-Enemies-with-Great-Violence-And-Feasts-Upon-Their-Carcasses motioned to two dragons carrying a wooden chest. They deposited it at our feet, and one of the dragons flicked the lid open. Gold, silver, and jewels coruscated in the sunlight.

"You earn," the emperor said.

I smiled. "Sire, I will look back on our time here with fond remembrance. Stories of your, um, power will amaze the galaxy."

I figured I couldn't lay it on *too* thick.

CHAPTER 11

THE PROMISE OF TALL BEERS led Fur and me into a tavern on our way back to the ship. An epidemic threatened the primary food and pack animal of Certis Prime, and we had assisted the world's small group of veterinarians vaccinating the last of their herds. The distress of thousands of animals hammering my psyche had taken its toll. Exhausted, thirsty, and in a foul mood, I was overdue for that cold brew.

The closest patrons looked up and wrinkled their noses, from the effluvia of herdbeast manure that wafted off our boots and coveralls, no doubt. Certis Prime herdbeasts were not the cleanliest of animals.

"Two pints," I told the barmaid. Despite our pungent condition, she smiled. She knew we tipped well.

As we drank, several men at a nearby table looked at us and laughed. I ignored them, as did Fur. Unfortunately, they did not return our disinterest. One man stood and approached our table with a smirk on his face. The sun beaming in through the windows into the dimly lit tavern gave me a good view of his attire. His ostentatious outfit, shiny black boots, fringed black leather pants, burgundy shirt with a frilly front, and multicolored bandanna around his neck, made me take an instant dislike to him. His aura of arrogant conceit may have contributed.

He cleared his throat and looked around the room before he spoke. "I say, fellows. You appear to be a bit bedraggled."

Laughs issued from his compatriots.

"There is a distinct...atmosphere about you. It is rather interfering with the enjoyment of our dinner. Would you mind moving closer to an open window?"

Laughter from around the tavern did nothing for my mood. I caught one comment, "Not *our* window."

I simply wanted to enjoy the rest of my beer without interference, but that was not going to happen. I pushed my chair away from the table and looked up into the man's vapid blue eyes.

He said, "Your smell is so pervasive, I would have thought that you would be more affected by it...considering the size of your nose."

Another wave of laughter made the rounds of the tables.

I felt Fur tense up, knowing my sensitivity about my outsized proboscis. I stood. The man was about my height and weight, and I looked him up and down before I spoke. "Excuse me. Did you say something about my nose?"

He smiled. "Why, yes. You have a *very* big nose."

More laughter.

"Is that all?"

His brow furrowed and the corners of his mouth turned down. "Enough, I think."

I stepped closer to him and grabbed his shirtfront so he could not move away. "Ah, no, sir. That is too simple. Why, you might have said a great many things. Why waste your opportunity?"

He tried to pull away, but my grip was firm. "For example, thus: 'I, sir, if that nose were mine, I'd have it amputated on the spot!' Or, 'Tis a rock, a crag, a cape.

A cape? Say rather, a peninsula!' Or, 'Do you love the little birds so much that when they come and sing to you, you give them this to perch on?'"

He struggled to disengage, but I grabbed his arm with my other hand. "Or, 'When it blows, the typhoon howls and the clouds darken. When it bleeds, the Red Sea!' Or, 'Was this the nose that launched a thousand ships and burned the topless towers of Ilium?'

"These, my dear sir, are things you might have said had you some tinge of wit. But since you are a *half*-wit, you could not. Before these good folks, you have made jest of me. Now, I say these things lightly enough myself, about myself, but I allow no one else to utter them."

"Let go of me, you freak." He grabbed the hand holding his shirt to free himself, and I allowed him that, while I kicked him in the left kneecap. He grunted and dropped as his leg gave way. On the way down, I used my grasp on his arm to guide him. My knee met *his* nose with a satisfying crunch.

His two companions leapt toward me, only to come up short when they faced Furoletto towering over them. "I think you had better see to your friend." Fur's deep voice added a layer of menace to his bulk.

The two looked at Fur and then at each other before they slunk back to their table.

My opponent's burgundy shirt turned black with blood that dripped from his nose. The exudation spoiled the pretty bandanna he used to staunch the flow.

Fur turned to the bartender who had appeared with a stout club in his pudgy grasp. "No need for that. I think the festivities are completed." Fur looked at our assailants who avoided his gaze. "See?"

"I think you might find another tavern after this." The bartender turned on his heel and retreated to the bar.

"Don't worry," I said. "We won't be back."

Fur and I reseated ourselves. Fur finished his beer, but I pushed mine away. I had lost my thirst to a churning stomach and aching head.

***

After we were clean and smelled sweet once again, we sat over coffee in the *GCVS* commissary. Levi was off on one of the secretive jaunts—what he called "fact-finding" missions, euphemisms for spying—that busied him on all the human worlds we visited. Fur was antsy. He hated having the rebbe out alone, not knowing what form of subversion he was spreading on this world.

"Relax," I said. "There's nothing you can do about Levi. You can't be on his tail constantly."

Fur heaved a sigh. "Okay. But while we wait for him, let's have the whole story. Your pretty speech was rehearsed."

I snickered. "That pretty speech isn't *mine*, at all. That was the wit of one Edmond Eugène Alexis Rostand, paraphrased from his play, *Cyrano de Bergerac*."

"You're kidding." Fur's eyes were wide.

"Do you have any idea *how long* I've waited to use that, to follow in the footsteps of Jose Ferrer?"

Fur shook his head. "What in hell are you talking about?"

I laughed. "Get a refill. You will now hear the unexpurgated version of my life story."

We both filled our cups and sat back in our chairs.

"My birth name is Cyrano D. Berger."

Fur pulled at his beard. "Cyrano, huh? What does the 'D' stand for?"

"Just wait. It will make sense. I hated that name until I was twelve when I stumbled across *Cyrano de*

Bergerac in my folks' vid files. It starred an actor named Jose Ferrer who won an Academy Award for his performance."

This led to even more confusion on Fur's part.

"I really need to get you into ancient vids. You don't know what you're missing. Anyway, this led me to the written version of the play. Cyrano, whose full name was Hector Savinien de Cyrano de Bergerac, was a real Frenchman who lived on seventeenth-century earth. Rostand romantically expanded de Bergerac's life in his play; he immortalized Cyrano. He also immortalized Cyrano's huge nose."

Fur snorted.

"At first, I couldn't believe that my parents would do such a thing, name me for a man with a gigantic nose. After all, they *knew* my family heritage guaranteed me that. I was mortified and incensed. Perhaps they didn't know about Cyrano, I'd thought, so I confronted them, filled with twelve-year-old indignation. Their response, far from contrite as I expected, as I *demanded*, was rather amused. I'll never forget that conversation.

"'So,' my father said with a straight face, 'you've discovered Rostand and your namesake.'

"*My namesake?* I deliberately had been named after a Frenchman with a huge nose? I was so upset I couldn't get a coherent thought out.

"My father looked at my mother and then back at me. 'Why are you upset? Didn't you like the story? Don't you think that Cyrano is a worthy model?'

"I was floored. *A model? For me?*

"My mother chimed in with her side. 'Cyrano de Bergerac is one of the great characters in literature, but he was based on a real man.' I hadn't known that. 'Admittedly, Rostand exaggerated many of his qualities and characteristics, but do some research on him.'

"My dad said, 'What did you think of Cyrano's character...as portrayed by Rostand, of course?'

"When I thought about it, Cyrano was the ultimate dashing, romantic figure, someone worth emulating...well, as much as possible. Cyrano was brilliant, a poet, a musician, a swordsman, possessed with the courage of ten, a man who exemplified fundamental honesty and integrity. Remember, I was twelve. Cyrano D. Berger—I wondered that they hadn't changed my name and stuck an '-ac' on the end. Big-nosed, Cy Berger."

Fur said nothing. No doubt he took into account my reaction to any slights about my nose.

"I realized that being named for de Bergerac was not an embarrassment, but an honor. An honor I would have to live up to. I admitted that to my parents and we had a good laugh.

"I worried as to what might happen if any kids put my name together with the famous figure, but my father put that in perspective.

"He said, 'There might be a dozen people in all of New Jerusalem that know Rostand and *Cyrano*, and they are academics at the university. No one you know will have an inkling.'

"They hadn't named me in an idle moment. They had planned that I would learn of Rostand and *Cyrano de Bergerac*, if not through my own explorations, then through their introduction. They wanted to force me to broaden my horizons, to not take the easy roads in life."

Fur sat back; his cup almost disappeared in his huge hands. A small smile played about his lips. "That's quite a story. And quite a figure to live up to. Seems to me that you've done an admirable job so far."

My face grew warm. I mumbled thanks and continued. "What happened in the tavern today mimics a scene in the play. A boob insulted Cyrano's nose and

Cyrano launched into his famous—and much longer—soliloquy. This led to a duel to the death. Cyrano composed a ballad as he dispatched his foe. I couldn't quite follow up on the last parts, but the rest came off almost perfectly."

Fur's laugh boomed across the small room. "You are something else."

"Wait," I said. "I'm not done."

"Let me get some more coffee first."

He did and I continued. "You can see my family heritage, goes back to my father and grandfather, this great hooked beak of a nose. Even farther, back to our Semitic ancestors. It got me into more than a few scrapes as a kid. Unfortunately, many of the other kids in my school also came from farms, so the strength I gained from chores did not save me from some nasty thrashings.

"Once I discovered Cyrano, I determined to emulate him. I wrote bad poetry." I smiled. "I took up martial arts."

Fur grinned and nodded. "As I learned on Beta Cygnus."

"You must understand that Cyrano is both a glorious and a tragic figure. On the tragic side, he loses his only great love through his own insecurity and ineptness, and he dies young."

"Impressive story, Cyrano. Do you have any more deep dark secrets?"

"No, but now that I've leveled with you, I want the story behind *your* name. You don't meet someone named Furoletto every day."

He smiled. "No, you don't, but I'm afraid that it lacks the drama of your story. My parents loved opera. It was their overriding passion, so I have a name that sounds operatic. Maybe Verdi's *Rigoletto* influenced it. They never said, but I like to think that." He spread his hands and shrugged.

I smiled. "I like it. I can picture you on stage and singing bass in *Die Walküre*."

Fur laughed.

"Let me give you my vidchip of Jose Ferrer's performance in *Cyrano de Bergerac*. You'll enjoy it. It will say more than I ever can."

***

The next morning, I met Fur in the corridor outside the commissary. Fur examined me with his head cocked to one side. A weird smile twisted his lips.

"Cyrano's great love. Roxanne," he said. "*Roxanne.*"

He then did a strange thing. He grabbed me in a bear hug and lifted me off my feet. He didn't say another word.

Before we left Certis Prime I could not resist a message to my folks outlining our experience. If anyone would understand the import of the barroom encounter to me, they would. I thanked them for my name, and I could not help grinning through the entire recording session.

CHAPTER 12

THE TIGER WAS TWICE THE SIZE of its Terran namesake. Its tawny-coat slashed with dark brown and yellow-green stripes was perfect for camouflage on the Cennesari grassland that stretched for thousands of kilometers. Humans and the sentient, although primitive, carnivores native to the planet existed in a fragile truce. A problem with the planet's domesticated native food animals had prompted the call to the *GCVS*.

Carel Foster, the head herdsman of a small settlement on the edge of the plains, sneered as he pointed out the creature. "Never used to see 'em this close unless there was to be a meeting. Better not to see 'em at all. Our grasslands are parched, and there ain't many wild herds left, so the tigers eat *our* cenoxen. Don't have nothing to spare for the damn cats." Intense enmity flooded his emotions. I fought a surge of nausea as I clamped down on my shields.

I knew that the drought endangered the peace between the Hunters—the tigers' name for themselves—and the human settlers. The loss of stock to starving cats led to killing of Hunters by ranchers. This had tension stretched to the breaking point.

"Now our cenoxen been dying off, and we don't know why," Foster said. "Can't afford that. We're already running on the edge."

"We can look into the mortality in your herds," I replied. "We've also been told that there's an outbreak of disease among the Hunters. Can you tell us anything about that?"

Foster grimaced. "Don't give a damn 'bout that. What's more important is that we have five thousand cenoxen confined to this fenced area"—he pointed to a fence twice as tall as a man— "and we've lost a tenth of 'em. In good years, the grazing is enough for the herd. With the drought, we've had to supplement their feed with hay. We have feed stations scattered around the corral. The dead animals didn't starve."

"How big is the fenced area?" Fur asked.

"Ten by twenty klicks. Big enough for a bigger herd under better conditions."

"What kind of signs do sick animals show?" I asked.

"Mostly we find 'em dead in the field. Reports say there's bleeding, but no one's been willing to take a close look. There's only one vet on the planet, and he can't get here. Everyone's afraid of infection. We've already had a quarantine slapped on us. Can't sell any of our stock. That hurts."

"And this is new, nothing you've seen before?"

"That's right. Never seen nothing like it."

I nodded. "We need to get out there and examine the cenoxen before we can do much more."

"We need your help, Doc. We can't afford to lose these herds."

***

Fur and I set out in our land drone with herdsman Foster as guide. He directed us toward one quadrant of the corral.

Stephen A. Benjamin

"Give you a look at the herds, first," Foster said.

We also got a good look at the effect of the drought. The native grasses in irrigated fields near the farm buildings stood more than head high, a rich greenish-yellow, with golden seed heads. Away from the cultivation, the grass was only ankle high. No doubt some of that resulted from grazing, but the ground was rock hard and we left a corkscrew of dust behind us as we drove.

When we found a group of animals, I saw why the settlers had used "oxen" in their name for these native grazers. They were the size and conformation of Terran beef cattle, except for an elongated muscular giraffe-like neck.

"I wonder if they evolved those long necks to keep watch over the top of the grass," Fur said.

I nodded. "Good thought. No way to see predators otherwise."

The cenoxen coats were a mottled brownish-gray that shaded to cream on the belly, and they sported a set of sharp horns that spread wider than my arm span.

"Those things look nasty," Fur said.

As we exited the land drone to get a closer look, Foster responded. "They're dangerous...especially if you rile 'em."

"You have my word. I'll avoid provocation," I said.

Fur snickered. I raised my middle finger behind my back.

As we approached a large, male cenox, the thought pattern I received took me aback. A specific, rational thought submerged the animal's emotions. I stepped back.

"What's wrong?" asked Fur.

"It's the cenox. There's something—"

"Wrong?" Foster broke in. "What do you mean? These animals are healthy. There's no sickness—"

~154~

I waved him off. "That's not what I mean. Quiet."

He huffed but shut up.

I took a step toward the beast, and the thought came through as clear as a hyperwave message: *<Flee or attack? See what it does.>*

No way. I never read minds, and no animal thinks that logically. I shook my head. I took another step toward the cenox while I tried to soothe it mentally.

<No closer. I attack.> The angry cenox lowered its head and pawed the ground with one forehoof.

My stomach twisted like it never did for a single animal's emotion. I took a good look at the hooves. They were three-toed with razor-sharp nails. Coupled with the horns, this thing looked like it could fend off a Hunter, much less a human. Still, I stood my ground.

"What are you doing, Doc?" Foster's voice had a panicked tone.

I shook my head again in confusion, but did not want to reveal what I just felt. I turned to Foster. "How do we get blood samples?" I motioned with my head toward the cenox.

Foster laughed. "We don't catch *him*. Not unless you want a week in the hospital—or worse."

At this, the cenox charged five steps toward me then stopped short. *<Go>* was the clear thought I got from him.

I backed up, but did not turn away from the animal. Animal? Maybe, maybe not.

Foster said, "We'd better leave him alone. We'll collect your samples from a cenox that's restrained." He laughed again. "You don't mess with the free ones."

What was going on here? These things were raised as food animals. Were they intelligent, and telepathic, to boot? My mouth felt like it was stuffed with cotton wads, and my heart raced at the thought that the cenoxen might understand their own fate but were powerless to affect it because no other humans could communicate with them.

***

Foster led us to a cenox confined in a pen that gave it little room to move. As I approached, the thing stank of fear, but despite its dread, it projected one clear thought: <*Trapped*>.

I gasped as nausea and pain fought for predominance in me.

Fur put his hand on my shoulder. "Cy, there *is* something. What is it?"

I looked up at him and said, "Later."

I shut down on my empathic reception long enough to get skin, blood, and saliva samples to create a baseline for tests. We repeated this on a second animal and returned to the drone to store the samples. Then we set out to search for sick or dead cenoxen. I wondered how the cenoxen reacted when they were ill.

"The dead animals been found scattered throughout the enclosure," Foster said. "But more in the areas around the feeding stations."

"Could be an infection, if it tends to be where the animals are concentrated," Fur said.

"If this outbreak gets worse, it will ruin us." Foster's mood was bleak.

"We don't know that it's an outbreak," I said. "But if it is infectious, we might be able to control it."

Foster pointed to a lump in the distance. Fur steered the land drone in that direction, and shortly we pulled up to a dead cenox. Fur and I donned isolation suits.

External examination confirmed what Foster had told us. "Look here." I pointed to the eyes. "Hemorrhages on the conjunctiva."

"Also around the anus," Fur said. "Could it be some

sort of hemorrhagic fever?"

I pointed to numerous large blisters, all on the lighter-colored and sparsely haired portions of the skin. "I'm not sure how the hemorrhages and these blisters fit together. Let's get skin samples and do a necropsy." I moved to the drone to get the necessary equipment.

We outfitted Foster with a third isolation suit, and he leaned over and watched us dissect the cenox. I opened the abdomen. Half-clotted blood spilled out onto the ground. There were hemorrhages involving just about every tissue and organ.

"This lady bled out," I told Foster. "We'll get tissue, but she's too long dead. We need to find a sick animal that's alive or dead only a short time. I want fresh samples to isolate any pathogen."

***

A male cenox staggered and went down on its front legs. I could feel the animal was more confused than frightened. The thoughts I received were more what I would expect from an animal. Nothing lucid or rational, thank God, perhaps because of its terminal state. We put it out of its misery and performed a necropsy.

"Same lesions on the skin and internal organs," I said. "The hemorrhages aren't as bad, but my guess is they would have been soon."

"What's happening, Doc? Why are they bleeding like this? I don't understand."

"There are several possibilities. Hemorrhagic fever is at the top of the list because it's most dangerous and even potentially transmissible to humans."

Foster stepped backward, away from the carcass, despite his protective gear.

"I'm not saying that's the case." I didn't want to blow the guy's mind. "But if it is a hemorrhagic fever,

Stephen A. Benjamin

quarantine becomes even more critical. I'm sure you've heard about Ebola virus."

He shook his head, his face ashen. As I tried to shunt off his response, my face might not have looked much better.

"Ebola was carried to Alpha Centauri in a shipment of Terran monkeys for a zoo. More than a million people died in that epidemic. Emigration from earth stopped for years afterwards. Medical personnel are always primed for that kind of thing."

"Now I remember. I learned about that in school," the herdsman said, voice shaking. "But why does it cause bleeding like that?"

"The virus damages blood platelets and endothelial cells lining the blood vessels. The platelet damage inhibits blood coagulation, and the unclotted blood leaks out through the injured vessel walls. Victims bleed from everywhere and go into shock from blood loss."

"That's horrible." Foster's voice was hoarse.

"It's as bad as it sounds. We need to get back to our ship to run these samples. Then we might know more."

"If it is Ebola—"

I cut the herdsman off. "This is *not* Ebola. There are things that don't fit, like the skin lesions. And Ebola does not affect cattle—and probably not cenoxen. So, *please*, don't panic yourself or start one among your people. From the description you've given us about the number of animals affected and the time span involved, this does not look like any hemorrhagic fever we know of that could affect people. And there have been no people involved, from what you've said."

I looked to him for confirmation. He nodded. I was sorry we had mentioned Ebola to begin with. "But we have an obligation to be sure. Let's head back to town."

I drove the land drone, dodging occasional large

potholes caused by some native burrowing creature. Fur sat in back and chatted with Foster about agricultural practices on Cennesari. He kept the discussion away from the outbreak as much as possible to calm Foster down.

When we left Foster and returned to the *GCVS*, Fur stopped me before we docked the vehicle.

"Okay, spill it. What were you so worked up about out there?" The furrows between his eyebrows looked about ready for planting.

"I'm not sure, Fur. I received concrete thoughts from those creatures."

"Exactly what does *that* mean?"

"I got the usual emotional broadcast, but it was overridden by specific messages, like 'Flee or attack.'"

"You mean like it was *talking* to you?"

I shook my head. "I'm an empath, but I don't read minds. I didn't lie about that. I don't receive verbal thoughts, from people or animals."

"But these were verbal thoughts?"

"It's impossible unless the cenoxen are telepaths. I've never encountered a telepath before, so I don't know."

Fur ran his fingers through his beard. "The cenoxen are livestock, but to use language they would have to be sentient."

"Right. That's what makes no sense." Sentient cattle? The implications were earthshaking.

Fur continued. "If the Hunters evolved sentience here, why couldn't their main prey do likewise to keep up?"

"That's possible."

We encountered Levi as we left the land drone. "What is possible?" he asked.

I was not about to tell Levi about the cenoxen. I did not want this to get back to the Cennesari ranchers. God knows how they might react if I claimed their herdbeasts were an intelligent species.

Fur jumped in before I could respond. "We were discussing Cennesari biochemistry."

I followed his lead. "Yeah. The Cennesari ecology is biochemically compatible with humans, so the settlers can utilize local flora and fauna for food. It's close enough that it should be easy to pick out any pathogens. We need to run the samples we took."

He grunted and turned away.

***

"There's nothing," I told Fur and Levi.

Levi was sticking close since we were far enough out in the sticks that his spy missions were not worthwhile. I could tell that this relaxed Fur, since he and I were so busy with the cenoxen, he could not have kept tabs on the rebbe.

"We can't isolate anything from the sick animal, RNA, DNA, or proteins that are different from the healthy ones."

"Nothing like the weird bug on Pronac?" Fur asked.

I shook my head.

"Not an infectious disease, then," he said. "That's good news, anyway."

"But what else would cause something like this?" Levi asked Fur. He was paying attention out of boredom, I thought.

"I'm not sure. You should ask the doctor." Fur suppressed a smirk.

Levi looked at me, a sour curl to his lip.

"I have some ideas, but I need to get out into the field again. Let's go see Foster."

When we told the herdsman we had ruled out an infection, particularly a hemorrhagic fever, he went from stiff to limp in seconds. He grabbed a chair and collapsed into it.

"I...I didn't sleep last night. I couldn't forget the cenox...the blood...the stories about Ebola. I know, I know. You told me. But I still envisioned everyone on Cennesari..." He shuddered.

"What is he talking about?" Levi whined.

I brushed him off. "I'll tell you later." I turned to Foster. "You didn't say anything, did you?"

"No. I didn't say nothing to anyone. I just..." He shook himself, as if to throw off the burden he had assumed through the night.

I placed my hand on his shoulder. "You can relax now, but if it's not an epidemic, we still have to determine what it *is*. Let's go."

***

Within the fenced enclosure, we searched for plants Foster did not recognize, that were not typical forage for the cenoxen, and collected those. Levi was not there. Such activity was beneath him.

"You think that this disease is related to the plants?" Foster asked.

"That's what we need to find out," I said.

"Are there more of these atypical plants than you usually see?" Fur asked.

"Yeah. There's always more weeds in a heavily grazed area. When there ain't enough forage, animals eat strange stuff. Might taste bad, but that ain't important if an animal is hungry."

"How much supplemental feeding are you doing," I asked.

"As much as we can. The grain fields under irrigation are for human use, but the extra is cenoxen feed. We harvest hay from unirrigated native grass fields for them, too. Why?"

"Some plants can have compounds that can inhibit blood coagulation."

"Some Terran plants do," Fur added. "But what about the skin lesions?"

"I'm not sure yet. Let's get on back and look at what we have."

***

I looked at Fur, my shoulders slumped. "There are no anticoagulants in any of these plants. There are molecules I've never seen before, but simulations on how they might interact with coagulation components or endothelial cells are negative. We're missing something," I told Fur and Levi, "but what?"

Fur said, "Terran sweet clover was one of the main causes of bleeding syndromes in domestic animals. There was no problem unless the clover got contaminated with molds. The enzymes in the molds metabolized precursor compounds to dicoumarol, which inhibits vitamin K production." He looked at Levi who radiated confusion enough that even Fur picked up on it. "Vitamin K is necessary to activate the blood clotting enzymes. If it's gone, you can bleed to death."

This did not seem to make Levi any happier.

"That's a very good point, Fur," I said. "We need to check the hay and test it."

***

"The hay isn't put up if it's wet," Foster said. "We know that wet hay can get moldy."

"We still need to rule that out," I told him. "We're running out of options."

The hay *was* mold-contaminated, much to Foster's

chagrin. "This wouldn't happen if we didn't have to use every last bale of feed because of the drought," he said defensively.

When we analyzed the samples, we had a surprise.

"Foster, Fur, look at this. There's still no anticoagulant, but this compound..." I pointed to the readout, "...is a photodynamic agent. Plants can produce these in response to fungal contamination. In the skin, they cause photosensitivity. They absorb ultraviolet radiation from sunlight, become active, and cause cell damage. They're likely the cause of the skin blisters."

"But the blisters didn't kill 'em, did they, Doc?" Foster asked, frowning.

"No, they didn't."

Fur asked the herdsman, "Do you always get the hay from the same fields?"

"The irrigated hay fields remain the same, but we cut lots of natural fields, too. Don't have enough, otherwise."

"The hay we just checked, was that from irrigated or natural fields?" Fur asked.

"Irrigated," Foster said.

Fur tugged at his beard. "I think we need to look at the natural fields you harvested before the bleeding syndrome began."

"I agree." I saw where Fur was going with this.

We drove out to the grasslands, the first chance we had to see the native flora and fauna away from the human cultivated areas. The grasses stood waist high, half what we saw in the irrigated areas, but still much taller than in the overgrazed enclosure. A few large animals were visible in the distance.

"Grazers, wild cenox and hoppers," Foster said. "Wouldn't see 'em as easily if the grass wasn't stunted by the drought." He directed us to a patch where the grass was shorter, about knee high. "This is an area that we harvested a month ago."

We searched through the cut section and found little that we had not seen before.

"What about the unharvested areas?" Fur asked. "Does the vegetation differ from the paddock or these harvested sections?"

"Normally, no, the grass grows thick and crowds out anything else," Foster replied. "But with the lack of rain, the grass gets invaded by weeds."

Fur wandered off through the tall grass, then waved and yelled to us, "Here."

We moved to his location, and he pointed to several holes about an arm's length in diameter. "We've seen these before. Some sort of burrowing animal?"

"Ground slinks. Pests. Their holes are dangerous for the cenoxen. Broken legs. We clear most of 'em from our enclosures, but we have to keep after 'em. They come back quick."

"What do they look like?" I asked.

"Something like a Terran weasel, but about five times as big. They're real snaky in their movement. That's how they got their name."

"Omnivores?" Fur asked.

"Yeah. They'll eat anything, small rodent-like creatures are usual, but they'll take chickens if we aren't careful. They eat the bulbfruit, too." He pointed to a bush that had large yellow blossoms and a few fist-sized green fruits.

"Bulbfruit? Do you cut those when you harvest these wild fields?" Fur asked as he picked a fruit and examined it. He threw it to me.

It was hard and smooth, like an apple.

"That one's immature," Foster said. "They're soft and purple when they're ripe. We do cut the bulbfruit plants, but we pull 'em out of the hay before we bale it."

"Do you know if they are toxic?" Fur asked.

Foster shrugged. "Plenty of native animals eat the bulbfruits."

"Let's get some of those plants," I said. "And anything else we haven't seen before."

Fur had a small grin hidden beneath his sandy beard. His satisfaction signaled he had come to the same conclusion I had.

***

Foster and several other herders sat around a table. They quieted as Fur, Levi, and I entered the room. Levi had insisted on joining the party to reap some of the accolades, though he had not done a damn thing. There were not enough Jews in this rural area to make his usual underhanded efforts worthwhile, so he stuck close to the ship. A healthy fear of the Hunters no doubt played a role.

"We have figured out the problem," I told them as we sat. "You can thank Mr. Cohen, here. As you know, we found a toxin in the moldy hay that's responsible for the skin blisters. Foster has filled you in on that, I assume?" As heads nodded, I gave the floor to Fur.

"We found nothing in that hay to explain the bleeding problem. When we checked the natural areas where the hay was cut, Foster showed us different plants among the grasses, like the bulbfruits. He said that animals eat the fruits with no ill effects."

"We have fed those fruits to cenoxen," said an older herdsman impatiently. "We know they aren't the problem." Again, heads nodded.

"From what I've been told, native animals eat the fruits, but they *do not* normally eat the leaves and stems. Those contain a compound that isn't toxic in itself, but is activated in the cenoxen to interfere with the clotting of the blood. It breaks down the Cennesari equivalent of mammalian vitamin K, which is needed for blood coagulation."

"But we take out the bulbfruit plants before we give them the hay," objected one in the audience.

Fur held up his hand, palm forward. "I understand that the fruits only grow where there is a more natural ecosystem, with no irrigation and no overgrazing. When you harvested the hay from natural areas on the plains, you pulled out the bulbfruit plants that were mature enough to have recognizable blossoms or fruit, but the immature greens remained. Cenoxen would not normally eat the bulbfruit greens, but your domesticated ones didn't distinguish between the grass and the immature bulbfruit plants in the hay. Those young greens contain the precursor toxin."

We left the group engaged in a heated argument as to why they did not recognize the problem and who was to blame.

***

A celebratory dinner that evening allowed us to meet people other than Foster and the herdspeople, so I looked forward to it. Dinner was a potluck affair for the local families. The hearty and tasty food brought back memories of my own farming community back home. This brought my thoughts to my parents; I could not help but worry about them. I succumbed to a bit of homesickness. I missed my folks and hoped to get a chance to send more hyperwave messages, and to receive some, too, when we got to the capitol city.

As I traversed the room with my dirty plate in hand, my ears perked up when I heard someone mention the Cennesari tigers. They were to be our next project, so I eavesdropped.

"I don't care what you say." A large man with an ample belly and a vein-splotched nose spoke. "The damned things are worthless. If not for them, we could harvest the wild grazers from the grasslands. Then all this poison garbage would be moot. Less work and cost, too. Damned treaty. We should get rid of the fucking cats for once and for all."

"Keep your voice down, Booth. This is not the time or place." A small, wiry man objected.

Physically, the two reminded me of the ancient comedians, Laurel and Hardy, but their conversation was not funny. I did not hear what the small man said next, but they had caught my interest. This went beyond Foster's negative comments about the Hunters; it was more than a frustrated shepherd protecting his flock. I eased over to the two men I had overheard. I stuck out my hand.

"Hello. I'm Cy Berger."

The big man, I now dubbed him Hardy, scowled at me. "Yes, we know." After a few moments of silence, he continued. "We appreciate what you have done for our community." He raised his drink in a salute, but his tone and feelings said anything but thanks.

"I'm just doing my job," I replied.

Laurel added, "And a damn fine job it is. Yes, we appreciate it. Really do."

This was bullshit, too, so I probed. "Are you stockmen?"

They both nodded. Hardy said, "Yeah. You've saved us a lot of credits. I hope your payment is good."

I assured him my pay was more than adequate. "You know, when we were out in the grasslands we saw very few of the Hunters. Is that usual?"

Hardy made a rude noise. "Hunters. Goddamn ugly cats."

Laurel made a chopping motion with his hand, but

the big man ignored the imperative gesture.

"No. You won't see them anywhere near town. They know better than to get near our stock. Shoot them in a minute. Damned things are worthless." He glared at me. "And you shouldn't stick your nose—"

At that point, the Laurel grabbed Hardy's arm and pulled him toward the door. "Sorry," he said over his shoulder, "but we have an appointment we have to get to. Glad to have met you."

They disappeared in the throes of a furious argument.

Curiouser and curiouser, as Alice said. I needed to learn more before we met with the Hunters. I spent the rest of the evening asking questions about them. Most people shut up after a short response, but I found one woman who would talk. Charl Cooper was an agricultural specialist here to give a series of lectures on the benefits of native versus Terran crops.

"You have saved these people a lot of money, Dr. Berger. This community was hurting."

"Call me Cy, please."

She smiled and nodded. She was a tall lean woman perhaps twenty years my senior. "No one had been able to figure out what was going on. We only have one veterinarian on Cennesari right now, Sammel Cressel, and he's located on the other continent. You can imagine what the demands are on *him*. We had three others, but two died and the third left with her husband to settle a new world."

"I'd like to get a chance to meet Cressel before we go. One of my jobs is to entice some of your young people to attend veterinary college on Dovid's World. Sounds like something you need."

"I'm sure Doc Cressel will appreciate that. I'll pass your interest on."

"Thanks. My next job is with the Hunters. From the

reaction of the people here, they aren't too happy about that no matter what I did for them. I'd like to learn more about the Hunters. Whom can I talk to about them?"

Cooper squinted one eye. "Come with me."

She marched out of the banquet hall, down a corridor, and out into the evening air. When we were well away from anyone else, she faced me. "You ought to get this straight. You are walking into a minefield."

"I already feel like I have," I replied. "It seems I'm unpopular because I plan to help the Hunters with their disease outbreak, despite what we did for the cenoxen."

"This is no secret," she said, "but many of the people in the agricultural communities hate the big cats. How much do you know about the history of Cennesari?"

"Just what's in the guide books."

She shook her head. "Propaganda. Do you have some time? Will you join me in my quarters?"

"Happy to."

We sat across a table, each with a cold bottle of beer. After a long swallow, she spoke. "When the first colony ships arrived here, they found an ideal planet, an earth-like atmosphere, and an ecosystem biochemically compatible with humans. The Hunters were the only large carnivores. The male Hunters are solitary, except at mating time. The females raise the litters, so are less solitary, but they never needed to coordinate their society. Humans changed that.

"While most Hunters stayed clear of human settlements, there were enough rogue cats to keep settlers on their toes. To many, they were simply dangerous animals to be exterminated, and they set out to do just that. It was only when the Hunters started coordinated attacks—essentially fighting a war—that people recognized their intelligence.

Stephen A. Benjamin

"An element of the human population fought for equality between the Hunters and humans. The cats were the original sentient natives, they'd argued. Another group wanted none of that. The cats were impediments on an agricultural planet. With communication established, the two species made a tenuous peace, but our populace remains very much split on this issue, even today. Our two political parties have grown around the pro or anti-Hunter sentiments. Of course, the pro-Hunter party calls the cats by their own name; the anti-Hunter party calls them anything other than that. They even bitterly contested the use of the name Cennesari for the planet. It's a translation of the Hunter name for their world. There is one extremist fringe that still tries to change the planet's name every few years."

I shook my head. "Every planet has its own skeletons in the closet. My own has its problems."

She nodded. "Many ranchers will still shoot any Hunter that trespasses on what he considers his or her land. There are stiff penalties for that, but it's hard to prove. The Hunters are very individualistic. After mating, the males and females go their own ways. If one is killed, no matter what the cause, there is little they will do about it. Unless, of course, there is a wholesale attempt at extermination like what occurred early on."

"Is there no Hunter government, then? How do humans deal with them?"

"There is a Hunter council composed of senior females. The males are too reclusive to participate. The council meets on an irregular basis as needed, and any senior female can act as a council member. They have learned from humans that such organization is necessary if they are to survive. The pro-Hunter party has people that meet with the cats and help represent them before the human authorities. The antis do not love those people, and there have been some nasty incidents, even one murder last year. After a court judgment had come down against him, a fanatic rancher who had killed a Hunter shot the human representative who spoke against his case."

"Sounds nasty." I swallowed. "There's one more thing I'd like to mention to you." I told her about my concerns about the sentience of the cenoxen.

She was silent for some time before she spoke. "This is very disturbing. I'm not sure what to say. You know the Hunters are telepathic, right?"

I was stunned. "No. I did not know that. Then the possibility that the cenoxen are also telepathic is supported by that."

"But why have they never communicated with us?" she asked.

I thought about that then told her about my empathic abilities, otherwise my story would sound totally phony. "My guess is that other humans just aren't sensitive enough to receive their communications."

Cooper's thoughts were grim. "What I *can* tell you is that if you make this public, you will turn a large percentage of the Cennesari population against you, despite what good you've done. These people have raised and eaten cenoxen all their lives and will not be happy to hear they've been eating an intelligent species. Also, if cenoxen ranching was shut down, it would devastate the economy. I understand your concerns, but consider the consequences."

"What do you suggest I do now?"

"With respect to the Hunters, talk to the authorities in Cennesari City. You need to check with them to get permission to have access to Hunter territory. The government is strict on this to try to minimize incidents." She looked me in the eye. "And watch your back."

CHAPTER 13

W E SEARCHED myriad gray, institutional hallways of Cennesari City's government buildings before we found the office we needed. The man behind the desk had thinning blond hair slicked back above a flushed round face. He sat behind a placard that read, "Chief Clerk."

"Hello. I'm Dr. Cy Berger from the *Galactic Circle Veterinary Service*. We have a contract to consult on the issue of the Hunter plague. This is Furoletto Cohen and Levi—"

"Dr. Berger, I am aware of your so-called contract, but you do not have permission to visit the Cennesari Hunters at this time."

My initial response was brilliant. "Huh?"

When the man did not respond, I pressed on. "Look. We came because the Hunters are dying. We were *asked* to give our assistance."

The clerk raised one pale eyebrow and smirked. "I cannot help you. Good day."

I stepped to the edge of his desk and leaned toward him. "You better have a good explanation for this."

The clerk stood and sneered. "I represent the Cennesari government, sir. I don't have to explain—"

"Like hell you don't," I shouted. "Your government asked us to assist with a deadly epidemic. So, either I skin you like a fish, or I let your superior do it, but someone is giving us permission to get on with our job."

The clerk's watery blue eyes rolled to the left and widened, ringed with white. He flopped into his chair as if shoved. Fur now loomed over the desk at my right side.

Levi broke the silence. "Berger, do not address the good man in this manner."

I ignored Levi. Why couldn't he have gone on one of his damned spy excursions? Chief Clerk's eyes bounced back and forth between Fur and me before he funneled his attention to a sheaf of forms before him.

Fur reached out and placed his large paw over the papers. Chief Clerk bounced in his chair.

"You were going to say..?" Fur rumbled.

Chief Clerk cleared his throat. "Um, er, ah, perhaps you should see Captain Snedecor." He buried his head in his paperwork before we left.

We found and knocked at Captain Snedecor's door.

Someone called for us to enter.

The office was twice the size of the clerk's, with a large desk of dark polished wood. A single sheet of paper sat squarely in the center. The man who sat behind it wore a crisp blue and gray uniform with a single star on both shoulders. His head jerked back in surprise. He frowned. "You must have the wrong office. Who are you looking for?"

"If you are Captain Snedecor, you," I replied. "Chief Clerk told us to see you."

His brow furrowed. "Chief Clerk? Do you mean Clerk Floof?"

"Is that his name?" I nodded. "Floof fits quite well. I'm Dr. Cy Berger. These are my associates. The Cennesari government asked us to assist in the diagnosis and treatment of the Hunter plague. Floof said we didn't have permission to do that. What in hell is going on here?"

A slight smile crossed his face. "Please sit." He waved us toward several wooden chairs arrayed in front of his desk.

He leaned forward, elbows and forearms on his desk. The chiseled lines of his face became grave. "There has been a slight problem with respect to your visit. Relations with the Hunters have been difficult, of late. It may be a while, perhaps several weeks, to get the arrangements in order. I trust that will not be a problem."

I detected a slight curl of his lip and a wave of hatred when he had said *Hunters*. He had no intention of granting us permission. My roiling stomach fed my anger.

"You *trust* that will not be a problem?" My voice rose. "Yes, that's a problem." I ticked off points on my fingers. "One: we have a schedule to keep and are due elsewhere. Two: the Hunters are dying. They don't *have* time. Three: We already have permission. We had that before we landed. Who countermanded it?"

Snedecor sat back in his chair. His eyes narrowed. "I don't think that it's any business of yours *who* has given these orders. They are orders. That is enough."

Levi broke in. "That is very clear, Captain Snedecor. We will pay attention to your orders, as we should. We will be no further bother to you."

"Bother? *Bother?*" I looked at Levi as my voice rose toward the stratosphere. I turned back to Snedecor. "You're absolutely correct, Captain. That *is* enough. Enough bullshit. Who's at the top of this flea-bitten organization?"

"Sir! Your tone and words are insulting. Remember that you are a visitor on our world. You are here at our indulgence. Your invitation can be revoked. Come back in one week and we will see whether the situation has changed. You are dismissed." He punched a button on his desk. "Get me security."

As I stood and started to move toward the desk, Fur grabbed my arm and pulled me back and out the door.

Levi closed it behind us and rounded on me. "Doctor Berger, that was an inappropriate performance, as usual. You could endanger our mission by such antagonism of our hosts."

"I don't give a shit about your fucking spy mission," I screamed as Fur dragged me down the hall. I shook off his grasp. "If these *putzes* think—"

"Not here," Fur cautioned. "Something is going on that we don't understand, and we need to find out what it is."

"Why were we asked here in the first place?"

Levi's darkened face looked as if he were going to have a stroke. His voice trembled. "We have fulfilled our contract, which was about the settlers' cenoxen. This tiger business came up after we agreed to come to the planet. I refuse to have us waste time on a bunch of worthless cats."

It was Levi's usual refrain with respect to anything nonhuman. My temples pounded with rising blood pressure and pain.

Fur must have seen this in my face, because he squeezed my arm—hard. "We probably were asked to help the Hunters by the pro-Hunter people. It is just as likely that the anti-Hunter faction is trying to block us."

I took a deep breath as I tried to control my emotions. "If they think—"

"All the more reason to leave now," Levi broke in. "I order you to forget these aliens. Do not disobey me again, Berger." His fists clenched in front of his chest, his body stiffened with fury.

I looked at him, pursed my lips, and said, "*Kish*

mein tuches," loud and clear. I ignored Levi's strangled response, spun, and stalked down the hall.

***

Cennesari City was the planet's largest city and the seat of its government, so we spent most of the next week sightseeing. At least I did. Fur surreptitiously followed Levi on his usual spy missions. I used our forced break to get a message off to my folks and to Roxanne. When Levi tried to view my recording, I flipped.

"Look," I told him, "there's nothing I can tell anyone that could make the slightest difference to you. I don't know a fucking thing about your spying at every place we land, and I don't care. Let me have my own life for a change."

His red face got even redder. His scar seemed to pulse in time with his eye twitch. "You have crossed the line, Berger. I have not forgotten what you said to me at the Captain's office. Remember—"

"*Remember*? I remember everything you've said. How could I forget? You threaten me at least five times a day. That's on a *good* day." I dropped my voice. "Please, Reb Levi, I can't continue like this. I'll explode if I don't get some room."

The rebbe stepped back and pulled at his scar, as if to stop his eye spasms. "Well, perhaps I have been a bit too forceful with you. This visit has been somewhat stressful. I will allow you to send your messages, but I assure you, someone will watch at the other end, so do not think you can get away with—"

"I don't want to *get away* with anything. I just want to correspond with my parents and with Dr. Simon."

"Hmph. Agreed. But I expect an apology for your manner toward me in the past few days."

"Okay. I apologize. I'm sorry I mouthed off. I'll try to be a good citizen. That enough?"

"Your actions will tell if that will be enough." He turned on his heel and marched off.

I suppose an apology I did not mean didn't change anything, but it still rankled. I had pushed our relationship to the limit, maybe beyond, but I didn't care any longer. I felt that nothing I did would satisfy the bastard or make a difference in what happened back home. I tried not to let this color my message to my mom and dad. I'm not sure if I was successful. I had no doubt that Levi's colleagues intercepted what I sent home, so I stuck to facts and assured my folks that I was fine and enjoying my adventures.

The recording for Roxanne was more difficult. I feared putting my feelings into words that might be either trite or presumptuous. I could not be sure she felt as I did.

Hi Roxanne,

It has been a while since I could get to somewhere I could send a message. Some of the worlds didn't have accessible hyperwave equipment. I enjoyed your last message. It sounds like you have the EPD epidemic licked; that's great news. I know that wasn't easy. I told you already about our visit to Pronac, but that was almost topped by our visit to Dragonworld...

I gave her a short version of those adventures, and then explained our trials on Cennesari. Then came the hard part.

I look forward to your communications, but more than that, I wish I could see you again, in person. I love your hyperwave vids, but it's not the same. Our time together on Sammara was far too short. I feel like we barely started to get to know each other, and I would like to get to know you better. I hope that you feel the same, but if I presume too much, just say so. I'll back off. Though I can't be much farther off as it is. Joke—ha, ha. I should be here on Cennesari for several weeks from what I can tell. Longer than we had planned, but as I mentioned, there have been complications. Despite roadblocks, I'm determined to help the Hunters. We need to gain access to them or we won't be able to forestall the epidemic. I have no idea what the disease is yet. I think you'd be with me on this if you were here. I hope everything is well for you, and I hope we can stop by Sammara on our way home. Until then, you'll be in my thoughts.

Cy

The delay engendered by the recalcitrant bureaucracy had one positive side. We were on Cennesari long enough to get a response from Roxanne.

Hello Cy,

Since you said you would be on Cennesari for some time, I thought I'd try to catch you before you left. I hope this gets to you. That was very clever of you and Fur to figure out the plant poisoning in the cenoxen. I wish I could have cases that were such challenges. Since the end of the EPD epidemic, things have slowed down here, and I spend most of my time on paperwork. Not that I'd rather have EPD, you understand, but I could use something to liven up my days. I do hope that you can figure out the Hunter problem. They sound like a fascinating species. I've always thought our own domestic cats can border on sentience at times, so a thinking cat one hundred times as large tickles my fancy. Would I ever love to meet them. And dragons? Wow?

Cy, I have to agree that our time together was far too short, and I would like to know you better, as well. It is hard to gauge one's feelings after a few hours

*together, but I feel as you do. I look forward to your
return to Sammara. I miss you.*

Roxanne

For days afterwards, even Levi's usual jabs did not
penetrate my enraptured state. That was probably good
because it defused our escalating conflict.

***

A week later, Chief Clerk Floof scowled at us from
behind his desk. He looked like he had lemons for
breakfast. The intensity of his hate hit me like a splash
of acid.

"The authorities have approved you to take your
ship to this location." He threw a map across the desk.
"The red circle shows where you will be met by a
government representative who will conduct you to the
Hunters."

I ignored his hostility and asked, "Can you tell me
anything about the nature of the problem?"

He shook his head sharply. "I know nothing about
that. You will have to talk with the representative."

And you don't *want* to know anything, do you?

***

A breeze caused the tops of the golden grasses to
shimmer as we put down on a landing pad on the plain.
The tops of the native plants were well above our
heads, and we could see little once we were on the
ground. It was a startling contrast to the drought-
ravaged areas we had seen. A couple of silvery metal
huts sat in a clearing. A short, stocky woman in a blue
and white uniform met us.

She smiled and extended her hand. "Dr. Berger. We
appreciate your willingness to come." We shook hands.
"I'm Lieutenant Stannard, the Intermediary on duty.

We have heard wonderful things about what you accomplished with regard to the cenoxen deaths. We hope you'll have as much success helping the Hunters."

"Thank you." Refreshing to meet someone who cared about the giant cats. "Happy to help in any way we can. This is Furoletto Cohen and Levi Schvartz." I pointed to my companions. "They are my veterinary technicians."

Fur smiled. Levi scowled.

"A pleasure to meet both of you. If you would come with me, please?"

We followed her into one of the buildings where the four of us took seats at a table in a room lined by file cabinets.

"Please excuse me while I send out a rover to call a conference with the Hunter representatives." She spoke for a few moments on a communicator.

When she finished I asked, "How long?"

"It will be perhaps an hour, depending on how far away the Hunters are. Can I offer you some refreshment? Coffee? A cold drink?"

We all asked for coffee. When our drinks arrived, I quizzed her about the Hunters and their problem.

"We don't know much other than they are losing many cats of all ages," she said. "You must understand that while the Hunters interact with us, it is limited. They are solitary and don't share personal information."

"How do you communicate? Will we have a problem that way?"

"You have a translator program, I presume?"

"Yes. Ruthie, er, our AI does that."

"Yes. And I can translate telepathic communications long distances," Ruthie said.

My head jerked back. I had never really thought about Ruthie's capabilities or her range for such things. We were several hundred meters from the ship now, and although I wore one of the translation devices with which we communicated to our AI, her voice seemed to emanate from speakers atop a cabinet.

Lieutenant Stannard gave me a quizzical look and asked, "Was that your AI? It sounded almost human."

I grimaced. "Yeah, almost."

Fur grinned and Levi frowned.

Stannard shrugged. "That should suffice. Most of our words and ideas will translate well with the Hunters' telepathic capability. The telepathy obviated the need for them to develop a complex spoken language. We can't receive from them telepathically and must rely on computer translation of their speech, but most concepts seem to get through just fine."

I wondered if I could communicate directly with the Hunters as I did with the Cenoxen. Obviously, other humans could not. It had taken the war to learn the Hunters were intelligent. I wondered if other species that evolved on this planet, beyond the Hunters and cenoxen, had telepathic capability, and even sentience.

"Uh, can I ask you a difficult question?"

She nodded. "I'll answer if I can."

"We've gotten a lot of different vibes regarding human-Hunter relations from the human side. We understand that there are different factions. How about from the Hunter side? How do they see humans—and human politics? I mean, we have to get pretty personal with them if we're to help. How will we be viewed?"

"Is there any danger?" Levi's belligerence caused Stannard to inspect him before she answered.

She pushed mousy brown hair out of her eyes. "There should be no danger to any of you, Mr. Schvartz. The Hunters are rather shy. There has never been a case of a Hunter injuring a human except in self-defense. That said, they are large and successful carnivores. Most humans who come face to face with them find them intimidating. To answer *your* question, Dr. Berger, the Hunters wish only to be left alone. They care little for human politics, although it affects them severely, I'm afraid. They have a minimal social structure, as I said, they are individualistic. If they agree to your assistance, you'll have no problems." I noted her stress on "If they agree."

"And how do we get their approval?"

Stannard smiled. "That is my job, Doctor. If you tell me what you will do, I will explain it to them. They know and trust me."

"Thanks, Lieutenant."

"Please, call me Anne."

"Good enough, if you call me Cy."

"And please call me Fur."

Levi was silent until Fur looked at him pointedly. "Yes, you may call me Levi."

Stannard gave him another questioning glance. Her confusion was understandable.

***

The Hunters flowed out of the tall grass as we stood outside the post's buildings. Despite their size, they had all the grace of their Terran feline counterparts.

"There were four senior female Hunters within range for a meeting," Anne said. "Remain motionless until all four come to a halt. This demonstrates lack of fear, something critical if the Hunters are to deal with you as equals."

Face to face, however, I could not suppress a visceral response to the giant cats. My scalp prickled and I attempted to conceal the reaction. According to Anne, these cats could read fear telepathically.

I noted that Fur placed a hand on Levi's shoulder, no doubt to keep him from bolting.

After introductions, I addressed the Hunters. "We are honored to meet you and hope that we can help. Can you tell us of your sickness? I am experienced in medical treatment of beings of your type." Of course, I meant teeny Terran domestic cats, but they did not need that information.

A Hunter female spoke in a sibilant purr. She was emotionally flat, almost unconcerned, with a touch of superiority. Typical cat. *<Hunters are dying. They need help.>*

I received the message on two levels: one through Ruthie's translation and the second mind-to-mind from the cat, much like my experience with the cenox. A thrill coursed through me.

"Can you describe this illness?"

<Bowels run. There is pain. And shivering.>

They would have no way to deal with those effects, I supposed. "What do you do with the Hunters who die?"

<Nothing.>

Stannard added, "Their society recognizes nothing beyond death. They have no religion."

I heard Levi mumble, "Of course not. They are not God's creatures."

I hoped the Hunters would not understand that. I shook my head, heaved a sigh of exasperation, and addressed Anne. "Would it be a problem if we performed a necropsy on a dead Hunter?"

"I don't think so. They leave their dead for nature to process. But I'll ask."

It turned out they did not care. They granted permission to travel into their territory to examine sick Hunters. The four of us took the land drone and followed the Hunter emissaries.

***

The big cat was prostrate and unresponsive, his respiration shallow.

"He isn't communicating with his fellows," Anne said as she motioned with her head to the Hunters who accompanied us.

Diarrhea befouled the hindquarters. When I lifted a pinch of skin, it stood in a fold, rather than springing back, a sign of severe dehydration.

"He's comatose," I said. "I'm not sure we can do much for him, but we have to try. Let's get some electrolyte fluid into this guy."

With Fur's help, I installed a venous catheter and drew a blood sample. A quick analysis showed that our standard IV fluids were compatible, and I took more blood before I started an IV drip. I gave the samples to Levi to store in the drone. He grumbled as he did. "I'm not your lackey, Berger," but I sensed that he would rather be in the vehicle than with us. As I expected, he did not come back out.

The cat had improved when we finished, but I was doubtful he would make it. I gave directions to keep him hydrated; at least to place water where he could drink. The Hunter I spoke with turned away with no reply. The cats were not big on nursing care.

We saw several other sick Hunters at various stages of the disease and did what we could. One died despite our ministrations.

"May we perform an examination of the dead Hunter?" I asked one cat.

<Dead. Is of no use.>

I supposed that was a "yes" and went ahead with the necropsy.

"Look here," I said. "The intestinal mucosal lining is atrophied—thinned—as if the agent has specifically attacked it."

"And that causes the diarrhea?" Anne asked. She

hung right with us.

Levi, as usual when there were blood and gore, stayed in the drone, probably studying the scriptures he always carried with him.

"Yes. Normal intestinal lining prevents excess fluid loss into the intestine and reabsorbs fluid from the contents. If it fails, then fluid runs right through the gut."

"How does that kill someone?" Anne asked.

"If you lose too much water, blood pressure drops below what's needed to maintain blood flow to critical organs. That takes a lot of fluid loss, but there's a complication in intestinal disease like this. There's also loss of electrolytes—sodium, potassium, and bicarbonate, among others. Fluid loss and electrolyte imbalance disrupt many systems and can be fatal. Let's get organ samples for analysis."

***

I lifted my eyes from the microscope and faced Fur, Levi, and Anne.

"There's necrosis where the intestinal epithelium replaces itself in the deep mucosa. If the epithelial cells die and don't renew themselves, the lining is lost. We saw that atrophy earlier. This pattern fits with two things. The first is high dose ionizing radiation, like x- or gamma rays."

Anne gasped.

"I doubt this is radiation injury, though. The second is infection by a parvovirus. There are many parvoviruses, often species-specific, but not always. Parvoviruses are minor problems in humans, but major problems in Terran dogs and cats. In cats, the disease is feline panleukopenia, also called feline distemper. It's contagious and deadly."

Anne asked, "Could this be a natural disease here on Cennesari?"

"Something akin to parvovirus could be natural, but I thought that this disease was never seen here until recently."

"That's true," Anne said. "Importation of Terran domestic cats stopped because of concern over possible dangers to the Hunters. There are no Terran-stock felines on the planet and haven't been for several hundred years."

Fur waved a piece of paper. "Look at the blood work. Leukocyte counts are severely depressed."

I nodded. "Parvoviruses attack rapidly dividing cells that have constant replacement, like the intestinal epithelium and the stem cell precursors of the white blood cells. The loss of the leukocytes causes inability to fight bacteria that invade the tissues from the compromised gut.

"It's a double whammy.

"My guess is that this agent, whatever it is, is *acting* much like a parvovirus, but it might be a different organism. Let's run the isolations and the genetic scans. We'll get back to you when we know more, Anne."

***

I faced Anne and Fur across the table, a cup of coffee cradled in my hands. My forefinger tapped out a staccato beat against the mug. Levi had declined to join us. His concern for the Hunters was nonexistent, despite what I had told him of our discovery.

"There's no question. This is a Terran parvovirus, not some new alien bug. The antigenic profile is identical to feline panleukopenia—the Terran version."

"What does panleukopenia mean?" Her face screwed up in perplexity.

"The word simply means that all the leukocytes counts are very low."

"A Terran disease? Are you sure about this? *Absolutely* sure?" Anne asked.

I nodded.

"How could that be?" She was dumbfounded.

"That's the question, isn't it?" Fur said.

Silence hung in the air like a shroud.

"It's no surprise that this disease is so deadly in the Hunters," I said. "They've never been exposed to this or any similar virus. They have no resistance. It could destroy the vast majority of the population."

"Will it kill them all?" Anne's voice was soft. Her horror sent a frisson down my own back.

"That's hard to say. If the population numbers drop too low, it might collapse completely, wiping them out. It's also possible that there will be enough animals that survive to save the species."

"Why is that?" asked Anne.

"There's usually enough genetic variability in a population that some percentage is resistant to any particular disease. Back on earth, immigrants to the continent of Australia imported rabbits and, with no natural predators, they multiplied to become a plague. A viral disease, myxomatosis, was imported to control them. It killed off ninety-nine percent of the rabbits. But that resistant one percent repopulated the continent in short order, so the effort came to naught."

"Ninety-nine percent." Anne exploded. "Is that what will happen to the Hunters?"

"That I can't say. We don't know their immune response, whether all who come in contact are susceptible, what the fatality rate is. Too many unknowns."

Fur added, "We can't treat all the cats, and the treatment is only supportive anyway. There is no cure."

"What we *can* do is supply the Cennesari government with stock virus for the panleukopenia vaccine," I said. "The Hunter population must be vaccinated."

"Do you have enough for that?" asked Anne.

"No. This will take a concentrated effort on the part of your medical community. I have enough of the modified live virus vaccine to serve as a culture stock. You will have to produce enough vaccine for the Hunters. The cats can't do it themselves."

Anne shook her head. "I don't know. The current government is anti-Hunter. It won't be easy to get that kind of commitment. I'm afraid many of them would be happy to see the Hunter population thinned out...or worse."

I did not voice the thought that the disease had to get into the Hunter population in the first place. And there was only one way for *that* to happen.

"Is there anyone to talk with besides the Yahoos we saw before? We got nowhere with the bureaucrats in Cennesari City." I described our interactions with Chief Clerk Floof and Captain Snedecor.

"Yahoo? An interesting word. Obviously derogatory. Does that come from your home world?"

I rolled my eyes and shook my head. "No. Way back before, from earth. An ancient novel. But what about other help?"

"I'm afraid that's the tone of the Cennesari bureaucracy right now," she replied.

"There must be people on the opposing side in government."

"Yes, but our political system does not afford them much power if they don't control the government."

I gritted my teeth and ran my hand through my hair. "Anne, can we keep this quiet for a while? Until we figure out what to do next?"

"I'm not sure I can do that. As a military officer—"

"Please. If you care about the Hunters, we need to do *something*. If the anti-Hunters get hold of this, they might suppress what we have learned."

"Are you suggesting they are involved in this?"

"Yes. I am. This epidemic didn't start on its own. I think it was deliberately planted."

"Good Lord. I can't believe—"

"I'm sorry, Anne, but I *can* believe. And I intend to do something about it. I know you can't, in your position. All I ask is silence. We didn't tell you any of this. You can't be held responsible."

She was quiet for a long time before she responded. "For the Hunters' sake, I'll keep my silence. But I can't do more than that."

***

Charl Cooper sat across the table from Fur and me. Her lips were thinned, her face pale. I knew that her sympathies were with the Hunters; she was the only person I met before Anne Stannard who would discuss the human-Hunter conflict openly.

"Yeah," I said, "there's no question that this is a Terran disease, and there's no way it could have gotten here without help."

Fur added, "It's unconscionable. We've got to catch the bastards."

Cooper's mouth turned down at the corners before she spoke. "Let me talk to some people. If this is a deliberate attack on the Hunters, we must learn who is behind this—and how high it goes. Based on your experience with Captain Snedecor, I fear this might go much higher. If nothing else, we need to move the medical community to work on the vaccine."

She paused and looked me straight in the eyes. "I

warned you once before and it's even more pertinent now. You are sticking your head into a hornet's nest."

Stephen A. Benjamin

CHAPTER 14

F UR AND I STOOD at the door of a tavern in a seedy part of town. Half of the arc lights in the street were broken. The sign said, *The Skinned Cat*, accompanied by an illustration of what could only be a flayed Hunter.

"Cy, this isn't a good idea." Fur's glance bounced around like ping-pong balls. "Cooper said pro–Hunter people aren't welcome here. She said a couple of activists disappeared last year and have never been found."

He had a point. I recalled Cooper said there was no solid evidence of foul play, only suspicion about what happened.

My reply was a bit too emphatic. "Hey, it's not a problem. No one will recognize us. We might have been celebrities out in the sticks for the cenoxen business, but no one in the cities knows about that, much less cares. We may be able to glean information that the locals can't. The authorities obviously won't help."

Fur tugged his beard. He had no lack of courage, but he was more circumspect than I was. I stepped through the door and he followed. A miasma of thick smoke hung in the air, and the place had a sinister mien. Or, perhaps that was my own preconception.

Eyes swiveled toward us like laser targeting systems. As we moved toward the bar, I felt those eyes as if they locked onto my soul. We ordered a couple of drafts from a surly bartender and made our way to a table.

After a few moments, a body detached itself from a nearby group and approached us. The man was middle-aged with grizzled hair and beard. His burly body rolled as he walked, but he was light on his feet despite his bulk. His broad, blunt hands clenched, and the muscles of his arms corded as he stood over us.

"New here. Who be ye?" He was as blunt as his hands.

"In from Crescent City," I responded. That city on the opposite continent was a safe place to be from, I hoped.

He nodded. "What brings ye *here*?" He pointedly looked around the room.

"Looking for a friendly place. Told this was one."

He nodded again. "For some."

Fur raised his mug and examined the dark reddish-amber beer. He took a big swallow then finished the very large mug. "I like that. The malt and hops are well-balanced, and it's got a smooth, creamy head. Served at the perfect temperature, too. Think I'll get another."

The man raised his eyebrows. I wondered if he was impressed by Fur's knowledge of beer, or more so by his capacity. I had seen the latter before and it *was* prodigious.

When Fur returned, the man said, "Cal Brooking," and stuck out his hand, his thoughts suspicious and dour.

Fur shook it and introduced himself and me with fictitious names. I let Fur lead.

"Good beer," he said. "We were told to come here

for it. Brewed locally?"

Brooking nodded. "Yah. Anselms. Brewed over by the river."

"Can you only get it here?" Fur asked.

"In a few places. For the right people."

I raised an eyebrow. "Right people?"

"Two other taverns. Like this one." He paused. "Again, I ask. What brings ye here?" He glanced at the mug in Fur's hand. "Not the beer." This guy was as mistrustful as a raven eyeing a scarecrow.

Fur launched into our fabricated story. "We're professional hunters. We have contracts from people who desire certain types of trophies. Good money. Wealthy clients will pay for bizarre or dangerous creatures to display in their houses. Some even claim they collected the animals themselves." Fur chuckled.

Brooking, poker-faced, did not ask any questions. Fur knew when to stop—not like me—and the silence grew oppressive. Finally, Brooking stalked off.

I looked at Fur. "Do you think he bought it?" I asked in a low voice.

He shrugged. "My guess is we're about to find out." He motioned with his head.

Brooking returned with another man, a head taller than Brooking, slender, with sandy hair and beard, and a weather-lined face. His ice blue eyes glinted as the two men sat across from us.

Brooking said, "This is Kev Strindberg."

Strindberg nodded to us. "Cal says you be hunters. Tell me about that."

Again, Fur took the lead. We had done as much research as possible for our cover, and he launched into a description of trophies we had bagged and sold.

"We're just at the start of an expedition, so we don't have anything yet," Fur said, "but past hunts have been profitable." He described a hunt for the nonsentient cousin to the dragons of Dragonworld. Since we had been there, he could add touches of verisimilitude.

Strindberg asked, "Interesting creatures. Sound dangerous. What about others?"

Fur pursed his lips before speaking. "Well, there's the Jinxian Bandersnatch, a slug-like behemoth with crystal teeth as hard as diamond and just as valuable."

"You have to see them to believe it," I added. "Those teeth can slice a land drone in half. The crystal is like a prism and glows with every color of the rainbow. We got good money for that."

Fur continued. "The Rigelian hyperbeasts are even more impressive. They're invisible while they're moving, they're so fast."

"Then how do you hit them?" Brooking asked.

"You wait," I said. "You set up on a known trail and wait. If they move by, you never see them. It took us ten days until one paused long enough to get a shot."

"What weapon do you use?" Strindberg asked. He was still skeptical, one eye squinted at me.

I said, "We use tranquilizer darts. We can't mess up any part of a trophy or the value is less than the cost of the expedition."

"How do you know what will work?" Brooking again.

"We research each species—what's known about the physiology of each world. We can run tests on related species and come up with an effective tranquilizing agent."

Strindberg cut in. "What if it *doesn't* work and it's a dangerous animal?"

Fur answered. "One of us always carries something more lethal—a laser."

"Which model?" Strindberg was not easily convinced.

"General Dynamics XXV," Fur said.

I added, "I use a Beretta Slingshot gas carbine for the darts. I think it has better long-range accuracy than the Win-Rem. The Beretta costs a lot more, but it's worth the money."

Strindberg nodded and continued the questions on worlds and hunts. After a half an hour, he grunted, got up, and left.

Brooking stood. "I be going. What do you two do now?"

"We'll be around here for a few days. We'd like to see the country a bit. The grasslands, the animals." After a moment's silence, I added, "Maybe see some of the local wildlife? You know?"

He nodded. "Perhaps we'll meet again."

I put out my hand, which he ignored.

Fur and I made our way back to the *GCVS*. We made sure no one followed.

***

We sat in the commissary and dissected the evening.

"Do you think they bought it? Was I too obvious about the 'local wildlife'?"

"We'll find out soon enough," Fur replied.

Levi glared at me. "What do you think to accomplish by such behavior? *Gott in Himmel*, you're acting like spies."

Even *he* had the grace to blush after that statement. He cleared his throat—a couple of times—before he continued. "This is too dangerous. Miss Cooper said that two people were murdered by these anti–Hunter people."

"That's not what she said," I replied. "Two pro-Hunter types went missing. No one knows what happened to them."

"Bah. You mince words. This does not further our mission." He grunted. "We have gone as far as we should now. It is time to return to Dovid's World."

With that pronouncement, he sat back and nodded his head as if he would brook no disagreement. His *yarmulke* shifted and he readjusted it.

I looked at Fur, then back at Levi. "We have two more worlds we agreed to visit. We can't back out of those commitments."

"Those stops will add little useful information to what I have already collected. It has been long enough. I cannot send my, er, data by hyperwave—it is not secure. I must return home."

Fur stepped into the breach once again. "Reb Levi, I can understand your impatience to return home, but if we don't keep our commitments, our veterinary service could lose all the goodwill it has attained in this sector of the galaxy. It could even impair Dr. Berger's success in recruiting new students for the Academy."

Levi grimaced at that, but couldn't argue. I had made good contacts on Cennesari, and we would likely pick up a dozen or more students here.

"We shouldn't throw that away. You might want to use the *GCVS* again in the future, right? As it is, Dr. Berger is welcome on every world—"

At Levi's snort, Fur hesitated. "Well, except Beta Cygnus. But isn't the service's reputation important to maintain? It could be an invaluable resource for the Rebbinical Council and Dovid's World, whether it was you or another Rebbe on board."

I silently thanked Fur as I waited for Levi's response.

"I suppose you have a point, Mr. Cohen." He fixed me with his black-eyed glare. "Berger, Cohen's argument has merit," he repeated, as if I hadn't heard it. "I will agree to complete the commitments we have made. That is all. There will be no other stops. None.

"Now, I think you would benefit from some tutelage in the finer points of *Torah* interpretation. You have been lax in your studies, of late."

I watched a slight smile bend the corners of Fur's mouth as I rolled my eyes.

***

Fur and I sat in *The Skinned Cat* across the table from Cal Brooking, Kev Strindberg, and a new acquaintance, Ryle Landsman, a wilderness guide. The talk wove a circuitous path around and through a number of subjects, including the flora and fauna of the Cennesari grasslands, trophy hunting, local beer, and the Cennesari tigers. These people would *not* use the term Hunters.

"Yes, I can guide you through the grasslands," Landsman said. "Would you be interested in anything in particular?"

"Well, the tigers are fascinating," I said. "Could we see them?"

"And your interest would be?"

"You know of our business, right? We get, um, vid images of exotic animals to sell to collectors and vid companies."

He nodded. I did not need to hit him over the head with more. Brooking and Strindberg would have clued him in.

"Can you meet me at this address in two days?" He handed me a piece of paper.

"What time?" I asked.

***

Charl Cooper introduced us to a man and a woman who represented the Pro-Hunter faction in the legislature. The man was my height, with carefully coiffed, wavy silver hair, and a phony smile. The ultimate politico. The short, slender woman wore a no-nonsense business suit, had shoulder-length graying brown hair, and a quick smile. She radiated sincerity.

She spoke in a gruff voice. "You realize there is considerable danger. These are not people to be trifled with. Are you certain you want to do this?"

"Yes," I said. "We think the epidemic was introduced into the Hunter population. It's nothing less than attempted genocide."

"This is not new for humans, you know." The man's voice was as smooth as his appearance. "Back on earth, settlers in the Americas deliberately introduced diseases like smallpox into the native populations to clear the land for themselves."

As a student of history myself, I knew this was not totally true. Yes, disease brought in by the European explorers devastated the Native Americans, but the earliest introductions were not deliberate. Later, in the westward movement of the United States' frontier, there were incidents of intentional introduction of disease, but these were isolated. The real damage had occurred hundreds of years before.

He continued. "In the twentieth and twenty-first centuries, earth countries developed chemical and biological weapons to be used on their fellows, who differed only in ideological or religious beliefs. Is it any surprise that we would inflict such a thing on an alien species?"

"Perhaps not," I replied, trying to keep any hostility out of my voice, "but that does not make it any less abhorrent. Criminals like this must be brought to justice."

The woman broke in. "That's all well and good, but this does not help the Hunters with their affliction."

"No," I replied, "but the issues are tied together. The government claims that it's not responsible for the panleukopenia epidemic, and it can't—or won't—intervene. Cennesari has the capacity to mount a vaccine program for the Hunters. This could blunt the epidemic and prevent effective genocide, but the government won't do that unless forced to. The powers *want* the epidemic to succeed."

Smoothy interrupted. "I wouldn't go that far. I cannot believe—"

"I can. I do. Someone deliberately introduced this disease. The fact that your government refuses to help is proof-positive that they don't care if the Hunters are decimated."

"Those are harsh words, Dr. Berger."

"Then why won't they even let me go out and help where I can. The sons-of-bitches we met with stymied us at every turn. They don't even try to hide their interference."

The woman countered, "But how do you expect to get proof of this genocidal intent?"

"If we are seen as willing to kill a Hunter as a trophy, then maybe they'll be willing to talk about what is happening to the cats. We'll be sympathetic listeners. We've got to try."

"Well, if you can bring back proof," she said. "I believe we can reverse this stand—at least at the political and bureaucratic level."

"If you do that, I can get your medical infrastructure started on a mass vaccine program. It won't be quick, but we can save the majority of the Hunters."

"It does not seem likely to me you can get that information out of the anti-Hunter extremists." Smoothy shook his head and frowned as he spoke.

"I'll tell you this," I said, "I'll do my damnedest. Humans created this disaster, and we need to fix it—

soon."

***

Landsman glared at us over the steering wheel of the land drone. A small, wiry man with dark brown hair and a handlebar mustache below a long nose spoke only when addressed directly. He made no pretenses about being a nature guide.

"You have the equipment you need?"

I looked at Fur and then nodded to the man. "Yeah. Everything we need to... *sample* the wildlife."

He nodded and pointed to the back seats of the land drone. "Get in." His aura was hostile, even though we were "paying customers." I wondered if he ever got repeat business.

An assistant, introduced as Ric, was more garrulous. He hopped in the copilot's seat. "You guys are going to bag a—"

Landsman slapped Ric on the shoulder—hard—which shut him up for all of two minutes.

Ric chattered on and took the role of nature guide that Landsman refused. He pointed out herds of grazers and named shrubs and trees scattered among the grass. He did not refer to the Hunters again.

"How long will we be traveling?" asked Fur.

"We need to get beyond the regular patrols," Landsman said. It was as close as he would come to acknowledging the illegality of what we were doing.

"We'll set up camp at Three Buttes tonight," Ric said. "Then we'll head up the Carrion River."

"Quite a name," Fur said. "Where did it come from?"

Ric laughed. "Early on, some settlers wanted to clear the area of tigers, so they decided to wipe out their food supply. Slaughtered thousands of wild cenoxen before they gave it up as impossible—just too many. Carrion birds, big and little, blackened the skies for weeks. That stuck the river with its name."

The guy actually thought it was funny. I shuddered at the image. These people haven't changed all that much, they just used a different method now.

We set up camp at the mouth of the river canyon, a lovely place with the rocky stream spreading out among tall umbrella-like trees as it left the canyon's confines. I had to fight to keep down cenoxen stew and Anselm's beer when I thought about what Rick had said about the site, and what had been done to the sentient cenoxen. Never again would I eat anything from those animals, but I could not give myself away here. As the beer worked on our thirst, Fur broke out our ace in the hole, a bottle of fifty-year-old Rigelian whiskey. Famed for its spirits, this particular Rigelian vintage was a gem.

Even Landsman's dour façade lifted when Fur handed him a generous portion. "Very good. Thank you."

"Hopefully, we're just celebrating before the fact." I smirked at him—at least what I hoped was a smirk.

Fur refilled the glasses. I sipped at mine, while Fur made a point to down his in one gulp.

He smacked his lips and poured himself another. "More?" He motioned with the bottle to Landsman and Ric.

Both downed what they had and held out their glasses. It was futile to try to keep up with Fur, so I sat back and watched the fun.

Halfway through the bottle, Landsman quit and staggered to his tent. Ric was young enough and foolish enough not to know when he had enough. While Landsman had gotten quieter, if that was possible, Ric got giddier and even more garrulous.

"Whatcha got t'do the job?" he asked in a low tone,

now that Landsman was gone. "Can I see it?" He belched.

"Well...I don't know," I answered. "I'm not sure your boss would like—"

"Shcrew that. I wanna see it."

I motioned with my head to Fur, and he stood and walked to the equipment cache. He lifted a long case and brought it back to the fire.

Ric stood, then staggered backward. I caught him before he fell. We wanted him conscious and unharmed—and talkative.

Fur uncased the gas-powered rifle. It gleamed in the firelight. I had to admit that in the darkness on the wild grassland, it was an impressive instrument. To me, it was an implement of my profession—used to tranquilize animals when needed...and an occasional fat asshole. The barrel and the receiver were titanium alloy, the latter topped with a torpedo-shaped gas cartridge and a laser targeting scope. The stock was dark gray composite with a bipod mount below the forearm. A pistol-grip trigger completed the piece.

Fur handed the unloaded gun to Ric.

"Wow. That'll do it for sure."

He wobbled a bit as he sighted down the barrel. "Those damn cats won't have a chance."

Until now, nothing had been said about the real— what they thought was real, anyway—reason for this little jaunt. The closest we had come was the issue of payment. We had agreed on a price ten times the cost of a nature tour. Far more than we could afford if we were not to sell our "trophy" for an obscene sum. Although the pro-Hunter movement bankrolled us, we haggled enough to convince them of our roles and make us look pecuniary.

Ric looked down at the case again. His eyes surveyed the hypo darts in their clear cartridges. Even to me, they looked evil in the firelight.

"Do you think I...*burp*...I could shoot one?"

"I don't think we'd better, Ric," I countered. "We can't waste them. Each dart is worth three hundred credits. Unless you can pay for one."

Even at his advanced stage of inebriation, the thought of shooting off a week's pay was out of the question. He settled for another half glass of whiskey. I figured that we'd better cut him off soon. We wanted him drunk—not dead.

We had fitted both Fur and me with the microrecording devices that the Rebbinical Council had foisted on us. I could not think of a better use for them. It was pure luck that Ric had showed up. I realized now that we had no chance of getting anything out of Landsman.

Ric blathered on for a few minutes about the rifle. Then he moved on, with some prompts, to the subject of the Hunters.

"You'll get one of them fuckin' cats, for sure. They're easy. Not expecting to be hunted. Just stand there and look at you. Pick 'em off like that!" He tried to snap his fingers, without success.

"You shoot them often?" I asked.

"No. Got t' be careful. Bad stuff, if we get caught. But kill 'em all, I say."

"Don't like the tigers, Ric?"

"Hate 'em. Take our space. Ours."

"What can you do about that? Besides killing one or two with a rifle?"

"We can do something. Kill 'em all."

Fur and I exchanged glances.

"How could you do that, Ric?" I asked. "There are a lot of the tigers, aren't there?"

"Kill 'em off. Doin' it now." His head wobbled on his shoulders as if it were fitted with a loose ball joint.

"How, Ric? How are you killing them off?"

"Sick. Got 'em sick. Droppin' like...like flies."

"How did you do that, Ric?"

"Cat dishease. We brought in cat dishease. That will kill 'em all."

At that, his eyes rolled up in his head and he collapsed backward to the ground.

I suppose I should have been elated. We had the proof we set out to get, but the vileness that exuded from the young man nauseated me. It was time to put the next part of our plan into action. Unfortunately, this would take my nausea to a whole new level, but we did not intend to kill, or even scare, one of the Hunters.

***

The next morning I knelt behind our tent with nothing left to throw up but bile. At least I had gotten rid of the cenox stew. Fur and I had argued about who would have to endure this indignity. He claimed that he had to maintain his image as a hard drinker. As I usually did when I argued with Fur, I lost. A drug cocktail that would make me sick, but not so sick as to run the risk of dehydration and electrolyte imbalance, induced the vomiting.

"What's wrong with him?" Landsman asked Fur.

"I don't know. He complained of a stomachache early this morning. Then this started." Fur motioned to me with his massive head.

"Did he drink too much?" Landsman's mouth turned down as he glanced at Ric who sat by the small breakfast fire, his head in his hands. Landsman had chewed out the young man when he saw his condition this morning.

"No," Fur replied. "He didn't drink that much. Must have picked up some local bug."

At this, I ran for our latrine. The second half of my affliction came right on schedule. I cursed Fur silently as I crouched. The pain had now become all too real. That was enough for Landsman. I heard him say, "Whatever it is, I don't want it. We better cancel this. Get him back to Cennesari City. Be hard to explain a dead offworlder out here."

Fur argued to continue, but Landsman was adamant. It worked as we planned. Too much so, from my point of view.

***

I picked up the microchip on Senator Schwab's desk. The woman we had met with before now had a name and she did not hide her position or inclinations. After she listened to Ric's drunken statements, her face became beet red and her dark eyes smoldered.

She was silent for long minutes. I did not interrupt her thoughts. I had left Fur at the *GCVS* to placate Levi. The rebbe had been vehement in his demands that we leave for our next stop when we returned from what he viewed as a frivolous sightseeing trip. He did not care what we had learned.

Schwab waved her hand and a woman's voice issued from her desk.

"Yes, Senator?"

"Get Scott in here. Reesling, too." Now she turned to me. "You have done our world a great service, Dr. Berger. I'm not sure how we can repay you. I know you said you want no remuneration, but there must be something."

I shook my head. "Senator, routing out these assholes and saving the Hunters is reward enough. I apologize for my crudity, but there are few other words that fit."

She smiled. "No apology needed."

"We still have a lot of work ahead before the Hunters are out of danger. When can I start work with your microbiologists to mass-produce a vaccine? Every day brings more deaths."

"I understand your impatience, Dr. Berger, but it will take some time to convince the right people that there is a problem. That's my job and I assure you—"

At a knock on the door she called, "Enter."

A woman and a man came in. The man looked to be in his forties, the woman about ten years younger.

"Scott, Rees, this is Dr. Cy Berger. He's just leaving, but keep in mind that he has given us the opportunity I'll tell you about. Scott," she motioned to the man, "is my chief of staff. Rees is my scientific adviser. She'll work with you to accomplish your goals." She stood. "Dr. Berger, again I find it difficult to thank you enough. We will be in touch."

I stood to leave then stopped. I looked at the Senator and bit my lower lip. "Senator, you know, there is one more thing you can do for me."

I gave her a capsule summary of my relationship with Reb Levi, of the situation on Dovid's world, and mine in particular. Her face grew even darker as I spoke. I sensed it partly related to my briefing, but something disturbed her beyond my own personal problems. I shrugged that off. "Can you keep Levi happy if we stay on Cennesari? He's chomping at the bit to move on. I can't delay him forever. My parents and I are still at his mercy."

Schwab frowned, then said, "Scott, get General Poulous here first thing in the morning." She looked at me. "If he likes military intelligence, we will give him all of that oxymoron he can handle. It sounds like your world could use some help, too."

"Yeah. Feel free to tell Levi that I set this up for

him. That will help."

"I can do better than that. Tuesday is the first night of Passover. How about if you, Mr. Cohen, and Reb Levi join us for our community *Seder*?"

I was speechless, not a condition I found myself in often.

***

Turned out that Cennesari had the largest Jewish community of any of the worlds we had visited. Levi knew that but had not mentioned it. Traditionally, many of the locals had a communal *Seder* in a banquet hall in Cennesari City.

Levi was happy as the proverbial clam. He could not believe his good fortune. Not only would we have a real, live *Seder*—no vid chip congregation here—but also his new connections to the military had him gushing with good will.

As we traveled to the hall, Levi said, "Berger, sometimes you surprise me. Your efforts will stand you in good stead. You may take whatever time you need here, at least until I am done with my...research."

The *Seder* is the Jewish ritual feast that marks the beginning of the holiday of Passover, and commemorates the emancipation of the Israelites from slavery in ancient Egypt. But the *Seder* did not go exactly as Levi would have it. The descent to lunacy began when we walked in the door.

Senator Schwab greeted us accompanied by another woman. "Welcome. Captain Berger, Mr. Cohen, Mr. Schvartz, let me introduce Rabbi Pearlman." She nodded to the tall, gray-haired woman beside her.

Pearlman smiled and put out her hand. Fur and I shook hands, but Levi took a step back.

His thoughts were black. "Unacceptable. A woman

cannot preside over a holy day service."

I knew the Test-Lit brand of fundamentalist orthodoxy did not recognize women as suitable to make a *minyon*, much less be rabbis, but I did not expect this.

"Excuse me?" Pearlman frowned and looked at Schwab.

The senator said, "I'm not sure I understand, Mr. Schvartz. You have a problem?"

Levi nodded emphatically. "Women cannot be rebbes. I will conduct the service."

I cringed. Oh, God. What is he going to do next? My stomach did a flip-flop.

Pearlman laughed, but there was little humor in her voice. "I'm afraid that will not be possible. And what gives you the right to make such a demand?"

Levi caught himself in his own trap. If he admitted he was an ordained rebbe, he would blow his cover. If not, how could he justify his demand? He threw his caution to the wind.

"I am Reb Levi Schvartz, a leader of the Rebbinical Council on Dovid's World." He puffed out his chest. "That gives me the right. My standing is higher than anyone here on Cennesari, especially *women*." The last word dripped with contempt.

After a few gasps, there was silence in the room as all present watched the confrontation.

Rabbi Pearlman's face reddened, but Senator Schwab spoke first in a firm, but calm voice. A politician, for sure. "Reb Schvartz, you may have your beliefs and traditions on Dovid's World, but on Cennesari we follow our own traditions. We will begin our *Seder* shortly. If you would like to leave, you have my blessing."

Levi grumped and grumbled, but after a large number of people gave him dirty looks, he backed off. But not for long. He next protested when he saw the shortened *Seder*, a consideration for the many families with children present. There are many versions of the *Haggadah*, the Jewish text that sets forth the order of the Passover meal. I remembered the interminable, very traditional *Seders* at my grandparent's home. By the time we got to the meal, the younger kids were sleeping under the table. There is an apocryphal story of the Rabbis whose deliberations at the Passover table lasted until their students had to tell them that dawn had come and the holiday ended. Levi did not believe in the short version, but he shut up again after sharp words from Rabbi Pearlman.

The final blow came when Rabbi Pearlman omitted the cup of wine poured and placed at the open door for the Prophet Elijah to drink. Levi became apoplectic.

"We must fill the cup and recite the invitation to the Prophet Elijah. His presence foretells the coming of Messiah," he screamed. His red face, white scar, and twitching eye had half the kids at the meal hiding behind parents.

The rabbi stood and fixed Levi with her own, equally scary glare. "Reb Schvartz, we welcomed you to help us celebrate a sacred portion of our traditions as Jews, and you do nothing but denigrate and berate us for our hospitality. Our own rabbis have spent much time interpreting the *Torah* and the *Talmud* in the light of new knowledge gained from our spread through the galaxy. Tradition is one thing, fantasy another. This is the fourth millennium, time that ghost stories are put away from our religion."

"Pfeh." Levi spat. "You are no better than a bunch of heathens. You call yourselves Jews? I have met aliens that were more observant than you."

A laughable statement considering the depth of Levi's xenophobia.

"I cannot tolerate this travesty a moment longer. We

will send a mission here to bring you back to the true religion. You will learn what the true faith means." He turned and stomped out of the hall, leaving an enraged congregation behind him.

Unfortunately, the congregation turned their anger towards Fur and me. I thrust my gorge back down and shouted over the multitude of furious voices. "Friends. Please. Listen to me."

Senator Schwab raised her hands, and things quieted down.

"Please let me apologize," I said. "If I had known Levi would act like this, I would not have brought him tonight. He does *not* speak for me, or Mr. Cohen, or for most of the forward thinking Jews of Dovid's World. Unfortunately, a few reactionary and parochial people like Levi dominate our world's government. That is our problem, not yours. This is a solemn holiday. Let's not allow a closed-minded fanatic spoil it for the rest of us. Your service is wonderful. Please, let's complete it in the spirit of our ancestors."

Senator Schwab added, "It is my fault, not Dr. Berger's. I knew of Reb Schvartz's nature, but did not expect such narrow-minded hatred." She turned to me. "Dr. Berger, sometimes one must *experience* something to truly understand it." She turned back to the assembly. "Let us continue."

After the *Seder*, Senator Schwab spoke to Fur and me. "It is truly my fault that this happened. After you informed me of the nature of your world's government, some puzzling events became clear. Your Reb Schvartz has been fomenting dissension in parts of our community, amongst people who form the lowest rung of our society. His threat about a *mission* to convert us was not bluster. From what I learned, this man and his thugs truly plan to invade our world. He should not have been invited."

Fur responded. "I'm glad you've seen through his duplicity, Senator. You should know that he has done this on every world with a Jewish population that we have visited. I am a member of the main resistance organization to the Testamentary-Literalists, and I have kept tabs on and worked against Reb Levi throughout this voyage. We have thwarted his attempts to create an environment ripe for conquest on other worlds. I would have contacted you about this had you not learned of it yourselves. From your reaction, I think that Cennesari will be prepared."

I watched Fur, wide-eyed. It amazed me that he had come into the open like that.

Schwab looked at Fur with newfound respect. "You surprise me, Mr. Cohen. And you, Dr. Berger. There is more to *your* mission than meets the eye." She fixed me with her steely gaze. "There may be more we can do for you in the future, Dr. Berger. A threat to invade our world may require a response. We will discuss this further."

***

It took a week before the news of the introduced epidemic hit the vids. When it did, the current Cennesari administration came down with a crash. You could almost feel the city reverberate. The scandal stripped out bureaucrats from top to bottom.

Scott told me, "We used the recording to approach the Premier first. We had reason to believe that he would never have countenanced such a barbaric action. He was appalled. He put his entire staff to work, and they pinpointed the functionaries who had thwarted efforts to help the Hunters. While not many, they held strategic positions in the bureaucracy. A few of them broke down, and that opened the floodgates. People pointed fingers in every direction. Most of the extreme anti-Hunter politicians have been forced to resign."

The cadre that had smuggled in and released the virus was not in government, but had ties to it. Some of those responsible escaped. I worried that the anti-Hunters might learn of our complicity in their downfall and come after us, but Scott told me that they kept our part in the operation secret. Fortunately, I doubted Ric would remember what he had said, or admit it if he did remember.

***

I met the Cennesari veterinarian, Sammel Cressel, who came over from the other continent to assist. We collaborated with the scientific and medical community, and managed to mass-produce the needed vaccine.

When we had some time alone, I raised the question of the cenoxen. When I told him about my suspicions, he was somber.

"Your talent is quite extraordinary. I can only imagine how useful that would be. On the other hand, in a case like this, I'm not sure I envy you. Are you sure?"

"Yes. I don't receive clear, rational thoughts from animals or humans, just emotions. The Hunters and the cenoxen are both telepaths. We know the Hunters are sentient. If the cenoxen are not sentient, they are damned close to it. I feel like I should do something, but I was warned off by Charl Cooper. She said it would devastate the economy of the planet."

"Charl is a sharp woman." Cressel was silent for long moments. "She's right, you know. The export of cenoxen meat is the keystone of our economy. If that stopped..." He shook his head. "I'm not sure I have a good answer for you. Right now, you have half the humans on this world who love you and half who hate you for what you have done. You drop this on them and you would probably push it to ninety percent against. As far as this world is concerned, the cenoxen are cattle. I can't tell you what to do. That has to be your decision."

***

With the vaccine ready, we headed for Hunter territory. Cressel and I instructed the medical personnel in how to treat Hunters with dehydration and electrolyte imbalances. While too many of the Hunters were beyond help, we did manage to save a significant number. We set up field clinics for mass vaccination and sent out Hunter representatives to have as many of their compatriots as possible gather at the clinics. After two weeks, we had vaccinated over eighty percent of the estimated remaining Hunter population. That was all we could do, but it would break the back of the epidemic.

I told Sammel that I had to raise the question of the cenoxen. I could not live with myself if I did not. After putting forth such an effort to save the Hunters, how could I ignore the cenoxen? I saw them in the same light, both sentient telepaths. I wrestled with the recognition that I might cause a major upheaval and untold hardship for an entire world and I did not sleep well the rest of my stay on Cennesari.

Senator Schwab made the official announcement regarding possible sentience of cenoxen in their parliament. Give her credit. She agreed to make the unpopular disclosure even though she knew it could damage her own political career. The response was quick and overwhelming: The vast majority of the

Cennesari population vehemently disbelieved that the cenoxen were sentient. Of course, there were no other empaths who could confirm or deny my assertion, so I was portrayed as a rabble-rousing nut case. The media denounced my so-called "telepathic ability" as prevarication. Fortunately, I was off in the wilds; otherwise, I might have been torn limb from limb by an angry mob.

As it was, Levi's wrath came down on me doubled because I had not told him of my abilities. I blew that off as best I could and looked to Fur for needed support.

"You've done what you can," he told me. "What happens from here is up to the Cennesarians."

"Yeah, but I doubt they will do anything about it. They'll keep on eating and exporting the creatures unless pushed to change."

He pulled at his beard. "You're probably right, but do you want to take on a galactic campaign against them? There are a lot of good people on this planet that you would harm, as well as the bigots and xenophobes."

I leaned my elbows on the table, my head in my hands. The small *GCVS* commissary felt claustrophobic. "Many worlds would stop cenoxen imports if they knew, but that could cripple this planet. I just don't know what to do." The painful knot in my chest would not go away.

"Cy, leave it. I understand where you are on this, but you can't be the final arbitrator of what is right and wrong with the universe."

I looked up at Fur and took a deep breath. "You're right. I can't even do anything about our own little corner of it back home." I stood and turned to leave. "I need to take a break. I'll see you later." I wanted to cry alone.

***

We wrapped our vaccination efforts up late one evening and found that a celebration had been prepared. As we approached, a huge bonfire roared, as did the Hunters who surrounded it. I even saw a few male Hunters present. The sounds caught my breath. The fire's heat distorted the atmosphere. Monstrous shadows from even the smallest members of the celebratory party danced like drunken wraiths against the night. It recalled some of the ancient African jungle vids I had watched. I half expected Tarzan of the Apes to swing down out of a tree—though there were no trees here on the edge of the Cennesari plain. Beer flowed like liquid gold—not the Anselms' variety, but good enough. The Hunters brought in fresh game, exotic-looking and -tasting meats. No cenoxen, thankfully.

At the end of the evening, after many libations, the Hunter elders gathered and one ancient tigress addressed me. *<You have saved the Hunters. You are ones without fear. You are now Hunters. You may lope the grasslands, kill the game, live among our people. We come if you call, as you came for us. We offer you game for your lifetimes.>*

I heard gasps from the humans present. Anne Stannard, who had joined us at our request, leaned toward me. "Get up. You've been made honorary Hunters. You need to respond. Nothing like this has ever happened before."

Fur and I stood and I stammered through thanks I could not recall afterward.

Fur was more articulate. "You honor us. To live among you would be a life of joy. Your offer of food is beyond our expectations, although we will be leaving your planet and won't be able to accept. Having been able to assist you is reward enough."

Levi did not stand or speak. I sensed that the title of honorary Hunter insulted him.

Lieutenant Stannard stepped forward and addressed the Hunter clans. "We have already uncovered many of those who were responsible for the atrocity that has been delivered upon the Hunters. Some are still at large, but make no mistake, we humans will find them and bring them to justice. When we do, we will ask the Hunters to assist us in judgment."

This created a major stir among the small group of humans present. These people stood behind our work for the Hunters and my plea for the cenoxen, but the idea of Hunters standing in judgment of humans was unheard of. I had discussed this with Anne earlier, but others were not prepared. Anne had forewarned the Hunters. This message would move through the human population with alacrity; that was deliberate. The party wound down after that, perhaps cooled a bit by the thought of what lay ahead for those responsible.

Then the eldest of the female Hunters approached me, dropped to her belly, ears back, and rolled onto her back. I recognized this classic demonstration of submission, that I was dominant.

Stunned, I was not sure of the proper response. I knelt, put my arms around the massive head, and spoke. "You are among the most magnificent beings I have met in our galaxy. You are strong, brave, and wise. If I can be half so much, I will face my end in peace and honor."

The elder stood and voiced her thanks. <*Well spoken, brother.*>

At this distance, I could examine her extremely red and swollen gums; her breath was foul enough to turn the stomach of a carrion bird.

I addressed her again. "One more thing I might

accomplish for the Hunters and for you. May I *please* clean your teeth?"

CHAPTER 15

"**I** WILL TOLERATE NO MORE of these useless diversions." Levi's face was even redder than usual, and his white scar slashed his face like an exclamation point. "Worlds of lizard-men—if you can call them 'men'—and dragons do not add to our knowledge."

Of course, he meant *military* knowledge, or worlds that might be targets for the Test-Lits' evangelical activities.

"We will stop only at the two human worlds we have contracted with. And you..." He looked at me and squinted to stop the twitch of his eye. "You will refrain from alienating the people of these worlds. We left Beta Cygnus with nothing after your outrageous act of attacking Master Fredo. You alienated most of Cennesari with your insistence on helping a bunch of cats, not to speak of your insane insistence that their cattle were intelligent." He spat the words like a curse.

It seemed that his alienating the Jewish community on Cennesari didn't count.

"They would have paid us much more, if not for that. You seem to forget about your parents, Berger. My hyperwave reports to home keep your parents unconfined and unharmed. This could change."

I ignored the pounding in my head and kept my

voice even. "I agreed to schedule human worlds, but we won't avoid nonhuman worlds if they are in dire need of our services. That's both unacceptable and immoral. If we do, we'll lose what credibility we've gained, and that won't help *your* mission."

I could read the conflict within the rebbe; greed warred with his xenophobia. Greed won. "Hmph. So long as they are willing to pay well."

Hypocritical *putz*.

Even if Levi's avarice won out—he had about orgasmed over the treasure from the dragon emperor—his xenophobic harangues did not let up. We were on the next leg of our voyage, and we sat around the dinner table, over dessert and coffee. Fur leaned back in his chair and propped his size-fifteen feet on a stool. For the most part, he stayed out of my verbal battles with Levi unless things started to take a nasty turn.

The Rebbe leaned across the table toward me, his black eyes intense. "Can you not see this, Cy?" he asked. "*Neshama*, the Hebrew word for breath, describes the soul or spirit. God gives the soul to a person in his or her first breath. It is written in *Bereshit*." He used the Hebrew name for Genesis:

"'And the Lord God formed man of the dust of the ground, and breathed into his nostrils the breath of life. Man became a living soul.'

"Nowhere in the *Torah* does it say that souls exist in other species than humans."

I kept my voice tempered. "That may be the literal translation that implies the existence of souls in men. It does *not* specifically say that animals do not have souls, does it?"

He narrowed his eyes, but I continued before he could respond. "The *Torah* was composed by humans millennia ago. They didn't have a clue that there were other sentient races out among the stars. How could the writers even consider whether they had souls if they didn't know they existed?"

Levi sat up straight and lifted his chin imperiously. "The *Torah* is the word of God." He looked at Fur. "I recall Mr. Cohen made *that* point to you the night we first met."

"Why are you so determined to look down on every race we meet as inferior to humans? That's bigotry, plain and simple."

"You call me a bigot?" He removed his *yarmulke* and wiped beads of sweat from his bald dome with his sleeve. His eye spasmed and he rubbed it. I figured that he would unleash one of his threats, but he surprised me. "*You* are biased against the true religion. God handed down his laws to his people. His *chosen* people. Not to lizards, manlike or dragon-like, to cats, and Lord knows what else out there."

"Ha. You just said it better than I could. 'Lord knows what else.' Isn't that an admission that God does know, and care, about these other sentient species? Just *listen* to yourself."

He huffed, rose, and turned to leave the commissary, but he could not pass up a parting shot. "You and yours will regret this attitude, Berger. See if you do not."

True to form. My help to get him ingratiated with the Cennesari military had already lost its charm. I looked at Fur and shook my head. "What a *schmuck*."

"Our keeper is getting antsy," Fur said. "My guess is that he'll demand again that we return home before we finish our contracts, even though he agreed to go on. What do we do then?"

"I've thought about that a lot." I looked at the hatch and went to it. I checked the corridor outside, and closed the hatch before I returned to my seat. "If we return to Dovid's World now, it won't change Levi's, or the Inquisition's, view of me or my beliefs. It won't get me or my folks out of danger. I don't know what to do."

"Have you thought more about the resistance?" Fur asked. "You know the situation at home, the excesses of the Test-Lit regime, and the activities of the Sons-of-David. You could be a valuable ally—"

"Yeah, but if I openly oppose the regime, my folks are in deep shit."

"The resistance could hide them."

"And they would be hunted like criminals. Can you guarantee their safety? At least they're free now." I thought about that a moment. "Unless Levi is handing us a pile of *drek* and they're already prisoners."

"We have no reason not to believe Levi on that one." He fixed me with his brown eyes. "I wouldn't ask you to openly oppose the Test-Lits. You could help in other ways. If we are to have a free future on Dovid's World, we have to take action."

"But you've said yourself that the SOD does not have the strength to take on the Test-Lits. What have you accomplished? Tell me."

Fur chewed at his lower lip as he combed his fingers through his whiskers. "Cy, you know that my hyperwave messages to and from colleagues at home are censored just like yours. I can't get good information on what is happening there. But I have been able to get some messages through secondary sources. The latest, on Cennesari, said the SOD is close to taking action. The people of Dovid's World have reached their limit. We know the Sammarans will come in and fight with us because many Sammarans either are refugees from Dovid's World, or have first-hand reason to hate the Test-Lits for their invasion. The other worlds that rescued Sammara are sympathetic. They appreciated my information about Levi, but they won't commit troops in a civil war on Dovid's World unless they are convinced that we will win. On the other hand, we know that Reb Levi has gotten precious little out of this trip. If anything, he's pissed off just about everyone he has met."

"Great. We can go home and tell everyone that Levi is a *schlemiel*. That helps us a lot."

Fur's face colored. "You could help. Maybe if you were to—"

"*Maybe? If?* Maybe if we had salmon, we could make lox. Give me a break. To foment rebellion without offworld support besides Sammara is sure defeat. That does me or my parents no good."

His face got even darker, his voice tight. "Is that all that matters? You and your parents? How many millions on Dovid's World live under repression unknown to Jews for over a thousand years? I feel responsibility to do something about that. Every day, the Test-Lits torture reasonable people who resist them. Every day, people disappear without a trace. How long does this go on before we rise up and stop it?"

A vein in the side of his temple pulsed as he screwed his thick eyebrows together. He stood, stalked out of the room, and slammed the hatch behind him. That was more raw emotion than I had ever seen from the big guy.

I sat for a long while and thought over what he said. Was I really selfish? Was I not supposed to care about my family? I wondered if more lay behind his feelings than the idealistic objections to the Test-Lits that Fur and the SOD professed. I knew there was more I could do. Senator Schwab had as much as said that Cennesari might help to fight the Test-Lits, but most of her world hated me now, so what good was that? Fur was right, though. We had reached a point where backing down was no longer an option. But what could I really do, I wailed silently? I was scared shitless.

I returned to my cabin and picked a vid to watch, appropriately enough something called *Exodus* about the formation of the independent state of Israel after one of earth's world wars, after a Holocaust had nearly wiped out the Jews on the continent of Europe. About midway through, I heard a knock on my cabin door.

"Come," I called.

Fur's bulk filled the opened door. "You busy?"

"No. Take a load off your feet." I motioned to my one chair, an archaic wooden construction I brought as a little piece of home. It creaked ominously as he sat. I sat up on my bunk and put my vid pad aside.

Fur said, "I want to apologize. I was out of line to get angry at you."

"Are you kidding me? I'm the one who's out of line. You were right. I *have* been self-absorbed. There are a lot of people at home who are in dire straits besides my folks."

"I'm glad that you acknowledge that, but there's more." He looked away from me, then back. "You've been open with me. It's only fair to respond in kind."

I sat on the edge of my bed. He had my attention.

Fur glanced at the floor, then at me. He took a deep breath and let it out as he fingered his beard.

"This goes back much farther than your problems, to when the Test-Lits first took power. My grandparents were prominent political figures and opposed the archconservative wing of the ruling party. Years of drought had devastated our agricultural society and the economy was in shambles. We imported food from other planets at a high cost and our debt was astronomical.

"This was fertile soil for those who invoked the images of biblical plagues and retribution against a society that had moved away from the teachings of

Yahweh. History has taught us that fundamentalism is popular when people face circumstances beyond their control. The Test-Lits rose to political power, but didn't have the kind of domination they have now. That evolved over time as they passed law after law that infringed on the rights of the people.

"They drummed up nonexistent threats to make their point. First, at home, they outlawed groups and parties that disagreed with their tactics. That gave them a 'criminal' element that they fought in the name of safety of the realm. Of course, this created the very groups that opposed the repression of the Test-Lits."

I nodded. "A self-fulfilling prophecy. The Sons-of-David was one, I presume?" His history differed from what we got in our textbooks.

Fur nodded. "An early one and still the most effective. Then the Test-Lits trumped up supposed threats from offworld, specifically from Sammara. You know that many Dovid's Worlders emigrated there to escape the oppression. The Test-Lits wanted them back under their collective thumbs. They claimed that expatriate Dovid's Worlders planned to invade their home world. In truth, the evangelical wing of the party pushed the need to export their brand of belief to other, 'heathen' worlds."

"The invasion of Sammara," I said. "Makes sense."

"Yes. Of course, that went awry for Dovid's World. We became pariahs throughout our sector of the galaxy. Anyway, getting back to my grandparents, they lost their parliamentary seats due to a smear campaign against them. Accused of treason, they became outspoken opponents of the government. Of course, that seemed to confirm their seditious activities. They were arrested and imprisoned."

"Wait. I didn't think that the Inquisition formed until much later."

"True, but there was a judiciary that had been put into place by the Test-Lits. Trials were a sham. My father was five-years-old when his parents were incarcerated. Released when he was twenty-five, they were broken and old beyond their years. They died a few years after their release. An uncle and aunt raised my dad, but they all lived in constant fear of the increasingly repressive government."

"I'm sorry, Fur." That sounded lame even to me, so I continued. "I understand better why you feel as you do. My family's problems seem minor in comparison."

Fur shook his head, a sharp movement as if to throw off my sympathy. "No, you don't understand yet. My father's hatred of the Test-Lits was intense, though he never let me see that as a child. I learned the story later, from my mother. Father became a prominent activist in an underground organization, the FRF, Fighters for Religious Freedom."

"I've never heard of them," I said.

"You wouldn't...now. The FRF was a terrorist organization, for all intents and purposes. They were overcome by the Test-Lits' military in a major campaign. You won't find that in your schoolbooks. I was eleven when my dad died. Mother told me there had been an industrial accident. He worked in a farm machinery manufacturing plant." Fur halted here and stood up. He rolled his shoulders as if to shrug off a great weight.

I suppressed the urge to say, "I'm Sorry," again.

After a few moments, Fur sat and faced me. "I didn't learn the truth until I graduated from high school. Before I went off to the university, my mother sat me down and told me the story. I had been raised a devout Jew. Although my parents didn't hold to the kind of strict interpretation of the *Torah* that the Test-Lits demanded, outwardly we toed the line. My parents never criticized the government in public, but we did discuss alternative beliefs and interpretations of scriptures in our own home. I was cautioned to keep such discussions private." He paused and I detected a slight smile. "I learned that lesson."

I felt my face heat, but he forged on.

"Because my father's participation in the FRF was covert, he was not known to the Test-Lits by name. The accident at his plant was an explosion attributed to the FRF, and many mangled bodies were never identified, my dad among them."

"But would the FRF have done that? I thought they were the good guys."

Fur shook his head. "They didn't. This was a real accident, not a terrorist attack, but the Test-Lits executed some of our friends and neighbors anyway...as a warning. When I went off to school, I had a spotless record insofar as the government was concerned, but Mother died a year after I entered veterinary college. After my dad's death, she faded. I know physiologically you're not supposed to die of a broken heart, but *she* did." He whispered the next words. "I think having me at home kept her together. When I left for school, she..."

Fur was silent for long moments. His fingers smoothed his mustache over and over. He stared at the wall as he spoke. "I vowed to do everything in my power to help bring down the regime that had devastated my family. I quit veterinary school and went to work as a farmhand. Somehow, the physical labor helped to assuage the fury that simmered inside me. With the help of a classmate who finished vet school, I became a vet tech. Later, I sought out the SOD and I became a member of that organization." He looked at me. "You know the rest. You were an opportunity too good to pass up."

What could I say? I saw Furoletto Cohen in a new light, one that did not reflect favorably on me.

Fur hadn't finished. "There is one more thing you might like to know. It's about our rebbe."

I perked up at that.

"You say that I keep my temper and don't react to his behavior. True, but he directs most of his antagonism at you. I've given him no reason to suspect me. For good reason."

"What do you mean by that?"

"Reb Levi Schvartz is the grandson of the rebbe who oversaw the torture of my grandparents while they were imprisoned."

"No shit?"

"No shit. I've made it my business to learn about this family. Levi's grandfather was a brutal man. Not just to opponents of the Test-Lit regime, but to anyone who questioned his extreme religious views. He inflicted his brutality on his own family, Levi's father included. In turn, no doubt to get his own father's approbation, Levi's father became a bully. He was instrumental in the formation of the Inquisition."

I got the picture. "And I suppose that Levi got the same treatment? Like father, like son?"

Fur nodded. "Levi was abused just as his father had been and followed the same path. That's not an apology for him. We all make our own decisions as to what to do with our lives."

I shook my head in disbelief. "Nothing is ever as simple as it looks, is it?"

"No. You might find the story of Levi's scar of interest. As a child, if Levi didn't toe the line with respect to following strict, ultraorthodox Test-Lit Judaic doctrine, his father beat it into him with a belt. The story goes that Levi once rebelled and tried to fight back. His father caught him across the face with the belt buckle, and he almost lost his eye."

I sighed. "I suppose that ought to make me feel sorry for him and to help me excuse his behavior, but it doesn't. As you said, 'We all make our own decisions.' I appreciate the information. Maybe it will help me understand the bastard a bit better."

It did explain the vision I had gotten from Levi when he was enraged: the buckle flying at my head. But again, understanding did not necessarily lead to forgiving.

**

I mulled over Fur's revelations. I recalled Rabbi Pearlman's statement about the evolution of religious belief on Cennesari, the reevaluation of tradition to fit modern circumstances. Evolution was an integral part of life. Tradition was a wonderful thing, but I knew religion had evolved on earth over several thousand years as societies changed. Even to the formation of new religions, Christianity and Islam, for example, that worshipped the same God but in different ways. The concept of God had changed. Many Jews had discarded as impossible the idea of God as a just or benevolent being after the European Holocaust. Yet, the Test-Lits took that to the opposite extreme, not accepting any change from the rules laid out thousands of years before. They were strangling Judaism on Dovid's World. Levi's family was a microcosm of that process. Generation after generation remained rooted in a single behavior, unwilling or unable to change.

I thought hard about my return to Dovid's World, how I might play a role in the overthrow of the Test-Lits. I never gave Fur a chance to say it, but I knew where his thoughts went. I now had four worlds indebted to me for the services we had rendered them:

Pronac, Dragonworld, Certis Prime, and, at least in part, Cennesari. Four possible allies against the theocracy that throttled my world and threatened my family. How to use this was a conundrum I had yet to solve.

CHAPTER 16

THE ANTIQUATED yellow whirlydrone dipped and rose like some giant moth evading a fly swatter. Our pilot, Grof, yelled, "We get lots of up and downdrafts out here. Don't worry."

Easier said than done. The condition of the machine did not add to my confidence. I leaned toward Petor Steckel, the head of Ulm's Agricultural Bureau, and asked, "Is this thing safe?"

"Um, certainly," he replied. "We are not a rich planet. We may not have all the modern equipment that we would like, but what we have we keep in good operating condition. We, um, must."

The next sudden descent left my stomach fifty meters higher than the drone and dropped my confidence an equal distance. We passed over cultivated fields and pastures dotted with Terran cattle before copses of red, blue, green, and purple alien vegetation appeared. These grew denser, and Grof brought down the whirlydrone in a clear area near the edge of the jungle.

As I jumped out, I knocked large flakes of paint off the fuselage. I cringed at the thought of the flight back. Fur ducked under the rotors, his face pale. True to form, Levi had stayed behind to gather information as he called it.

Steckel continued the orientation he had begun at the spaceport. "The ecosystems of Ulm are quite extraordinary. Jungle covers both the equatorial and temperate regions of the planet. Original exploration scans showed no, um, animal life: mammalian, amphibian, reptilian, avian, piscine, or even insectoid. The basis of existence for all life here is photosynthetic, and that is accomplished by a symbiotic microorganism we call algoids."

"So the plants themselves aren't photosynthetic?" Fur asked.

"No. The algoids perform their functions in cellular structures analogous to, um, mammalian mitochondria. The microorganisms draw their own sustenance from byproducts of the host's metabolism."

"Interesting biology," I said. "And no animals at all, huh?"

"There are mobile creatures, some quite large and, um, predatory. The hydra is one of those. It is a plant that eats other plants."

"And this is your problem?" Fur asked.

Steckel said, "Yes."

"That's fascinating," I said. "But if you have a problem with plants, why not call in an agronomist. I'm a veterinarian."

"Dr. Berger—"

"Cy, please."

"Well, yes. Cy. Call me Petor. Our husbandry people, veterinarians, and agronomists have attempted to figure out the problem, but we work with Terran animals and crops imported by the colonists. The native algoids are toxic to Terran life, so we cannot utilize them. We do not know how to deal with the Ulm flora. The *Galactic Circle Veterinary Service* has the reputation for solving problems with, um, unusual species."

He wasn't lying, but there was something unvoiced. That came through in his thoughts, his hesitations, and his furrowed brow.

"Petor, you're leaving something out. What are we getting into here?"

He seemed startled by my insight. The corners of his mouth turned down. "Perhaps the best thing to do is to go see the, um, problem. Then my answers will make more sense."

Steckel led us down a path into the jungle, an odd mixture of giant fern-like plants and towering broad-leafed trees, with dense undergrowth between them. The multicolored riot of growth was disorienting. Grof brought up the rear and carried a plasma rifle. Fur looked at Grof, then at me with raised eyebrows. I shrugged.

A plethora of bizarre, psychedelic flowers exuded heady, almost narcotic odors that made my head swim. I noticed a slight buzzing in my ears, and my stomach twinged. I attributed those symptoms to the perfumes. An elongated scarlet bell, shaped like a trumpet, swung slowly in a slight breeze. For the size of the flower and the lightness of the zephyr, I wondered at the movement, and I stepped closer to examine it.

Petor stopped me with a cry. "I wouldn't do that. The trumpet plant is a predator."

I turned to him. "You're shitting me."

"It is not big enough to seriously, um, harm a human, but its secretions are corrosive and can give you a bad burn if they get on your skin. And it can spit those several meters."

I took three steps back. "Hmm. Is poison typical of Ulmian plants, Petor?"

"Yes...for the predators."

"Great," I muttered.

Crevasses cut Fur's broad brow.

I followed Petor down a path through the thick undergrowth. I took care to stay in the center of the cleared area and cast my eyes from side to side, but saw no trumpet plants close enough to do damage. I wondered about some others, but Petor and Grof did not seem concerned, so I kept my anxieties under control. The buzzing and queasiness stayed with me, but I wrote them off to the pungent flora.

As Fur followed, he muttered something about unnatural plants in his guttural voice.

Steckel stopped at the edge of a less densely vegetated area and pointed. "A hydra."

I stared at the thing in the clearing in disbelief. It stood twice as tall as Fur, the top half composed of nine stalks that resembled Terran lamprey eels. The stalks terminated in gaping round maws ringed by razor-sharp teeth and corrugated grinders that no doubt made short work of the indigenous vegetation. A mental picture of what those teeth could do to a human did not comfort me. The necks and mouths formed a circle about the circumference of the two-meter wide trunk. With nine of them, the name hydra was appropriate.

More radially arranged, tentacle-like appendages poked out from the base. The creature was a mottled red-brown that shaded more toward red at the necks. The inside of the mouths was the color of human blood.

"Cute bastards, aren't they?" Grof said.

I shuddered and turned to Petor. "Are these things dangerous?"

"Not usually."

"What in hell is *that* supposed to mean?"

I stepped back to the edge of the clearing. So did Fur. The thing had done nothing but sit there, yet it raised an instinctive fear and loathing in me. Fur's frown was prodigious.

"It is quiescent now and no danger," Petor said.

"But some have attacked and eaten our livestock."

"How in hell could this thing catch a cow?" I demanded.

"Um, just before this stage."

"*This stage?*" My voice rose.

Before I could speak again, Fur's deep voice asked, "Just what is the problem here, Petor? What is it you haven't told us?"

Petor physically cringed as he answered. "You see, they are also, er, eating people."

"What?" Fur and I exclaimed simultaneously.

"They have taken to attacking and eating colonists. This has never happened before in our two hundred years of colonization. We don't know why."

Both Fur and I edged farther away from the beast. Who knew how fast it could move when it wanted to? I glanced behind me to be sure I had not encroached on some other Ulmian monster.

"Have you provoked them?" Fur asked.

Petor shook his head. "Not that we are aware. Their nervous system is not as complex as in animals. Responses to stimuli are quite slow in comparison, but still far faster than the responses of Terran plants or even the non-mobile Ulmian plants. They are hunters, but their normal prey is sessile vegetation. Their movement is slow. Slower than a large tortoise."

That was a relief. Even I could run faster than that.

"The first attack occurred two years ago. We thought the person stupidly got in front of a feeding hydra, and the beast could not distinguish between its normal diet and the unfortunate farmer. Then there were other incidents scattered over the next year. We puzzled over that, but still did not see it as a general pattern. Now, it appears that the hydras have taken to hunting people and animals, um, deliberately."

I stared at the hydra. Given Petor's history, my

mental picture of what it could do to a person was no longer so imaginary. I almost felt the teeth as they rended my flesh. First, they would eat off my arms, then my legs, like some giant gingerbread man. Fur's voice interrupted my descent into daymare. Ever practical, he asked, "How can these things hunt people if they are so slow?"

"They position themselves at doorways during the night. Then they, er, grab someone as they emerge in the morning. Once they have seized a person, unless help is immediate, it is too late. The mouths bite off anything they touch. Usually, um, several places at once."

Why this was so much worse to me than any other form of violent death, I didn't know, but it was.

"But as slow as they move, that's got to be disaster for the hydra as well as for the person," I said.

"True," Petor said. "The hydra is dispatched by rescuers, but the damage is done."

"Okay, so these things know enough to set up an ambush, but they can't connect actions and consequences, that they'll be killed if they do that."

Petor nodded. "There is more that I must tell you. I said that they are not dangerous at this stage..." He motioned with his head toward the creature in front of us.

"You did say something about stages," murmured Fur. His instinctive horror of these monsters seeped past my shields and added to my own queasiness.

"Yes. It is just *before* the stage you see here that the hydras are most mobile and, um, dangerous. Once that stage passes, the creatures become sessile and their headstalks become rigid. They stay paralyzed like this one and die. We have no idea why any of this has occurred. That is the reason why we asked you to come to Ulm."

I asked, "These 'stages' you mention, are they a normal phase for the hydras?"

"We did not start evaluating their behavior until after attacks began, but nothing like this was reported before."

I thought for a moment. "This one seems pretty dormant. You say it's paralyzed. Can I examine it without risking my ass?"

"Well, I should think so."

I took Petor's ringing endorsement of my safety into account and picked up a seedpod. I stopped and said, "Oops. I didn't ask whether this was dangerous or not." I waved the pod at Petor.

"Well, no, but ask before you touch anything else."

"Right." I flung it at the hydra and hit one of the necks. Not so much as a tremor.

I decided to approach Hell's representative on Ulm. I kept my sphincters clenched and moved to within an arm's length of the thing. So far, so good. I reached out and touched its trunk. Nothing. I felt up and down the side I could reach. It felt like any other plant stem I could recall, smooth with a slightly fuzzy surface, some sort of hairs for transpiration, I supposed. That brought to mind another question.

"Do these things move around all the time or do they set down roots?"

"When they are young, they begin as a rooted plant. When mature, they become mobile. They have never been observed, um, taking root after that. They just stop moving."

"How do they get water if they don't have roots?" Fur asked.

"We assume they get everything they need from their, um, prey."

Fur continued. "If the biochemistries between the Ulmian and Terran species are incompatible, how can they eat and utilize humans? Or cattle?"

"We surmise that the reason they go immobile and die is because we are toxic to them."

"So why in hell are they eating us?" Fur's voice rose as he spoke.

While I mulled over this information, I walked around the hydra. There did not appear to be any back or front. I reached up again and ran my hand over one neck. I could have sworn it twitched. My leap away from the hydra might have put me in contention for the interstellar Olympic broad jump—if they had a backwards category—and if I hadn't slammed into Fur's massive body.

"Did you see that?" I screeched. "It twitched. It's alive."

"Well, yes," Petor said. "I said it was dying, not dead. Decomposition is rapid when they die. They lose color within minutes. Ulmians have evolved to return to the ecosystems very, um, efficiently."

Fur muttered, "So, colorless, dead; colorful, alive. That helps."

There was no further activity from the hydra, so I walked up to it again. Fur accompanied me and ran his hands over the trunk and the necks.

"I feel no movement," he said.

"It's probably afraid of you," I answered.

He did not respond. He could reach quite a bit higher than I could and extended his hand almost to the mouths without eliciting any reaction from the beast. I wouldn't have done that.

"How long will it stay like this?" Fur asked.

"We are not sure. They have been observed in this state for as much as three days."

I pointed to a large branch that had fallen from a nearby tree. I looked at Petor. "That okay to use?"

He nodded.

I grabbed the branch, wound up, and whacked the hydra in the side of the trunk.

Fur let out a squawk. "What in blazes are you doing?"

Grof laughed.

I watched the hydra before I answered. It moved neither leaf nor stem. "I wanted to see if this thing would object."

I threw the branch at one of the heads. It bounced off the open mouth. Again, no reaction. I perceived no emotional aura from the hydra. This could be because it was too far-gone, or because it was a plant. My talent did not work with Terran plants.

"Good enough. Petor, if these things decompose so fast, we need a live one to start with if I'm going to do a dissection."

"Yes. I would think so."

"I want one in this stage, where it does not respond to external stimuli. Can you get one to our ship? Or can we transport His Stiffness here to that location? I need our instrumentation."

"We will have a, um, specimen for you tomorrow."

As we walked back to the whirlydrone, I shook my head to clear a strange fuzziness in my mind that accompanied the buzzing in my ears. The odors nauseated me. I would be glad to get away from these plants.

***

Except for some green mottling over its trunk, this hydra seemed identical to the first specimen I had seen. The beast had been whirlydroned to the spaceport and deposited near the *GCVS*. Onlookers, including spaceport personnel and a large contingent of military types, surrounded us. One character with lots of braid on his shoulders barked orders to everyone. I ignored him until he pushed his way to my side. The side *away* from the hydra, I noted.

"Are you going to tell us why these things have attacked our people?" he demanded.

I glanced at him. "Maybe."

He harrumphed. "What do you mean, maybe? We brought you here for that reason."

His arrogance nettled me. I turned to him. "Look, *Sir*. I came because you people asked me to assist. You haven't been able to learn anything useful, from what I gather. I'll do my best. I can't promise any more."

"But we are paying you—"

Steckel pushed his way through what had become a military cordon. "General? Petor Steckel." He held out his hand, which the general ignored. "We are pleased you were able to, um, attend. Dr. Berger is being most helpful. Why don't we allow him to do his work? Yes?"

It surprised me that the general allowed Steckel to lead him off. Maybe Steckel had more clout than his personality suggested.

Levi had toured the city on one of his usual espionage jaunts. This was his first chance to see a hydra, and it left his usually red face more of an ashen gray. "This cannot be a Godly creature," he muttered.

I ignored him and looked around. "Do I just start cutting on it? Does anyone know if it feels pain?"

"I know plants can react to outside stimuli, but they don't feel pain, do they?" Fur asked.

One bystander piped up, "My ma used to talk to plants and said they had feelings. Does that count?"

I rolled my eyes. "Thanks, I'll take that into consideration."

Even if it did feel pain under normal circumstances, the tree-branch whacking I had given the other one suggested it should not be an issue now. But a paralyzed human or animal might feel pain and not respond to it. Argh. Worrying about this had paralyzed me.

"Get that crane over here and let's lay that thing on the ground."

That done, Steckel returned. Alone. Fur and I approached the hydra. I had a knife and Fur wielded a small cutting laser. We both wore isolation suits but breathed ambient air. Based on Petor's description of the trumpet flower, I worried about the toxicity or corrosiveness of the thing's fluids. I made a cut across one of the base tentacles. The consistency was like a piece of very soft wood. Pink fluid oozed from the cut. It had a sharp, nutty, but not unpleasant odor. I dropped a piece in preservative fluid.

A deep vertical cut in the trunk with the laser yielded more ooze; lots of it—sort of like blood-tinged sap. I hoped that this particular specimen had eaten a cow, not a human. I shuddered.

The internal tissues were uniform except for some longitudinal tubes that looked too much like blood vessels for my comfort. I took more samples for preservation. Just below the necks, my efforts hit pay dirt.

"Look here. The tubes are larger." Even more sap exuded from the cut surfaces. "And there are solid white ones, too."

"I'll bet you anything that those tubes are a circulatory system," Fur said. "And maybe the solid white cords are the nervous system."

A cut in one of the necks revealed a hollow central tube about as large as my wrist.

"Aha. Feeding tube, I'll bet," I said. "There's got to be a stomach of some kind where these come together from all nine necks." I gave Fur pieces of esophagus to preserve.

"Shit," I cried. "The thing is starting to lose color. It's dying."

I cut samples from around the mouth and threw them to Fur. I cut out a couple of teeth, then stopped.

"What the hell is that?" I looked at a coiled black rope. Its surface was smooth and it glistened. I followed the coils with my eyes and saw that the rope disappeared down the throat into the neck. Even as I watched, the inky blackness paled to gray. Fast decomposition didn't even *begin* to describe this process.

"Good lord. I think it's a tongue," I said. "How can a plant have a tongue? And we haven't seen any organs of vision. How in hell can these things get around without eyes?"

Fur walked over to a mouth, reached in, and dragged out a tongue. I shuddered again. I would not have done that.

I heard a retching sound and when I turned, Levi had disappeared.

The front end of the tongue was as thick as two of Fur's fingers, and tapered to a point. He pulled it hand over hand until he had a three or four body lengths stretched out. The tongue's middle was as thick around as his wrist. Now, the whole carcass slumped like a grotesque mound of melting ice cream.

"I've wondered how they captured prey," he said.

"Prehensile tongue? What other surprises do these things have for us, Petor?" I demanded. "We were well within the thing's range where we stood yesterday."

He cleared his throat and looked away. "We have observed the hydras feeding, so we know about the, um, tongues. But I assure you they are no danger when they become, er, immobile."

"So *you* say." *Schmuck.* I turned back to the hydra. "You're a bundle of surprises, aren't you?"

I made a few more cuts where the necks swelled as they merged with the trunk. Delving downward, I hit an empty cavity, likely the stomach. Below that I hit a node of soft, white tissue with a cauliflower-like shape. The thin threads of white that looked like nerves spread out from there.

"I haven't found anything that looks like a circulatory pump," I said, "but this will be hydra soup in a few minutes." I looked at Petor. "What do we do with this mess?"

"It will be gone by morning. Just a bit of, um, staining on the ground."

I shook my head. "Every species we meet seems to get weirder. Let's get those samples to the lab and see what we can find out." I looked at Petor. "I'd like to have a chance to see the hydras in the wild. Normal and abnormal ones. Can we do that?"

Petor grimaced. "It might be, um, dangerous. But if you need to."

"Yeah, I need to. And you make sure that it's not dangerous...to *me*."

***

Levi and Fur looked over my shoulder as I examined the photomicroscopic image on the screen.

"The tubes *are* some sort of circulatory system. These cells surrounding the tubes are muscle, just like our own smooth muscle cells."

"But we still need our heart to pump blood," Levi said. "Don't we?"

"We do, but maybe these things don't. They probably have low fluid pressures in this vascular system and don't need a heart to get enough pressure to move the sap. Rooted plants suck up water from the soil. This gives pressure for the upward movement of fluid from roots to leaves, but that's not enough for tall plants or trees. The pores on leaves must be open to take in carbon dioxide for photosynthesis and they constantly lose water to the atmosphere. The water loss causes negative pressure that helps draw the water up from the roots.

"I think this is a combination of factors. The adult hydra may harvest its water from whatever it eats, but there still has to be circulation. We can see here that each hair on the surface contains tubes just below it. I'd say the hydra loses water to transpiration through the hairs, and this helps the fluid move through the body. If the muscle cells direct movement of fluid, they can use that to help them move the root tentacles. That gives them mobility. Also, the directed fluid movement is likely to make the movement of the necks and mouths possible."

"And the tongues?" asked Levi. His slight nausea as he spoke affected me, too, but he seemed interested despite his usual disdain for anything nonhuman. Maybe he didn't have to worry about souls in plants.

"There, I'm not so sure," I replied. "That movement would have to be rapid, from the descriptions of attacks on prey. I don't think fluid movement could account for that."

"That's where the nervous system would come in," Fur said. "They have to have some way to interact with their environment, to perceive the presence of prey, and to get them to move in that direction. The white mass and fibers look like nervous tissue. But we still have found nothing that resembles eyes."

"Yeah," I replied, "how do they perceive their environment? No eyes or ears rules out sight and sound. I suppose that taste is possible with that tongue, but that doesn't get them from place to place. Touch is possible. The root tentacles are in contact with the ground and other vegetation. But that still doesn't get them to prey that's a distance away."

"That leaves smell," Fur said. "I can see how the hydra could operate on scent. Prey plants might emit distinctive molecules that the hydra homes in on. Since the prey plant is rooted, it doesn't matter if it takes the hydra all day to cover a hundred meters. It will get there eventually and eat the emitter. That could even explain how it homes in on people if we are stationary all night."

"Yeah," I said, "we give off enough noxious fumes to attract a variety of predators."

Fur chuckled. "Nice image. Maybe you should lay off the garlic on Ulm?"

I did not grace him with an answer. "Let's see if we can find anything that resembles chemoreceptor cells."

After further examination, Fur cried, "That's it. These cells are similar to mammalian chemoreceptors. They're on the tongue and around the inside of the mouths. A white filament from each of them goes straight down and merges into the nerve bundles. That's the olfactory system."

I nodded. "But why do they go from a sluggish beast to a stage capable of relatively rapid movement? And then why do they become comatose and die?"

Fur added, "And why do they go from a creature that did not even recognize humans, to one that attacks and kills people?"

I hoped we could learn that without the need for first-hand experience.

***

We arranged for the field trip to observe the active hydras. Two men in uniform carrying laser rifles accompanied us. Grof was our pilot again. More paint flaked off the side of the whirlydrone as I climbed in. The rotors were dull, pitted metal, rather than the gleaming graphsteel of new blades. We crammed too many people into the old bird for my comfort.

We headed in a different direction than we had taken on our first trip. The cleared fields were not as extensive, and we flew over the jungle within minutes. When we landed, Petor briefed us.

"We have located a hydra that is in the, um, active stage of its problem. We will view that specimen first. Then we will go to an area that has a high concentration of normal adult hydras. It should not be difficult to find some that are in, um, feeding mode."

"Sounds like a good plan." I hoped that would be true. "Thanks for the help in this."

I glanced at the soldiers with their weapons. Tran was middle-aged and a bit paunchy. Worden looked fit and maybe ten years younger.

I asked, "Is there any real danger? After all, these things move like a snail. As long as we keep out of reach of the tongues, we'll be okay, right?"

Tran answered. "No doubt, Doctor, but we're charged with your safety and don't want to leave anything to chance. There are other predators on the planet, you know."

I looked at Petor with raised eyebrows. "Besides the spitting trumpet plants?"

"Well, yes," he replied. He would not meet my eyes. "There are two other mobile predators, but they are not, um, usually dangerous to humans."

"What the fuck does 'usually' mean?" My pulse pounded in my temple.

Fur muttered something under his breath. For all his lack of fear of animals and his ability to handle them, these alien plant forms spooked him maybe more than they did me.

Petor was silent for a few moments before he responded. "There is the creeper. It lives where the heavy undergrowth gives it a place to hide. It is mobile, but moves only to find a place where an ambush might be successful. Its vines can, um, whip out and grab a passing prey item."

"A 'passing prey item'," I mused. "And, pray tell, what might this prey be?"

Fur groaned.

Petor said, "Well, their favorite prey is the hydra."

"*The hydra*? You tell me there's a beast that preys on the *hydra*? Good Lord. Next you'll tell me that some creature preys on the creeper." I looked at his face. "No!"

"Well, um, yes. The other mobile predator does feed on the creeper."

Now, *I* groaned.

Petor continued. "But it is a smaller beast that gnaws away at the creeper vine, ultimately killing it."

"How does it avoid the creeper tentacles—or whatever you call them?" Fur asked.

"The untouchable—that is our name for it because it is very poisonous—is avoided by the creeper. Its touch is deadly to both plants and animals."

"And I presume 'animals' includes humans?" I asked.

He nodded.

"And you know this how?"

"Well, there have been a few unfortunate instances where an untouchable has come in contact with a domestic animal or a human. Those were, um, fatal."

I drew a deep breath before I spoke. "And the creepers? Have there been attacks by those, as well?"

"Yes, but those have been less, um, injurious. If the people have companions, they are able to cut the victim loose."

I followed up with the obvious question. "What about if they're alone?"

"Well, then they are in more difficulty. You see, the creeper has a toxin, too, and it paralyzes the prey. But if released, the paralysis wears off quickly."

"Great," I muttered. I looked at Fur, whose face was a shade I had never seen before: sort of avocado with peach overtones. My stomach felt like he looked.

I glanced back at Petor. "And tell me where we are headed. To the deep, thick jungle, where these creatures are most numerous and at home, right?"

Petor said nothing, nodded, and averted his gaze.

"Petor, you've been dribbling out these bits of information—critical bits to me, by the way—instead of giving us the whole story. I'm fed up. I'm ready to say screw you and your planet. We don't need this kind of shit."

Fur muttered, "Hear, hear."

Petor's face turned red as he cleared his throat and looked at me. "Dr. Berger, you have a valid complaint. I will be honest. I was ordered not to tell you about our, um, dangerous Ulmian flora for fear that you would not agree to help. That you would find it too hazardous a duty and leave."

"That sounds good to me," Fur said.

"I understand your feeling, Mr. Cohen. It seems that this approach has had just the opposite effect. Our withholding of information may be what drives you away. I apologize and promise to cooperate henceforth."

"Just who is it that gave you these instructions?" I asked.

"The military commander." He colored again. "We have a rather, er, authoritative military on our world."

As I took that in, Steckel and the soldiers headed into the jungle. Fur and I followed with Grof in the rear again. Fur's head swiveled like a weathervane as he surveyed the multicolored undergrowth.

Petor turned to me and Fur. "The, um, active hydra was seen a short distance from here. We should be able to find it with little difficulty."

He directed the soldiers to move off to the north. I must admit that I now viewed the jungle with different eyes than I had on our first trip to see the hydra. I flinched at every movement in the tangle of alien plants. Again, I felt a strange, almost subliminal rustling in my brain and buzzing in my ears. I shook my head and muttered, "These things have me so spooked I'm hearing things." With what I just learned, no surprise that my guts felt like a nest of snakes.

"What was that?" Fur asked.

"Nothing".

Petor stopped our escort at several points and had them laser plants he felt were too close to our path. None was a creeper or an untouchable, he'd assured us. I really did not want to know what they *were*.

After the third such incident, I asked, "Those rifles are fully charged, right?"

"Yes, Doctor. There's plenty of charge to handle whatever we might meet," Tran said.

Fur muttered, "Can I go home now?"

Our escort stopped suddenly, as did Petor, and I nearly ran him down. Fur almost obliterated me, in turn.

"There's a feeding hydra, Doctor." Worden pointed.

I peered over his shoulder at a hydra that was dismembering a bush covered with plump, glistening leaves.

Petor commented, "They prefer the plants that store the most water."

My acquaintance with immobile hydras did not prepare me for what I saw now. The hydra stood with four of its necks bent over the unfortunate shrub. A tongue shot out, wrapped around a branch, and ripped it off. It retracted, carrying the foliage to its mouth. The grinding sounds were gruesome. While that mouth chomped, another tongue fired out and repeated the process for a different mouth. The process continued like that. From what I could tell, the tongues seemed to trigger in sequence. After one latched onto a branch, another tongue discharged. I wondered if it ripped off a human limb, like the branches of the bush, or if it lifted the entire human to its mouths. I would see this during my sleeping hours for the rest of my life, even if it *was* only a plant that it dismembered.

I whispered, "It can't hear us, can it?"

Petor looked at me. "Well, no. Didn't you tell me that it has no, um organs of hearing?"

"Yeah, but...right."

Fur grinned at me. He enjoyed my discomfort. It took the attention away from his.

Petor cleared his throat. "This is an active hydra, and its feeding behavior is not typical. A normal hydra would be much more deliberate, much slower."

"How fast will they move when they are like this?" I asked.

"Perhaps as fast as a very slow human walk, much faster than their usual, um, ambulatory mode."

"Would it be dangerous to get it to move?"

Petor looked at the officers with a raised eyebrow.

Tran replied. "I don't think it will be a problem, Doctor. But how will we do that?"

In response, Fur stooped and picked up a rock the size of a grapefruit that sat by his right foot. He hefted it a couple of times and then hurled it at the hydra. His aim was excellent and he hit one of the mouths dead center.

The hydra froze. That showed the nervous system could respond instantaneously. It stood that way for about three or four minutes, and then the mouths resumed munching on their repast.

Fur found several more rocks in the undergrowth. He carefully examined their locale and questioned Petor as to whether there was anything hazardous within reach before he picked them up. He pitched three more sizeable stones, hitting the hydra in two necks and one head.

This time, the beast pulled all its heads upright and held them there, shivering in the slight breeze. Then it began to move. For a fearsome creature more than twice as big as a large man, the locomotion should have been comical, but it only added to its repugnance. The root tendrils writhed as they reached forward and grasped at the ground. Then another set would move forward as the first set moved back, pulling the trunk with them. I shuddered as I backed up. I wanted plenty of space between those tongues and me.

"Remember those larger hairs on the roots, Fur? I'll bet internal fluid pressure activates those to grab the ground and help it move."

In the time we watched, the hydra moved almost two meters away from us. It did not seem to recognize the source of its torment.

"I wonder," I mused. "There's not much wind, but we *are* downwind here. Let's move upwind and see if it responds."

"Is that a good idea?" Fur asked.

"We'll stay back so it can't reach us. But I'd like to test your chemoreception theory."

When we moved upwind, the response was almost immediate. The hydra stopped its movement, then, after a delay of a minute or so, it began to crawl in our direction. It definitely recognized human scent.

"Enough," Fur cried as he backed up, both hands in front of him as if to push the hydra away. "Point

proven. Let's get the hell out of here."
   We did.

CHAPTER 17

INVITED TO DINNER with the local dignitaries, Petor ushered Fur, Levi, and me into a large dining hall. A different host appropriated each of us and trundled us off to separate tables. Petor took my arm and waved me to a chair next to a well-endowed woman bedecked with a profusion of what had to be costume jewelry. If real, it might have equaled the gross national product of Ulm.

Petor looked at the woman and said, "My dear, this is Dr. Berger, whom I have told you about." He turned to me. "Doc—um, Cy, this is my wife, Belinka."

I made a brief bow. "Delighted to meet you, Belinka, if I may be so bold as to be familiar."

Her eyes crinkled and crows' feet tracked outward as she smiled. "Oooh, Doctor Berger, you are just as gallant as I imagined. I have so wanted to meet you since Petor told me of your arrival." She turned to her husband, her lips twisted in a sneer, and said, "Took you long enough, didn't it."

"I did my best, my, um, sweet." Petor's smile went rigid.

"Please sit, Doctor Berger," Belinka cooed. She leaned toward me, baring cleavage that rivaled an oceanic abyss. "Doctor—ooh, may I call you Cy?" She gave me no chance to respond. "Cy, I have a question for you. It's about Punkums."

I raised my eyebrows. "Punkums?"

"Oh, yes. You see, he has this problem."

"Punkums. Problem. I'm not quite sure that I—"

"Yes. He has been scooting. On all our rugs, you see."

I groaned inwardly. A server who deposited a warm roll before each of the diners interrupted us. Before she spoke again, Belinka buttered her roll, then nibbled daintily at the edges. When done, she smiled at me and said, "Punkums?"

"Ah, yes," I said. "Punkums. Scooting." Why is it that every pet owner that meets me thinks I desire nothing more than to talk about his or her pet and that free consultation goes with social events?

"This happens *all* the time, Doctor—ooh, I mean Cy."

The way she oozed out my name gave me the shivers. I wished I had never used *her* first name to begin with.

"It looks very uncomfortable. Is it uncomfortable, Cy? Punkums, I mean."

I shook my head to clear my thoughts. "Um, yes, it can be uncomfortable, Mrs. Steckel." Maybe I could get a bit of distance back.

"Oh, please let's not be formal. I just *love* when you call me Belinka."

I imagined that the look on her face might have been an attempt at coyness. I looked away. I tried my damnedest to block out her emotions with only partial success.

"Well, I just *knew* it had to be uncomfortable." She straightened her back and lifted her head, eyes narrowed. "Didn't I tell you that, Petor? I *told* you poor Punkums was in pain. Just swooning with pain."

Petor did not respond. He gazed around the room as

if looking for a path by which to escape. The delivery of a bowl of purple soup kept Petor in his place. Borscht, I wondered? I tasted mine. Definitely not borscht. The strange flavor was like nothing I recalled. I ate it, if for no other reason than to put our conversation on hold.

"Quite nice," I said to Petor to fill the silence that had descended as Belinka finished her soup.

Belinka sat back and sighed. "Now, back to Punkums. His pain must be excruciating, mustn't it?"

"Well, Mrs. Steckel, if Punkums is your dog, I don't think 'pain' is the right description. Discomfort would be more accurate."

"But *severe* discomfort." The corners of her full mouth turned down before she smiled again. "And, of *course*, Punkums is my little doggie. You are *so* perceptive, Cy. Punkums is my Antarean Ploofle. Don't you think they're the most adorable breed? So much better than those awful Cockriers and Shihtzhunds. Don't you agree?"

"Um, certainly. They're quite delightful." Disagreeing would accomplish nothing. In fact, mini-Ploofles were vile creatures with a nasty temperament. I hated the little bastards with a passion. A couple had used my hand for a chew toy in vet school.

"Wonderful," Belinka said. "Then you will have no problem if Petor brings you home to take care of Punkums." She glared at her husband. "Soon," she barked. Then she smiled at me again. "Our regular vet only checks Punkums once a year for his physical and that's surely not enough to relieve the poor dear. He always says it's his—" She shuddered theatrically, then whispered "—anal sacs."

The main course arrived, Ulmian prime rib, surrounded by unidentifiable mashed orange and wilted greens. Conversation ceased as everyone tucked into their meals. I stared at mine as my stomach squirmed. Belinka, and the soup, whatever it was, disagreed with me. When dessert came, I excused myself. "I apologize, but I am feeling a bit poorly tonight. I need to return to my quarters."

I had never even met the person who sat on the other side of me. When I glanced at him, he could not suppress a smile. I nodded and stood.

"Oh, do take care, Cy." Belinka's obsequious voice pulled my attention back to her. "Petor will bring you to take care of Punkums." She turned to her husband, voice dripping with acid, and said, "You *will* do that, Petor, won't you?"

"Yes, dear," was his toneless reply.

I made my way to the exit. I had gained some insight into Petor's diffident and indecisive personality.

***

Petor's face was a mask of indifference, but his thoughts were in turmoil, embarrassed over his wife's performance the previous evening. I could tell that he wanted nothing more than to retreat to his work and block the entire incident out of his mind. He radiated that thought so clearly that I almost glanced around me to see if others were aware.

He looked at the floor as he spoke. "Cy, I apologize for last evening—"

"Hey. No apologies necessary, Petor."

"Yes, they are. Belinka can be, er, intimidating. But I must ask you for one more thing."

I knew what was coming and cringed inwardly.

"If you would do me the great kindness of seeing to Punkums, I will be indebted to you."

I could not refuse. It was a small enough favor, and Petor was trying his best to help us now, so I followed him to his home.

Belinka answered the door. A huge smile cracked her face when she saw me. "Oooh, Cy. You're here for Punkums, aren't you?" She beamed at Petor, and said, "Thank you, dear." Those were the first civil words I had heard from her toward her husband.

She led us back to the kitchen where the Antarean Ploofle lay on a gold-embroidered cushion next to his food and water bowls. As I approached the dog, he growled softly, a warning I did not need. I kicked myself mentally. Why in hell didn't I think to bring Fur along?

"It's okay, Punkums," I spoke in my most soothing voice while I tried to calm the little beast with my empathic ability, but he got even nastier. Wouldn't you know he would be one of those where my talent had the opposite effect? I turned to Petor. "Could you please pick up Punkums and put him on the table?" I motioned with my head to the kitchen table.

Petor paled. "Um, I don't think..." He looked at his frowning wife.

Belinka shook her head. Her disdain was tangible. "Petor is afraid of Punkums. I'll hold my little sweet."

Oh, great. Just what I needed. Maybe I *should* beg off and get Fur. My procrastination allowed Belinka to sweep Punkums onto her lap.

"I'll just hold him here. Is that all right, Doctor?"

I stared at her. "This could be messy, you know. And it will stink. Maybe I should go and get my assistant?"

"You mean that huge bear of a man?" Belinka shook her head. "He would scare poor little Punkums to death. No. I'll hold him." She cradled the Ploofle to her ample bosom.

Despite my misgivings, I donned surgical gloves, and said, "Petor, would you please get some towels and put them under Punkums on Belinka's lap?"

Wielding large gauze pads to catch the odorous secretions, I went to insert my lubricated index finger in Punkums nethermost orifice. As soon as it met skin, the Ploofle yowled, spun, and turned my hand into a chew toy once again. Fortunately, he did not hold on, or I might have throttled him right then. I peeled off my glove and examined the four neat punctures. The crimson blood matched my state of mind. I applied pressure to my hand with a gauze sponge, then wiped the bites with alcohol and bandaged it.

I did not look at Belinka as she crooned to the little monster. "Oh, poor Punkums. Did the doctor scare you? That's okay little one. Mommy's right here."

I opened my bag and loaded a hypospray with a liberal dose of tranquilizer. I slapped it on Punkums' rump before Belinka could move.

"What are you doing?" she yelped.

I dropped my bedside manner. "What I should have done to begin with. I gave him a tranquilizer. Give him a minute or two and we'll finish up here. It won't hurt him, just put him to sleep for a few minutes."

She crooned over the dog until it collapsed in her arms. I took it, placed it on the table, and expressed the anal sacs. As I cleaned up, Belinka tapped me on the shoulder. I turned.

"I suppose I should have told you that the veterinarian always puts Punkums to sleep before he works on him."

"That might have been nice." I now knew why her vet wouldn't see Punkums more than once a year unless absolutely necessary. "Mrs. Steckel, I must be going now. Have a nice day."

"I *am* sorry for your injury, doctor. I apologize." She was actually contrite.

I looked at Petor and sensed his chagrin. "I can find

my own way out," I said.

***

The next morning, I arose early. Bleary-eyed and half-asleep, I stepped out of the bunkhouse I shared with Fur and several Ulmians. The sharp, nutty odor took me a moment to recognize, and that was almost my undoing. I halted in mid-stride and looked up. Right into the mouth of a hydra.

As I turned to leap for the door, I heard the tongue whistle past my head and felt it wrap around my arm. I grabbed onto the doorframe and screamed. I felt another tongue seize my leg. People boiled out of the bunkhouse, Fur in the lead. He grabbed me as the hydra's tongue ripped loose my grasp on the doorframe and hauled me toward its mouths. I faced away from the monster, but my mental image of those mouths made me lose control of my bladder. Even with Fur's strength, he was losing the battle, and I waited for agony as the teeth came together on my body.

Suddenly, the thing released me and Fur stumbled and fell backwards, with me on top of him.

"Oh, phew." were his first words. "You pissed yourself."

I rolled off him onto the ground. I looked up to see two men with heavy-duty lasers. The hydra was now just a trunk, its nine necks scattered on the ground around it. Pink sap oozed out of the severed neck stumps and down the sides, like some bizarre fountain. It had already started to lose its color. I looked away. I had seen enough of that process.

Fur reached down and helped me to my feet. I noticed a weight on my ankle, looked down, and saw a decomposing mass of black hydra tongue still attached. Bile rose to my throat and I bounced around like some berserk groundhopper, until I dislodged the disgusting mess. I retched, then I collapsed.

***

I stood at the rail of a corral that confined hundreds of cenoxen. At the opposite end of the corral was a chute, much like the one on the Sammaran crematorium during the EPD epidemic. The cenoxen, one by one, funneled into the chute. As they walked, they cried. Shed actual tears and sobbed.

"Help me. I am just as human as you," they wailed.

My stomach heaved and I puked down the front of my tunic. Not for the first time. The fresh acid-laden vomitus formed a new layer over the coagulated remains of previous episodes. Every cenox in the corral turned and stared at me. Their communal telepathic voice cut through my brain like a scalpel.

"We will die because of your failure. We are not cattle. You know this but have done nothing." They turned away as one, dismissing me and everything I stood for.

" No," I screamed. "No. I tried. I tried."

Then I felt a tap on my shoulder. I turned. Levi stood before me, holding one of the lasers used for euthanasia. Crimson light strobed from his twitching left eye, and his scar opened to reveal a mass of writhing hydra-like tendrils that latched onto my face. I could not move. He raised the laser to the side of my head.

"This is what you deserve, Berger," he sneered. "For all your failures."

I startled awake and cried, "No. It wasn't my fault..." I stopped as I realized it was a nightmare.

A nightmare. "That's all," I whispered to myself. "Just a nightmare." My eyes stared at a white painted ceiling. Sweat poured down my face.

Opposite my bed, pale blue curtains fluttered feebly in an open window that showed a darkening sky. I rolled over and screamed as waves of agony coursed through my body.

Voices outside the room preceded an influx of bodies, Fur in front.

My entire attention focused on my arm and ankle. It felt like a demented goblin troop was sharpening their teeth on me.

Fur grabbed me by my good shoulder and said, "Stay still. Movement only makes it worse."

"Makes *what* worse?" I gritted my teeth as I spoke.

Petor came to stand by my bedside. He would not meet my eyes. "It is the, um, secretion of the hydra. A digestive enzyme. On your skin, you know."

I didn't know. I didn't *want* to know.

Another voice broke in. It came from a tall, fair-haired Ulmian woman. "I'm Dr. Schaffler. The hydra's saliva, if we may call it that, is quite toxic. You are very fortunate that only one tongue contacted your skin on the ankle. Your sleeve protected your arm, to a degree, so it's not as bad. You were rescued quickly, otherwise, you might not have survived."

"Have I been out all day?" I asked.

Schaffler gave me a rueful smile. "You've been unconscious for three days."

Good lord. Three days? I tried to sit up. A thousand hot irons pierced my flesh. I held in a scream with difficulty.

Schaffler said, "Please remain as still as possible. I've ordered a powerful painkiller. My assistant is fetching it now."

"Did the toxin put me into a coma?" That would be some powerful stuff.

"No," replied the doctor. "I had you kept under. The

pain would have been far too severe for you to tolerate."

"You mean worse that it is now?" I asked, incredulous.

"I'm afraid so. We have had enough experience with attacks that we know how best to handle those who survive."

I mulled over *that* thought as I lay immobile. Fur gave me a few words of encouragement and, surprise, surprise, Levi came in. He got a perplexed look from the doctor as he began to rock back and forth in prayer—in Hebrew, of course. I wondered if he prayed for my recovery.

Schaffler gave me a shot in my good arm and I faded from consciousness.

***

A week passed before I recovered enough to be mobile. Even then, it hurt to walk. My arm blistered and peeled like a bad sunburn, but the surface tissues of my ankle had sloughed. It looked like a case of gangrene. Even Levi was sympathetic. At least he did not make his usual snide comments about my family's safety. Thank God for little things.

Worse news, the hydras had become more active; the number of attacks had increased in the time since my encounter. Whatever lay behind the behavioral change affected more and more of the creatures. The communities near hydra territory had gone into panic mode. People were evacuating, even though the likelihood of attack was quite small for any individual. It was more the horror of the phenomenon. I could relate to that. Some vigilante groups penetrated the jungle and took vengeance on any hydras they found, but this did little to resolve the problem.

Fur, Petor, and I racked our brains for reasons to explain the activity of the hydras, without success. We sat over fresh, real coffee—the tropical climate here grew wonderful beans—and strategized.

"The way this is spreading, it seems like an epidemic," I said.

"But we haven't found anything in the hydras that even resembles an infectious organism," Fur said. "Not even like the weird enzyme bug on Pronac."

Petor's eyebrows rose in question, so I related the story of the Pronacian epidemic.

"You have had rather unique experiences, to say the least."

I grimaced. "I guess 'unique' might describe them. But there has to be something that's spreading, moving from one hydra to another." A piece of the puzzle was missing. "Are there areas where *no* hydras show the disorder?" I asked Petor.

"Yes. On Astrasia—that is the southern continent—this does not seem to be a, um, problem."

I thought for a moment. "Can we take our ship down there?"

"I think so. I will get the necessary military clearances for you."

"Good. Let's do it. But that raises another question. What's with the military? Who in hell are you fighting or even worried about here? You seem to have a peaceful society...except for the hydras."

"Ah. That goes back a bit in our history. Our planet was settled relatively recently by immigrants from the New Prussian worlds. There were groups of settlers from Rhineland, Bavaria, and Holstein who, um, did not quite agree how to divide the land and how to govern it. This led to a period of, er, civil warfare. The Bavarians were victorious and consolidated Ulm to the system we have now. The military retained the governmental authority."

I shrugged mentally. Humans managed to foul their nests no matter where they built them.

***

Pctor came with us, and Ruthie landed the *GCVS* at a tiny jungle outpost a couple of thousand kilometers south of our first location. Fascinated by our AI, he had a long conversation with her about the meaning of intelligence during the flight. "Your technology is rather, um, spectacular, Cy. I did not know something like your AI existed."

"Yeah. I suppose spectacular is one way to describe it."

"I should be granted a higher status than 'it,' Cy," Ruthie complained.

"Just take care of the ship," I muttered, as we exited via the ramp. The anthropomorphizing of Ruthie made me distinctly uncomfortable. I made a mental note to ratchet down her higher functions a notch.

The jungle did not look much different to me, and Petor confirmed that the ecology was consistent on all the continents.

Fur speculated, "The continents must have drifted apart fairly late in the evolution of life on the planet for this to be the case."

I wondered at that. There should have been *some* variation.

We toured the jungle and observed a dozen hydras at play. None of them exhibited any of the signs we had seen in their northern counterparts. That subliminal buzz and queasiness I felt whenever I was in the jungle was present here, too. I had the nagging feeling that I was on the verge of understanding something, but *what* I couldn't fathom, so I shoved it to the back of my mind.

"Petor," I asked, "can we sample a few of these guys?" I added, "We would have to kill them first, of course." My heart rate shot up and I started to sweat when I thought about getting close to one of the things again.

"We can have them, um, dispatched if you desire."

"Yeah. I desire."

He had the courtesy to turn a bit red. Although he had apologized multiple times over the past week for underestimating the dangers of dealing with the hydras, I was not about to let him off the hook.

We 'dispatched' four of the beasts: two young ones that were sedentary, and two adults that were mobile. I took tissue and fluid samples so that we could compare them with their 'sick' analogues. Then we headed back north.

***

"Damn it. There's not a thing that's different between the southern and northern hydras that we can find."

Fur nodded and pursed his lips. "Not that could explain why the ones around here have changed behavior. But there has to be *something* that's caused it."

I shook my head. "I'm still bugged about the incredible similarity between the hydras and the entire flora on the two continents. The data on continental drift show it's been at least fifty million years since the two landmasses split. There ought to be *some* evolutionary variability."

"I wonder," Fur said, his brow creased. "These are plants, after all. Maybe they didn't evolve on the two continents. Maybe they evolved on one and then spread to the other."

"Are you thinking airborne seeds?"

He raised his eyebrows and shrugged. "That, or carried by some other vector. We haven't seen anything like a bird analog, though. I wonder what *might* move between continents. Let's ask Petor."

***

Petor introduced us to Anna Zeller, a middle-aged botanist with curly, graying hair. Tall and slender, she had a brusque demeanor, but answered our questions with the thoroughness that bespoke her knowledge of her subject. She reminded me a bit of an older Roxanne, and I recalled I was overdue for a hyperwave message. I sighed inwardly.

I pulled my thoughts back to Zeller when she answered our query about the jungle.

"You are perceptive," she said. "I surmise that the floras of both continents are similar because they have emigrated from one to the other relatively recently. It is not certain which continent the hydras and the other flora originally evolved on and to which they emigrated. The ecosystems are now almost identical."

"Do you have any idea of just *how* this migration took place?" I asked.

"That is more difficult," Zeller answered. "The jungles were established in both places when humans arrived." She paused. I sensed suspicion. She was not quite sure whether to trust us, and I wondered why. "I'll give you my own speculations, but they are not accepted by the Ulmian bureaucracy."

This might be interesting.

"From the early descriptions of the planet, I believe that the jungle flora was better developed on the southern continent. There, the forests were unbroken from one coast to the other. Here, there were open areas. Since the jungle growth is rather rapid, I think that the flora moved north, rather than evolving here. Humans took over the open areas and have kept the jungle at bay. If we were not here, I think the jungle would fill in what was open."

"But that still does not answer how it might have gotten here?" Fur prompted.

"That's even more speculative," she said. "There are no flying creatures, although many plants do have seeds and spores that are airborne."

"But not the hydras and other predators?" Fur again.

"No. To get the entire ecosystem reproduced as it is, something momentous must have occurred. I think..." She stopped and her expression froze.

I read her misgiving. "Excuse me, Doctor Zeller. Is there a problem with telling us?" I recalled Steckel's military-enforced reticence. "We don't mean to put you on the spot."

"No. That's fine." She straightened her back and looked into my eyes. "I believe that the jungle is a single entity, a group mind with a basic sentience."

"It's *what*?" I could not believe what she said.

Zeller's face darkened. "Your reaction is much like all the others." She stood. "If I have answered your questions, I'll be going now."

Fur jumped up and towered over the fragile-looking woman. "Please, don't. I'm sure Dr. Berger was just startled. As I was. It's not that we don't believe you."

I followed suit. "I'm sorry. Please, sit down. We want to hear what else you have to say."

Mollified, she sat and continued, but her thoughts remained defensive, with a touch of bitterness. "I admit that my theories aren't believed or considered important. This is a very insular and pragmatic world. If things work, there is little interest other than to keep them working. Science, other than what applies to agriculture and the engineering necessary to our basic lives, or what applies to military matters, is a luxury. My work does not contribute to the *needs* of our society.

"But I believe that there is a very basic, instinctual sentience that underlies the flora of Ulm. It's not at a level that we can communicate with it, at least for now. I...I have tried. I haven't told others of this. They already think me strange. This would only make it worse."

I sensed her plea to keep this quiet. There was a long silence as I processed her words. Then I blurted, "My God. That's it."

Both Fur and Zeller looked at me as if I had nine heads.

"Dr. Zeller, what you just said makes all the sense in the world. You've leveled with us. I'm going to return that favor."

I told her about my empathic ability.

"So you aren't crazy," I finished up. "I didn't know what I was hearing and feeling when I was in the jungle so I just shoved it aside, attributing it to my nervousness about the weird predators or the narcotic perfumes. But I was hearing the jungle—its thoughts. And feeling its emotions, if I can call them that. The consciousness is incredibly diffuse, but it's there. I never had contact with plants before, and it was nothing like what I receive from animals."

Zeller's eyes were wide. "You're serious, aren't you?"

I nodded.

Fur grinned. "He's serious, all right."

She took a deep breath. "I think that the colonization of this northern continent was a deliberate and conscious act. That the entity knew it had filled the available ecosystem on Astrasia and looked to continue its spread north."

"Amazing," Fur said.

I felt the tension drain out of her.

"I never had incontrovertible proof of this theory," she said. "Just suggestions of a preexisting flora in a few places. Others wrote that off."

Fur asked, "But how did the...thing, whatever you want to call it, move itself?"

She stared at him and said, "I believe it grew rafts."

It grew rafts? I had trouble getting my mind around that. "A sentient ecosystem, capable of a decision to spread to another landmass. Amazing is right."

"Dr. Zeller, you said your evidence is not conclusive," Fur said, "and the rest of the Ulmians aren't inclined to believe you."

"But you have given me hope that I can prove this." Her voice projected that hope.

Fur turned to me. "Are you willing to go out on a limb based on your talent, Cy? Remember what happened on Cennesari. I don't think even Levi truly believes you have such power. He dismisses your cenoxen claims as prevarication."

"I'm not sure how far to take this." My heart still ached over the cenoxen. "I certainly didn't receive anything that was conscious thought from the jungle, nothing that communicated with me. But there is definitely something there." I shook my head in frustration. "Anyway, I don't see how this applies to the main problem of the hydras, which is confined to this continent. The behavior seems to be spreading, which suggests something infectious, but we've come up with zip."

Fur stood and stared out the window. Neither Zeller nor I interrupted his thought train. I, too, puzzled over what our next step might be.

Fur whipped around, his mouth open in an O.

"What?" I said. His excitement was contagious.

He leaned toward Zeller and me. "Try this on. Human settlements and agriculture are only significant on this continent. Might the entity be responding to specific human activities?"

I sat back, perplexed. "What do you mean? They said they were doing nothing different to trigger this." I turned to Zeller. "Right?"

She nodded.

"We saw that the human intrusions on the southern continent were small outposts," Fur said. "Here, with each passing year, the settlers clear more and more jungle for agriculture and towns. Does the jungle sense this? Could it be responding with its only defense mechanism?"

Now my mouth hung open. "You think?"

"It makes sense. Terran plants have defense mechanisms, from toxic chemicals, to mechanical deterrents like thorns, to mimicry and camouflage. Those developed in an evolutionary fashion for each plant. And it's not just evolutionary. Even individual plants can respond to being munched on by insects and produce deterrent chemicals. Why would this jungle not have *its* responses to threats, especially if it has some degree of sentience?"

"I never thought about such a reason," Zeller said.

"But why now?" I asked. "Why has it taken hundreds of years to respond? Why didn't it happen soon after humans got here and started their settlements?"

"What has changed that wasn't the case even twenty years ago," Fur asked.

"I can evaluate changes that relate directly to the jungle," Zeller replied. "Changes in agricultural practices and engineering would be in the records."

"Let's follow up on that," I said.

***

Zeller, Fur, and I pored over the data sheets we had collected. A map of the northern continent laid out all the settlements, and industrial and agricultural areas. A second map pinpointed all known instances of hydra attacks on humans. These, of course, clustered around human-occupied regions.

Zeller said, "Something is missing."

I looked at her. "What do you mean?"

"We don't know whether there are deranged hydras *away* from the human-occupied regions. If this is specific aggression directed at humans, rather than random attacks, there shouldn't be affected hydras out in the wilderness, like there weren't any on Astrasia."

"Good point," Fur said. "The other thing we don't know is whether there have been instances of human-directed aggression from the rest of the floral community. Have any of the other dangerous plants responded in a similar manner?"

I looked at Zeller. "That would give credence to your contention that this is a coordinated, intelligent entity, wouldn't it?"

"Perhaps." Her caution was perceptible. I could sense her fear of ridicule, but when we looked at the map overlays on the computer screen, she became excited. "Look. There's no question. All the activity is around the agricultural sections. Surveys have shown no aberrant hydra activity away from those. Furthermore, there *have* been increased attacks on humans from other plants. These are far fewer than the hydras and have been ignored in the uproar over the bigger creatures. They are also clustered around human agricultural areas, but not around any technical facilities without agriculture."

Zeller looked at me. "With this information, I'm willing to stick my neck out and go public. At the least, I think that it's hard to refute that this is a defense mechanism of the jungle. It still does not explain why it has taken this long for the entity to respond, or what we can do to stop the attacks, short of destroying the entire jungle and creating a wasteland."

"Let's lay this out to the community and then we can brainstorm about the next step," I said.

"Agreed. And thank you," Zeller added. Then she smiled. "I don't think we need to invoke our attempts at communication with the jungle. To just prove a coordinated effort will be enough."

I nodded, relieved.

***

Military brass, politicians, and people representing scientific, medical, agricultural, and industrial interests filled the room large room. Fur and I sat on a stage and Zeller stood behind a podium and explained our theory. The responses ranged from incredulous to ecstatic. Several scientific types jabbered about the possibility that another intelligence inhabited their planet; others were resistant to the concept. A couple of beefy types in coveralls demanded that the military destroy the jungle to protect their farms and families. The room quieted when a military official with lots of stars on his hat stepped to the podium.

"Atten-*shun*." His voice boomed over the loudspeakers. His rather expansive abdomen made it difficult for him to bend over the microphone. In frustration, he wrenched it off its stand. "These discoveries put a new light on what has occurred. We can't decide what to do until we have made a full study, looked at strategic options, and determined the necessary course of action. Be assured you that your government will consider the good of all of Ulm. If you have concerns, please direct them to Councilman Richter here in Stannispoort. The High Command will issue a directive immediately on completion of its deliberations. Thank you."

He stood down from the podium and swept out of the room, flanked by a couple of soldiers bearing military lasers. I looked at Fur and shrugged. That performance gave me as much comfort as crawling into bed with a hydra.

Petor sidled over to me afterwards and said, "That is my wife's, um, father."

Ah. A bit more of Petor's background revealed. That's why the brass at the hydra necropsy had listened to him.

Fur and I strolled back to our quarters and talked.

"I'm not encouraged by the generalissimo in there. His kind of mentality is more likely to blast opposition than try to solve the problem." I saw too many similarities with the Test-Lit government.

"Can't argue with you on that," Fur said. "I hope there's someone in those 'deliberations' that recognizes the significance of the sentience in the jungle. There will be more than those few farmers who will want a 'Final Solution.'"

I didn't respond. No Jew anywhere in the galaxy would ever forget the twentieth century's Nazi Germany and the Final Solution, its plan for the systematic genocide of our people that ended in the Holocaust. The Hunter episode on Cennesari had sensitized me to that even more than usual.

I was silent through dinner, despite Fur's attempts to draw me out, and he gave up. I could not allow any government to destroy a sentient species, plant or otherwise. We had to do *something*.

***

A week later, we had accomplished nothing. We had gone over our data again and again, but could not see how to connect the attacks, other than our theory that the jungle protected itself.

The sentiment for wiping the continent clean of the native flora was overwhelming. Some pled for a lesser option, creation of a "kill zone" of up to fifty kilometers around every settlement. While not genocide *per se*, it was still murder of millions of the individuals that made up the whole of Ulm's native intelligence.

Fur and I argued in support of Dr. Zeller and a bloc of Ulmians who wanted to spare the Ulmian sentience. To my great surprise, we had an unexpected ally: Belinka Steckel. Perhaps she felt obligated to me in some way for the debacle with Punkums, but she interceded and pressured her father. I imagined the form that pressure might take and would not want to be the general. This helped, and they adopted a "kill zone" approach to begin with. Broader destruction was still under consideration, but tabled for now.

Acid rose to my throat as I watched military drones sweep over the jungle around the settlement we inhabited. A red cloud of defoliant resembling a blood bath submerged the spectacular colors of the foliage. I turned away, determined that I would not give up.

***

Fur was ready for bed when I burst into his quarters. We had opted to sleep in the *GCVS* after my hydra incident.

"Get dressed."

"What for?"

"Come on. Be quick."

Fur pulled on clothing and shoes and followed me.

"The tissue samples, I want you to look at them."

"We've been over those data a dozen times. There's nothing that explains the change in the hydras. Everything looks the same in all of them."

"Not quite." I waved my hand. "Just wait."

Fur shrugged and gave me a look that promised revenge if I had ruined his sleep for nothing.

In the lab I said, "Look at the trace mineral readouts for the different groups of hydras."

He fixed me with a steely glare, on the verge of losing his temper. "We've done this already."

"Humor me. Just look."

He did. "So? It's the same in all the groups."

"No. It's not."

"Shit. Do you mean the fact that the hydras here on the northern continent are marginally lower in some of the trace elements? That is *not* statistically significant. We agreed on that already. What's wrong with you?"

"Think about it. I agree it's not statistically significant, but let's forget statistics and think *biologically* significant. What do crops do when grown on the same fields repeatedly? They deplete the soil of minerals and nutrients. Farmers replace the nutrients, the carbon and nitrogen. Sometimes they worry about the trace minerals, but often they don't. Micronutrients like boron, molybdenum, cobalt, and nickel are just as critical as carbon and nitrogen."

"We looked at those. There's just not enough difference there to be important." He rubbed his hands across his eyes. "Is this going anywhere new? I'm exhausted."

"Yeah, I'm going somewhere new. Look at this." I handed him a new sheet.

His eyes flew open. His fatigue melted away.

"Good lord. How did you—?"

"I don't know how we missed this for so long. I couldn't get these trace elements out of my mind, even though we agreed there was no difference. Then it hit me that some elements would be below detection levels of our instruments in *all* of the hydras, normal and abnormal."

"So, if there were differences, we would never see them," he continued.

"Right. But if I used radioactive tracers, we should be able to detect differences, no matter how small." I held out my open hand toward the data sheet.

***

I explained to a group of scientists, including Anna Zeller. She beamed with my news.

"The trace elements that are depleted by farming have affected the health of the plants in the surrounding jungle. Although we saw negligible differences between the hydras here and on Astrasia, we couldn't pick up trace amounts of elements like the rare earths cerium and lanthanum. They're below the detection limit of our equipment. But they're important even to Terran plant growth."

"Then how did you evaluate that?" a short, balding agronomist asked.

"You know that many elements have a tiny fraction that is radioactive. Carbon is a well-known example. We use the amount of radioactive carbon to date archeological specimens. The amount of decay tells us how long it has been since integration of the chemical into the organism. I used the same concept. Both cerium and lanthanum have radioactive isotopes, so I looked for those. We can detect minute amounts that way. And we found what you see."

"So there's a difference in cerium and lanthanum levels in the northern and southern hydras. So what?" This came from a thin crops specialist. "I can't see how this would cause the beasts to attack people and animals. Even if there is rudimentary intelligence, and I wonder about that." He sent a belligerent glance toward Zeller. "It wouldn't be enough to direct those things to attack specific targets."

I responded without rancor to his contentiousness. "I agree with you that any normal plant defense mechanism would be pretty diffuse, but there's a very good reason for the attacks on humans and our animals. Our tissues contain the very trace elements depleted in the jungle, including the rare earths like cerium and lanthanum. Our studies of the hydras show that they have very sensitive chemoreceptors. I think the attacks are because the hydras sense that they can get the needed elements from mammalian tissues. That also explains why the hydras become sessile and die after consuming mammalian tissue. It has nothing to do with toxicity of mammalian tissues to them. The hydras die and decompose on a signal from the jungle, so the critical elements get back into the soil."

This pronouncement caused quite a stir.

A man in back called out, "Why did it take so long for this to happen? We've been farming here for hundreds of years."

Zeller answered. "Remember we are dealing with plants here, not animals. My guess is that the jungle perceived this for decades before it could conceive and implement a plan. Then, even that might take decades to bring about. The jungle may be sentient, but its mind is not centralized. It is likely distributed throughout the entire ecology."

I added, "More important, if the response of the jungle *is* to a depletion of such elements in the soil, we can reverse that. By being careful to replenish farmlands, you can live in peace with your neighbors." I sent a lidded glare around the table. "This creature has as much right to life as you do. Maybe more on *this* planet."

Zeller broke in before I could antagonize my audience any more. I tended to be good at that.

"Dr. Berger, Mr. Cohen, what you have done is nothing short of amazing, and we can't thank you enough. For now, what we need to do is test your hypothesis. That shouldn't be difficult. We can seed a trial area as you suggest. The response of the hydras and other plants should give us our answer."

***

Our hypothesis proved correct. When trace elements, particularly the rare earths cerium, lanthanum, and praseodymium, were added back to the farmlands bordering the jungle, the hydras dropped back to their normal behavior, and the attacks stopped. I wished there were some way to communicate with the jungle entity, but maybe that would come with time. I knew that Anna Zeller would never give up on that. She now stood at the top of the scientific hierarchy on Ulm. She deserved it. Without her insights, we would never have solved the mystery of the hydras.

I took the time to get a message off to Roxanne and my folks, but I started to worry a bit since I had not heard from mom and dad for a while. That concern stuck with me as we prepared to depart Ulm.

We were the guests-of-honor at a huge celebration. I was annoyed no small amount that Levi thrust himself into the midst of the congratulatory events. He had spent the majority of his time holed up in *GCVS*, afraid of the hydras and anything that remotely resembled a daisy. I made a mental note to present him with a Venus flytrap at some time in the future.

Other than that, he had gone off and done his spy thing. There were no Jews to harass on Ulm, but he did his best with the military. Part way through the evening, I noticed that he was face-to-face with one of the generals. Both were red-faced and animated. I moved over to where I saw Steckel and pulled him aside.

I motioned to Levi and the general. "What in hell is going on over there?"

He laughed. "Your Mr. Schvartz is quite a, um, character. I have trouble believing that he is a veterinary assistant."

I had to laugh, myself. "Pretty obvious, eh? He's more of a watchdog, sicced on us by our government at home." I gave Steckel a short version of Dovid's World and its problems.

Steckel nodded. "His intrusions into military matters here on Ulm have not been received well. His bull-in-a-china shop approach to military intelligence has rather, um, angered a number of the Ulm brass."

So be it, I thought. While I had no love for either side in that conflict, such a well-developed military might be useful in opposing the Test-Lits. Perhaps a few words with Petor and Belinka might be in order.

I found a chair to rest my bad leg, and listened to overblown politicians and military types praise Zeller and the *GCVS* crew. I reflected I would be happier if one of their scientists would come up with an antihistamine that worked against the allergic effects of the damn hydra toxin as I scratched at the ankle I had propped on my knee.

CHAPTER 18

Our FINAL SCHEDULED contract planet, a small agricultural world where we supplied routine veterinary services, was a welcome departure from our previous experiences. Nothing weird, thank God. I did get a message from Roxanne that brightened the stop even further, but the lack of contact from my parents continued to worry me. Approaching Levi about that would not help much; I did not trust him to give me an honest answer. I broached the subject with Fur. It bothered him, too, but he had no better suggestion than to give it some time.

Roxanne's missive was delightful, as usual:

Hello Cy,

Before I get your messages, I believe that there can't be anything that could top the experiences you have already told me about. Then you bowl me over with new ones. First, I think it is just fantastic that you were able to resolve the Hunter epidemic. Those big cats sound like such a wonderful species. The galaxy would have been much poorer without them. The attempted genocide is beyond appalling. It makes me sick just to think about it. I understand how cenoxen issue was just the opposite. The thought of another nearly sentient species used as food animals is even more dreadful. I suppose I can understand the stance of the Cennesarians to deny your claim. They don't have any proof other than your empathic ability, which you have no way to document, so they cannot see the reality themselves. And such an admission could devastate their economy. My point is that you did everything you could and you should not beat yourself up over what you can't control. You made a huge difference on that planet. Take away the good and don't dwell on the bad. I wish I were there to support you.

How many nights had the recurring nightmare about the cenoxen destroyed my sleep? I imagined Roxanne in bed with me, holding me when I awoke sweating and trembling. Would her support banish that failure? No, nothing could do that, but her arms and her care would go a long way toward lessening the pain. I pulled myself back to her face and her words:

Then, you move on to Ulm and prevent an even bigger genocide of a totally unique species: A sentient jungle. I truly hope that success has lifted your spirits. It should. I have to admit, though, that I would much rather meet a Hunter than a Hydra. While the sentience of the jungle was worth saving, your description of the Hydra gave me the shivers. I'm can't begin to tell you how glad I am you are recovered. The thought of losing you before I ever had you... Oops. That sounds rather presumptuous, doesn't it. But I've already stuck my foot in my mouth, so... It is hard to know how you feel about someone when you have spent so little time together, as we have. But I feel I have come to know you through your messages. Not even so much as what you say, but as what you do, what you have accomplished. That shows me your character, and it is a character that I want to know much better. And closer. Okay, I think I have said enough. I'm going to sign off before I dig this hole any deeper, but please do come home soon. I miss you.

Love, Roxanne
Love? *Love?* My chest felt like it would expand outward and burst. Tears flooded my eyes and spilled into small rivers that cut courses down my cheeks. I sat for many minutes staring at the blank holoscreen. I was afraid to rerun the message, afraid that I had heard it wrong. That somehow the ending would have changed while I waited. I wiped my eyes and decided I would not watch the message again until I was safe in my own quarters. Why that would make a difference, I didn't know, but I wanted that privacy. I wanted to scream out my own love for Roxanne across the galaxy. Surely, she could hear me. I shook my head at myself, rose, and left the hyperwave messaging booth smiling.

***

We received a request from the natives of the planet Lupus IV before we left for home. Levi was beyond himself when I told him we would respond.

"No. No, no, no. We will not go anywhere else. You agreed we would return to Dovid's World after this one. Berger, this is the last straw. Do I need to tell you—?"

"Tell me what? How you'll torture my parents? How you'll ruin my life? How you and your cronies will continue to destroy what was once the hope of a new beginning for our people? What else can you do besides destruction? That's what *you* live for."

He stood with his mouth open, speechless, black eyes wide.

"I have another opportunity to *help* someone. To make a *positive* difference in the lives of other beings. I won't turn away. I want to help *build* better lives, not destroy them."

Levi moved toward me, fists clenched, murder in

his soul. The wave of hate nearly dropped me to my knees, but I readied myself for a fight.

Before that could happen, Fur stepped between us. "I think that you two need to cool it. Violence is not going to solve anything. Reb Levi, perhaps you might retire to your cabin for now? That will help."

Levi looked up at the stern visage of the big man and retreated. After that, he refused to speak with me until we reached the Lupan solar system, and had little to say to Fur, either. He finally relented, and had been oddly congenial since we landed. That was uncharacteristic, and I wondered what it meant. I still avoided broaching the subject of my parents, afraid of what I might learn.

***

Ghosts, ghouls, demons, and zombies had no basis in reality. Vampires were fictional, though they had roots in the bloodsucking vampire bats of the Terran tropics. Shape-shifters, like werewolves, were another story.

Fireworks of supernatural dread burst behind my optic nerves as I gazed at the welcoming committee on Lupus IV. The Lupans—our name for a species that called themselves "the People"—were the only known race of shape-shifters. They could change from their humanoid form into sleek, four-legged beasts that resembled huge Terran wolves, hence the name. Bright yellow eyes, unclothed fur-covered bodies, and the exuberant fur mane over the heads and necks of their bipedal humanoid forms were enough to give me the willies as I watched them approach the ship on the viewscreen. We had little information on the Lupans. The one exobiologist who spent time on the planet left in a state of post-traumatic shock. His reports were almost useless. Their world was earth-like in atmosphere, climate, and gravity. So many of the worlds we had visited with alien sentient species were similar in that regard, that I had to wonder if those factors were critical in the evolution of DNA-based life.

As Fur and I moved toward the airlock and ramp, Levi said, "I will remain here. No need for all of us to meet these...things." His hands trembled as he gazed at the natives in the viewscreen. You did not need to be an empath to feel his angst.

Face to face, I took note of three things: First, the Lupans' manes varied considerably. Colors ranged from almost black to reddish blonde. Styles included fluffy, smooth, wavy, kinky, and even braided, and almost all were neatly coiffed. Second, they were all very obviously male. Third, a somewhat disheveled, mousy-colored Lupan twitched and scraped at his neck, a movement that was reminiscent of a dog scratching with its hind leg. He would then dart a glance at the others, as if to see if they had noticed. The braided Lupan snarled at the scratcher, baring impressive canines. Scratch cowered and retreated several body lengths behind the others.

Curious. What did that mean?

I addressed Braid. "I'm Captain Cy Berger." I made an introductory wave of my hand. "This is my Co-Captain, Fur Cohen. How can we be of assistance?" The growls that emanated from our pinned-on translation speakers startled me.

The entourage of five Lupans stared at me, then at Fur, and then back at me. I sensed that they were surprised I was the one who spoke. Then Braid growled at me. I flinched, even though I felt no aggression. When Ruthie cut in with a translation through my earbud, I understood that growling was their speech.

"The People welcome you. You must speak with our

leader. Follow." They took off, side by side, toward a small cluster of wooden buildings at the edge of the forest. Scratch slunk along, well in the rear.

Minimalistic did not even *begin* to describe the audience chamber we entered. The circular wooden building was a single room that contained no fixtures or furnishings. The only light came from a large opening in the roof. A dozen Lupans, again all male, stood around when we entered. At a bark from a large individual with a luxurious dirty-blonde mane, they formed a semicircle and squatted. I noticed that Scratch had not entered the hall with the rest of our welcoming committee.

"Greetings. I am Captain Berger of the *Galactic Circle Veterinary Service.* You asked for our assistance."

I got the same reaction from the assembled host. They looked at Fur as if they expected him to speak. Then Barker addressed us. *"The People need help."*

A few untranslated growls met this pronouncement.

Barker looked around the room with bared teeth, and the vocalizations subsided. *"We learned you have helped others and ask for aid."*

I sensed a mix of curiosity and aggression from the group. My stomach cringed, and I strengthened my shields. "Sir, do you have a name I may address you by?"

"I am Leader."

"Yes. Leader. Of course. What is the nature of the problem? Is it a disease of some sort?"

A rumble of low-pitched growls shook the room, and my head ached along with my rebelling stomach. Had I said something wrong?

Another bark quieted the circle. I shivered as Leader's yellow eyes glared into mine. If they were this scary in their humanoid form, I was not sure I wanted to

~285~

meet them in the lupine mode.

"You will talk to lower caste for this information."

Lower caste? I sensed that Fur's perplexity was as intense as mine.

This seemed to be a dismissal, since all the Lupans rose and moved toward the entrance. Fur and I looked at each other. I shrugged and shook my head. I did not have a clue as to how these beings would react to some misstep we could not even imagine.

A Lupan with a fuzzy auburn mane motioned for us to follow him. He led us to another wooden dome. *"Enter."*

As we did as we were told, he remained outside.

The small dim antechamber did nothing to soothe my nerves. Fur's head almost brushed the ceiling, so he scrunched up his shoulders. He looked like a turtle, albeit a very large one. His aura wavered with fear, far more than the circumstances warranted. He wiped sweat from his face, though it was not hot.

I had no time to wonder about that as a figure materialized in the doorway opposite the one we had entered. He stooped as he moved into the light. He had a short, sparse, dull mane.

"Welcome to the People."

"Hello. I'm Dr. Cy Berger."

"I'm Furoletto Cohen."

The Lupan looked at Fur. *"You are Leader?"*

"No. That's him." Fur motioned to me with his thumb.

The Lupan's pupils dilated as he looked at me. *"Interesting."* He motioned for us to follow as he moved toward the interior door.

The next room actually contained benches, a wooden table, and an open cabinet that contained an ancient hyperwave set. A small window illuminated the room. We sat.

I began. "I'm a bit confused—"

"Yes, no doubt." He bared his teeth—a grin, I hoped. His teeth were smaller than Leader's, but still impressive. *"I am Healer. I may discuss what is not possible for the upper caste."*

I glanced at Fur and back to healer. "We need information if we are to help. Is there an illness?"

"There is a malady, but you may not be allowed to help."

"Then why did you call us?"

"To help, you must be recognized as worthy. To accept the assistance of one not proven worthy is taboo."

I shook my head. "I'm sorry, but this makes no sense. We have proven our worth on multiple worlds, with many different races—"

Fur broke in. "I don't think that's what Healer is talking about."

"Then what?"

Fur continued. "Correct me if I'm wrong, Healer, but we must be proven to a standard of your society. Is that right?"

He nodded. *"That is correct, large one."* He looked back and forth at Fur and me. *"Your standards differ from ours."*

"What? Proven how?" I demanded.

"Only Leader can tell you."

"What is this? Some kind of shell game? First Leader, then you, now Leader again. If you people need help, I'm happy to oblige. If you don't want it, we have plenty of other worlds that need our services."

Fur put his big mitt on my arm to calm me. "Let's hear Healer out. Okay?"

I took a deep breath and let it out. I nodded.

Healer stood and walked to the crude window, gazed out, then turned back to me. *"The People have little contact with offworlders. I am Chosen to speak with strangers, here and far away.*" He motioned with his head toward the hyperwave set. "*I cannot be contaminated any further by interaction.*"

Contaminated? What in God's name—?

"*If you wish to help the People, you must prove yourself. If not, you must leave our world. To stay would invite harm.*"

I bolted to my feet. "Is that a threat?"

"*I do not make threats. I say what is true. You must decide. Please return to your ship. If you wish to stay, inform the guard.*"

"Guard? What guard?"

Fur grabbed my arm again, more forcefully this time, and it hurt. I swung around to him, but the warning in his thoughts cut off any retort. He gave a sharp shake of his head and said, "Let's get back to the ship. We can talk there."

Maybe he picked up on something I missed. It would not be the first time.

***

"They're a pack-oriented society," Fur said.

He, Levi, and I sat in the commissary over cups of Ulmian coffee. I would be sorry when that ran out. Levi's face scrunched into his usual scowl as he looked at Fur.

Fur continued. "You could see that in the way they responded as a group. Maybe I'm oversimplifying, but I liken it to Terran wolf packs. An Alpha male lords it over the others. He stays dominant by demonstration of his ferocity and strength."

"See," Levi broke in. "They are nothing but beasts. We waste our time here." He looked at me. "Your parents suffer with each delay." It was like an automatic response from him, but it seemed to be underlain by more menace this time, as he had cracked the mask of congeniality he had been wearing. Coupled with not hearing from them for too long, this caused my empathic nausea to bring acid to my mouth.

I tensed, but Fur pressed his hand on my shoulder to keep me from reacting violently. "Remember how the one that scratched himself was glared down and then became submissive?" he asked.

"Yeah. And he was excluded from the meeting," I said.

"The references to 'lower castes' by Leader, and the need to 'prove' ourselves to be worthy, suggests a hierarchical society." Fur sat back and sipped his brew.

"Okay. Even if that's true, we should be careful about drawing direct parallels. It can't be that simple."

Levi poked his nose in again. "This is useless speculation. They will not allow us to assist them. This world was not on our schedule. We have finished our travels. I demand we leave."

I ignored him and turned to Fur. "But if they need help, why this 'proving' business? How can we not be good enough to help when we have knowledge and technology? That makes no sense."

"Think about the Caste System of ancient India," Fur said. "The Untouchables were the lowest members of society and suffered from religious, economic, and social discrimination. Even their touch defiled high caste Hindus. They couldn't draw water from Hindu wells. Maybe it's something like that here."

"Ha. You even compare them to a religion with false, pagan gods. We will leave them to their heathen ways." Levi sat back, radiating triumph.

Why anything this bigoted *schmuck* said surprised me, I don't know, but this one did. I turned on him. "Now you imply that even *humans* that follow any other religion than Judaism aren't worthy of God's recognition?"

"That is not what I meant." He glared at me. "I—"

Fur interrupted. "We're getting off the subject. We need more information. First, what's this proof we need for them? Second, what's the malady that has them upset? Then we can make a rational decision whether to help them or not."

I couldn't argue with his logic, and it prevented further escalation of the conflict between Levi and me. We would follow up in the morning.

***

The guard at the ship's airlock was Scratch. His mane was unkempt, his shoulders drooped, and he did not walk with the grace we had seen in the other Lupans. It seemed that his transgression, whatever it was, had dropped his state so far that we couldn't further pollute him. He led Fur and me to the Healer's building.

Healer met us at the door. *"You have made a choice to stay? To be proven?"*

"Not quite," I said. "Before we make any decision, we need to know what this trial is. And what the problem is, whether we can help at all."

"I cannot inform you, but the trial will be both a physical and a mental challenge. You must make your decision now, or leave."

I looked at Fur. "I guess this is it? Do we stay or go?"

Fur tugged at his beard. "I'll undertake whatever trial they have in mind. I can handle the physical stuff."

"Maybe we can split it up," I said. "You do the physical and I'll do the mental."

Fur's eyebrows rose. "Oh, you don't think I'd be up

to the intellectual challenge?"

"You started it."

Fur grinned. "Let's go for it. If worse comes to worse, we leave with our tails between our legs and don't accomplish anything."

I rolled my eyes, but grinned back in spite of myself.

We followed Scratch to a building we had not entered before. A Lupan at the door did not deign to look at our guide, and Scratch slunk off. If he'd *had* a tail, it would have been between his legs.

Inside, Leader sat at a table covered with piles of paper, the first sign of written language I'd seen.

He rose and approached us. *"You undertake to prove yourself."* It was not a question.

"Well, we thought that Fur..." I waved my arm in Fur's direction, then cut off at the almost subsonic growl that emanated from Leaders throat.

"What..?"

His yellow eyes bored into mine. *"You are Leader?"*

"Yeah, but that does not—"

"Then you undertake proof. Not the inferior one." He looked at Fur. I fought to hide a smile as a frown creased the big man's brow.

Fur turned his palm upward toward me. "Your call."

It was hard to back down now, so I concurred. "What do I do?"

Leader looked at Fur. *"You return to your ship."* He looked at me. *"Follow."*

"Go ahead. I'll be fine," I said. Fur continued to frown as he turned and walked toward the ship. I followed Leader toward the edge of the forest.

When he stopped, Leader ordered, *"Unclothe."*

"What?" I cried.

Fur turned back, but a cordon of Lupans surrounded

him and urged him toward the ship.

"You go as the People go," Leader said.

Shit. I didn't expect *that.* "Wait a minute—"

"Unclothe."

I shrugged and stripped to shorts and a T-shirt. The temperature was comfortable, but I wondered how long that would last. Nighttime would be chillier.

"All clothes."

This was ridiculous, but backing down now would blow the whole deal. I reluctantly complied. Somehow, with my privates uncovered, I felt far more vulnerable, though undershorts were no real protection from anything *but* cold.

Leader stared at the hydra scars on my arm and leg but said nothing. I did get a mental wave of something akin to approval. Respect for battle scars?

Leader made a motion toward the woods, and three Lupans stepped out and approached us. Leader voiced a series of growls to the newcomers.

Ruthie said, "I can't translate, Cy. There were tones that were outside the range of my audio pickups. I must say, you look fetching that way."

Leader turned back to me and pointed to my ear. *"Remove."*

My earbud? How in hell could he have heard that? "No, I need that to maintain contact with my ship. It's policy. I can't leave it behind."

A chorus of growls accompanied a visible erection of the manes of all four Lupans. I felt the hair on the back of my neck rise in response. What was I getting into? Was it too late to back out?

Leader took a step closer to me, followed by his companions, and held out his hand. *"Remove!"*

I could refuse, head back to the ship, and be off this planet within an hour. Something made me demur, possibly anticipation of Levi's inevitable smirk when he won. I reached up, removed the earpiece, and handed it to Leader.

He showed his teeth and stepped back. He turned to the three other Lupans and growled. Without Ruthie's translation, I felt far more naked than I had from removing my clothes. Now I couldn't even communicate with the Lupans, much less the *GCVS*. How would I understand the trial?

It shocked me when Leader spoke to me in rudimentary Common. It was too easy to think of the Lupans as naked savages, but their intelligence surpassed their outward appearance.

"You follow." He pointed to the three newcomers. "Three days, nights."

Three days and nights?

"Kill, eat. Face danger. Then accepted."

Kill? Eat? Danger? There seemed to be an echo in my head.

Before I could do more, Leader waved at his cohort. I stood mesmerized as the three Lupans started to melt. This raised a crop of goose bumps all over my body. The figures transformed before my eyes from humanoid to brutes that more than matched their human-given moniker. They were longer and leaner than Terran wolves. The domes of their skulls were larger; the size and shape of the brain did not seem to change. I assumed that their intelligence did not desert them in their lupine forms. I hoped so.

The muzzles were long and narrow, more like a crocodile than a wolf, and the teeth were even much more prominent than they had been in their bipedal form. The legs were long and they looked as if they could cover ground like a Terran cheetah. The claws were canine-like rather than lizard-like. The eyes had not changed at all, piercing yellow stares that scared the shit out of me.

Now, thick fur the color of their humanoid manes covered their bodies. One was black, one a grizzled grey-brown, and one a rusty red. Their manes were even more prominent in the lupine form, and resembled the Terran male lion. Tails were very wolf-like. Altogether impressive beasts, although I might have appreciated the display more if I didn't stand bare-assed in front of them.

At a motion from Leader, the pack bounded off for the woods. If I had thought they were graceful in their humanoid forms, I was now astonished. They seemed to flow across the ground, almost without contact. They were gone in an eye blink, and I was alone with Leader.

I looked at him. "Exactly what am I supposed to do?"

"You learn. Part of test. Go." He pointed to the forest, then turned and walked back toward the village.

I stood with my mouth hanging open for a moment, before I shut it with a snap. "Idiot," I muttered, "what have you gotten yourself into now?"

An eerie howl floated back to me from the direction the beasts had flown.

***

Thankfully, the dim forest was not like the Ulmian jungle, whose psychedelic, toxin-spewing inhabitants still haunted my nightmares. Here, boles of great evergreen trees blended into the mist, with sparse undergrowth due to the shade. I heard or saw no birds and wondered if they had not evolved on this planet.

At least it was open enough to preclude an ambush. My eyes lit on a dead tree branch that might serve as a weapon. I picked it up and hefted it. It was twice my height and as thick as my wrist. I broke it in half over my knee and hopped about for a minute or two as the pain subsided. I discarded the thinner portion. That would do for now, but I needed something more lethal if I was to follow Leader's instruction to "kill," presumably to "eat." I hoped I could find plenty of nuts and berries before I got to that point.

I walked until the sun reached its zenith. Soft pine-like needles covered the forest floor. My bare feet were sore, but not cut. I hoped they would toughen with use, but knew that one false step on a sharp object might cripple me. I moved slowly. Fortunately, the hydra wounds had healed and did not hamper me. Although the trees shrouded me from the sun, the air was warm. I avoided bushes as much as possible to minimize scratches and possible contact with anything poisonous. Ulm's floral monstrosities taught me caution.

My breakfast had been meager and my stomach rumbled. I had not seen anything that resembled food, other than seeds that looked like an aborted acorn with a red fan sticking out of the top. I was not *about* to test those. Previous reports said humans could eat Lupan flora and fauna, but there were plenty of toxic Terran plants. Nothing to do but keep going. They didn't send me out here to sit on my bare ass.

Leaves soughed in the breeze. Maybe I was supposed to *smell* out something. No doubt the Lupines had great olfactory senses. As if this thought was a trigger, I heard a crash in the underbrush and a rank smell assaulted my nose. I hid behind the trunk of the nearest tree.

The noise moved closer. The thing emanated hunger and curiosity, but no fear or aggression. Certainly nothing sentient. I gagged at the thing's odor, somewhere between a skunk and marsh gas. It stopped on the other side of the trunk. The tree was wider than I was tall, so we remained hidden from one another, but I could tell that it sensed me. Maybe it could hear my heart pounding like a kettledrum. The only emotion I could perceive now was curiosity. The standoff lasted moments, but it seemed like hours.

My curiosity got the better of me. I moved to the edge of the bole and stuck my head out. I'm not sure who was more surprised, but both of us jumped backward. I stepped on a broken limb and fell on my ass. My heart rate rose as I went down.

The beast looked like a cross between a hippopotamus and an elephant, other than the color. Irregular red, vertical stripes slashed the bright yellow body from the back to the abdomen. It swung its broad head from side to side. Its arm-long nose swung like an elephant's trunk. No tusks, thank God. It snorted and pawed with its sizable hoofs. Still no fear or aggression. It stood no taller than my shoulder, but outweighed me at least several-fold. My branch felt like a toothpick as I levered myself to my feet.

"Hello there." I kept my voice low and sent out a thought of calmness. "You're a strange one. I wonder what they call you."

The thing stood immobile, curiosity still its primary emotional scent.

What in blazes did I do now? Back away?

I did. The beast obliged and mirrored my move. Okay, another step. Same result.

Strange. I took a step forward. Hippophant did the same. I stopped. He/she stopped. I bent over to look and confirmed this was a she, or at least lacked obvious he-ness. She sort of bent her stubby legs and cocked her head in response.

Come on. Was this some sort of joke? I lifted one leg. So did she. I lifted both arms and stood like a crane, then hopped on one foot. Her eyes widened and she snorted. My heart fluttered.

She jumped, lifting her bulk perhaps a few

centimeters off the ground. The earth juddered when she landed. It was a bizarre game of *Simon Says*.

Then I felt more judders. Bigger ones. Something else approached. I backed off, but now Hippophant followed me. *Not* what I wanted. I stopped short as huge bulks materialized between the big trees.

Oh, shit. She was a *baby*! That explained the curious behavior and lack of fear. The rest of the family was not similarly inclined. When the lead hippophant saw me, it let out an elephantine bellow and pawed the ground, gouging up clods of dirt the size of my torso. Its anger swamped the curiosity I had received from Baby. Baby turned and ambled back to Momma. In turn, Momma nuzzled Baby with her snout, before she returned her attention to me. Now flanked by a dozen other adult hippophants, none of which looked or felt friendly, she lifted her short, flexible snout in the air, as if questing for my scent. A large male—maleness was obvious on this planet—opened its mouth. Typical herbivore dentition reassured me I was not on the dinner menu, though they could make quick work of me with their broad hooves if they so desired.

I backed away again. Momma then started toward me, so I picked up my pace. She did, too. I got a tree between us, turned, and sprinted for all I was worth. I came up short when I reached a cliff edge and could go no farther. The hippophants were no longer in sight, and I felt no emanations of hatred. I gasped as the stitch in my side receded. The bruised ball of my right foot where I had stepped on the limb hurt like hell.

I had been lucky. Undoubtedly, those things could have outrun me, but they probably saw no need since Baby was unharmed. I wondered, was I supposed to kill one of them as my trial? Good luck. No way could I do that, short of digging a stake-lined pit with a stick for a tool. I was pitted against the three Lupans, though I could not fathom how. Probably not a physical conflict, but I could have been wrong. I did not see how I could win something like that.

I stood perhaps three or four hundred meters above a broad grassland that extended to the east as far as I could see. Copses of trees dotted the landscape, and a serpentine, tree-lined river ran from east to west, paralleling the cliff, but several kilometers away. A herd of animals grazed near the river, and I saw movement within the trees, as well.

I limped along the cliff face, looking for a way to get down. I heard chittering in the trees, but whatever they were, they would move off when I got too close.

As the sun was halfway through its decline to the west, I came upon an outcrop of rock that resembled flint. Pieces had flaked off and I examined one. I smacked it against a tree bole and it shattered. Probably useless as an axe head. I picked up one of the shards and tested its edge against my fingernail. It left a slight groove. Maybe a knife?

I took several more flakes of rock and beat them against one another. After a dozen pieces shattered in my hands, I got the hang of it and fashioned something long and thin enough to be a serviceable dagger. I made a couple of spares and used one to whittle the end of my staff to a point. After admiring my new spear, I threw away the blade that now resembled a butter knife. I felt better with weapons, prehistoric though they were.

How would I carry my tools? I could manage the knife or the spear; I wanted to have one hand free. A tough vine twined its way up a tree, and I cut a length with my second knife. One segment made a belt. Thinner vine strips made handles for the knives. Then I wove a crude sheath and attached that to the belt at my side. The two knives fit in it. Just what the well-equipped caveman would carry.

As the sun sank into the trees, the temperature dropped with it. I shivered. A hide tunic and some sandals to match would have been nice. As I hobbled along, I watched for a place I could hole up for the night. Predators liked the dark hours. I shivered again, but not from the cold.

I found a dead tree that formed a hollow within its massive roots. After making sure that nothing lived there already, I scraped out the accumulated decayed wood and rotted vegetation to make a cozy little cave. I collected branches with needles for a bed and to cover myself for warmth. My hunger and thirst would have to wait until tomorrow. The opening was small enough that if anything did desire to investigate, only one thing could get to me at a time. Big mistake, thinking only of large animals as a threat.

***

A sharp pain on the rear of my left thigh woke me. I sat up, groggy, and ran my hand down my thigh to where it hurt. My hand encountered a squiggly and I bolted out of my hole with a scream.

Shit. Something bit me.

Creepy crawlies were okay, so long as they didn't sneak up on me. I wasn't sure what had bitten or stung me, and I danced around the tree, hopping from one bad leg to the other, in case there were more of the things. There were. I felt one more bite on the left ankle, swiped at it, and dislodged the deliverer.

In the blackness, I could not see what form my adversaries took or how many there were, so I moved away into the forest. No way was I going back to the tree for my spear. I stayed within the trees so I would not stumble over the cliff in the dark.

The wounds were a fiery torment. Both my legs

were now lame. Despite the cold air, sweat poured off my body. My arms and legs trembled. I kept a steady pace until the dawn light filtered through the trees, then I sat to examine my wounds.

Bites, for sure. A small chunk of flesh had been gouged out at each site. The wounds were not large, but they burned, and I worried about infection. I used saliva to clean them up a bit. I had to find some water soon, to drink and to clean the bites better.

I checked the bottom of my right foot. The painful area was blue-black, but at least there was no open wound. My arms and legs trembled even worse now. Even my eyelids twitched.

Did those things have some sort of neurotoxin? Venomous creatures seemed to have a thing for me lately. I was lucky I only had two bites. A pack of those things might have brought me down permanently.

The sun had reached the level of the treetops when I found a small stream that dropped over the cliff edge in a waterfall. I moved to the edge of the water and peered at it. What I expected to see, I'm not sure, but my two experiences so far had engaged my paranoia reflexes. There was no way to test or purify the water, so I scooped some up with cupped hands and drank my fill. Then I washed the bite wounds. Fortunately, they showed no signs of festering. I scrubbed them and let them dry before I moved. The pain that had started to subside renewed itself. Thank God my trembling was no worse.

When the pain had lessened some, I found another branch that would make a decent spear as well as a walking stick. When I tried to sharpen it, my shakiness threatened more injury to me than to the stick, but I persevered then threw away the dulled second knife.

I rested for a bit, then moved to the edge of the waterfall. The cliff was not as sheer here. Rock falls and scree sloped outward toward the base, as good a place to climb down as any. I had no doubt I needed to do so. Other than the hippophants, the only animals I had seen were down there. Aside from the creepy-crawlies, but I had not *seen* them. Maybe there was some sort of fruit on those trees. There certainly wasn't anything up here.

It took about half an hour to make my way down. Again, I checked the area out from the bottom of the cliff before I moved. The herdbeasts did not seem as large as the hippophants, but I did not want to take chances. Any animals can be dangerous if they felt they or their offspring were threatened.

As I stepped out from behind a rock, a small, furry creature bolted from beneath my feet. I caught a hint of the animal's fear as it scampered. That it was potential food came to mind only after it ran up on a rock pile a dozen meters away. I had half a mind to chase it, but I could not have caught it even on good legs. It disappeared into the rocks, in any case.

Okay, patience. My stomach rumbled so loud it would probably scare off anything that got close. I squatted down and stayed as motionless as I could. All the stories about how hunters remained motionless for hours at a time had to be exaggerated. Besides the pain of the bites and my tremors, I must have itched in a thousand places within fifteen minutes. My reward came when the animal, or its brother, stuck its head out and peered around. The size of the ubiquitous rabbits of my world, the plump brown little guy sat up on two stubby hind legs. The short forepaws held what looked like a tuber of some sort. His large front teeth munched contentedly as my mouth watered. I wondered if the salivation was for the little beast or the tuber it fed on.

What to do next? He was too far to throw my spear. Well, an arm's length was too far to throw my spear, even if I didn't shake like a belly dancer. I'd have to get closer, maybe try to brain him with a rock. But even the *thought* of that caused my empathic circuits to twinge. I had learned to euthanize animals for whom the act was a kindness, but that still left me a nauseated, pain-wracked wreck. Could I kill a cute little animal like this? I couldn't see that I had a choice. "Kill and eat" Leader had said.

I started up from my crouch and he was gone in a blink. So much for the great stalker. I moved over to where I had seen the creature, and found a burrow within the rock pile. I positioned myself above the burrow where he would not see me when he first stuck his head out. Then I waited, knife in hand, motionless like the books said.

And I waited. The sun rose toward noon before I heard some rocks move behind me and felt a tickle of wariness. I whipped around just in time to see my fat friend pop down. I moved up the slope. Sure enough, another hole.

Crap. He probably had a dozen of these to get away from predators. I laughed. Me? A predator? Not a very good one. Time to move on. I put away my blade, climbed down the rocks, and moved off toward the plain. I looked back after a few steps and saw a half dozen furry faces watch me go. No doubt it was my imagination, but I could have sworn they were laughing.

As I followed the creek from the waterfall, I saw several small herds of grazers near the big river. As I walked, they moved away from me at a distance that made any thought of hunting them moot. The trees along the creek were scattered and not thick enough to serve as cover for anything large. They resembled the imported cottonwoods of Dovid's World, with thick boles and a spreading canopy of dull green leaves.

Maybe when I got to the river corridor, I'd have the cover I needed. As the sun baked me, I assuaged my thirst in the cold creek. It was now a day and a half since I had eaten. I knew this was not a life threatening issue, so long as I had water. I could go many days without food, if necessary, not that it appealed to me. Plus, Leader had said I must kill and eat something to pass the test. I wondered if plants counted. You *could* kill and eat them, after all, but this skirted the issue. The Lupans were carnivores.

Of greater concern right now was sunburn. Yesterday, I had been in the shade of the forest, but now the sun broiled me like an Antarean rock lobster. I scooped mud from the creek bottom and smeared it over as much of my exposed body as I could reach. I would have a nice red spot in the middle of my back, like a target. Not the most comforting image.

I studied the trees along the larger river before I moved toward them. I did not want any more nasty surprises. The outer trees were acacia-like umbrellas, and formed a verge with thin underbrush. Then came a band of tall, thin trees with spiky, reddish-green leaves. These tapered off into a willow-like thicket that would be hard to maneuver through, interspersed with the cottonwoods. A game path paralleled the smaller creek where it fed into the river, and I followed that.

The river flowed brown, peppered with leaves and debris, certainly not the crystalline beverage of the stream I had drunk from earlier. As I examined it, I heard something move in the brush. A dun-colored animal about my size moved into the open and stopped. It looked toward me, but its gaze slid past as if it did not see me. A black stripe down the front of its face terminated in a grey-pink nose, nostrils flared. Arm-long black horns spiraled upward above mobile ears several times the size I thought should fit the head. I let out the breath I held, and the ears locked onto me like radar dishes. This thing obviously depended on hearing rather than sight. I shifted a foot, and a leaf barely crackled beneath me. With a squeal like a dying cat, the beast took off. The leap was at least twice my height and covered more than five times that distance, like a jet-propelled kangaroo. With those ears, it reminded me of a character I had once seen in an animated vid: Dumbo, the flying elephant.

I shook my head. I had as much chance of catching one of those as I did one of the planet's moons. I drank as much as I could hold from the clear stream, before I moved on along the main river's course. A while later, I heard wood crack in the brush, and I dropped into a crouch behind a bush. Another alien nightmare slunk out of the willows no more than fifty meters from me. The creature looked in my direction and a wave of ravenous hunger washed over me. It was not my own.

CHAPTER 19

THE ANIMAL WAS vaguely feline, but taller and leaner than any cat I knew. The head had an elongated crocodile-like muzzle, like the shifted Lupans, but with canines that resembled those of the extinct Terran saber-toothed tiger. The legs seemed too long and thin for the tawny, black-spotted body. Even crouched, its head towered above me. Saliva dripped from its mouth, like some rabid beast.

I almost panicked and jumped up to run, but caught myself in time. My heart pumped panic through my veins.

The beast lifted its head and snout toward me, and audibly snuffed the air.

Shit. I was upwind of the thing. Did it catch my scent? Oh God, please no.

After an eternity, it turned away and moved to the river to drink.

It didn't smell me. It must've been the mud I'd smeared on me. I breathed a sigh of relief.

Then a goat-sized brown gazelle-like animal startled me when it bounded out of the thicket. It stopped between the cat-thing and me and swiveled its oversized ears like antennae. It looked toward where the predator crouched behind some small bushes, but did not seem to see the cat. The gazelle moved to the

Stephen A. Benjamin

water, stood straddle-legged, and drank.

The felid crept closer, then roared and sprang. The gazelle went rigid at the sound. A bite to the neck made quick work of the grazer, and the cat dragged the carcass onto the bank and into the brush. I could hear twigs snap as it moved away. I did not move until I could no longer hear or sense the beast.

When I stood, my knees were rubbery and my hands trembled even more. *I* could have been the target. Now every bit of cover seemed to hold a cat-creature or something even worse. Should I hide in the brush or stay out in the open where I could see any dangerous beast though it could see me? I sat down with a thump.

"Get hold of yourself." I spoke aloud. "You have another two days out here, and you can't be scared shitless the entire time. You have intelligence: *think*."

I listened and watched as I followed the grassy bank along the edge of the river. After I traveled perhaps a kilometer this way, I saw movement ahead of me. I squatted behind some brush. An animal the size of a fox moved to the river's edge to drink. It was brown with grayish spots, had cloven hooves, a long face, two small white nubbins of horns on its head, and the typical, huge ears. I could feel its wariness, but it did not spook.

At five meters, I would never hit it with my spear, even though my tremors had decreased. I recalled the reaction of the gazelle to the cat-thing, and wondered if I could freeze it. Maybe the acute hearing that seemed to be the primary protection also was its weak spot. I leaped up, gave my version of a predator's roar, and sprang. The little creature froze, just as I had hoped, and I drove the spear into its chest.

Its pain and fear cut through me as if I had been the one assaulted. My stomach cramped and acid rose to my throat.

I had to kill it. The empathetic agony made me want

to scream, but I suppressed that and pulled my knife. Hot needles of pain stabbed behind my eyes when I slashed the creature across the throat. I staggered away from the animal as it died, and vomited water, acid, and bile, all that remained in my stomach.

It took many minutes to gather my strength and my will. I had to do something with the carcass, but I could not bring myself to touch it.

"Come on. You have no choice," I chided myself. "You killed it. Don't make that sacrifice for *nothing*."

I gutted the animal and then skinned it. Even a small hide would be useful when night came again. I scraped the skin clean of as much fat and tissue as I could, then thought about the meat. My stomach rebelled. With difficulty, both physical and emotional, I cut off the head. Somehow, it was better without those glazed eyes staring at me. With my now dull knife, I sawed off several strips of hide that I wrapped around my feet, hair side in, and secured them with thinner strips to make sandals. I cleaned myself of blood as best I could in the river, threw the bloody carcass over my shoulder—which negated much of the previous effort—and set out away from the water. After two steps, the remaining grease on the hide caused my feet to go out from under me, and I landed smack on my coccyx.

I cursed, tossed away the sandals, and moved away from the river as I rubbed my tailbone. When I reached the outer trees, I sat gingerly on the hide with my back against a bole and tried to regain my equilibrium. I pushed the carcass out of my field of vision and closed my eyes.

The next thing I knew, I awoke with a start. The sun was half way down. I had slept several hours. I stood and stretched out my cramped muscles. The bites hurt much less now and the tremors were gone.

I brushed some insect-like creatures off the carcass

of the grazer and lifted it and the hide to my shoulder.

"I'm lucky that nothing scented the blood and found me while I slept." I shook my head. "That was stupid."

I had to think more clearly. As I looked around me, the next part of my dilemma hit home. I had no way to cook the thing. I had killed, but I still had to eat. Raw?

The retching that accompanied that thought resulted in nothing more than a cramped stomach.

How do you make a fire? Ah, twirl a stick in some tinder, right? The way our ancestors did it. With twigs, dead leaves, pieces of bark, and a small stick placed as best as I could remember from old vids, I twirled the stick between my hands. Long before I saw anything resembling smoke or fire, my hands hurt like hell and my arms trebled with fatigue. I rested and tried again. Nothing. Maybe I didn't have the right ingredients, but this was sure harder than it looked. I gave it one more try before I gave up and slammed the stick to the ground.

"Shit. This is ridiculous."

The sun approached the horizon. I needed a place for the night, but I didn't want another hole. I found a climbable spiky-leaved tree. With the carcass and hide tied to my belt, I worked my way up through the lower branches. I wedged myself into a sturdy fork, hoping I would not fall if I slept. I also hoped I was high enough to be safe from terrestrial predators. I did not even want to *think* about anything that climbed. Once settled, I untied and stared at my dinner. At least I no longer retched at its sight, maybe because I was as bloody as the damned meat, but I decided I was not quite ready yet. I tucked it in a nearby, smaller fork.

The past two days unrolled before my mind's eye. I had given my adrenal glands quite a workout. I had done the "kill" part and had to steel myself for the "eat." Somewhere ahead were the three Lupans. I wondered if I already had done the "face danger" bit—I sure as hell hoped so. Well, first things first. I used my knife to hack a chunk of meat off the rear of the carcass. I stared at it for a long time before I raised it to my mouth.

***

The howls woke me. Two large bright moons hung above my tree. I rubbed the sleep from my eyes and squirmed to a place where my back and butt ached less. The howls came again, a chorus of them. My guts squirmed in time to the sound.

Sleep banished, I wondered if that was my three adversaries. It seemed logical. Tomorrow was the third day and though I had seen or heard nothing of them, I guessed that they knew exactly where I was. No doubt they had kept tabs on me the whole time, as they waited for me to fulfill my charge. I alternated between being pissed at the Lupans for my trial, or elated because I had made it this far.

The howls were closer now. Did I stay in my tree and risk getting stranded, or jump down and get on the move? One thing I did know: the little carcass would stay behind. I had managed to choke down a half-dozen chunks of the bloody meat, but that was it. Even then, they had threatened to seek release more than once during the night, but they stayed put and would give me some nourishment for the final day.

As I dithered, the howls cut off, replaced by a series of barks and deep growls and a loud bleat. The sounds of snapping jaws tearing meat and crunching bones made my decision easy. I tried to find some comfort on my branch, but it eluded me. I wrapped my arms around myself and shivered, partly from the cold and partly from the grisly sounds that came from nearby. The little hide was as useless as the rest of the meat.

It seemed to take forever for the moons to saunter across the sky to the horizon. The forest had quieted by then. As dawn raised the world's nightshade, I slipped down from my tree and stretched to work out the kinks that invaded every joint in my body. I started a vigorous set of calisthenics to get my blood warmed, but that did not last long; I had little energy to spare.

I crept toward the scene of last night's party. The dismembered body of a large herdbeast lay scattered in a small clearing. The meat was gone and the bones cracked open. There was no sign of what brought it down other than some piles of scat. Though I assumed it was the Lupans, I really had no idea how many different predators were out there.

As I walked around the clearing, I looked for some clue to inspire me as to what to do next, but it eluded me. I backtracked to the small stream and quenched my morning thirst. My stomach was the only water container I had. I washed up again, but some mixture of blood and mud remained. As I followed the creek back out to the plain, I scared up a bevy of small rodent-like animals in the process. Thank God I no longer needed to think of them as food.

I stopped at the edge of the trees. A herd of the same kind of beast I had seen dismembered in the forest grazed just outside the woods. A constant alertness overlay a feeling of satisfaction with their food. When I stepped out of the shelter of the foliage, the entire herd wheeled to look at me. Fear hovered on the verge of panic, but I tried to send a message of calm and moved away from them. They watched for a while and then went back to grazing, although two of the largest kept me in their sights. I walked on, at a loss as to what to do next. It turned out I did not have to decide.

I neared the cliff when a pack of Lupans in wolf

form stepped out of the trees. There were six of them and they advanced on me, hackles raised and growling. Two were female, the first female Lupans I had seen.

"Look guys, I'm not sure what it is you want me to do, but I'm trying my best."

This elicited more growls. Suddenly, it hit me that these beasts could not be the Lupans. For one, they lacked the luxurious manes. The ruff of fur around their necks was sparse and the same color as the rest of the body, a dull gray-brown. Second, the brain cases were distinctly smaller than the Lupans', even in their wolf form. Third, my empathic reception did not feel like what I'd gotten from sentient beings. Their emotions were a mixture of hunger, aggression, and even a bit of fear, but they did not cause me undo distress.

I stepped backward and the pack stepped toward me. I tried to send my own message. *Be calm. I am no threat. There is no reason to attack.*

If anything, the response was of increased aggression. What a time for my reverse empathy. Hackles rose; legs and tails became rigid.

What *were* these things? Whatever they were, I could not back off, not show fear. That might trigger an attack.

Now they started to encircle me. When I moved toward an opening in the circle, they darted to close it.

Not good. Not good at all. My heart thumped as I hefted my spear.

"Know what this is, beasties? This is a spear. It can skewer you. One false move and..." I made a thrusting motion with my arm.

No response. Hunger and aggression had all but drowned out the initial fear I had felt from them. Their fear had transferred to me. My breath came in short gasps.

The pack now dropped down, bellies close to the

ground, and edged toward me.

I figured I was finished. Even if I broke through the circle, no way could I outrun these things. Hungry, thirsty, and pressed to the point of exhaustion, my blood boiled over.

"*Stop, Goddammit*. I'm *tired* of this shit. I don't know what my test was supposed to be, but getting eaten by a pack of overgrown plooﬂes is not included."

The pack came up short. A quiver of fear returned to their emotions.

That was it. I needed to show dominance. That worked with some predators.

"All right, enough," I barked in as gruff a voice as I could manage. "You." I pointed and stepped toward the wolf in front of me. "Sit!"

I felt confusion, and a bit more fear. The thing's hackles lay down and it backed off.

I pointed and moved again. "You next. Heel!"

A similar response. The creature tucked its tail between its legs. They could not understand the directives I gave, but the tone of voice and command was the thing.

I turned and waved my spear at a third. "Play dead!" I almost laughed at myself on that one, but suppressed it. I could not show any chink in my dominance display.

When that wolf backed away, I stepped toward it and threw my knife, a calculated gamble. I knew it would not hurt the animal. Even if it had been a throwing knife, I had no clue as to how to launch it. The ﬂat of the knife hit the wolf on one shoulder. It yelped, whirled, and with a ﬂash of fear, zipped off across the plain. The others followed.

My trembling legs barely kept me upright. Just then, three Lupans—real ones in their humanoid form this time—stepped out from behind some trees and approached.

I faced them, recognizing the three from my trial. "Okay, what the hell was that all about? Those things could have torn me apart. What *were* they, anyway? They looked like your wolf form, but they're not sentient. So, now do I fight you, too?"

My body tensed. I was mad enough to take them on despite the fact that I knew the hopelessness of such a fight.

Rusty ruff raised a hand and growled in Common, "Complete portion of challenge. Follow."

"*Portion*? What—?"

Before I could even think further, the three melted into their lupine forms—I would never get used to *that*—and loped across the grassy sward toward the cliff.

When I couldn't keep up with them, they slowed their pace to a comfortable jog, and I hobbled behind as best I could. A cavern at the cliff's base led to a tunnel to the plateau's top. Beat climbing the cliff. The trip back was surprisingly short. I had not gone as far as I had imagined.

My guides let out a few howls as we approached the village, and Leader met us. He had both Fur and Levi in tow. Levi's usually ruddy face was bloodless.

I bent over and gasped for breath as Fur grinned at me. "Glad to see you back in one piece, Captain." He looked me up and down. "Though your attire leaves something to be desired."

I did not have breath to spare for an answer, so I just glared at him. I straightened up and motioned with my head toward the rebbe. Levi's left eye spasmed frenetically as his glance ricocheted from one Lupan to the next.

Fur snorted. "We watched a few of the Lupans go through their shapechange."

I understood. That could scare the shit out of anybody. Levi's cowering acted like a challenge to the Lupans, and they displayed far more aggression toward him than they ever had toward Fur or me. When my companion Lupans changed back to humanoid form, Levi bolted in the direction of the ship to a chorus of barks and howls. He screamed obscenities at the Lupans as he ran, but no one pursued him.

Leader stepped before me. "You pass trial, Captain Berger." It was the first time he had addressed me by name. "Welcome to People."

A chorus of barks and howls deafened me, but they were congratulatory, rather than threatening. I could not help but grin. Fur followed suit.

I donned my returned clothes. I had thought that shoes would be a blessed relief, but my swollen feet did not fit into my boots. My socks gave me a bit of cushioning, which helped. I reinstalled my earbud.

"Okay. What next?" I asked.

Leader stared at me; his golden eyes seemed to see through to *my* thoughts. He reverted to his own growled language, and Ruthie translated. *"You will be informed of our needs."* They were more fluent in their own language.

They took me to see someone called Former Leader, one of the elder statesmen, I presumed. The Lupan that sat on a stool in the middle of the room was the sorriest specimen I had seen on their world. Patches had fallen out of his dull dandruff-flecked mane, showing the raw red scaly skin beneath. There were bare patches elsewhere on his body.

He stood, but with hunched shoulders, body angled away from me. He would not meet my eyes. This was a far cry from the confident, almost domineering figures of the other People. Especially for one who had been top dog.

My Lupan guide had not even stepped into the room for an introduction, as if Former Leader was now taboo...or considered contagious.

"Greetings," I said. "I'm Dr. Cy Berger."

Nothing.

"I'm told that there's a disease problem that threatens your society and that you can help me understand it. Does it have to do with your coat?"

Former Leader straightened up, met my eyes. *"You are a healer?"*

"Yes, I am."

"You see me as I am? I was not always so. I was Leader. I stood above all others. Then this." He waved a hand at his mane, then his body. *"You can fix this?"* His voice was as close to plaintive as I had heard in these beings.

"May I examine you?"

He nodded.

I examined his skin, mane, and coat, then asked, "May I take samples of your skin and hair? I only need to scrape the surface. It won't be painful."

He made a noise something like coughing up a hairball. *"Pain is meaningless."*

"I need to go back to my ship and get some materials. I'll be right back."

He nodded again and sat on his stool.

***

"That's it," I told Fur. "I suspected as much as soon as I saw Former Leader. He has a bad case of mange. The parasites aren't the same ones as on Terran animals, but they're comparable. Microscopic mites that burrow into the superficial epidermis and cause inflammation and hair loss.

"It will be no problem to treat. What I don't

understand is why this is such a big deal. Former Leader is the only one we've seen who is badly affected. And even then, this isn't a life-threatening condition."

"Yeah, but remember the guard we first met?" asked Fur. "The one that scratched at his neck and was then shunned?"

"So?"

"What strikes you about Leader, other than his tone of overbearing superiority?"

"His appearance," I replied. "His mane is by far the most luxurious of any of the People. And *Former* Leader is just the opposite. You think that their mane is their main status symbol? No pun intended. That it determines superiority?"

"I think that's a major factor. Probably not the only one, though." Fur smoothed his beard. "I can't believe that physical prowess doesn't play a role, but you have to have both to reach the top—and stay there."

I nodded. "That makes sense. That's why they expected you to be the leader, with your size and beard. Like the dragons did. Mange is contagious, so they isolate and shun those infected by the parasite. I'll bet that's why we didn't see any others who were infected. They banish them to the forest or some isolated place. Everyone else is afraid of loss of *their* status."

"Yeah. In a community where personal dominance is everything, a disease like this undermines the entire structure of the society."

"We need to speak with Leader again."

***

Leader listened to my explanation without change of expression. When I finished, he said, *"This is good, Captain Berger. That you can cure this affliction will relieve the People. But that is not the entire problem.* "

"Oh, what else is the matter? I've seen no other—?"

Leader growled, *"Look at the People. What do you not see?"*

As I glanced around, Fur nudged my arm. "We've never seen a female. Or kids, or cubs, whatever they call them."

Fur was right. I had assumed that they were kept isolated from the influence of us offworlders, but maybe not. I looked at Leader. "Where are your females and young?"

There was a low, almost subsonic rumble from the surrounding Lupans.

"There are none," Leader said.

"None? That's not possible?"

"There has never been a female. And for many, many turns there have been few cubs. Captain Berger, the People die."

***

Back at the ship, we puzzled over the plight of the Lupans. To help me think it through, I explained the problem to Levi.

He asked, "Where could the Lupans come from, if there are no females? Or children?"

I shrugged. "I thought you would have no difficulty imagining them *created* that way."

"Do not push me, Berger." His glare could have melted ice.

Fur kicked my leg under the table. That had become an unpleasant habit.

I winced and rubbed my ankle. "There were things about my trial that puzzled me. The pack of feral wolves that threatened me looked like the sentient Lupans in their wolf form. Also, the Lupans watched me from hiding, and I sensed that if I had not driven the wolves off myself, they would have extricated me without significant harm, or at least before any damage was fatal. But they *desired* that encounter."

Fur asked, "Do you think the sentient Lupans evolved from those creatures?"

I nodded. "Anatomically, except for the coats and manes and cranial capacities, the wild wolves appeared too similar to the Lupans to be coincidental."

"So they are beasts," Levi exulted. "These things are abominations. We should have no more to do with them. Fix their skins and we will be gone."

I took a deep breath before I spoke. "We need some more information from Leader."

***

We met him in his hut.

I said, "The pack of animals that cornered me was almost identical to the People in your shifted form, except for minor features like their heavier coats and sparser manes and smaller skulls. What's their relationship to you?"

"They are our sires and dams," Leader said.

I was not sure I heard him right. "You mean you were born of them?"

He nodded.

"But you said there were no females among the People. And I didn't detect anything like sapience. How can that be? Do they think logically and plan? Can they communicate with speech?"

"No."

"Can they transform, shape-shift?"

"No."

"This makes no sense," Fur said. "How do you get from a non-sentient wolf to a thinking wolf-man?"

I did not believe they had some magic elixir that transformed them, like the fictional Dr. Jekyll and Mr. Hyde. "This has to be biological, a major evolutionary step."

"The basis of evolution is a selection and accumulation of genetic changes—mutations—over time," Fur replied. "It doesn't happen overnight."

"How many of you are there—the People—on your planet?" I asked Leader. "And how many of the wolf-only forms are there?"

"There are uncountable sires and dams to every one of the People. Once there were twice as many People."

My heart pounded. "And there are no females among the People."

It was not a question, but Leader nodded.

"Then there can only be one answer," I said. "Every one of the People represents a genetic mutation, one that confers both sentience and the ability to change shape on the carrier of that mutation."

Leader stared at me without comprehension.

"It's in your seed," I explained. "There must be a change in your seed that confers thinking and shape-shifting."

Leader said, *"Our seed is changed to make us different? How does this occur? Can it replace our People?"*

"Before I know for sure, I will need some of your seed."

***

Fur, Levi, and I sat in the laboratory of *GCVS*. I waved the genetic analysis readouts in frustration.

"Levi, can't you see it? All of the species we have encountered have DNA or a closely related molecule.

And they have structures analogous to chromosomes. Not to mention physiological forms congruent with Terran biology. The People are no different. Evolution wouldn't work differently with Lupans than it does with us."

Levi scowled. "Blasphemy. God created all these forms after he created man." Before I could jump on that one, he rushed ahead. "If he *did* create these aliens, which I question. In any case, they do not have souls. They are *not* human but no more than animals."

"I can't deal with your steadfast ignorance and bigotry anymore," I snapped.

Levi's face darkened, and his stocky body became rigid. "You don't speak to a rebbe like that. You don't speak to *me* like that." He rubbed his scar so hard I thought he might draw blood. "I am your spiritual advisor, and you risk your soul."

I stared at him in amazement as my stomach churned. "*My soul*? Oh, of course, Rebbe. How foolish of me, Rebbe. You have my most abject apologies, Rebbe. I don't know what came over me, Rebbe." I glared at him. "Why don't you just fuck off?"

His eyes widened to black pools of hate. He looked at Fur, who clearly was poised to step between us, looked back at me, but said nothing. After a few moments, he turned on his heel and marched out, his back as straight as if he had a steel post rammed up his *tuches*.

Fur said, "I think you just might have pushed him past his limit. You may regret what he does."

I sighed. "I can't help it. The man is beyond comprehension. Let's finish this up."

Fur took the readout from me and gazed at it. "The People are only males. Therefore, the mutated gene has to be on their version of the Y chromosome, so every time this mutation occurs, it creates a new member of the People. Leader said that they watched the wild wolves and when they identified an affected cub, they removed it and raised it themselves."

"Yeah," I added. "The cubs were recognized when they shape-shifted spontaneously. It seems to take a couple of years to get that under control. But why all of a sudden are there no more mutations and no more affected cubs? That's what makes no sense."

Fur's brow creased. "Well, what are the usual causes of changes in DNA? Radiation. Chemicals. Viruses. I suppose that if any of those were responsible, they could have been removed from the environment, but that's hard to imagine in this civilization."

I nodded. "Viruses don't cause mutations. They insert their own genetic material into cells. Most of the mutations important for evolution occur when a cell divides and it makes a faulty copy of its DNA. I agree that chemicals and radiation are not likely here. In any case, most mutations are random, not something this specific. It has to be something else."

We puzzled silently for a few minutes until a thought hit me.

"Wait a minute. What if we're dealing with a segment of DNA that is inherently unstable? There are plenty of examples of that in humans and animals. Like the fragile X chromosome in humans. Say some Y chromosomes have a fragile area that can mutate to the sentience gene. Every time that occurs, that particular defective Y is removed from the wild wolf population because one of the People is born."

Fur added, "So, over time, there will be fewer and fewer carriers with the defective Y until there are no more. And no more sentient cubs."

"Right. But how do we fix this?"

Fur smiled. "What they need is a population of sentient females who carry the critical gene on their X

Stephen A. Benjamin

chromosomes. Then the People are self-reproducing and no longer rely on a chance mutation in the wild wolves."

"That's it, Fur. Brilliant. And it won't matter if the gene is dominant or recessive, because it will be on all X and Y chromosomes."

"What is 'brilliant,' Berger?" Levi couldn't stay away, but acid dripped from his words.

I grimaced. "We have figured out a way to solve the People's problem. The male Lupans carry a mutated gene for sentience. We'll isolate and copy it, then insert it onto the X chromosomes in ova from wild female wolves. Once we fertilize the ova with sperm from the sentient males, we will have offspring, both males and females, who all carry the critical gene. From there on, the People will be a self-reproducing population, not one that depends on a rare chance mutation to survive."

"But this would take years." Levi's face went from dark to pale in seconds.

I laughed. "Not what you think. The forced embryonic maturation incubators we got on Sammara can accomplish what we need to do in a couple of weeks. The People can take care of the babies from there."

"Weeks? We should never have come at all. Now you tell me weeks?" His black eyes bored into mine. "You deny God, Berger, but now you endeavor to *play* God for these abominations. So be it." His eye did not twitch, and he made no threats. He turned and left.

This behavior worried me more than his usual belligerent ravings. Well, I could do little now.

***

I explained our plan to Leader and a cohort of his pack, simplifying as much as I could. There were many perplexed thoughts, particularly when I told them we would have to tranquilize and collect ova from wild females and fertilize those with "seed" from themselves. I would have bet anything that some of the more recent sentient offspring were the result of breedings between the People in their wolf forms and the wild females. This behavior would not have been widespread since, if discovered, it would cause permanent loss of face in their stratified society. I wondered if the mange might have been picked up from the feral wolves after such an encounter and passed back to the People.

The collection of ova was not difficult. I had Ruthie set the *GCVS* down on the plain in the area of a wolf pack, on directions from a guide Lupan who came with us. Fur and I followed the Lupan to a grove of trees. We stayed downwind and crept up to a clearing where the pack rested. Fur raised the trank rifle and shot two females in quick succession. We had decided to take no more than two from any pack to diversify the gene pool. The rest of the pack jumped up in confusion, but when our Lupan guide stepped into the open and growled, they dispersed into the wood.

I did quick laparoscopies and harvested eight ripe ova from each female. We repeated this effort five more times, so we had ova from twelve females, then headed back to the settlement.

When we met with Leader again, I explained the plan. "We will use four eggs from each female to produce young. All of the young, males and females, will be of the People."

"That is good," Leader said. *"You will use my seed for all. We will have strong cubs."*

I frowned and glanced at Fur, who suppressed a smile.

"Um, no, Leader. That won't work." I plunged

ahead despite a growl from the Lupan. "Every ovum must be fertilized by a different one of the People. We need to diversify the gene pool as much as possible."

Leader shook his head, mouth open. I didn't think I was getting through to him.

"Think of it this way. If we used your seed to produce all the pups, then they would all be just like you."

"Yes. Good."

"No. Not good. You are the strongest and most impressive of the People. If every one of the males from this breeding produced you, no one would be dominant. They would fight each other for control, perhaps killing each other off until only one remained. Then this whole effort would have been wasted."

Leader shrugged. *"We would have females. We could breed them."*

"And this would be done by a few dominant males and you would have the same problem again. The whole point here is to give you a new population of young males and females. The rest of the People are aging. Yes, you can breed the new young female People, but you need those young males for your future."

Not convinced, Leader grunted and turned away.

Before I lost him, I said, "Leader, you must be the first to donate your seed. You may have the first choice of eggs. We have images of the females that match the eggs. Then you may choose the other forty-seven males to participate."

He turned back to me. *"I will look at the images."*

I breathed a sigh of relief. Nothing like selling a little alien porn.

As we walked back to the *GCVS* to prepare the lab and incubators, Fur grinned at me. "This one might surpass anything we have done yet. Cy Berger, father to werewolves."

I snorted and punched him on the arm.

He laughed. "As impressive as the People are, shape-shifting and all, these relative Goliaths were in danger of being brought down by a bunch of microscopic Davids. Before we 'play God,' we do have to deal with a bunch of mangy curs."

CHAPTER 20

<We must have help.>
<We do not need help. Do not impinge on our hive.
If you—>
<Beware. Danger in burrow. Danger—>
<What manner of beings are you?>

THE MESSAGES THAT bombarded us projected directly into our minds. My stomach heaved.

"What insanity is this?" Levi screeched.

The transmission centered on a system only a short distance off our route home.

I turned to Fur. "What do you think? Whoever they are, they don't seem to agree on whether they want help or not."

"We must return to Dovid's World. We are finished with helping creatures on useless worlds." Levi's voice stroked my nerve endings like fingernails on a chalkboard.

"Yeah. Curious." Fur pulled at his beard. "Can't hurt to head in that direction and see what's up. It's not far."

Levi erupted. "I forbid it. Absolutely forbid it. Computer, do not take us anywhere but back to Dovid's World." He looked at me, his black eyes scorching my soul. "You are playing with fire, Berger. I have already had your parents arrested because you have disobeyed my commands."

This was news to me. My stomach turned over again, and I squinted against the incipient headache.

"They will be tortured unless I countermand the orders."

Pain pulsed in my temple. My voice shook. "If one hair on my parents' heads is touched, your own loved ones—if you have any—will be saying the *Kaddish* for you, you son-of-a-bitch."

Levi stepped toward me and grabbed the front of my tunic. "I will—"

I brought my forearm down on his wrist. He loosed his grasp, but then went for my throat with both hands. The bastard was strong from all his weight lifting. His fingers cut off my breath, and I tried to knee him in the groin. I was not successful, not having room to maneuver. He squeezed tighter.

I slammed the heels of both my hands on his ears. He grunted and relaxed his grip momentarily, but then squeezed even harder. I grabbed his wrists but could not budge them. The blaze of his fury cut through my shields, adding nausea and vertigo to the lack of oxygen to my brain. His suffused face started to waver, and my vision faded before I felt another set of hands intervene.

Fur pried the rebbe's fingers loose. As strong as Levi was, he could not match the big man. Fur put his post-like arms between us and pulled us apart. "I think you had better come with me, Reb Levi," he said.

"You've threatened me and my parents at every turn," I croaked as I rubbed my throat, "but you are not going to have a chance to give more fucking orders. You're not in charge of this expedition anymore."

Levi stood with his mouth open, face purple. His white scar seemed to throb in time with his twitching eye. "You cannot—"

"Ruthie, activate my override, execute program

Levi Lockout."

"What are you doing? Computer, ignore that command," Levi screamed.

I stared at the rebbe. "As of now you have no rights to operate anything on the *GCVS* outside of the food machines. Ruthie, I don't want him on the bridge without Fur or me, so lock it if we're gone. Let him access the comm to us if we are off ship, but that's all."

"You can't do that!" Levi struggled against Fur's grasp.

"Just shut the fuck up. *I* programmed the AI interface. It takes *my* commands. I don't know what's happening on this world, but we're going to find out and see if we can help." I glared at Levi.

Ruthie broke in, her dulcet tones at odds with her words. "Command sequence activated, Cy. You know, I never did like the way Reb Levi insulted me, so I am happy to keep him under control. That will be fun."

I about swallowed my tongue on that one. The first image that hit my mind was that of Hal, the computer in *2001: A Space Odyssey*. What kind of monster had I created here?

The rebbe's black eyes went wide. He stared at the comm board, then stopped struggling and said, "Let me go. I will leave." When released, Levi broadcast hate that would have immolated my brain if he had the power. Then he wheeled and stalked off the bridge.

Fur gave me a long, hard stare. I could feel he was worried about the repercussions of what had just occurred, but he said nothing more. I rubbed my neck, anticipating the bruises that I knew would appear, while I tried to get my stomach and head under control.

***

As we settled into orbit around an unnamed world.

Ruthie said there were no records of the planet in any of the databases. I hailed the planet on the comm and myriad voices assaulted our senses again.

"Whoever you are, please, stop contacting us all at once. Our minds can't tolerate it. If you persist, we must leave."

The assault paused, but it then resumed even more frenetically.

<Help. You must—>

<No. Stay away—>

<Danger. There is dang—>

<Who are you? What do you intend?>

"Shit. Ruthie, can you do anything? Shield us somehow?"

Levi stormed back onto the bridge just as I gave this direction. "What is happening? I am going mad."

I could only wish. "We're trying to get a handle on it. These things are incredible telepaths." My writhing guts agreed.

Fur groaned. "I can't think straight."

Silence descended. Ruthie said, "I have erected a barrier, Cy. It will work at this distance, but I can't say what will happen on the surface of the planet."

I breathed a sigh of relief. "Thanks, Ruthie. You're a godsend." I ignored Levi's sputter at what he considered blasphemy. "We need to figure out how to communicate rationally with these beings."

Fur frowned. "It almost sounds like there's some sort of civil war going on. The last voice seems to be the only rational one, wanting to know who we are and what we want."

"Yeah. Maybe we can contact that one to start."

"Contact no one," Levi screeched. "This is too dangerous. They are warning us themselves. We must leave."

I clearly had not gotten across to him. "Levi, why

don't you just go back to your cabin and stick your head up your ass for a while? When you're ready to be useful, you may come out. If not, just stay there."

Levi's face resembled a bruise. "Cohen. You are a devout Jew. You understand. Stop him from this madness." He turned back to me. "Your parents are already suffering. That I guarantee you," he screamed.

My head pounded as I stepped forward with balled fists, but Fur grabbed Levi's arm first. He bodily picked the rebbe up by both arms and said, "It's time for you to learn some truths yourself, Levi. Guess who I am?" Then he slammed the rebbe down on his feet, eliciting a grunt of pain, and hauled him off the bridge. "It's time for a chat." I heard Fur say before they disappeared down the corridor.

I sat back down and breathed deeply, pressing on my abdomen with crossed arms. Levi's final words reverberated in my brain, but I needed to concentrate on the matter at hand. The mental voices were gone so I activated the comm.

"They are killing us. You must—"
"You have no hope. We will kill—"
"Hide. We must hide. Run—"
"We must communicate."

"You," I barked, "the one who wants to communicate. Can you shut down the rest of the voices?"

After a moment, the comm went quiet. Then the last voice came through from the speakers. At least Ruthie kept it out of our heads.

"Is this acceptable?"

"What's going on down there? It sounds like a disaster."

"We are having difficulties. Our mind is fractured."

"'Our mind is fractured?' What in blazes does that mean? I don't understand."

Fur walked back in and said, "I left Levi to cool off, but I doubt he will. He was rather incredulous when I told him who I was."

"I don't doubt that a bit."

The voice spoke in my head and interrupted us. <*It is confining to speak through your electronics. I will speak directly, but will not allow others to do so.*>

"I'm sorry, Cy," Ruthie broke in. "The being has overridden my block."

<*If this is not acceptable, I will withdraw. I will keep the other voices out.*>

"So long as it's just your voice. Who are you?"

<*I am the Overseer.*>

Fur looked at me and shrugged. "That helps a lot."

I responded. "Greetings, Overseer. Can you explain what the problem is so we can understand it?"

<*Our society is fragmenting. We are no longer one. Our parts are at war, seeking dominance, where none is possible. We are doomed if this is not corrected.*>

"Okay, you're at war. There's nothing that we can do to assist in that case. We are a veterinary medical service, not peacekeepers. I'm sorry, but that's the way it is."

<*You mistake my words. There is fighting, but that is not the difficulty. I need the kind of help I see in your mind: you call it 'medicine'.*>

I glanced at Fur. "Shit. The thing reads minds, too? Overseer, we can help the wounded, but not at the risk of putting ourselves in the middle of a civil war."

<*That is not my intention. It is not help for the wounded that we need.*>

"Then what?"

<*I need one who manipulates brains.*>

"You need *what?*"

<*One who helps with consciousness alteration.*>

Fur's murmured, "I *think* it means a psychiatrist."

"A *psychiatrist*? I'm not a psychiatrist. I'm a veterinarian, for crying out loud. I can't help you."

<You can. I have looked at other worlds, and you have assisted others who are different.>

I looked at Fur, eyebrows clawing their way up my brow. "You've contacted *other worlds*? If you have that kind of mental capability, what do you need us for?"

<I believe you can help.>

I let Overseer's words dangle in the air for long moments. "Maybe we can do this from the ship?" I said to Fur. "Then we don't have to put ourselves at risk on the ground."

<You must land to assist us. This is not what it seems.>

I did not have a clue as to what the thing meant. Our voyage had stretched the meaning of veterinary medicine. I expected that we might run into some unusual situations, even a strange animal or two. We had far exceeded our allotment in *that* regard, but this promised to be the strangest of all. Playing psychiatrist to a warring species—if it *was* one species.

<We are one species. You have helped all those other species you thought about.>

"This thing can read minds and *I'm* supposed to be the psychiatrist?" I sighed and dropped my chin to my chest.

Fur grinned. "Pull this one off and you'll be famous throughout the galaxy."

***

The planet had no discernible cities, or even settlements large enough to identify as such. The seas were muddy green and covered about half the planet's surface. The landmasses were uniform ochre except where mountain ranges thrust bedrock toward the sky.

The Overseer directed us to a spot on the northern hemisphere that was indistinguishable from any other as far as we could tell. As we got close, we saw a series of earthen domes that jutted above the ochre plain. Overseer directed us to land near one of the domes, and Ruthie brought us in.

The atmosphere was not breathable—high in methane and ammonia—so Fur and I donned our suits and armed ourselves. At the Overseer's direction, we exited and moved toward the nearest mound. Gravity was a bit higher than Dovid's World, but not enough to be a problem. The vegetation resembled splotched brown, olive, and gray lichen. I had Ruthie shut the airlocks.

"For all the telepathic communication, we still have no idea what these aliens look like," I said.

"I think we're about to find out," Fur pointed to an opening in the side of the dome.

What emerged might have been the communal offspring of a daddy longlegs spider, creeping Kudzu, and belly button lint. The central body was a ball of grayish-green fluff that stood about head high. A multitude of long thin legs covered with greenish leaf-like structures stuck out from the body. Two pairs of thicker bare legs—I assumed they marked the front of the thing— were tipped with hand-sized pincers. A mass of glittering black spheres spun within the body lint.

The three beings moved to the edge of the mound. One raised its front legs toward us.

"There is danger here. You must hide." The translation came through my suit's speaker. At least the Overseer was keeping his promise to stop the mental voice assault.

They constantly pirouetted their bodies on their myriad delicate legs as if on lookout for the danger they feared.

Fur had his hand on his blaster. "I have a bad feeling about this."

I did a double take. I didn't *think* he had been watching my old *Star Wars* vids. I shook my head and addressed the spider-things. "We were invited by the Overseer. We're here to help."

"The Overseer no longer commands us. We cannot stay in the open. Follow us."

They turned and moved toward the entrance to the dome.

I saw Fur's face blanch, even through the suit's faceplate.

"What's wrong?"

"Cy, I...I don't..."

"What is it? Are you sick?"

"No. I just can't...I can't go in there."

This was not like him. "Why?"

He shook himself like a dog trying to rid himself of fleas. "I can't abide underground places." He looked down at the ground. "I have claustrophobia."

I stood open-mouthed. In all the time I had known him, this had never reared its ugly head. Then I recalled how uncomfortable he had been when we entered the tiny hut on Lupus IV. "Okay, I agree. Let's get back to the ship."

Then our conversation came to an abrupt close.

"Flee! Flee! They come."

Levi, listening on an open comm, screeched, "What is happening? Who is coming?"

A howl of fear from the beings battered my empathic sense like a physical blow. I had no time for Levi. "Ruthie, shut him off."

I looked for the source of the creatures' panic. A horde of even larger beasts galloped around both sides of the ship. They resembled our greeters but with a denser core and stouter legs. Wicked-looking spines glinted on front legs that had pincers the size of my torso. The telepathic emotional message was one of hate and destruction. That moved me more than the panic of the dome dwellers. The oncoming monsters were between the ship and us.

"We've got to get in there," I yelled at Fur, and darted for the entrance of the mound.

Fur followed, but hesitated at the underground entry. I grabbed his arm and tugged. It was like trying to move a land drone, but he relented before the horde reached us. One spider did something on the wall with two legs and a rock barrier slammed down behind us.

"This will give time, but they will enter. We must go."

Fur shuddered.

There were many more spiders clustered in the tunnel we had entered. In response to their combined fear, I doubled over and almost vomited before I got myself under control. At least our guides were friendlier than the things outside. A blaster might take down a few of those creatures, but there were dozens. Maybe more.

"We must go." I could not tell which spider was speaking to us, but we followed the horde.

The tunnel's earthen walls were smooth, hard, and slick as glass. Eerie greenish illumination seeped from patches of a fungus-like growth and bounced off the burnished walls. The passage was tall enough for Fur, but he still walked with his head down and his shoulders scrunched together. I described our progress to Ruthie as we walked.

"We need you to keep a trace on us. We'll never find our way out of these warrens if you don't. We've passed at least a half-dozen intersecting tunnels already."

"Cy, you are breaking up. GPS read...cannot follow..."

"Shit. Keep trying, Ruthie."

I wondered how Fur would respond to our loss of communication, but he seemed oblivious. When we marched out into a spacious cavern, Fur straightened up a bit, but not completely.

A host of creatures awaited us and the block on mental communication that had been protecting us disappeared.

<Danger.>

<They come.>

<We must flee.>

<Who are outsiders?>

<To the catacombs.>

<Kill strangers.>

At the last thought, Fur quivered. I couldn't say I blamed him. Pain lanced through my temples.

"*Quiet*," I screamed. "I can't make sense out of anything you're saying." I instinctively held my hands to my ears, a useless gesture.

The voices subsided to a dull roar. I looked at Fur. His eyes were wide as he stared off into space.

"What were those things outside?" I asked the spiders. "They resembled you, but were more threatening."

<We are the workers. Those are the soldiers.>

"Whose soldiers? Some other army? Where are yours?"

Confused thoughts fleeted through my mind. Then something spoke again. *<We do not understand. What is 'army'?>*

"Well they can't be *your* soldiers, can they? Why were they attacking you?"

<Only one soldiers. They kill. Take control.>

Fur spoke for the first time since we had entered the

dome. His voice was hoarse. "Maybe there's been a military insurrection. Maybe some sort of coup."

<Catacombs are filled with nurses.> Another voice.

<We will kill. Take their space.>

<Now. Go.>

<Kill.>

"Wait a minute!" It seemed like the only way to get their communal attention was to yell. "What in hell are you talking about? Those things out there are trying to kill you. You ran in here to be safe. Now you want to kill someone else? Nurses, yet?" I looked at Fur. He wrapped his arms around his chest.

<They are nurses. Not workers. We need the space for protection from soldiers.>

"What is this? Does everybody just kill everybody else here? If so, I want out. We can't help you."

"I second that," Fur muttered.

The clamor in my head ceased. I could still hear the movement of the creatures around us, but internally the constant chatter of voices in my head disappeared. Then Overseer spoke.

<Humans. I sense you do not object to that appellation. You begin to see some part of the problem that faces us.>

"Faces *us*?" I retorted. "I don't understand it or want any part of it. I said we wouldn't get involved in a civil war. We won't take sides. And there seems to be more than two sides. I want you to get us out of here. Now."

Then the clamor broke through Overseer's silence.

<They have broken through.>

<The soldiers come.>

<Danger. Danger.>

<We must take flight. The catacombs.>

<Flee. Flee...>

Stephen A. Benjamin

The entire herd of workers stampeded for the smaller tunnels at the opposite side of the chamber from where we had emerged.

Fur stood rooted to the spot.

Overseer spoke again. *<You must follow them. Haste is necessary. The soldiers come.>*

I grabbed Fur's arm again and pulled. "Come on." I couldn't budge him.

He stared at the even smaller tunnel entrances. "I can't," he moaned. "I can't."

His distress hit me like a blow.

He said, "You go," as he unholstered his blaster.

It seemed that facing a ravening horde of giant spider-things was preferable to the unknowns of the cramped tunnels.

"I won't leave you, Fur. If we're going to die here, we do it together." I pulled my blaster and clicked off the safety.

That brought him back to himself. He whirled to me and said, "No. I can't let you..." He grabbed me by one arm and pelted for the tunnels.

"Ow. Let me go, you big oaf. You're dislocating my arm."

"Sorry," he gasped.

As we reached the first tunnel, I looked back and saw the soldiers enter the cavern at the other side. That added to our urgency, and we sprinted through a downward-sloping tunnel with no end in sight.

It was a descent into madness. Tunnels filled with a seething mass of workers branched to the left and right. Some workers attacked us with mental cries of *<Different. Different. Kill.>*

Despite their size, they lacked significant mass. After collisions with us, the aliens careened into walls or others of their kind. We easily fended off the workers who did assault us. The major danger was a rip in our suits from their pincers, but the suits were tough, carbon nanofiber-reinforced fabric. We heard sounds of battle and screams behind us, giving further impetus to our flight.

We broke into another cavern. A different group of aliens huddled in the center surrounded by the workers. These were smaller, no more than shoulder tall. While their basic body and leg anatomy was similar, they had large, gray-white, bulbous protrusions from their rear.

I said, "Nurses?"

Fur shrugged.

After a few straggling workers rammed their way into the crowded cavern, rock doors again slammed down over the entrances. The shriek of thousands of voices in my head tore at my sanity. An almost palpable miasma of fear surged up from the huddled creatures in the center of the packed cavern. Then the workers waded into the mass of nurses and started to flail about with their pincers. The terrorized mental anguish dropped me to my knees. Fur scrunched down and grabbed my arm, whether in support of himself or me, I couldn't say. What an ineffectual pair we made.

"Stop it," I screamed. "Stop it!"

Again, my yell seemed to get through to these beings as nothing else. Perhaps I unconsciously transmitted through my empathic ability. Whatever, it stopped the slaughter.

The Overseer's voice came through in the ensuing silence. *<Be calm. There is room enough for all. The soldiers cannot gain access to your refuge; they retreat. Soon all will be safe.>*

Rather than soothe the mass of spiders, the Overseer's words seemed to provoke the throng to even greater violence. Fur and I worked our way over to a wall. When the nurses started to fight back, the bedlam accelerated.

"We have got to get out of here," I yelled to Fur. "This is insane."

Fur shuddered. I felt his internal battle for control, which he had won for the moment. "Look at the structure of this society," he said. "What does it resemble?"

"Insects. Ants."

"Right. Nursemaids, workers, soldiers, an overseer, like a queen, maybe."

I nodded. "But they're no longer working together. They've fragmented into separate hordes that are at war."

"They're a hive-mind consciousness. They communicate telepathically. And the Overseer is the hub of that consciousness."

"But then why is this happening?" I asked. "The Overseer seems to be okay. At least it seems to be rational."

Overseer interrupted our discussion. <*I am not well. I am ill. That is the cause of this strife.*>

"What's the cause of your illness?" I asked. "Is it something we can treat? Do we need to reach you physically in order to help?"

<*It is not a physical disease. My brain parts have separated. They no longer are under my control. They vie with one another for dominance.*>

My mouth hung open as I looked at Fur. "Good Lord. I think the damn thing has Multiple Personality Disorder."

***

We stood alone in a chamber big enough for the two of us and the two aliens who brought us. These were smaller yet than any creatures we had seen, resembling little workers with tiny pincers. His servants, Overseer told us. There were no walls as such, just a pale gray, cottony substance that pulsed with an uncanny green light. The Overseer seemed to speak from all around us.

<This is the nexus. The centrality. This is where the Overseer oversees.>

"Great," I muttered. "Do we do a dance or pull a rabbit out of a hat?"

Fur looked more harried by the minute. His hands twitched, and his head jerked about, as if convinced something was always right behind him.

<I am the Overseer.>

<No, I am the Controller. There is no life without my nursemaids to succor the Queen.> That was *not* the Overseer's voice.

<The soldiers are mine. *We fight. We kill.>* A different voice.

A deeper, gruff voice. *<We must work. Our labors are lagging. We cannot survive without our labors.>*

<Silence! I am the Overseer. I will have control.>

The other voices faded. I wondered if they responded to the Overseer's command, or if it just blocked their transmissions, as it had done earlier.

<Not long ago, there was one mind. All its pieces worked harmoniously. All were subordinate to the Overseer. The Hive worked together, nursemaids serving the Queen and the larvae, workers providing the needs of the nursemaids, soldiers protecting from outside threat. Now predators can attack the Hive and destroy the Queen.>

I did not want to know what those were if they were worse than the soldiers.

<Now, the castes are adrift. With no direction, they falter at their tasks and turn on one another, as if they were strangers. I, the Overseer, see this, but my fragmented mind has descended to warfare for control.

<At times, I, the Overseer, can exert control, at

least enough to speak with you. At other times...> The Overseer went silent.

Fur's body twitched. Eyes closed, he mumbled something I had to lean close to hear.

"I don't know how long..." His voice trailed off as his head bowed to his chest.

I probed the Overseer for ideas on what we might do. "When did this whole thing start? Was it sudden?"

<It came over time. First, there was recalcitrance by the soldier command. An unwillingness to guard the burrows. Then the workers slowed, despite the cries of need from the nursemaids. I was able to set these right, but then I lost control. All became chaos.>

"Did anything happen just before then? Some event or injury?"

<None.>

"What about illness? Has there been any sickness in the colony?"

<None.>

This was singularly unhelpful.

I tried to engage Fur. I poked his arm. "What do you think?"

He started. "What? Uh, sorry. I wasn't listening."

"Come on, Fur. I need your help. There's been no injury or illness that seemed to precede the breakdown," I reiterated. "Do you have any ideas?"

"Ideas? No. No ideas. Um, do you think we can leave now?"

I had never seen Fur so forlorn. Not even when he injected me with Pronacian plague while trying to inject that lab lizard.

I shook his arm. "The tunnels are shut off because of the rampaging soldiers. We can't get out until we solve whatever is affecting the Overseer, so it can take back control. Get a grip, man. You're good at solving problems. Think."

We stood silent for long minutes; my mind whirled with uncertainty. I spoke hoping to get Fur functioning again.

"The only things I know about psychiatric disorders come from old vids, and they aren't known for medical accuracy. In humans, several distinct personalities can vie for control of the organic mind, the person switching from one to another. The submerged minds are not aware of what transpires between times.

"But this doesn't seem to be the case here. The Overseer's mind is aware of everything, but it's not in control of the consciousness of the soldiers, workers, and nurses who are organically separate entities themselves. There's paranoia in the separate castes. So the Multiple Personality Disorder analogy isn't a perfect fit."

I got no response. It did not look like Fur would be any help. The one vid that kept coming to mind was one where the characters were denizens of an insane asylum, a type of institution that disappeared a thousand years ago with medical advances dealing with mental illness. It had "Cuckoo's Nest" or something like that in the title. What stuck with me was electrical shock used to cure patients. That barbaric image had burned itself into my memory, and I had researched it out of curiosity. Apparently, it could be a valid and effective treatment according to some medical sources.

I wondered about drugs. Would I have to give them to every one of the individual creatures in the Hive? Or, could I somehow treat the Overseer itself? That was useless speculation. Even if I knew, I had nothing that I could use with me. We were stuck here with no hope of getting out unless the Overseer could bring sanity to his minions.

"Overseer," I said, "I have one idea, but don't know if it will work. Or even if it won't harm you in some way."

Fur perked up and looked at me.

<There is no hope without help. My minions are reduced to half their number. If we do not stop the carnage, there will be too few for life. Then all die.>

"Do you mean you, too?"

<Yes. My subsistence is dependent on the efforts of the workers and nursemaids and my personal servants. Without them, I die.>

Fur woke up and asked, "If you die, can we get out of here?"

<If our colony protection is lost, it will be invaded by predators. They hold back because the soldiers are here. If they are gone, all die.>

Fur turned to me. "Do something. Please, *do something.*"

***

I contacted the ship, passing messages via the Overseer's telepathy since Ruthie couldn't reach us. The Overseer passed on the incoherent, rage-filled rantings of Levi, as well as Ruthie's responses.

I addressed the Overseer. "Can you block out Levi, the one you say is screaming hate-filled oaths? And still let us talk to the other member of our crew?" I wasn't sure if I should reveal Ruthie's nature, although why I felt that was unclear even to me.

<You mean the silicon mind? Yes, I may do that.>

So much for my caution. "Can Ruthie, the silicon mind, hear me, then?"

<I will transmit your words.>

Fur remained silent, curled into a ball against one wall.

"Overseer, does any part of you go to the surface?"

<My workers and soldiers do this. The nurses and

the queen remain below.>

I shook my head. "No. That's not what I mean. Does any organic part of *you*, the central brain, extend out from this place? Like nerves, or conduits, or something?"

<Yes. I must have sensors throughout the Hive. I cannot rely only on the transmissions of my subjects.>

"And they bring in what? Light? Sound? Smell?"

<I receive auditory and visual input.>

"I guess it will have to be enough. Okay, here's what I want you to do. Give Ruthie the detailed location of some of your surface sensors. Then give her these instructions."

***

"Levi, you are going to have to go outside. There's no other option."

I pictured Levi outside the ship dragging heavy electrical cables and plugging them into the Overseer's sensory inputs. He had panic attacks just landing on alien worlds, much less having to face inhabitants like giant spiders.

"I will not help you, Berger. Under any circumstances."

"If we don't get out of here, you don't either," I said. "If Fur and I don't make it, you can't control the ship. Ruthie, if we die, cut off the air scrubbers. Remember that lesson, Levi? If those fail, you suffocate. When Levi is dead, you can return to Sammara and give them a report on the unfortunate loss of all your humans."

I suppose it did not reflect well on my nature that the thought of Levi's face purpling from lack of air buoyed my spirits, but after what he told me about my parents' torture, he deserved it. I wished I could be there to watch.

***

<*All is in readiness,*> the Overseer said. <*The silicon mind has used the organic one to connect cables to my sensors. We may begin.*>

I supposed if this worked, I might be glad that He-Who-Eats-With-Gusto didn't munch on the rebbe back on Dragonworld. I crossed fingers and toes and gave the word. "Okay. Pull the trigger."

I could feel the puzzlement of the Overseer.

"Tell Ruthie to switch on the current." I held my breath.

Nothing happened for long moments, and my heart plummeted. Stomach acid geysered into my throat. Would it end here, as we were close to the end of our voyage? Would I never see my folks or Roxanne again?

Then I felt a tremble, a minuscule tremor in the floor beneath my feet. It gained strength and I saw movement in the cotton wall fluff that composed the Overseer's organic body.

Fur stood, and his head jerked about him. "What's happening?" he croaked.

"I *hope* we are looking at our salvation. Ruthie is giving the Overseer electric shock therapy."

His eyes gleamed for the first time in hours, replacing the dull, flat, hopeless gaze that had clouded the big man's countenance.

A strident ululation battered my senses. It seemed to come from all around us. The intensity of the sound, coupled with a severe quaking of the floor, knocked me to the ground. I pressed my hands to my ears.

"Overseer, what's happening?" I screamed.

No answer. Pieces of the body fluff broke off and dropped to the cavern floor. The sound became unbearable. I continued to scream wordlessly, adding to the rawness of my acid-bathed throat. Fur's mouth formed a wide O, but I heard nothing.

Then there was silence, but it lasted no more than seconds before a cacophony of voices replaced it.

<Protect the Queen and the larvae.>

<Soldiers, to the surface. The Hive is attacked.>

<Workers, collect carcasses. Supply the nursemaids to feed the larvae.>

<Work together. Save the Hive.>

Then silence again.

"Did we do it?" Wonder tinged Fur's voice. "Did *you* do it?"

The Overseer's voice broke in, with an auspicious confidence it had lacked before. *<I am one again. The Hive functions. You have succeeded. The hive is beholden to you. I am the Overseer!>*

"Thank God," I breathed.

<Is God another member of your crew?>

I grinned. "I suppose so, in a manner of speaking." I could imagine Levi's reaction to that little exchange.

<I will have you directed to the surface now, if you wish.>

I said, "Yeah, but there's one more thing. You might be able to help us with a problem of our own."

<If it is within my power, I will help.>

"You can contact worlds at great distances, right? Could you reach our home world, Dovid's World? Get messages there?"

There was a momentary silence, then the Overseer spoke. *<I see the coordinates in your mind. Yes, I can reach your world.>*

"I want to get a message to my parents. See if they are okay."

Fur broke in. "Cy. We need to find out the status of everything at home. I told you that the revolt was imminent. We must learn if that's begun."

I nodded. "Yeah. All of the above. Overseer, we need to contact Dovid's World and Sammara to determine the status of the rebellion on Dovid's World. We also need to contact a number of other worlds we visited. You said you had already done that, so it should not be a problem. I need to find out if those worlds will support our rebellion."

<This will be done,> Overseer said.

Fur grinned and slapped me on the back. "*Our* rebellion, huh?"

I staggered at the blow but smiled back.

CHAPTER 21

THE PEOPLE AROUND the table included me, Fur, Colonel Glazer, Lieutenants Clarrett and Ranu, General Finster—a severe-faced, grey-haired woman in a uniform with lots of stars—and two men introduced as top members of the Sons-of-David. Most importantly, Roxanne sat next to me.

Despite the number of people, I could not keep my eyes off Roxanne. Colonel Glazer cleared his throat, and I wrenched my gaze to his face.

"If we are ready to begin, Berger?"

"Oh, yeah. Sorry."

Fur muffled a snort of mirth.

General Finster addressed us. "You know that Sammara has been the target of the expansionist plans of your home world, and we have no love for your governing party. It's also clear that the people of Dovid's World no longer want the Testamentary-Literalists to remain in power. They have rebelled against the government."

I knew this, but the statement of it still gave me chills. The Overseer had made contact with the SOD and we learned that the rebellion had started. Fur was ecstatic. I was not as thrilled. We could get no information about where my parents were or how they fared. Levi's torture threats had given me a new set of nightmares on the trip back to Sammara.

I glanced at Fur. He was as tense as I was. My heart raced as I asked, "Do you know anything more about my parents?"

Finster said, "We are aware of the situation regarding your parents." She looked at one of the SOD representatives, Charles Shapiro. "Please explain."

Shapiro looked at me. "Mr. Cohen apprised us of your parents' arrest. One of the efforts of the rebellion is to free all political prisoners. There are many more than just your parents, but I understand your concern. We will do the utmost to rescue them."

"Thank you," I said. A knot the size of a pumpkin throbbed in my chest.

Fur's and Roxanne's faces and emotions were somber with support.

Finster spoke again. "Those actions, while important to you, I understand, aren't the main issue. The rebels have neither the numbers, nor the armaments necessary to bring down the Test-Lit theocracy. They have undertaken their attacks with the promise of reinforcements from offworld."

The two SOD representatives nodded.

"Sammara is committed to supporting the rebellion and is sending troops now. We have good reason to want the Test-Lits gone from power, but our population is much less than that of Dovid's World. Our support for the rebels gives the combined forces no better than an even chance to overthrow the Test-Lits; there is no guarantee of victory. Your world has spent inordinate funds and efforts to build its military. We need more help."

There was silence around the table. Fur looked at me and said, "Your turn."

I addressed Finster. "You've read my report. I assume the others have, as well." There were confirmatory nods. "Okay. While Reb Schvartz demanded payment from those worlds where we assisted, that fell far short of the actual degree of aid that we provided. On some of these worlds, our assistance went beyond simple veterinary care, and what we did was crucial to the survival of the worlds' inhabitants. I secretly extracted promises of aid from some of those humans and aliens before we left their planets. After I confined Levi on the *GCVS*, through the Overseer we contacted all those we had assisted, including those I had not asked for help originally. They will supply troops or supplies to assist the revolution on Dovid's World."

Fur broke in. "It helped that Reb Schvartz insulted the inhabitants, human and nonhuman, on just about every planet we visited. Most couldn't believe that there was a world where people like him were in power."

Finster frowned. "Just how will these worlds be able to assist, Dr. Berger? They are scattered through this sector of the galaxy and some are primitive, without space travel."

"Yes, some of these worlds and beings have rudimentary civilizations with no spaceflight. This is what Fur and I propose. Pronac, Certis Prime, Cennesari, and Ulm are spacefaring worlds. The Pronacians will supply a substantial army in their own spaceships. Though their atmosphere was marginal for us, they can function in ours. Certis Prime is a human-settled agrarian world. They don't have a large military, however, their herdbeasts are excellent pack and food animals, especially the latter. Certis Prime will ship their herdbeasts with a contingent of their human handlers."

There were nods around the table. Always have to keep an army fed.

"The main contribution of Cennesari will be a force of Hunters." I looked around the room. "I assume you recall the Hunters from my report. Make no mistake. This is a formidable fighting force. A number of those humans who work with the Hunters will bring them in their ships."

"What about the rest of the human Cennesarians, or whatever you call them?" asked Glazer. "Seems they owe you something, as well."

"The Cennesari human population is not as happy with me. When I informed them that their livestock were sentient, it alienated the great majority of Cennesarians."

My mind flashed back to Cennesari, to the cenoxen and their plight. My gut cramped but I fought it off. Would I never be free of the pain of that failure? Perhaps not.

"The Hunters will assist us. I'm more than happy with that contingent."

Glazer harrumphed. "They coulda done more."

I paused and drew a breath. "Ulm is another difficult one. The planet runs on a proverbial shoestring. Their technology is dated and their space fleet far from modern. They'll send a couple of ships of their military. That aspect of their society is top notch. The flora of Ulm has an amazing array of protective mechanisms, including a variety of toxins. The Ulmians have adapted some of these for their military use."

Murmurs around the room made me stop.

"Do you suggest that we use toxic substances as weapons?" General Finster's voice held an edge.

I noted a frown on Roxanne's face, as well.

"Please. Let me continue. The use of lethal poisons, whether food, water, or airborne, is not acceptable. The same is true of biological warfare. But the Ulmians have one compound that we might consider. I'm not quite sure whether to call it a hallucinogen or a tranquilizer. It has some features of both. It's non-lethal and incapacitates the exposed person for a matter of hours. There supposedly are no deleterious aftereffects of exposure. It is most effective in confined spaces. Consider the potential loss of life—on both sides—if we have to clear out heavily defended buildings. Something like this could be useful. It's a much more effective analog to our tear gas. I don't urge its use—I am as reluctant as you to use biochemical weapons—but it is an option."

Finster leaned over and spoke to Glazer. He grunted a response I could not hear.

"What about the non-spacefaring worlds?" Lieutenant Clarrett asked.

"That means Dragonworld, Lupus IV, and the Hiveworld," I said. "Certis Prime has offered more than their herdbeasts. As an agricultural planet, they have a substantial cargo fleet. Their liners have large storage bays that will be suitable, after some modification, to convey a force of dragons to Dovid's World. From our first-hand experience, I can tell you that a battalion of dragons is a force to be reckoned with. The dragons live to fight and are thrilled by the opportunity. They also particularly dislike Reb Schvartz.

"Next, we need to find some way to convey a troop of Lupans from their worlds to ours. They will be another intimidating fighting unit."

Finster and Glazer conferred for a moment, then Finster spoke. "We can send a troop ship. How many do we need to transfer?"

"Several hundred, I'm guessing," I replied. "They are a small population."

Finster nodded. "No problem, then. One troop ship should do it."

"Then we have the Hiveworld dwellers. Their

soldiers would be an incredible strike-force, but I don't believe that they could function outside of their hive society or their own atmosphere."

"Then what—?" Glazer began.

"Some of the beings who have offered help don't speak Common, or have limited knowledge of our language. We need some form of general communication, lest we have a mob rather than a coordinated army. The Hive's overriding consciousness, The Overseer, is a telepathic mind of incredible power. It can read minds and can communicate across vast interstellar distances. As I mentioned, we used that capability when we contacted Dovid's World, Sammara, and the various worlds we had visited. It has agreed to join our army as the central nexus for communication."

A burst of clamor followed that announcement. When it calmed down, I said, "The Overseer itself won't come, but it will send a small clone who can manage our needs. It will accept a ride only if Fur and I supply it, though. We leave for the Hiveworld as soon as we can fit a *GCVS* compartment to contain its atmosphere. It will stay in the ship and work from orbit around Dovid's World."

Finster sat back and motioned for quiet. "Dr. Berger, Mr. Cohen, I commend you. What you have put together is nothing short of miraculous. While you travel to get this Overseer, we will alert all the other participants and get the space-lift underway. When you return, we will commence final operations." She looked around the room. "If there are no other questions—"

"Wait," I cried. "I do have one. Where is Reb Schvartz and what are your plans for him?"

Glazer replied. "Since you turned him over to us, he has been incarcerated in our maximum security prison. In isolation. I'm not sure he would last long in a prison full of Sammarans who well remember the atrocities of the Test-Lits. We plan to take him to Dovid's World. When we are victorious, he'll stand trial with the rest of their ruling council for crimes against humanity."

"And against every other form of sentient life," Fur said.

I nodded. As much as I would like to take personal vengeance against Levi, I recognized the need not to descend to his level.

As we exited the meeting room, Roxanne caught my arm. "I'm going with you."

I stopped and looked at her. "We'll go directly to Dovid's World and into battle once we get the Overseer."

"I'll be a field medic. Especially for the nonhuman contingent of your army. Your efforts over the past year have proven that will work."

I grinned. "The trip will be a hell of a lot more fun with you along instead of Levi. Hyperwave transmissions didn't quite do it for me."

She threw her arms around me and planted a sweet kiss on my lips. I found it was hard to return a kiss while I had an ear-to-ear grin.

***

On our trip to and from Hiveworld, Roxanne and I started out tentatively, hesitant to be demonstrative, especially in front of Fur. He seemed to find that hilarious, but gave us plenty of space. One morning we sat in the commissary, cradling cups of coffee, and gazing at one another.

"It's not really fair, you know," Roxanne said. "You know exactly what I'm feeling. I can't read you."

I huffed. "You know how I feel, even if I don't know how to put it into words. Somehow, around you, my tongue gets all twisted up."

She threw me a mock frown then twisted her lips in a sly grin. "I know one way to straighten out your tongue."

I felt heat rush to my face.

Roxanne didn't give me time to reply. "Well, I expect you to do better. After all, a girl deserves a bit of fawning."

I kept my face serious and said, "How's this?" I recited:

"How do I love thee? Let me count the ways.
I love thee to the depth and breadth and height
My soul can reach, when feeling out of sight
For the ends of Being and ideal Grace.
I love thee to the level of everyday's
Most quiet need, by sun and candlelight.
I love thee freely, as men strive for Right;
I love thee purely, as they turn from Praise.
I love thee with the passion put to use
In my old griefs, and with my childhood's faith.
I love thee with a love I seemed to lose
With my lost saints. I love thee with the breath,
Smiles, tears, of all my life!—and, if God choose,
I shall but love thee better after death."

Roxanne's mouth hung open by the time I finished and tears glistened in her eyes. She shook her head. "Cy. Oh, Cy. That is so beautiful. Did you actually write that? For me?"

Unfortunately, I had to break the spell. "I could only wish I wrote that. I meant every word, but they aren't mine. The poem was by Elizabeth Barrett Browning from nineteenth century on earth. To me, it's one of the most beautiful pieces ever written. And I do love you."

She rose, placed her cup on the table, and reached

for my hands. "Don't say another word. Come with me."

I kept my mouth shut, for once, and followed, heart beating like the cadence of a poem.

***

Shortly after that, I noted a change in our AI. Ruthie's responses to me became very formal, almost like they were when she responded to Levi. Her responses to queries by Roxanne were even brusquer. She followed my commands to the letter, but did not engage in her usual banter. I wondered about that, but put it out of my mind. Between Roxanne and the transfer of the Overseer's clone to the ship, I had enough to worry about.

One day, Roxanne crooked a finger toward me and motioned to her cabin. We entered and closed the door. She put her lips to my ear and said, "Can your AI hear us all the time? Even if I whisper in my quarters?" She never called Ruthie by name.

My eyebrows rose. What was she talking about? In full voice, I said, "I don't—"

"Shh." She put her fingers to my lips. "Whisper."

I felt foolish, but followed her direction. "I have no idea. I've never thought about it."

"I don't trust it," she said. "It doesn't like me."

I pulled away from her, eyes wide. "You're serious?"

"Quiet," she snapped. "I'm serious," she whispered again. "I can tell when a wom...someone doesn't like me. It's creepy. I feel like I'm watched and listened to all the time. I want someplace where we can be and talk without being seen or heard."

I nodded. "Okay. I'll do the programming." Easier to reprogram the AI that than argue with Roxanne. She never struck me as paranoid before, but this seemed a bit over the top.

But as I thought that, the uncomfortable feeling I had gotten about Ruthie resurfaced: Her disturbingly anthropomorphic characteristics, her bizarre responses to Levi, and my recollections of *2001: A Space Odyssey*. Oh well, I would give Roxanne her privacy. A weird AI was the last thing I needed to worry about now. First, we had a war to win.

CHAPTER 22

I HUNKERED DOWN behind some boulders just outside Jerusalem City, flanked by Roxanne and the dragon, He-Who-Eats-Enemies-for-Breakfast. The faces of my companions shone with a hellish glare as ruby laser fire reflected from the protecting granite. I flinched as the dull whump of a missile detonated nearby, and cringed at the thought of our casualties, both human and nonhuman. I had never held my empathic shields so tightly before, but it worked. All the emotional battering I had taken on our journey had forced me to develop them far beyond my previous capability. I worked hard on that during our trip to get the Overseer' clone. Without it, the fighting would have incapacitated me.

The populace of Dovid's World had rallied to the SOD once they rebelled openly. My people had had enough of despotism and terror. Things had been dicey to start until the Sammaran military force came in. Then there had been a stalemate. As General Finster had suggested, the Sammaran support alone was not enough to win the war. When Fur, Roxanne, and I arrived back on Dovid's World with the Overseer clone, we found our alien entourage in place and eager to do battle. The Dovidian people greeted us as saviors. In the two months since, assistance in the form of munitions and supplies had come from other planets, but only after they were convinced they would be on the winning side. We had beaten down the Test-Lit forces and now had them confined to a last stand in the capitol city.

I felt like anything *but* a savior. I still had no word on my folks who were in the main prison adjacent to the Test-Lit headquarters. My level of anxiety had steadily risen. If not for the support of Roxanne and Fur, I would have been a basket case.

And my "army" was stymied. I felt totally incompetent as a military leader. I was a veterinarian, for crying out loud. I turned to Roxanne and Fur and yelled over the tumult of the battle. "We can't stay pinned down like this. They have our range and are decimating us."

"Right," Fur shouted back. "Got any more bright ideas?"

I cringed again, this time at his words. The spot we were in was my own fault. I had thought to break our troops off in a flanking maneuver and attack from the west side of the city where the buildings were smaller. I thought the dragon "air force" would be more effective there than amongst the city center skyscrapers that were the main objectives. It turned out that gave the defenders a better look at the open sky and the incoming targets, and the open spaces on the ground where our main forces were. We took far too many casualties. The dragons and Hunters, effective in close combat, were vulnerable at long range. Pronacians and Lupans could use weapons—at least the Lupans learned to in their humanoid forms; they shape-shifted for hand-to-tooth fighting.

A thought cut through from the dragon, transferred by the Overseer's mind. *<We must reach the forest; hide and spread out. Missiles will be less effective.>* The dragon had proved to be a surprising strategist.

Certainly better than me. My command consisted mostly of me taking suggestions from my comrades.

"Okay," I said. "If we all move at once, it'll be harder for them to pick out single targets. Overseer, pass on the plan." When I saw He-Who-Eats nod, I yelled, "We move. Now!"

As I jumped up, accompanied by Fur, Roxanne, and the dragon, I could see an eruption of forms on the ground and in the air, all moving in the same direction. There were humans: Dovid's Worlders, Sammarans, and the soldiers from Ulm. Outnumbering them were the nonhumans: Lupans; Certis Prime packbeasts and their herdsmen; six-limbed Pronacians who reminded me of Edgar Rice Burroughs' green Martians, Cennesari tigers that raced in front of everyone else, and the dragon air force.

The woods gave us a respite, and I gathered the command group, including Roxanne, Furoletto, the Sammaran Lieutenant, Clarrett, Sergeant Stiegman commanding the Ulmian force, and the commanders of each of the alien groups.

"We won't have long," I said. "Whoever is manning this sector is better armed than I expected. We're taking too many casualties."

A missile detonated just within the edge of the wooded area we occupied.

"They're homing in on us again. Anybody got a plan?"

<*Cyberger,*> He-Who-Eats broke in, <*I suggest a flanking maneuver by my dragons, and a frontal assault by the rest of the force.*>

"They'll target you and decimate your dragons," I said.

The dragon rumbled a laugh. <*To die in battle is valiant, but we will come from all directions.*>

After a brief discussion, we agreed. Overseer

transmitted the plan.

"Okay, people, Go!"

The dragon force split and wheeled to the north and south. The armed humans, Pronacians, and Lupans moved forward and laid down heavy covering fire. The Hunters brought up the rear, by my command, despite their desire to charge in regardless of the losses they would take. We used the rubble of buildings and out-of-commission vehicles as cover, and made our way toward the Test-Lit defense perimeter. We moved within a couple of hundred meters and halted. Return fire was heavy. We huddled behind whatever cover we could find and waited for Overseer's signal.

<Now,> came the mental cry.

The dragons soared in from the rear and sides of the Test-Lit lines, darting erratically through the city's concrete canyons to take the defenders unawares. As the defensive fire moved from our positions to target the dragons' attack, we assaulted the front line. The Pronacian troops loped toward the perimeter faster that any human could, as they wielded their assault rifles. The Lupans followed, again faster than any human, firing as they ran. Finally, covered by the initial assault and the firepower of the human soldiers, the Hunters streaked through the defense lines and leaped the barricades as if they were not there. The rest of our contingent followed.

By the time I reached the battle line, the Test-Lits were in retreat. The three-pronged attack of the dragon air force wings and the frontal assault of the lizardmen, werewolves, and tigers had engendered panic amongst the defenders. The speed and agility of the nonhuman troops made them difficult to hit. Even when hit, if their wounds were not fatal they dealt out horrific injuries. If dragons, four-armed lizardmen—each wielding two weapons, a pulse rifle and a longsword for hand-to-hand fighting—and giant tigers wasn't enough of a shock to the defenders, when the Lupans reached the battle line and shifted into their werewolf forms, many Test-Lits screamed, dropped their weapons and fled.

"Overseer. Call off the troops. Let those soldiers go," I yelled.

There were cries of dismay from the dragons, Lupans, and Hunters.

<Kill them all. Now. Hungry.> That was the dragons.

<They are weak. Not deserving of mercy.> The Lupans.

<Prey must be killed.> The Hunters.

"No," I cried. The thought of such a massacre nauseated me.

"I agree," Lieutenant Clarrett said. "They'll do our cause more good if we let them go. They'll bring word to the rest of the defending forces of what has happened here. The stories of our fighters will scare the shit out of the rest of them. Those who have fled will magnify their defeat. That will demoralize the Test-Lits. What we need to do is secure this section of the city."

"Thanks, Lieutenant. We need your experience here," I replied. "Overseer, contact General Finster and tell her what we have accomplished."

The Overseer transmitted Finster's reply: *<Well done, Berger. You'll make a soldier, yet. We've breached the defense perimeter on the east and south and will proceed toward the city center. That's where they're making a final stand. If your troops move in that direction, we should connect up by day's end. Good luck. Over.>*

"Right, General. Will do."

Clarrett said, "Let's set up a perimeter and take a break. Bring up the medics to take care of the wounded."

Roxanne grabbed my hand and led me away. I was one of those medics, of course.

***

Fur moved up beside me as I gazed down a long, seemingly deserted avenue. "I don't believe they have all pulled back," he said. "This could be a death trap."

"I wonder," I replied. "They were pretty spooked by our allies, here. Clarrett, Stiegman, you're the soldiers. What do we do?"

Clarrett spoke first. "I agree with Cohen. We're dead meat for snipers in those buildings and we aren't equipped to clear each one out as we go."

Stiegman added, "Sir. We need to send out a probe."

"And you suggest?" I asked.

Clarrett pursed his lips. "I think we should—"

He got no further. Overseer transmitted He-Who-Eats' words. *<I go. They cannot hit me if I fly swiftly.>*

He did not wait for a reply, lifted into the air, and wove rapidly from side to side down the avenue. Several volleys of laser fire splashed off the buildings opposite their origin. One hit the dragon, but most of its effect reflected off his polished scales.

<Exhilarating,> He-Who-Eats remarked as he cupped his wings and landed. *<These are unworthy opposition for dragons.>* His licked at a scorched spot where a wisp of smoke rose from his flesh.

The Hunter elder growled agreement.

<They would not pass trial,> added the Lupan leader.

"Right," I muttered, recalling my bare-assed days on Lupus IV.

Stiegman stepped forward. "Sir. Permission to speak."

"Um, sure." I was still not comfortable with all the military protocol.

"My troops are equipped with special grenades that can incapacitate anyone within a building if we fire them through upper story windows. The gas will settle down through the lower floors. We have enough of these to clear a path through the city, if necessary."

I looked around. "Okay. We've talked about this before. This stuff is derived from one of the less noxious Ulmian plants and is supposed to be non-lethal, the equivalent of tear gas, but more effective. Do we go with it?"

Clarrett spoke. "We can't destroy the buildings. There might be noncombatants in there. If we try to clear out these buildings one by one by conventional means, we'll take too many casualties."

Roxanne said, "We've barely been able to keep up with the injuries we already have. If this stuff is non-lethal, like tear gas, I say use it."

I looked around me. I found it hard to get past my own experiences with the hydra on Ulm; that colored my thoughts and made me reluctant to use something derived from the Ulmian toxic flora, but I understood the need.

Fur said, "If this will save lives, I vote to go with it."

Clarrett nodded.

I said, "Okay. Stiegman, do whatever you need to do, and let's see how it works on this block. Then we can decide further."

Ten minutes after the Ulmian troops fired their grenades into the six buildings on the block, two dozen Test-Lit soldiers and twice that many civilians staggered out onto the avenue. The enemy combatants were now slumped against a wall. Some mumbled incoherently, but none seemed mortally injured. An

Ulmian medic who had an antidote ministered to the non-combatant victims.

"How long does this last?" I asked Stiegman.

"A few hours, Sir. It will vary in individuals. We should bind the soldiers, leave a couple of troopers here on watch, and move on. We'll take it block by block."

Again I was thankful for the genuine soldiers in my supposed command.

We met uneven opposition the rest of the way, but at one intersection, resistance was spirited as armored artillery and laser tanks blocked the road.

As we debated the best way to attack the fortification, one of the dragons dropped out of the sky onto a defender and ripped him limb from limb. Blood spattered everywhere. The spectacle froze the opposition troops; they didn't even fire. When the dragon began to gulp down body parts, the rest of the defenders screamed and scattered for cover in every direction. I couldn't blame them. I had trouble keeping *my* last meal down.

I turned to He-Who-Eats-Enemies-For-Breakfast. "That was very brave of your dragon, but can you please ask them to refrain from eating the enemy?"

There was a low rumbling from him that did not translate.

"I know this is what you do on your world, but it discourages our own troops. I promise you a full feast of herdbeasts tonight."

<Agreed, Captain Cyberger,> the dragon said.

While the Certis Prime herdbeasts were fine pack animals, more critical had been their use as a food source for the Hunters, Lupans, and dragons. We would have stripped Dovid's World of its livestock, otherwise.

When we met up with Finster's forces, they had the main government buildings surrounded. Finster approached as I collapsed onto the fender of a burnt-out land drone.

"Has anyone got word about my parents yet?" I asked her. The lump in my throat and pressure in my chest made it difficult to breathe.

"No, but we assume they're in the prison, there." She pointed to the concrete block building that I knew too well as the headquarters of the Inquisition. "That's our next objective. But the remains of the Palmach, their best fighters, are in there."

That did little to make me feel better.

***

As we moved toward the doors of the Inquisition building, there was heavy fire from some of the windows. Fur, Roxanne, and I were in the vanguard of a group of only human troops. I did not want any cases of mistaken identity by any of our toothy allies. I wanted in there to find my folks, and refused to be left behind. Fur and Roxanne would not let me go without them.

My heart pounded as if it sought exit from my chest. "God, please let them be okay," I muttered.

Roxanne put her hand on my arm. I appreciated that support, but nothing anyone could say or do would suffice until we knew.

We moved up to the main doors, and a couple of Sammaran soldiers placed charges. When the doors were blown, we rushed into the lobby. Projectiles whanged off the walls amid the splash of laser fire. I dropped to my belly and looked for a target. The seasoned troops with me were more effective. They cleared the lobby of opposition before I fired once. Four of our men were down. My gut clenched. Of course, it would have been much worse if *I* actually had killed a human. Killing the gazelle on Lupus IV had just about incapacitated me. I never felt less like a soldier.

We worked our way down a hallway toward the cellblock where the prisoners would be. A giant vise squeezed my chest. I bent over and gasped.

Fur took my arm. "You going to make it?"

I stood up. "Yeah. Let's move."

When we got to the locked cellblock, a fighter who led the SOD contingent said, "The guards are likely holed up in here for a last stand. They might use the prisoners as shields."

I tasted bile.

"Then how do we get the prisoners out without harm?" Fur asked.

Roxanne answered. "What about the Ulmian gas grenades? Do we have any more of those? It won't harm the prisoners and there is an antidote for them, anyway."

I gave her hand a squeeze. "Good Idea. Get Stiegman up here."

The few minutes he took to arrive felt like the longest of my life.

The Sammarans blew the doors and Stiegman tossed in the grenades. After a couple of minutes, we heard lots of coughing and then what remained of the Palmach and the Test-Lit guards staggered through the doors. We were fitted with gas masks and, after we relieved the guards of the keys, we charged into the cellblock area. We opened every cell that had prisoners, and half-carried, half-dragged them out where the air was fresh. We left them with the medics and continued the process. Panic had set in by the time we came to the last cells. I had not found my folks.

Where are they? Where? I screamed silently. They can't be—

Then I heard a yell from Fur. "Cy. Over here."

I ran toward him and saw that he carried the limp

body of my dad in his arms.

"Oh, God, no," I wailed.

"He's alive," Fur said. "So is your mom."

Roxanne knelt and cradled my mom's head, but did not have the strength to lift her. I bent, picked Mom up, and rushed after Fur, Roxanne trailing in my wake.

Fifteen minutes later, I crouched next to my folks. They had received the antidote and were conscious, recovering from the effects of the Ulmian toxin. Dad was his usual stoic self, but tears ran down my mother's face...and mine, too. They had been tortured to a limited degree, Dad said, but they were okay. I was not sure what "a limited degree" meant, and I did not I *want* to know. They were alive. That was enough for now.

A soldier tapped me on the shoulder. "Excuse me, Captain, but General Finster needs you right away."

My dad's eyes opened a bit wider at that. He turned to Mom. "Sounds like our boy has risen in the world."

Mom responded with more tears.

***

When I reached Finster, I had stopped crying. Not appropriate for a hardened soldier, you know?

The General said, "Berger. Can we use this Overseer of yours to communicate with those inside the Parliament building? It's supposed to be what's left of the Test-Lit government."

"It's not *my* Overseer, General. And it will transmit anything you like."

She nodded. "And we've got somebody else with us you might like to see."

A Sammaran soldier dragged a struggling figure forward. It was Levi.

"Unhand me, you Godless buffoon," he cried. "You will pay for this. I promise you."

I could not help but smile. The last I had seen him was when I turned him over to the Sammaran military police. Levi's basic nature manifested even now. He stopped short when he saw me.

His hatred struck me like a physical assault. His stubbled face, twitching eye, and disheveled appearance made him look even more demented than I remembered.

"You. Berger. This is all your fault. When we defeat this paltry army of unbelievers and heathen creatures, you will—"

"Oh, shut up, Levi. You can't see the nose on your face. You're finished. You and the whole revolting crew that tyrannized our world. The rest of them are in there." I pointed to the government building. "The only question is whether they want to come out upright or feet first. Frankly, I couldn't care less which it is."

General Finster ignored our little sideshow and said, "Overseer, please tell those in the building this:

"This is General Cara Finster of the Sammaran Army, allies of the free Dovidian people, also commanding forces from Pronac, Certis Prime, Dragonworld, Cennesari, Ulm, Lupus IV, and Hiveworld. Your army has been defeated. You are under arrest for crimes against humanity, both on Dovid's World and Sammara. We prefer that you surrender peacefully, but we will use whatever force is necessary. We give you fifteen minutes to exit the building, without weapons, with your hands in the air. That is all. There will be no parlay or repeat of this ultimatum." She looked around. "Now we wait."

"General, Sir." The Ulmian sergeant spoke. "We have the means to extricate them with no need to put our troops in danger."

Finster looked at me, eyebrows raised. I nodded and told her about our use of the Ulmian toxin grenades.

"Let's see what they do, first."

"General," I said. "Do you mind if I add something?"

She shook her head. "You've earned that right."

"Overseer. Please transmit this:

"I'm speaking to what remains of the Test-Lit government and the Rebbinical Council. This is Cy Berger. Remember me? The guy you exiled a year ago? Well, I'm back, and I have some friends with me. You may have heard a bit about them. If you don't surrender within the fifteen minutes that General Finster has given you, I'll send my friends in. No holds barred. That includes the dragons, the Cennesari tigers, the Lupan werewolves, and the Pronacian reptilians. And just remember, they have not had lunch yet."

There were loud guffaws from amongst Finster's troops until she leveled her steely glare at them.

Fur smiled and said, "Way to go."

Roxanne slipped up beside me and grasped my hand. "It's almost over." She breathed a deep sigh.

Fur bracketed me. "You should be proud. You've been a major force in helping to free our world. Thank you."

"Hey, you did just as much, or more. Keep some of that thanks for yourself."

A few minutes passed before the front doors to the building opened and a string of people moved out, arms above their heads. Plaintive cries emanated from the group.

"Don't shoot."

"We surrender."

"Don't let them eat us."

"Keep the monsters away."

Fur laughed. "Sounds like the stories about your shock troops made the right sort of impression." He pounded me on the back hard enough to make me gasp.

Then I heard someone behind me yell, "Stop him."

The next thing I knew, a screaming, biting, kicking lunatic bowled me over. I managed to extricate myself, and jumped to my feet. Levi stood before me, his face purple, his lips pulled back in a snarl every bit as feral as one of the aliens he hated. His eyes were like black holes in his face. Two soldiers held his arms as a tsunami of hatred surged over me. Fortunately, my enhanced empathic block protected me from my usual responses.

I took a deep breath. "Let him go. This one is mine."

The soldiers glanced at General Finster, and she nodded. When released, Levi grabbed a knife from one soldier's belt and lunged at me. I sidestepped and watched him, balanced on the balls of my feet.

"Fur, no," I said as the big man moved toward Levi. "I said he's mine and I mean it. That goes for everybody."

"But he has a knife," Roxanne cried.

"So give me one," I said as I moved laterally to keep Levi in front of me, not taking my eyes off him. "And a jacket. He's forfeited any right to General Finster's surrender terms. That's his choice."

I felt the handle of a knife thrust into my right hand and a leather garment into the left. Someone understood what I wanted. I twisted my left arm to flip and wrap the jacket around my forearm as a knife shield.

Levi chose that moment to drive toward me again, knife hand outstretched. He knew nothing about knife fighting and grasped the handle as he would a hammer, with the point down. He slashed at me, but I warded off his blows with the leather guard. I danced aside to maintain the distance between us. I had trained to oppose knife fighters, and he had no clue. I could take him. I waited for the inevitable opening. I brushed aside the fleeting worry about whether I could bring myself to kill someone. A flash remembrance of the little gazelle on Lupus IV reinforced that, but I had no choice now. And if anyone deserved killing, it was Levi.

"This is all your doing, Berger," Levi screamed. "You have fought me at every turn. We may lose, but I will have my satisfaction. I will *kill you*." After the last two words, he threw himself at me.

I held my shields at full to prevent his hatred from getting through and slowing me, but as I pivoted, my heel caught on something, and I stumbled. I twisted to my right, and felt Levi's body hit my left shoulder. A searing pain shot out from there. I heard Roxanne scream. I rolled and came up on one knee. I felt wet blood running down my torso. I firmed my grip on the knife in my right hand as I watched Levi.

"I want no help," I barked, as Fur and two soldiers moved toward the rebbe again.

Face livid, Levi could not help but taunt me, even now. "A fool now as you always were. I hope your parents died in agony like I ordered they should. Like you will. Now you die."

As he stepped in, foolishly thinking I was incapacitated, I kicked out with my right leg and swept him off his feet. His arms windmilled, and he twisted as he came down. As he fell, I could have raised my arm and administered the coup de grâce. But I pulled my knife back and let him hit the ground. I could not do it, as much as I hated the bastard. He rolled over and pulled himself up, so we were face to face.

"As I thought," he breathed. "A fool."

I tried to move as he raised his knife, but found I could not. My whole body trembled; I had no strength left.

A huge shadow loomed over us. Levi's arm halted, wrist grasped by an unmovable force. I looked up. Fur's great paw held Levi's knife arm tightly enough that the rebbe dropped the weapon. He reached down, grabbed the rebbe's collar and leg, and lifted him off his feet.

"Cy is too good a person to kill you," Fur said, voice tight as a bowstring. "He's a healer, after all, not a killer. *I* don't have that compunction, Schvartz. This is for my family. My grandparents. My parents. And me. I told you about them on the ship, remember? And for every Dovidian that has ever been harmed by you and your abominable party."

Levi squealed and squirmed and fought. Fur shrugged off blows from Levi's flailing arms. His prodigious strength held the rebbe fast. Fur lifted Levi to eye level, so that the two men stared into one another's eyes.

"I am the last thing you will ever see in this life. I hope you see me through eternity." Fur lifted one knee and brought Levi's back down against it with incredible force.

I heard a sickening crack and Levi's body went limp. Fur dropped the rebbe to the ground and turned away.

Another body hit me from the side, but gently this time. Roxanne moaned, "Cy. Oh, Cy."

"Watch it," I said. "You'll get blood all over your pretty uniform, silly."

I looked at Roxanne and followed her saucer-sized eyes downward. My uniform was soaked with an incredible amount of blood. The last thing I remembered was Fur bellowing, "Medic. *Medic!*"

***

When I opened my eyes, I smiled. In my vision were the three prettiest sights I could hope to see: Mom, Dad, and Roxanne.

I tried to raise my head, but it was too difficult. "I see you three have met."

Roxanne giggled like a schoolgirl. "Of course we have." She looked at them, a grin plastered on her face.

Mom put her hand out and stroked my brow. "We almost lost you there, son. Don't strain yourself."

I looked at Roxanne.

"The knife hit an artery." She grimaced. "You were a fool to do what you did. There was no need—"

"Yes. There was *every* need. You didn't live with that sadist month after month. You didn't listen to him threaten your parents every day, enjoying every word. You didn't—"

"Enough." Dad's authoritative voice. "It's over now. You need to rest and get back your strength. You have more work to do."

I closed my eyes. Work? What in hell did I have to do now? How could I top the past year? And what was I going to do with the rest of my life? Being a rural veterinarian as I had planned would be an anticlimax, for sure.

A shadow blocked out the ceiling lights. I opened my eyes to the looming visage of a bearded giant. Fur grasped my good shoulder and smiled.

I grimaced and felt a wave of shame. "I couldn't do it. As much as I hated Levi and what he did—" A wuss: That's what I was. But my stomach roiled at the thought that I might have killed another thinking being.

"Hey, you did what was right for you," Fur said. "How are you feeling?"

"I'm fine...thanks to you."

Roxanne inserted her face back into my picture. "You're fine, huh? Then I have a bone to pick with you."

"Huh? What have I done now?"

"It was because of my name, wasn't it? You didn't

care about *me* when we first met. It was my *name* you were enthralled with." She frowned at me.

"I... What are you talking about?"

"Hmph. You should know...Cyrano D. Berger."

"You know?"

"Of course I know. *Roxanne*. Your folks gave me *Cyrano de Bergerac* to watch and read. They said if I was going to...I mean, if you and I..."

Laughter filled the room as Roxanne blushed.

Fur poked his hairy snout into my sight again. "You need to get better. In the meantime, we'll revamp the equipment and restock the *Galactic Circle Veterinary Service*."

"Restock the *GCVS*?" I felt like I was two steps behind everyone else.

"Well, of course," Roxanne said. "And Fur has to train me to fit in as the third member of the crew before our next voyage."

"Our next voyage?"

A Cheshire grin crossed her face. "You had far too much excitement flitting around the galaxy. I intend to get out from behind a desk and join the fun. Because of what we did...what you did, really...I'm getting a dispensation to join the *GCVS*. It will count to paying off my government service."

I couldn't help but mirror her smile.

"That's all well and good," Mom said in a severe voice, "but Roxanne isn't some tramp to go off with an unmarried man." A smile lit her face. "We'll just consider that little jaunt to Hiveworld as practice for the main event. Don't you have something you want to ask her?"

It took more than a moment to gather my wits. I looked into Roxanne's eyes for a long while before I asked, "Will you marry me?"

She squeezed my good hand. "Of course I will."

"It's good that you brought home a nice Jewish girl," Mom said.

I frowned at Roxanne. "You never told me you were Jewish."

"Oh, stop babbling," she said. Then she planted a delicious kiss to make sure my mouth stayed shut.

Stephen A. Benjamin

About the Author

Dr. Stephen A. Benjamin was born and raised in New York City. He received his A.B. degree from Brandeis University, and his D.V.M. and Ph.D. degrees from Cornell University, and he's a board-certified veterinary pathologist. He has been a university teacher, researcher, and administrator, and is currently Professor Emeritus at Colorado State University's College of Veterinary Medicine. His interests in human and animal health are reflected in most of his short stories and novels. He lives in Colorado with his wife, and enjoys traveling, especially visiting his family, fishing, golf, skiing, cooking, and writing fiction.

www.twbpress.com